If you enjoyed *Yes we live on a boat,* I'd really like to hear from you – richard@rw2.co.uk. Here are details of my other titles.

Loft Island
The Island and the Town

Set on the Salcombe (Devon) Estuary in the 1950s. Rescued from a flood, Mary (11) comes to live with the father and 13 year old son who saved her, though her parents and brother were drowned. The land they farmed is now an island. Practical and emotional help with their losses comes from unlikely sources. They are faced with a variety of attitudes from authorities, from friends and from a relative.

The long established friendship between the children develops slowly, innocently, with neither of them realising. Gradually life becomes stable, only to be ripped apart again before normality returns. The sequel, *The Island and the Town,* continues the family's story, examining character types of the era as well as its evolving social standards.

Change at Tide Mills

Near Seaford, 1963: a chance, fleeting glimpse of a girl from a train brings Owen running back from Seaford to Bishopstone Tide Mills. His interest is matched by his father's interest in the Mill, for the Tide Mills in the story is still fully built.

The youngsters explore, finding evidence of the past which leads to a search for the past inhabitants. It unearths a story of lost love, a tyrannical husband and his mistreatment of a wife and the child.

Gradually the Mill is restored and ready for its next chapter. The characters of its past are brought together and find surprise after surprise.

This is a tale of families, of the ups and downs of life, of some little adventure. But it's also a tale of the real Sussex of the time, with its old customs, its history, and some of its Characters.

The Suspects

A mainly light-hearted story, with spikes and humour. A group of mid-teen friends camp illicitly in a wild, private estate. Despite being discovered and evicted, they later need to hide from an adult criminal gang and return to lie low.

Encounters with their evictor whose life they save, the gang, Police, hospitals, a hotelier, a dog, truffles and copious thorns and brambles bring a maturity they never realised. It also brings friendships and relationships.

Available online at Amazon - Search for *Richard Harbroe Wright*

Yes, we live on a Boat

Richard Harbroe Wright

Published by Richard Wright,
Seaford, Sussex
www.rw2.co.uk

First Edition 2023

Thanks

Dedicated to Judy Wright for… everything in life, but in this case the eradication of the stupid, the only-semi-readable, the multitudinous typos and any attempt on my part to murder English grammar beyond the level that I intended.

Also with grateful thanks to Gretta Harvey whose eagle eyes spotted even more that both Judy and I had missed. She also checked its geographical accuracy from personal knowledge and was good enough to say that she enjoyed the story.

Thanks too to the owner of King's Ransom, a good friend, for being himself. I hope he will not beat me about the head for including some of his delightfully non-fiction character traits within this work of fiction.

Real life and its inclusion

The English canal system is a wondrous thing and my description of some of its quirks are from personal experience and memory.

If you navigate the canals, please be an Attwood, not a Smith, thus avoiding being entered in the Red Book of Bad Hirers which, of course, doesn't exist. As far as I know.

Hockley Port Interchange in Birmingham is now a secure private moorings. It probably has been ever since working narrowboats abandoned it. To my knowledge it has never been a hire base or a Marina. Other than that much of its geography is as described. It's private, so please don't try and trespass except via Google Maps or similar.

You might find the map of the Birmingham Canal Network and a smaller scale map of the wider system of use whilst reading. Though the map on the following page which cover the boat's journeys may help, it's necessarily to a very small scale.

Right at the back is a sketch plan of the boat.

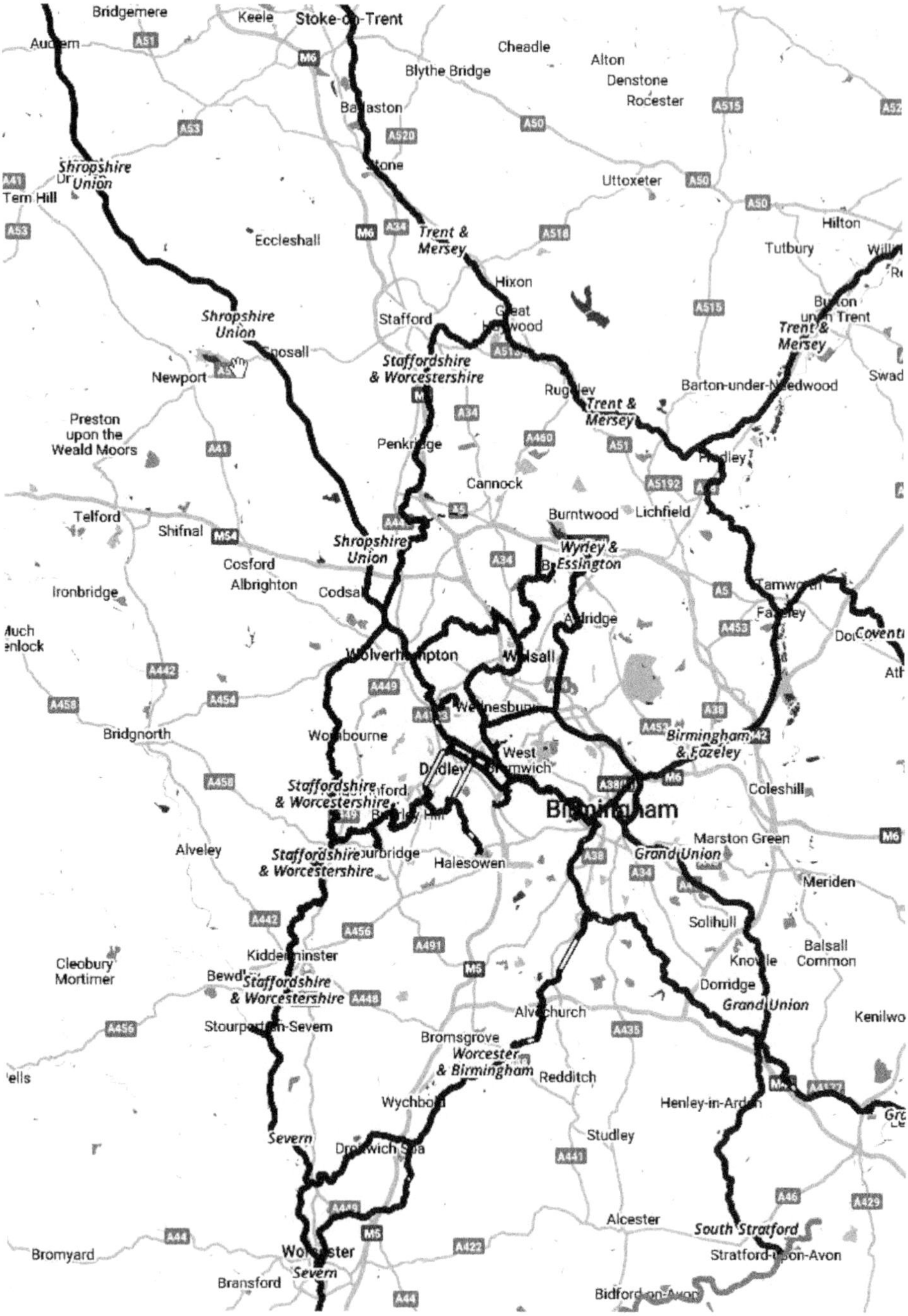

Map courtesy of the Canal & River Trust

Index

1 A deepening shadow

"Jack, if you feel that way about how I want to live my life, you'd better get yourself out of it."

Even now, the memory is a crystal. It sits deep in my mind; a point in my life that changed everything. I recollect the sick feeling of shock, remember how my mouth and eyes opened and that I stared at her, wordless. My mind backflipped, and registered that she still looked as she had the day we met. Oh, there were more lines on her face, and her skin was no longer the colour of clear honey that it had been. Indeed, my looks were similarly affected; the more so as I was five years the elder. On the rare occasions I bothered to think about it I regarded my older self as looking rugged, decisive (and of course good looking). When Helen and I had been talking, laughing at each other and laughing with each other as couples do, we had teased each other about our signs of age as being laughter lines, character lines. I had enjoyed thirteen years of being at ease, in love, with her.

But why should my mind, now of all times, be uselessly engaging with those thoughts?

Since my fortieth birthday and her thirty-fifth, cracks had started to appear, but so gradually they had field to register with me. My work had changed over the years as I followed my path, my career, in large scale diesel engineering. The job had increasingly absorbed me. Some years previously the post of senior engineering manager had been bestowed on me by the management of what was a significant player in the field of international power plant providers. Much was expected of my abilities. Those abilities and my time had both been readily given. In practice the post meant travelling widely, mainly on troubleshooting missions and often abroad. Absences from home came at ever more frequent intervals and for increasingly extended periods. Those long absences were the part of my seniority that I actively disliked.

For the previous two years I had missed an increasing amount of the growing up of our two sons. Helen was – I knew it and trusted her to be – a wonderful mother and I never had a reason to think otherwise. In fact the subject never even occurred to me. We had been thrilled when each of the boys was born, and welcomed them into the world with delight. We had shared the difficulties of those first years, the years that test every parent's patience. As the boys turned from infants to children and beyond we shared between us the inevitable problems they encountered or caused. By the time of the appearance of the shadow on our relationship the elder was thirteen, the younger eleven. The dreaded teen years were here.

Our home was a pleasant one. The house was detached, had a garden and a separate garage, was pleasantly but simply decorated with muted colours, majoring on inherited pictures to add interest. We preferred them to expensive wallpaper and intricate designing particularly as they held family memories for each of us. We were used to our surroundings; it was lived in, both in fact and in condition. It was comfortable. It was home.

Of late, perhaps over those two years of my work-required absences, Helen had occasionally started to look strained, even to my eyes; the eyes of one who thought to see no such change. I imagined it to be just the tiredness caused by work, two lively boys and the dirty sports kits that seem to breed around them. But over the weeks and months this strained appearance and a slightly strained mood had seemed to become a regular event. It was a niggle, an observation. If it should also have been an alarm bell for me, it was one I didn't recognise.

The fizz of our early married years had gradually diminished. To carry on the liquid analogy, it was effervescing less. When we first met we had indulged in that semi-crazy lifestyle that many couples follow from twenty onwards, maybe until the first pregnancy. We knew in advance that at the first birth we would need to settle down and to lose this wonderful, lively frivolity. Other couples, older couples, with whom we were on close, confidence-sharing terms, had hinted at it. They had described the onset of the more sober years as a change in taste from Prosecco to a still, mature, vintage wine. The active sparkle may have become just cherished memory of our young adulthood, along with the thrill of that house, those holidays, of those two births, but I believed and hoped that we should still have had the rounded wine of the middle years to enjoy.

It was difficult to put a finger on when, or why, or how that wine had started to become gradually less fresh. Maybe even stale. Less than the experience on the taste buds that the word 'vintage' should evoke. We still did the same things, thought the same thoughts – mostly – and carried on as we always had – mostly. But there was an invisible barrier being built. It was being done so subtly that I missed the start of its construction. It was not until we were relaxing on a family holiday that the realisation came that there was a problem. Helen and the boys were swimming together, leaving me on the beach having one of my occasional periods of self-examination. With a shock the existence of that embryonic barrier occurred to me. It unsettled me, and did so very considerably.

A holiday is not the time for a personal discussion of the sort that we needed. I fretted about it. Once at home again, because of the long working hours and absences, I was almost always too tired to engage in more than a quick cuddle before being overtaken by sleep. From her angle it seemed that at weekends there was always a headache or some other impediment to that night-time effervescence that still accompanies most of the years of ageing. Or maybe she had gone to sleep even earlier than usual.

There was also a reluctance to broach the subject, the potential barrier; it would have meant admitting a problem existed. And that I found that I could not do. Neither, obviously, could Helen.

Our family stayed at two.

One day in spring I had returned late from work tired – yet again – and found no welcoming answer to my homecoming hail. The house was completely silent. It was late winter, the weather was in one of those long periods of drear that reach up to haul down the spirits.

"Hallo?" I called from the shoes-off station by the front door.

Nothing. I called again. A door opened upstairs.

"That you, Dad?" Thank goodness. Nathaniel, the younger of them from the higher pitch of the voice.

"Yes. Sorry I'm late. Blame work. Again."

"It's ok. Mum's out. Said she'd be late and not to wait up for her."

This was new. At least it was acceptable now to leave the two alone. Phil was by then a confident and sensible fourteen.

"Where's Phil?" I called up, stowing my outdoor shoes in the allotted place. Odd, I'd not noticed the absence of Helen's shoes. In fact they were still there.

"In his room. Probably got the buds in."

The earbuds had been a compromise to stop Phil's taste in music from infecting the rest of the house. Half way through being thirteen he had started to 'enjoy' music in which I could really detect neither creative skill nor possible enjoyment for the listener. Discussions to try to turn him away onto a more acceptable genre proved fruitless. For once our usually compliant elder son had held his ground, but at least he had accepted the imposed use of earbuds "so long as they're the noise cancelling sort" (his stipulation). It had seemed unkind for me to tell him that if he wanted something to cancel out noise for his current choice of music it would involve the off button. I got a look of withering scorn. He got the earbuds. Our bank balance diminished more than I thought it should.

"Any idea where she's gone?" I asked, becoming a little annoyed, hoping that one of them might know.

You can't hear a pair of shrugged shoulders. I spotted them in time.

"Are you ok?" I asked. Then the trump card came to mind, one that was bound to get some attention and maybe a verbal answer. "And have you eaten? Are you hungry?"

"We had something before she went out. But if you're offering…"

"I want something," I announced, "so if you want to join in with it, come and help."

To my surprise they both joined me in the kitchen, Nat first, then Phil; the delay presumably being the time it takes for the near-surgical removal of earbuds.

"She doesn't usually go out without you, and not without us." Nat: was he uneasy, or was he actually upset? Was there a tinge of worry there?

"No, she doesn't. Maybe she's got fed up with the hours I'm having to work and wants some company."

"*We're* company."

"Company her own age. Like you have at school, or when you bring friends back. We don't see you then. You only have time for them. So you're not company for us then."

"Don't you want us to have them here?"

"Of course I do. It wouldn't be natural if you didn't." Our two are popular people and had a wide circle of friends, most of whom we liked too. "Friends of around your own age are the people you feel most at ease with. Your grandad used to tell me often that the affinity with people of your own age stayed the same all through your life." The remembrance caused me to smile.

"So it's all right for mum to go out with her old friends – friends her own age?"

"Well, she can, of course, and should when she wants. And none of the 'old', please! None of us should try to stop her. It's just that when you're married it's less usual to go out alone, and certainly not without telling the other one."

"Because you're not friends, then?"

"No, of course not. Husbands *are* friends. Or wives are. In fact they're *best* friends."

Phil was grinning. No, he was actually leering. What did he, at a tall fourteen years, suddenly know about couples that made him look at his younger brother with such a superior expression?

"So what do you want?" I asked, so as to avoid becoming a relationships adviser.

"Big boobs, a stunning face, and legs and a bum to die for." Phil, of course, the owner of the leer.

I swallowed. "To eat, dummy."

"Bacon sandwich." Nat nodded his agreement and it pleased me that we set to as a team. I added beans and an egg to mine as I'd had nothing to eat since lunch. Fortunately the boys didn't ask where their extras were.

After the usual negotiations in which Phil had to go to bed after Nat because of his two years' seniority but Nat thought it was unfair that he should and Phil needed to show he was superior… the boys went to bed. "Don't wait up," had been the message to me, but bed didn't feel as if it should be an option at anything like our usual time.

As eleven o'clock came and went I became uneasy. At one stage the eyes closed and it was only a loud motor bike from outside that woke me. The wall clock's opinion was that it was a quarter to midnight and I had work the following day. I was feeling aggrieved, not to mention tired. I went to bed.

Dimly there was awareness of movements, of stumbles, of a smell of alcohol and cigarette smoke. The bedclothes moved. I muttered something like "Good time?" and received a comfortable-sounding "Mmm" which added to the feeling of having been left out. I had not been there. I had not been told in advance or given details, let alone invited. Oh, neither of us controlled the other, but in any relationship it's good to know that the partner is safe and well and that they missed the other partner's presence in what they were doing. Certainly when there was a social event… but then I had been working. Still I felt that there could have been a message tome with the information, not a message left with the kids.

It rolled around in my mind until I dropped back to sleep.

"Sudden decision last night?" I asked as we met in the kitchen.

"Not really. I'd been invited some time ago."

"You never said." Did I sound accusing? Yes. I had meant to.

"Well, I knew you wouldn't be back, because of work."

"But there are times when I can engineer it differently. That could have been one of them. And the boys didn't know either."

"I need to have the freedom to go out with friends when I want."

"Yes, of course. It's just that it'd be nice to know in advance."

Further discussions were cut off by Nat's appearance. "Mum, where's my school jumper?"

It was the first of many of Helen's solo nights out. After that episode we were all told in advance when it was going to happen, to my relief. She told us that it was a gang of old friends of hers that she'd caught up with again. "They'd bore you silly, it's very girly stuff." Certainly that wouldn't interest me, and she knew it. And it was only right that she should have some respite from work, cooking, home, sleep, work…Maybe I should have done more around the house to start with, but my own work had just started taking more and more time, almost without my realising just how few occasions we had been out together.

I tried my damndest to arrange weekday evenings out, with or without the boys. But it seemed that each attempt resulted in a lack of interest on her part, and it seemed hardly right to take a twelve and a fourteen year old to the pub on my own, no matter how much they might like the idea. We did get out at weekends though, a few weekends, but not as many as I'd have liked.

"Why's Mum go out so often now?" Phil asked me after almost eight months of her increasing solo absences.

"It's these old friends of hers." I gave the stock answer.

"Don't you want to go as well?"

I hesitated. "I don't think it's really my crowd. They're her girlfriends from a long time ago."

His turn to hesitate. "Too old for me, then?"

"About three times your age, I should think." I smiled: he grimaced.

"Better off without, then."

Between Helen and me there seemed little said on the matter. There should have been time made; an attempt to start demolishing this increasingly high wall being built. The feeling grew on me. Should I look for a different company to work for? One that would require less time away from the family? For a year it had needed me to work later and later as more and more overseas clients were sought, clients that needed to be contacted during their own working hours, not the UK's. Faults and improvements need discussing when engines were being troublesome, not when they were working as expected, and when there were mechanics around at both ends with whom to work things through.

What should I do? The money was good – very good - but my career was genuinely turning into an issue about quality of life. And more and more often my mind would rebel against work, work, work and the strain of trying to persuade people at the end of a phone call or an email that I knew better about my employers' engines than they, the clients, did.

On quite a few times I tried to pin Helen down for a discussion about work and income, just the two of us, but eventually ran out of patience and raised it at a rare meal where all four of us were around the same table.

The opinions were that Phil thought I should do whatever was best, Nat thought that it'd be nice to see me home in the evenings – at least when he wasn't out with friends. Helen appeared to think nothing. She was silent when the other two had finished talking. I asked her again.

"How about the money?" she asked. "What would you do?"

"I've not even started looking yet. Almost certainly I'd be earning less, unless I wanted to work even longer hours."

"You'd need to be careful that we don't go into a downward spiral, financially, I mean." She had added that rather quickly. "We don't want to start having mortgage problems, and these two might want to go to university." There was more in the same vein. It almost sounded as if she didn't want me to return home at normal times.

"Well, if I did, at least I could get home in time for us all to go out sometimes during the week. That'd be good, surely."

The boys nodded. She was silent for a moment.

"I'd still want to go out with my friends when they go."

It was later that night, after the younger element's usual bed time negotiations and departure, that I raised it again, and met with quite a stone wall. The bi-weekly outings were important to her, she needed freedom and variety, and she needed them with her old friends who now meant so much to her. That stung, and I said in near-joke that it sounded as if they meant more to her than me; more than the boys and me.

"How can you possibly say that? It's nonsense, and really not something you need to interfere with."

I was taken aback. Voices rose. And then came the broadside: "Jack, if you feel that way about how I want to live my life, you'd better get yourself out of it."

It floored me completely. I was used to business negotiations, but not to emotional ultimata. Haltingly I asked questions and received some answers I never hoped to hear. Too many answers. Answers that meant that sharing a bedroom was, suddenly, no longer an option, or even a desire on her part. Even I, the communicative Jack Dyer had been rendered silent, although 'numb' would have been a better word.

The house is reasonably large and we had a spare room, scantily furnished though it might be. I slept in it that night. More accurately, I lay in its bed with my mind in turmoil.

"Are you in tonight?" I asked the following morning, trying not to allow the strain of the previous night's argument into my voice.

"Yes."

"I might be late."

"So what's new?"

Touché, I supposed.

My brother had been quite supportive when I was considering marriage all those years ago and had been very pleased to serve as my best man. We were still quite close; close enough to regress to teenager silliness when we'd had a drink or two. His own marriage had not lasted more than three years, to our sorrow, and we had been there for him when he needed support and, in my case, a shoulder to cry on. There were no children from the brief union.

I intended to chew over the problem with him. A call during the day discovered that Jonathan would be in later, so for once all the calls due to take place that evening were shelved. Why had I never just done that before and spent the time with my own family?

"It must be us, our branch of the family," he said when I'd arrived at his airy, modern flat; a perk of running a successful consultancy. Sitting, beer in hand, I had described Helen's row with me. "Jeanie soon tired of my having to be at work, and I was working fewer hours than you do now. It wasn't as if she was on her own all day, or tied to the stove, or some sort of slave, either. She worked, and we managed to get out quite a bit. But still she found it boring."

I knew all this and he and I had talked it all through before. "But Helen and I never argued before," I told him. "Not even when she spent so much time looking after the boys when they were toddlers. Although I wasn't as senior then, and got home at the usual time more regularly, I was able to help, and did. But in those days we did get out more, even during the week, and you babysat for us. It's only the last few years that we've each sunk so far into the rut of work and child care; especially me with work. And now of course Phil is old enough to look after himself and Nat. Besides, Helen really hasn't mentioned feeling... what? Left on her own? Not before this."

I didn't admit the gradual, mutual, cooling off in the relationship. It seemed too personal, even when talking to my own brother, and in any case I baulked at admitting it to myself.

"Do you think you *will* go? Leave home, I mean?" It was a sudden question, the words almost blurted out.

"Certainly not," I blustered. "I have my sons to consider. At least they still need me. I'm determined not to do anything that will upset their futures."

"Don't you think they'll pick up on it? Kids are pretty astute at picking up on adults' vibes, it seems."

"I don't want to tell them anything unless they do manage to pick it up. And even then I hate the idea of upsetting them. OH, I can tell that Phil seems to be getting more worldly-wise about relationships and the opposite sex than a fourteen year old should be, but he's made no mention of anything odd between Helen and me."

"You and I were pretty OTT about the opposite sex at that age," he reminded me. At only a year apart we had indeed swapped stories of what we then called eye-candy. "And really, apart from her wanting to go out on her own, you've not told me about how the two of you are getting on. I mean, not *really*."

It looked as if I was going to have to. So haltingly he learnt about the cooling off, the increasing lack of intimacy, all the other little signs that I'd never stopped to think about for myself.

It did me good to think, to confide, to get it off my chest, though I could still see no path through the issues, or out of them. There was little that he could say, really, but listened attentively to what I was saying and made the right noises. At about half-past ten I left Walsall and drove home.

The hallway lights were on. The front room was lit too. No surprises, except that the person asleep on the sofa in the front room was Phil, not Helen. He struggled to wakefulness as I opened the door.

"What's up, Phil?"

"Mum's gone to bed. She chased Nat upstairs and told me I could do what I wanted but she was going to bed. So I thought that if she wasn't going to wait for you, I would."

"You didn't have to, you know. It's a nice thought and I'm really pleased you thought of doing it, but you'll be no use in the morning."

"It's Saturday tomorrow, Dad."

I thought. So it was. I acknowledged defeat.

"Dad..." I waited. "It might be rude, but why are you in the spare room?"

I sighed, heavily.

"You're entitled to ask. We – well, we had a bit of an argument last night, and..."

"I heard."

I looked at him hard. "You *heard?*"

"My room's just above this. I couldn't help it. And it got a bit loud."

I sighed heavily again. Damn.

"All couples have arguments sometimes, Phil."

"Do they? But do they all finish it like you did?"

"What do you mean?"

"By Mum saying that you'd better get out of her life?"

His question froze my ability to think of what to say next. He was completely straight-faced, as well he might be with the potential of his fourteen year security – his world –grinding to a halt. To give her credit, Helen had also kept a normal gloss on things as we had gradually drifted apart. This was the first he had seen or heard that all was not well.

I took a deep breath, and let it out slowly.

"I don't want to get out of her life," I told him; though the truth of that was still untested in my emotions. "We have gone through so much. And... and we have a job to do. We have two sons to look after, and the best way of doing that is as a couple."

A smile flashed at me and vanished. He was silent.

"Are you really not in love anymore?"

I hesitated. He was being serious, mature. But he had no experience of emotions. Did he? Not adult, relationship-type emotions.

"As you get older, the first burning of love sort of gradually matures into a long-lasting fire. At least, that's what your grandparents used to tell me. It's meant to end up as glowing embers that fuel themselves and never really die.

"I honestly don't know what's happening at the moment. I feel..."No. that was enough. I could talk to my brother, an adult whom I'd known far longer than fourteen years, and know that he would – might – understand. And he wasn't as intimately involved with the relationship. It wouldn't be him who would be dragged through the trauma of a separation if it came to one.

"Confused, Dad?"

It seemed he was one up on me, despite my thoughts. I just nodded.

"Does Nat know anything of this?" I asked.

The head shook. "Don't think so."

"Be careful what you say. Don't... don't upset him. I don't like you being upset either. But – well, we're here, talking."

He yawned.

"And you – we – should be off to our beds. We'll be good for nothing in the morning, school or no school."

I rose.

"Dad?"

I looked down to where he was still sitting, on that comfortable sofa that was showing signs of its sixteen years of life and having to cope with two energetic youngsters.

"You won't just... vanish, will you? Promise?"

"Most certainly not. I mean, I won't vanish. That's the promise. I don't *want* to go anywhere, Phil. I want and intend to stay here. But if it gets..."

Enough.

"I promise that I will stay a part of your lives. I wouldn't go anywhere without telling you exactly what's happening, but I really don't think it will come to that."

How can you tell a look of hope when you see it? I don't know if that was it, but he looked a little less straight faced.

Life continued in the same way over the next two months, with Helen seeing as little of me as possible, or so it seemed. Weekends were difficult; it was obvious she was reluctant to come out and make a foursome, though she seemed reasonably happy with just the boys. It made me feel increasingly unhappy. Phil looked at me sometimes, with an expression I couldn't fathom. We bobbed along on the sea of life, even if Helen, Phil and I were floating lower in the water than we had before.

2 The darkness

"Uncle Jonathan looks well."

"Good," I said to Phil. "Been visiting, has he?"

He nodded. "Told us he wanted to talk to you but had to go before you got back from work."

Damn. "Did he say what it was? And why didn't he tell me before? I could have come home on time."

"He didn't say."

"Ok. Well, he knows where I work and he could call me if it's urgent. Mum in?"

"Yes, upstairs."

"Ok. Anyone want any food?"

"What are you offering?"

I called upstairs: "anyone want anything to eat?"

Nat's door opened. Helen's stayed closed. I cooked for three.

It was only when they had disappeared upstairs to bed and could have been expected to be going to sleep that Helen's – our – bedroom door opened. Steps on the stairs. She was there, looking strained as usual.

"You'd better sit down."

As a phrase it has the same meaning as "we need to talk", but somehow sounded more direct, more immediate.

"It's not working, is it?" she said. "We've known it for ages. And now you seem to have told Phil about it."

"He asked me. He heard us." I pointed to the ceiling. "Lies wouldn't have helped. I told him that all was not well between us. Which is an understatement, given what you've told me.

"You should have talked to me about it first. It's insulting to hear that your son knows about something you didn't know yourself."

My eyebrows raised. "You didn't know… Don't be silly. Of course you know. It was your comments to me that really took it to the stage it's at. I was suddenly unwelcome in my own bedroom and we both know why. And he heard you tell me to get out of your life."

"He still shouldn't have known first. We should have talked it over before they got to know."

"You never gave me an opportunity to talk when they were out of the way. Phil knows because he heard you." I pointed to the ceiling again. "Nat still doesn't know."

"You could have made an opportunity."

"I've been trying to get you to come out with me on our own for months and every time there's been an excuse. No, I told Phil the truth when he asked. There's been no opportunity to talk to you first, or even since. Until now."

"Until now. All right. Things are wrong. Put simply, you know I don't love you any more. I think the same is true for you."

There is nothing like being direct. This was an arrow shot, one that I had been dreading, and even expecting.

"We need… we need to keep going, for the sake of the boys," I told her. "If we separate, the trauma it will cause them will be immense. You know from others how much emotional turmoil it causes, and affects their happiness and education."

"What about *my* happiness? And it won't affect their schooling at all. They'd still live here and go to the same school."

I was horrified. "Of course it'll affect them! Emotionally it'll affect them, and that'll affect how they learn and how they behave. Besides, from what you told me it sounds as if you've found a replacement 'Happiness' already."

"The school can cope with that. God knows they're used to it." She ignored my accusation.

"Not with my children. I won't put them through that hell, and I'm amazed that you seem to care so little about them that you'd put yourself above them."

That was, I'm sorry to say, the start. From time to time I pointed at the ceiling, remembering even in my indignation and anger that Phil was trying to sleep above. Eventually there were steps on the stairs, the steps that I'd been half expecting and dreading. Phil. He opened the door, standing, bristling, in a dressing gown.

"Will you two please just STOP!" he shouted after a pause to gather breath. "Do you know what it's like to hear your parents arguing, knowing that whatever they decide is going to rule your future? It isn't fair. I'm tired. I can't get to sleep. And… and I'm upset. And disgusted with the pair of you."

This last was a sentence we had used on them when smaller. It sounded weird to hear it turned on us. He turned, leaving us no time to respond, left the room, slammed the door and we heard steps running up the stairs again.

Silence. She looked at me as if to say something, but didn't, and went upstairs herself. I was left to go, almost automatically, around the house locking the doors, switching the lights off and so on. On the landing I knocked at Phil's door.

"Go away."

"Phil, I'm sorry…"

"Go *away!*"

It hurt, those two words. I listened outside Nat's room, but he was silent. Thank goodness.

In the spartan spare room I lay, and thought, and stewed, and lay, and thought…

What to do? Leave? Stay and brazen it out? Insist she leave? If I left, what would happen to the boys? How could I find somewhere to live unless we sold the house? How would that affect them? If she left, how could she afford to live? Anyway, we needed our joint incomes to afford the mortgage and our comparatively modest living expenses – except for holidays, which were always spent abroad and which were expensive, given that we were a family of four. Had been four. And the holiday booking season was coming up.

She had no relatives to go to who lived near. I had Jonathan, who was only in

Walsall, and an easy drive or train journey from our part of Birmingham. To be fair to the boys, should I go there? But he had no room, and to be fair to me and to them, it should be Helen who went. But then, that *wasn't* fair on them either.

And on it went, round and round. I must have dropped off at some point, as I had after that first row, but it seemed as if I was awake for hours.

I woke late, very late. The house was empty. I phoned in to work to apologise and pleaded sickness. With that off the radar I moped around the house all day until Helen returned mid-afternoon, before the boys appeared from school. She was startled to see me, and looked alarmed, or so I thought.

"What are we going to do?" I asked.

"I'm going to make a phone call," she said, and walked abruptly upstairs. I went into the kitchen to put the kettle on to make her a cup of tea. It was an automatic reaction. Waiting for it to boil, I heard her laugh, a laugh that was shut off half way, as if she didn't want it heard. The tea was still brewing when she reappeared. I added the milk and handed her the cup.

"No thanks. I've arranged to go out. When you've decided what you're going to do, let me know."

"Now just a moment… it can't just happen like that. We've got to decide what to do about – well, everything."

"You mean *you've* got to decide. I'm staying here, of course, to look after the boys."

"I'm their parent too. I have duties towards them too."

"And you're never here in the evenings when they are. Fat lot of use you are as a father." That stung.

"What about all the weekends? What about the holidays? What about my contribution to the mortgage and all the other expenses – and the holidays? You can't manage them on your own. And I need to pay for a flat, or something. Better: how about you get a flat and I stay here and look after the boys? It's you who want me to go, don't forget."

She started at me, eyes blazing. It seemed like impasse, though why I should have thought that I don't know. But she had another surprise for me.

"This other man I've been with – well, it's become serious."

It was my turn to stare at her, and this time her gaze wavered first.

"Then you'd better move in with him," I said bitterly. "Why all this beating around the bush when you're going to live with your lover anyway?"

It's a mark that my opinion of our relationship had reached rock bottom that I could say that so levelly.

"That won't work. I need to be here for the boys. You said you didn't want them traumatised by a split. Well, think how much it would traumatise them if they had to move house as well."

"That's emotional blackmail!"

"It's fact. Recognise it."

"Ok, so the best thing is that we both stay here and maintain stability for Phil and Nat, at least for the next – what – six years until they've both reached adulthood." I was doing my best to keep us all together, even if the relationship between her and me was a lie.

"That won't work, and you know it, and it means… means I'll be stifled. And I'm not moving out. I need to look after them here, so they don't have that trauma that you're so scared of."

"So you think your boyfriend will be moving in? Huh! Think again. If you want to see him, you go out with him and start a love nest at his place. I suppose he has got somewhere to live?"

"He has, but I'm not living like that. The boys need stability."

"And that's what they'll get, with us living here and looking after them, or even with me living here."

"You're never here. You're always working. You can't expect them to be latch-key kids. Anyway, I'm not prepared for us to live together like that."

"Not even for their sake? That doesn't show you in a very good light."

The door opened. Both boys looked in, cautiously. Back from school.

"Are you having another argument?" asked Nat. "You're always arguing nowadays."

"We've got Uncle Jonathan with us," said Phil. Perhaps I was starting to get super-sensitive to his various tones of voice, but he sounded as if he was saying something he wasn't happy about.

But I was pleased. At least Jon's presence would still the atmosphere a little.

But it was a short meeting. It seemed that the person who was driving tonight was none other than Jonathan, and that is why he had appeared just as the boys came home.

"The girls have arranged to meet in Walsall tonight," he told me with the usual good natured grin, tinted as always with guilt when a meeting with anyone of the opposite sex was being planned. I took it that he was interested in one of the group of women that Helen had been meeting for the last several months. "We're having a meal first, with them."

It sounded almost as if the last two words were tacked on as an afterthought.

In a whirlwind the two made ready and vanished. I was left with the boys.

It was therefore my turn to cook a meal, helped by two straight-faced almost silent boys. They must have needed reassurance as usually they would go straight up to their rooms to unwind or start homework, or talk and text for ages to the people they'd just spent their school day with.

At last we ate, still in near-silence, and I even had two volunteers to wash up, a miracle in itself. When the last things had been put away there was the usual pause, which Nat interrupted.

"Daaaad…?"

I just knew this was going to be question time.

"Are you and Mum going to get a divorce?"

"We've really not thought about it or talked about it. And I really hoped that we hadn't made it too uncomfortable for you two."

"Oh, it's been obvious for ages."

I looked at Phil accusingly, but he shook his head.

"She's seeing ... someone else," Nat said.

How the hell did Nat know? I asked him.

"He... he comes here now and again."

Phil shot him a warning look, and it wasn't lost on me.

"You mean he comes here when I'm at work? What happens?"

"Oh, nothing *happens*," said the worldly-wise Phil, "but they cook and we get shoved off to do homework." Nat nodded.

"What's he like? Do I know him?" I was starting to seethe inside. My voice was becoming harder, I could tell. Nat looked worried.

"He's all right. But... we'd rather it was you."

That was something. But I was still angry, and not with them.

"Is that where your mother will be tonight? With him?"

Now they both looked uncomfortable, and stayed silent.

"It is, isn't it. And Jonathan knows about it and hasn't told me. And after I trusted him and asked him about what to do, as brother to brother." I was almost talking to myself now, but noticed the two of them looking at each other and wondered what they were thinking.

I was wondering what to say next when my mobile rang. Work. The last thing I wanted.

"Jack? We've got a major problem with that new generator installation in Ohio. I'm afraid you're going to have to spend some time talking to them out there – and please, please say that you've recovered enough to fly out tonight."

As if everything at home was just normal, I asked what the problems were and instinctively asked for accepted or new solutions. It was only when we'd been discussing it for some time I realised that the boys had gone upstairs and that I was the only one in the house looking after them.

I told my boss that I couldn't go immediately for that reason and he sounded irritated.

"When will you be able to fly, then? First flight tomorrow?"

"Is it that urgent?"

"You know it is. They're a massive client and we do have a reputation to maintain."

Part of me knew that I needed to stay at home and try to find solutions there. Another part told me that a trip to Ohio would help get me out of the situation and help clear my head. Reluctantly, with my increasing antipathy towards the ever-present requirements of my job, I agreed on an early start the following morning.

"Sorry, guys," I said when they had each emerged from their rooms onto the landing. "That was work, and despite everything I've got to fly to the States tomorrow.

"You're coming back, though?"

I looked at the asker, Nat. "Of course I am. Firstly I want to be with you two, at home; secondly I need to work out what to do, and thirdly I don't want to live in the States."

"It might be quite good," said Phil. "The girls are stunning."

"Almost as stunning as they are in the UK," I told him, glad there was a little normality returning.

They were asleep when I wrote my note to Helen to tell her that I was having to spend yet more time away, and why. I left it on the kitchen worktop before going to bed.

A desperately early start, the inevitable scramble at the airport, and mercifully a reasonable sleep on the plane. The journey was long and tedious, the reception in Ohio cool, and the problems testing – even for me with many years of experience with diesel engines. After days of almost no sleep, tests, phone calls, requests for urgent UK based tests to replicate the issues and a near meltdown with the client, we discovered the root causes. Fuel problems at the American end, problems so basic that it had occurred to no one that it they could be the fault. To the clients' question "why is there no built-in protection against damage from that sort of problem?" I could at least respond that fuel filters were fitted as standard but that everyone in the UK and the rest of the world takes greater care of their fuel so as to avoid damaging *all* engines, not just ours. And why had no one checked the quality of the fuel as I would have expected to have happened before calling a senior engineer from the UK?

Their MD was not happy, especially when I told him that my boss would be talking to him about full expenses.

I returned to the UK, knowing that I was going to be further deprived of sleep by the time zones, and already feeling edgy about returning to my marital situation. As the taxi dropped me at home I nearly changed my mind and asked him to drive to Jonathan's at Walsall. But there were two young gentlemen I needed to see. I paid him off. It was Saturday, mid-afternoon.

My key wouldn't work. It would even penetrate the lock, let alone turn. I fiddled with it and tried again and again.

With a sickened feeling I realised the locks had been changed.

The side gate goes in a covered alley-way down to the garden and the back door. I tried it but it had been bolted from the inside. The anger mounted.

There was no answer to the door bell.

The garage, at least, responded to my key. I put my luggage inside it and locked it in, then called Phil's mobile.

"Phil, it's Dad. Are you in? Someone's changed the locks."

"Sorry, it's a bit difficult to hear you. I'm in a noisy pub."

"Pub... Can you just nip home so I can get in, please?"

"I can barely hear you... let me nip outside... what? No, it's a mate from school. I won't be long."

It was a male voice asking the question, one that sounded vaguely familiar but thanks to the noise I couldn't identify it. I could feel myself getting angrier. On the phone, snatches of different conversations, steps, a door opening, peace.

"Ok, Dad. I can talk now. They've changed the locks and we haven't got keys yet. He says they're being cut and we'll get them soon. Sorry."

"Who's 'he'?

He hesitated. "You'll see when we get back. Look, we've been here ages. I'll tell them I've got to start homework and confer with someone from my class when doing it. I'll ask for a key, then run back. Don't go."

I didn't know whether that was 'don't hang up' or 'don't leave the spot'. I hung on. The sound effects of his return to the table came again, there was a discussion and again he must have gone outside, once again into the comparative peace of a Birmingham street.

"Hallo? We're all coming back. Look, Dad, I'll hang back with Nat and let them go in first. If they go in last they'll shut the door and you'll never get in."

I clenched my fists. Whoever this controlling bastard was I wanted to say things to him, then I'd chuck him out.

"I'll get out of sight somewhere, then be with you when you go in."

"There's a big tree on the bit of green. That's where we used to hide. I'll pick you up from there."

"How far away are you?"

"In the Engineer – about ten minutes' walk.

"Ok, Phil, and… thanks."

"See you soon, Dad."

That ten minutes was one of the longest, most frustrating periods of my life. The tree was a good idea, and hid me well enough, but I just wanted them all to go past – no, actually I wanted it all to be over, to be with my sons again and to have a rest from my jet-lag.

At last, as they walked past, I couldn't see properly but it looked as though the person Helen was with was Jonathan. So where, I wondered, had the other man gone? Nat was walking just behind them, but Phil was some way behind. He looked at the tree, checked ahead, and then beckoned me. I joined him, gave him a hug which, unusually, he accepted. Cautiously we followed them. When they stopped at the driveway and looked back for the boys I had anticipated them and had ducked behind a convenient bush; Phil continued dawdling. The three entered the house, I caught Phil up and went in in front of him.

Jonathan had just finished removing his shoes, straightened up, saw me, and a look of panic crossed his face. I looked at him, wonderingly, and then my eyes opened wide.

"Helen," he called in a tone that was higher than his usual permanently jocular voice. "Helen, can you come out here, please?"

"What's the matter, darling?"

That was enough. I pushed my brother in front of me into the kitchen where Helen was. Nat was in a corner, looking scared.

"Is this the man who you were talking about? The man who you want to have in your life? My own brother?"

She seemed to have difficulty knowing what to say.

"We're in love," was all she came out with.

"So were we. You and me. We married, if you remember. And you – " I shoved him against a wall. "You were the bloody best man. Some best man you've turned out to be."

"Jack, I'm sorry, but it just happened."

"Happened! I'll say it fucking happened! And you fucking let it happen.

How…"

I could feel the rage mounting in me. Twelve months of increasing sadness, of being in limbo in a declining relationship and confiding in this very man: my brother, my mutual companion to my life since birth, man of my blood, knower of my spirit, my helper with emotions; and now I learn that he is the cause of everything my emotions have suffered.

There is nothing so agonising as having someone who was a part of your life, for all of your life, turn round and spiritually stab you with the dagger of betrayed trust. My vision clouded. Rage boiled over.

All this time I had been staring him straight in the eyes, hoping even now that there was a joke being woven, that he would give one of those sudden grins of our youth and it would all be over. But he was not even meeting my eyes.

The words I shouted at him are now beyond my memory. As if operated by some automaton my right arm came up and connected – I think with his chin. There was a minor satisfaction of seeing him fall backwards and hit his head on the wall, but I turned away and stumbled from the house.

I walked away. Then I just walked anywhere. Oh God, how I walked. There is no saying where I went, what I did. I just walked. My mind was – well, I really can't describe it now, not in words. And I don't want to recall those swirling semi-thoughts, the numerous times I looked into the black pit of despair, at the black dog, because I'm scared even now that my mind could somehow return to that state.

When my feet hurt, there was a bench. When it became dark there was a bus shelter and my eyes closed, but the visions inside my eyelids were even worse than the semi-reality of being awake. There must have been sleep, but it was a tormented sleep if so; a sleep that neither refreshed nor healed. My eyes opened to the arrival of the first bus and I looked out at the supposedly cheerful lights inside it and the noncommittal faces of the early shift on its way to work.

Work! I should be at work! But the very thought of it was complete anathema. It made me panic. I would never be ready to face work. I had no wife, no children, no parents, no brother and no house. I had failed at life. I should be useless at work and fail there too. Sick to my stomach I rose, nearly fell because of the stiffness in limbs which were unused to being abused like that, recovered, and walked. And walked.

No memory remains of that day either, except for one thing. I found myself by water, by one of the city's multitudinous canals. There, ahead of me, was a Victorian building, incongruously flying a cheerful flag. There were boats, painted cheerful colours, moored against the wharf, parallel with each other, and stretching out to mid-canal. It was wide there, a basin.

By the building, on a seat, was a woman, bent over, her head in her hands. She was being comforted by a younger man who sat the other side of her, talking earnestly, his arm around her.

It was a tableau, a private moment. Even had it been appropriate to offer help I should have been powerless to do so. Most important to me then was my own turmoil, too great a turmoil to allow me to consider someone else's issues. My feet managed an about-turn and I regained the emotionally safer busy road.

Incredible to me now, I apparently managed yet more days and nights outside, walking blindly. The weather, until then kind, started to present one of those Midland drizzles that feels at first soft and kind, but nevertheless succeeds in soaking the sufferer to the skin. "There's no such thing as bad weather, just bad clothing choices": thus goes the lay. It would have helped had my mental state, when I had stumbled from the marital home, been capable of making a clothing choice. As it was I was equipped just with a shirt and a thin jumper.

At one point I managed to face a vending machine and extract a coffee from it, to drink the first liquid that had passed my lips since lunch two days previously. It made me feel sick, but it was warm and wet and gave me a little energy.

That night's hotel was another bus shelter near some smart houses. Sleep had overtaken me immediately I lay down, with the usual unease and trepidation. After a very few moments, so it seemed, a voice interrupted.

"You can't sleep here. Move on."

The opening of my eyes took in a dark blue pair of trousers and a high-vis jacket hung with all the equipment you see on a policeman. Another hovered just beyond.

I said the first words to another human since the conversation with my brother.

"Too tired."

"Can't help that. You'll have to move on. We've had complaints... hang on..."

He turned away to his colleague. Despite my frame of mind and my predicament I could feel my eyes closing again.

"What's your name?"

I woke again and shook my head. "Don't know. Don't care."

"Come on... sir. Please?"

The change of tone registered with me, just.

"Why? Does it matter?"

"It does to us, and if you're who I think you might be there are two lads who it really does matter to."

From the morass of my despondency a handhold of hope appeared, like the hand of the Lady of the Lake reaching up for Excalibur.

"Phil? Nat?" How he understood from my slurred, exhausted speech is a miracle.

The man in front of me conferred with his backup, who turned away and spoke into his radio. Impatiently I waited.

"Can you give us *your* name, please sir?"

If there was a chance... "Jack Dyer," I said.

He gave a sigh of relief. "Well, Mr Dyer, you've caused a lot of people some worry. I'm glad we've found you."

"My sons..." It was more of a plea for help, not a statement of fact.

"That's them," said the other officer. "Sounds like you have two good lads there."

I managed to nod, and to mean it. That, at least, was the one thing I could really latch on to, to know to be true. It was also the first positive mental image in my head that I recognised as such since I had confronted Jonathan. It was as if I had been able to reach out to grip that hand and to find it bore my weight.

"Are they all right?" I asked.

"I think it was them who reported you missing, so I'd guess they were as worried as hell, wouldn't you?"

There were no words I could think of to say. But I felt as if I was starting to pull on the handhold and to find myself gaining more substantial ground, hoping that neither my grip nor the handhold would let me down.

"Can you come with us, please?"

I was desperate to meet the boys, to find out… what? Whether there really was still a chance to regain some semblance of a life? I didn't know. All I knew was that I needed them. On the other hand I was physically weak, having drunk just a cup of disgusting machine coffee in days, eaten nothing for days and was still wet through. I tried to get up, but swayed and sat again., looking up helplessly.

They helped me up and found that my feet would hardly work.

"About time you arrested him. Bloody piss-artists. We don't like them around here."

One of the police turned and stared at the middle-aged man who had approached without our noticing.

"And you are?"

"I live over there."

"Name?"

I can't remember the name he gave. Or the address, which was the next question.

"We'll be visiting you when we have taken this man to hospital, so please can you write down the time when you first saw him, and the time when you called the Police. Thank you. No need to hang around now. Good night."

So I was going to hospital, was I? I'm quite a tall, broad person and they struggled to support me across the street and carefully sit me in the car. Once there, sitting on something more comfortable than a bus stop bench for a change I just slumped against the side window. My eyes closed.

3 Hospital

"Dad?"

It was a struggle, but that spiritual, emotional handhold was being offered again. Would accepting it, grasping it, pull me from sleep and, if even not irreversibly, from depression?

Eyes blinking in the light…how long had I been there?... and focussed on his face. Phil's face. He heaved a sigh.

"Where the fuck have you been, Dad? You scared us rigid."

I still had no words. But eventually one came to me.

"Language."

He snorted. "You'll hear worse than that from me if you *ever* do something like that again. And after you promised, too."

This was too much, even in my semi-awake state. "What promise?"

"You promised never to just vanish."

I closed my eyes again. He was right. I had made that promise. And I had broken that promise.

"Dad? Don't go off again." There was alarm in the voice. I deduced that he was scared I might drift off to sleep again, not that I'd just get out of bed and walk off.

"Sorry, Phil," I managed. "I've been… I don't know where I've been. But I know I've not been thinking straight."

"Is that because of Uncle Jonathan?"

That pulled me further out of sleep and into a distressingly familiar feeling of betrayal.

"Yes. What has he said?"

"Not much, so far. He's just home from hospital. He cracked his head when he fell, Mum said, so they've been treating him for concussion for the past few days."

I was silent.

"We visited him when he was there – didn't want to, but Mum told us we had to." He paused, then spoke softly. "His head was bandaged, and he had a wonderful black eye. How he got that from falling backwards, I don't know."

In a kind of flashback I recollected my fist swinging through the air and the sharp pain in my knuckles when it made contact. So my clumsy, unpractised and unbidden swing had found its mark, had it? And it seemed to have caused some more damage as a result. Something sprang to mind.

"Is that why the Police were after me?"

"He's said nothing about it. He'd just come round when we first saw him. And he just mumbled that he fell backwards. Nothing to do with the Police at all. It was us who called them."

"Who?" I wondered if Helen had relented.

"Nat and me. We were worried and called the Police. Mum was furious – she said you were old enough to look after yourself. That's what she tried to tell the

Police when they called, but they talked to us and asked her to leave the room."

Good God. How that must have hurt her pride.

"We really got shouted at when they'd gone. Nat..."

He swallowed. "Nat told her he hated her and rushed off to bed. I told her that I was sca... worried about you because you had promised never to vanish, and now that you'd done just that. I told her we knew about her and Uncle Jonathan. She said it wasn't our business. That's when I swore at her and went to bed myself. I checked on Nat and he was so unhappy I stayed with him."

Even from my mentally fragile state I could tell that she had gone completely off the rails so far as our marriage was concerned, that it was now not possible to go back. Nat – and Phil – were now the only people really in my life and who were very much still on the rails.

I gripped the arm nearest to me and told him so. But there was an interruption.

"Time, young man, please. He's only just woken and we really need to get the doctor to check him over properly. Come back after school and you can see him again. He'll probably be here for a few days."

He slid something to me: my mobile. The mobile that had been in my hand still when I'd made my wild swing. "Call me if you need me. See you later."

He was gone.

Of course, there was no doctor waiting. What did happen was that the mobile rang. I looked at it, and found, to my horror, a feeling of panic was mounting in me. I viewed it as if it was a bomb that was about to detonate, about to destroy me. And my family. The reaction was so intense that I could hardly breathe, and I remember calling, or maybe shouting, something incoherent. My eyes fixed on a clock on the blank white wall opposite as if it was timing a bomb detonation: it said 9.43. There should be a second hand, counting down the minutes to oblivion. It was puzzling, even in my desperation, that there was no such thing. Expecting any moment that whatever bomb it was would blow me to atoms and that I was physically unable to stop it or to escape, my eyes closed and a blackness overcame me.

At least Phil's escaped was my last thought.

When, eventually, the blackness dissolved again to light, I discovered that I was lying on a pillow, on my back. The ceiling was different. This time there *was* a doctor present.

"How are you feeling now?" He'd had the grace to wait until my eyes were focussed. I remembered the bomb and was about to ask if it had done much damage when something jogged my mind into the realisation that his was a hospital in Birmingham, UK, and that it was safe.

"I don't know," I said.

"Do you want to tell me what happened? I study the nervous system and its effects on people when things go wrong, so I really would like to know. Maybe I can develop strategies with you to bring you back to where you were."

To where I was... That was the last place I wanted to get to. The panic was starting again. It must have shown because his next words were more what I needed to hear.

"...assuming that's what you want, of course, maybe it isn't. You have had a rough ride, and I don't just mean physically. How do you feel about starting at the beginning?"

A silence ensued whilst my brain coped with where to start recounting the saga. A voice, almost separate from my consciousness, started from the nebulous point in time when there was nothing wrong with my marriage, and continued until all the wrongness surfaced. It had all seemed so sudden.

After about thirty minutes I trailed off into silence. There was nothing else I could add to the story, having told it up to the point in the police car when I ceased to be aware of anything. He allowed the silence to extend. Perhaps it was to see if I was going to continue with anything else.

Eventually: "How about your son? Was he helpful yesterday? Do you think you'd like him to visit again?"

I managed to look him direct into the eyes, having let them roam all over the very white, private room whilst the words of my experiences tumbled from me.

" I *want* him to visit. They're the best thing that could happen. Him and his brother."

"I don't know about both of them visiting, to start with. They might tire you. But one at a time, with a gap between them for you to rest."

"They're not tiring," I told him. "They are my future, now."

"Well, we'll see how it goes later. I gather that the nurse at the General said that – Phil, is it? – could come back after school. So are you happy about that? We'll need to pop in from time to time to make sure everything is ok, but apart from that, you just enjoy the visit."

I nodded, feeling just a shade more positive to anticipate a visit from my suddenly essential elder son. Another thought struck me.

"How long have I got to be here?" Despite Phil, I felt tired again after so much talking. Me! The one who talks on the phone or at a videoconference for a living.

"We'll see how it goes. We can chat again later, or tomorrow, and take it from there."

I was going to say something about work, and getting back to it, but the feeling when I even thought of the prospect of returning there brought a feeling of being out of control, and of an approaching panic. I could feel my eyes widening as something like a feeling of fear engulfed me.

He must have noticed it, because he spoke again, this time quietly.

"As long as you need to. You need to recuperate. Not just from the stress but from the hypothermia, the exposure that you suffered. But mostly you need to concentrate on the positive things; your sons, for example. Maybe their presence for a while will do you good. Anything else positive is good, but make sure it really is positive. Now is not the time to think of the negatives, or the things you dread. Don't forget that if you need, we can help you sleep. The brain can cure itself of a lot of hurt while we sleep."

I nodded. The effort of speech had all but tired me out anyway.

"Hallo, Dad."

The programming of the parent, hard-wired into the brain from the birth of the first offspring, works even when all other normality has been removed. A child addressing you whilst you are asleep usually means a problem. The effect is the same whatever the cause; instinct kicks in and the parent awakens.

In this case the interruption to sleep meant a distinct happiness. That was the emotion that came after a long pause to pull myself from near unconsciousness. A sort of happiness that returned even after all the adversity I had encountered.

"Hallo, Nat" I murmured half way between the two states.

"How are you feeling? I'm sorry if I woke you."

"I'd have been furious if I hadn't woken up and had missed you." I would have added more, but the look of happiness on his face, and the smile, told me that to say just that was enough.

"*We* miss *you.*" Again, a comment guaranteed to cause a smile of pleasure, this time on my face.

"I miss you too. All the time when I'm meant to be resting I keep thinking of you, and of Phil, of course. You're the two people who matter most to me now."

"Are we going to live with you?"

At that point my thoughts hadn't extended that far. All I'd had in mind were the good times we had enjoyed as a family: the boys and me; and the boys, me and their mother. After the doctor's instruction to make sure, I concentrated on the positives; the boys. I had been shying away from extended thoughts of Helen. It was the two boys and their antics that had kept me sane.

Sanity! Is it that that was wrong? Did they think I was deranged? Or just having a breakdown? If the latter, I realised with a jolt just how strong a mental breakdown can actually be.

Switching back to Nat's question, I thought.

"I'm going to do my damndest to make sure that you are. If that's what you want."

"Yes," said the twelve year old. "I don't want to be at home. Not with him. Not any more."

I reached out and touched the hand that was supporting him as he leant on the bed. He gave a start, which I thought was his trying to pull away. But there came a sob from above me, and before I knew it he was at an angle. There was a head beside mine on the pillow, in tears.

For myself, I felt inadequate. I was the one meant to be in mental turmoil. To the instincts of a parent the turmoil of a twelve-year-old son is something that has to be dealt with as a priority. The best way for a father to deal with it is to let the tears subside, but to stay with the child and maybe stroke the back until it does.

So that's what I did.

The door opened half way through this. Nat never noticed, but I shook my head decisively at the doctor who, to give him his due, gave a nod and just stood at the door, wordless and motionless.

My son finally lifted a red-eyed and blotchy face to mine. "Sorry."

I gave him a shaky smile. "It's been hell for both of us – all three of us. Hasn't it?"

He nodded. "It still is."

"What's happening?"

He hesitated, still emotional, and sat watching me, obviously wondering what to say next. The doctor cleared his throat, making him spin round.

"Sorry," he said. "I came in a moment ago but thought I should say nothing. Your father has been ill. And he still is. It's not an illness of the stomach or anything like that, though he has suffered from hypothermia – you know, exposure. He's had a shock and is so tired he's not been able to think straight."

"He's had a nervous breakdown, you mean."

"Well, something like that. He is still mentally very tired and isn't ready to tackle problems yet. We need to give him time to recover fully."

"I'm not a problem. Nor is Phil."

"No, of course not. And you're obviously good for him. But he can't choose what to do, not yet; not for himself nor for you two."

Nat's were not the only tears to be found between us. Some of my mental pain must have been released and I found the doctor's words condescending. I was by then reaching the state of mind that any father worth the name acquires when his son has been hurt by others.

"I can look after my own children, doctor. Remember that, please." I had raised myself from the bed to be able to look him in the eyes but wasn't ready for the unexpected feeling of weakness. I lasted about five seconds like that before having to give up and let myself fall back.

"Dad? Dad? Are you all right?"

"Just give me a moment," I mumbled. With an effort I opened my eyes. "Perhaps he's right, perhaps I need some time to recover."

The door had opened at Nat's anxious call. Phil.

"What's happened?" he asked.

"I'm just far more tired than I should be," I muttered. "Doctor, have I been drugged?"

"We gave you a sedative last night to help you sleep. It will still be in your system for the next few hours."

"I have that to blame, do I? Well, my sons need me, and by the sound of it, they need me now. What have they been saying to you both at home?"

Phil's turn. He looked angry in contrast to Nat's misery. "Mum says that you've probably gone round the bend. She and… and uncle… have told us that we can't visit you. So we came after school."

"You've not been back to eat yet?"

"No. We came straight here."

They are always famished when they get home. I knew what a struggle it must have been to disobey her – their – orders, not to mention the decision to go without a meal.

"Where are my clothes?" I asked the doctor.

"Mr Dyer, we can't release you yet. You don't have the strength…"

"I've discovered that," I interrupted him. "I want my debit card."

"We aren't allowed to interfere with someone's possessions..."

"Someone did when they brought me here, so that's already happened. I want Phil to get my card from my wallet. Please tell him where it is."

He pointed to a cupboard. Phil obliged and rummaged in my pocket, returning with the wallet. I carefully removed the card.

"There should be a cash machine somewhere. Go and get £100 from it – no more, or it'll make them suspicious. Buy yourselves a decent sandwich or a Sub or something. Something good, not junk food for a change, please. Then come back. Please."

"I'll need the PIN, dad."

So he would. I beckoned him closer and whispered it to him so that the doctor couldn't hear.

"Will you be all right?"

"Of course. Off you go, both of you, and get something to eat."

They both looked at me, each giving the sudden smile that had been one of the traits of their mother when I first knew her, and which they had inherited from her.

"They're good kids," said the doctor when their footsteps had receded down the corridor that I assumed existed was outside the room.

"None better," I said drowsily as I finally let myself drift off for a while. "But I want to see them when they come back." At least, I think that was what I managed to say before I succumbed.

"He's asleep again," were the words that started to bring me round: it was the doctor's voice. There was an argument: it was Phil's voice joining in.

"I'm not asleep," I managed, and it was just about true by the time I reached the third word. My eyes opened. "Better now?"

"Yes, thanks, Dad." Nat. Phil nodded and gave me the balance of the money.

"No use to me at the moment," I told him. "Hang on to it, would you?"

He looked uncomfortable. "He doesn't like us carrying too much money. Says we'd either spend it or it'd be stolen from us."

"But you've always had enough money to get what you need..."

"I know. But uncle's changed since he... since..."

He certainly had. My brain was trying to cope with the idea that my brother, my trusted brother, confidante and – yes, friend – had not just cuckolded me but had changed his stripes too. Something else occurred.

"He's out of hospital, then?"

"Last night. He's still got the bandage round his head, and the eye is something else."

Good.

"Poor chap," I muttered insincerely. Four eyes stared at me.

"You don't mean that."

"No, I don't. Are you sorry for him?"

Phil shrugged. "Never really thought about it."

"Well... Look, you two. What happens now is up to you at least until I'm better. Then we can sort things out. You need to know that you are both my reason for living and I draw strength from you. You'll both be able to draw strength from me again once I'm better. And that will be soon. I guess Mum will want you there. I want you with me just as strongly.

"I don't know what she'll do, whether she'll try to get Social Services involved, but you need to be very sure what you want and tell them what that is. And you have my permission to visit me when you want to, even if that means disobeying either of them."

That had exhausted me again and my eyes closed, though I wanted to hear the reaction. There was a pause.

"Dad, we're coming to see you every day, whatever they say. If we have to escape from the house, we will. Please keep that money for us, because uncle will take it from us if he finds it."

"Does he go through your pockets, then?" I had once again been jolted fully awake.

They were both nodding.

"Take a ten from it, each of you. If you visit and have to eat that'll tide you through. Make sure you get a decent meal at school, though. If things are said, ignore them. If either of them takes the money, you can tell him that I told you that I'll do them for theft... no, on second thoughts don't. Not yet. Tell them that I'm asleep most of the time and don't talk much. That won't get them worried. And can you get a laptop to me without either of them noticing?"

"Mr Dyer…" It was the doctor again. I managed to hold up my hand to stop him.

"It's essential that I start a bank account of my own that they can't get at. And it needs doing soon. Tomorrow. And no more tranquillisers or whatever they are. These two and I need to fight for our rights."

"Surely it's better left to the law…"

"Sod the law! Lawyers would milk us dry. No, this will be done by me. And by these two being strong – if that's what they decide."

By now I could feel that my brain was once again starting to feel like a battery running out of charge. I knew I was about to fade out on them and sleep, whether I wanted to or not.

"Good night, guys. Come tomorrow, and I'll be stronger. I promise."

I was a aware of one lightly rumbling and one more treble voice saying something, but what they were saying was beyond me.

When I next woke it was dark in the room, I felt stronger, thirsty and aching. What do I do? There was light in the corridor outside. I pulled back the covers and tried swinging my legs off the bed. Almost to my surprise I found they worked, were wobbly, but at least I could stand. There was no way I would want to be given that sedative again, the one that had made me as weak as a kitten.

I wobbled to the door and looked outside. Quiet voices came from one direction. Supporting myself against the wall I headed towards them. A male and a female nurse, chatting. One of them saw me and smiled.

"How are you feeling? Couldn't you sleep?"

I explained that I seemed to have been asleep for days and just needed to move. Also I needed a drink. Now upright, I was aware that I needed a lavatory too.

I found after being shown the latter and given the former that sitting on a chair and chatting quietly to the two staff was really rather pleasant. It showed that I was indeed stronger and more able to converse without my eyes closing. They seemed pleased to have someone to talk to, and equally pleased that I had recovered enough to oblige.

At last, at the end of a huge yawn on my part – which sent them both yawning too – I was persuaded back to bed, having declined a sleeping draught or anything else. The thought of getting back into bed was not pleasant, and I thought that I'd stiffen up again. But to my surprise, the next thing I knew it was morning.

4 Progress of a sort

"Your son came in with this early this morning."

It was one of my friends from the previous night. She handed me a laptop case which, to my consternation, contained Phil's school laptop. He had very considerately added me as a user. I supposed he didn't want me to see some of the files on his part of it.

Sitting up – carefully – demonstrated to me that I had more energy. There was a chair by my side so I levered myself out of bed and sat in it.

I tried logging into our online bank account, having had to beg details of the hospital's wi-fi from a passing nurse. Eventually the page opened. The delay between hitting 'enter' and anything happening had me almost sick with worry.

Good: the account was as I'd left it. I still had access to everything. Helen hadn't thought to change the passwords or to drain it of money. Hastily I changed my password, then started a new current account in my own name. Fortunately once your name is registered with a bank there seem to be fewer of the hoops to jump through that are presented when starting with a new bank.

The minutiae of details being presented to me on screen passed me by. All I wanted were the basics. The last screen told me that the account would be set up once I'd confirmed my email address, after which they would email me once it was available. Accessing an email could be an initial problem but I could download software to deal with that. Phil's email account was web-based and used grudgingly by him for school only. In common with just about everyone, I struggle to remember passwords that don't need entering often, but after a few wrong attempts my guess worked and a flood of emails presented themselves. Some were from work, asking where I was, and then in more conciliatory tones if I was all right.

I found that I could now think of work without panicking. What to do? The idiots I'd dealt with last – the U.S. ones – would probably try to start an argument which might lead to some stiff words being exchanged between me and my line manager. I found I no longer cared. My job had left me stale and had contributed in a major way to my now sitting in a hospital room next to a bed that I'd occupied for… how many days?

How many days had it been? I looked back at the entries on the secure messages exchanged with the bank and found my eyes opening wide. I checked the laptop's clock; it too was telling me something I could barely accept. I thought it had been Saturday when I'd returned home, punched my wife's lover and started to walk. It was now Tuesday, yet I knew that my mindless walkabout had lasted for more than three days. Surely I'd not been in here for over a week? I calculated. Eleven days, less three or four allowing for my slow marathon around the city. Seven or eight days in a hospital? How? Why? I didn't even know which hospital – though obviously my sons did. I even checked with the BBC's news page, only to find that the world had moved on from the stories I remembered from the supposedly normal times.

The BBC's date agreed with what the bank and the laptop said.

Where on earth had all that time vanished?

The door opened as I was lying back in shock, trying to fit together a time-line. The doctor looked tired. I had some sympathy with him.

"Am I right? It is Tuesday today? And I've been in here for about a week?"

"You sound better."

"I feel it, I think. But have I been here all that time?"

"You have, and recovering from hypothermia. Sleeping deeply was probably the best thing your brain could have done, given the circumstances you told to me."

"Have I been kept under with drugs?"

"No, Mr Dyer. You slept until your son came in, then when he left you were tossing and turning, and talking in your sleep, so we gave you a sedative to help peaceful sleep return. It affected you more than you think, which is why you were so weak and, of course, still tired, when you awoke next."

Only one dose, then. I supposed I could accept that.

"Am I better now?"

"That's what we need to decide."

"We?"

He smiled. "You and me, Mr Dyer. No one else. It's not as if you've been sectioned or anything. I need to talk about your life again, the life before you came in here."

"Where am I, exactly?"

"It's one of the Health Trust's mental inpatients' hospitals." He told me its current, sanitised name. I knew it by a different name, a much more historic and less politically correct name, and mentioned it.

His face twisted in a grimace. "That's what it used to be called by local people in the days before we knew as much about the brain and its workings."

"Okay…" I said slowly. "So if I'm not sectioned or anything, I could walk out of here at any time."

"You *could*, but I strongly suggest you don't. By default you've accessed some good, even specialist, mental health treatment by being brought here, and you'll obviously know how difficult it can be to accomplish that these days. I really suggest that you should make use of it until you can demonstrate to your own satisfaction that you can make decisions with what I'm sure is your accustomed incisiveness."

I must have looked surprised. He smiled. "We have had to research your identity from the few papers in your pockets, just so that we could find your medical records. I hope you don't mind, but it was essential that we knew of any previous medical events. We also discovered where you worked and your position in the company."

When I had remembered the US trip and the criticism I would likely face in its wake, it had hardly affected me. I had been dismissive of any criticism that might be coming my way. His approach to my job was from a different angle. To my horror I felt a shadow of the panic that had attacked me after Phil's first visit.

I stayed silent, but found that a hand was trembling gently, and there was nothing I could do to stop it.

"That is what I mean," he said, so quietly that I had difficulty hearing. "It may be that time will dilute that part of the stress you have been through, but it may not. Perhaps you could imagine life away from that company, and from that kind of stress. Such a life is possible for us all, you know, even me. The peace we gain through physically leaving the cause of the stress behind can be, and often is, enough to effect a cure."

I thought. He made no move.

"But if..." I started at last "...If that could cure the problem, it would mean that I could start at the same job again."

He smiled gently. "It's good that you are starting to retrieve your negotiating powers. But you also should know that it doesn't work like that. Besides, you have other issues to face, and those are stressful enough."

I thought again. He was right. Really, if I was going to resign from my very well-paid job and leave Helen to play along with my bloody brother – I shuddered at the thought – the only thing I really wanted to save out of it all was the presence of Nat and Phil in my life. And for that I needed a base. A home. Where were we going to live?

If Jonathan had moved into my family home, his flat would be empty. I baulked at any idea of moving into it; it seemed wrong on so many levels and anyway was too small. He had betrayed me. I found I no longer wanted anything to do with him. But I needed somewhere for us to live. This needed a lot of thought, and probably the money to go with it.

Money – it was nearing salary day. I needed that payment to go into the new account. Was I going to have to visit work to sign a form? Or just take the salary out before anyone noticed? That meant I couldn't remove a lump sum now for living expenses as had been my intention. She would doubtless try to put a block on my accessing the whole account if I did that.

There was nothing I could do until the account was ready, and I was starting to feel stress again after all this had been going round in my head. I laid back, thought of living somewhere nice with two ebullient young sons, and gradually persuaded my brain to calm down.

"Sorry, but I think I need to sleep again. Do you mind if I climb back into bed?"

He helped me as if I was four years old again. I slept. Again.

"Hallo, Mr Dyer. May we wake you up?"

You just flaming did, I thought and was about to say something rude but remembered where I was. It was the doctor again, plus Phil. A worried looking Phil.

"How are you feeling?" It was the doctor who asked, not Phil.

Better, I decided, and said so. I was starting to feel guilty about just lying down, something that always happens as I recover from something. I struggled awake, and sat in the chair again, thankful for even a hospital gown and a National Health dressing gown. Sitting up made me feel more alive.

"Well enough to talk to your son and maybe do a note for his school?"

"Well yes, of course," I said positively. I wondered what Phil had done now.

He put another laptop on the bed, my own laptop, and looked sheepish.

"What's happened, Phil?"

"School trouble for not having my laptop. They called home and asked if someone could deliver it to the school office. Mum said that I had gone off with it that morning, so I must have left it on the bus. I had to tell them I'd had to lend it to you in an emergency but couldn't say why. School didn't believe me, so I've got to give them a note explaining tomorrow. From you, or Mum."

So much fuss over a laptop belonging to a fourteen year old. There was less trouble made when he'd been ill and had to stay at home.

"I'm sorry, Phil," I told him. "Really sorry you got into trouble. Please could you tell Mum it turned up at school after all? Which it will, tomorrow morning, with you. And of course I'll write a note – or send the Head an email. That'd be better. I'll explain a bit more in that. I'll tell her something of the situation, and if she's got an ounce of decency she won't contact your mother any more about it."

He looked as if he was squirming. "She already has. She phoned Mum and complained to her when I was there. Said it was not acceptable for me to lend my laptop to you, that she couldn't reach you on your phone, and would Mum please ask you to call her."

He paused for breath. "When I got home I had an earful from both of them – what it's got to with Uncle Jonathan I don't know – but I told her you'd asked me to, and if she hadn't thrown you out she could have talked to you about it herself. Then I went upstairs and locked my door."

During this, the doctor's phone had rung and he had left.

"When they were eating I remembered where your laptop was and fetched it without them knowing. I was just leaving the house with it when she came rushing up and said I wasn't to visit you and what was I doing with your laptop. I just ignored her, and ran. A bit later I heard uncle running after me, but I know the area better than him and got out of his way. Then I hopped on the bus and came here."

He was looking at the floor after this. I realised just what that defiance had cost him, and how it must have gone against the grain of his upbringing, and what it was likely to cost him when he returned home.

"Phil?"

He looked up.

"Phil, you are wonderful. I'm so, so sorry you're had to be involved in all this, but I'm grateful beyond words for your help. One day, I promise, I'll repay you."

"All I want is for uncle to leave and for you to come back."

I pulled a face, paused and spoke gently. "And you know, of all the things we both want, that is the one thing we can't have. Not now. Not after all that's happened. I can't just go back and live there with my own brother... er... partnering my wife. It would be intolerable."

"I know, Dad, but why can't you just throw him out?"

"Because your mother has chosen him now, not me."

"I'll throw him out, then."

"It still won't change her mind."

"But that's not fair."

"I know. But you also know that she and I have been drifting apart for ages. It's not something we talked about until recently, but it's true. I just didn't expect my bloody brother to..."

I swallowed, suddenly tired again. My eyes closed for a moment. I felt a touch on my hand.

"I know, Dad. I really do. I don't want to live with her and him either. I know, really, that things won't go back to where they were, but you can't blame me for telling you what I really want."

I smiled again, tiredly. "What does Nat think?" I asked.

"He's very quiet. Hasn't really said much at all."

"That's not like him."

"I know," he said, looking worried. "I need to sit him down and talk, but we hardly have any time on our own."

"Can't he come here and talk."

"He's been told not to visit you, too. And he's scared of Uncle Jonathan."

"*Scared* of him? Why? They were always good together."

A sigh. "When he realised that the locks had been changed so you couldn't get back in, he said things to Uncle Jonathan that he didn't like at all. And when you hi... when uncle fell and hurt his head, Nat was pleased and told him it served him right. Since then, uncle has been very strict with him and tells him he's got to do everything he's told."

I was horrified. "Hasn't he tried the same with you?"

"Yes. I just ignore him."

"And poor old Nat can't."

"Well, he can, but he's scared what might happen."

"Has he made threats?"

"Not that I've heard."

I let the silence hang. Then:

"I don't want to live there any more."

My head snapped up. "I don't want... I want both of you... I want the three of us living together. You, Nat and me. The other two can go hang." I gritted my teeth. "Let me sleep off this wretched weakness or whatever it is, and I'll get things moving. That's a promise. Look, you'd better keep things sweet at home, as far as possible. Both of you. Let them think I'm still asleep most of the time and not doing anything. I'll start looking for something – a place for us to live. And I'll try and find a job that fits in with school times and holidays."

"But you won't have enough money. Will you?"

"Honestly? I don't know until I try. But try I most certainly will."

"Tell me how you get on, Dad. But don't call me. We have to tell them who we're talking to, and if it's someone they don't know they tell us to cut the call. It's like being in China."

I gave a wry smile and a thought occurred. "Can you start keeping a list of what they do? The things that affect you and Nat?"

"Why?"

"In case someone gets the bloody Social Services, and they start trying to throw their weight about."

He pulled a face. "Ok. Look, we can use WhatsApp. I'll set messages to vanish after ten seconds on mine, then no one will see them. I'll hide the app at the back of my phone. You can get an account too now. And make sure you only send them to me."

I thought about it. Though we didn't particularly like them using social media, Phil at least was over thirteen and it was legal. It was also inevitable. We were trusting of them and were aware that Phil used TikTok. Nat was often watching exchanges over his shoulder and so was probably almost as at home with it as his brother. I should say that it was Helen who had been trusting of them. I'd had little input because of my absences at work. But now it was different. We needed it for privacy reasons.

"Ok," I said, and dug my phone out. Inevitably he reached for it and I let him download the app.

"Username?" he asked. "We can't have your real one, just in case they *do* see it."

"What username?"

"For WhatsApp."

"It can't be 'Dad' then."

He laughed. "Along with the other million or so – Dad with a long number after their name! No. Something less obvious."

We tried various combinations of Jack and Dyer and went onto synonyms of each like 'carlifter' and 'colour-changer'. The amusement lifted our spirits a lot and resulted in a unique username. It made me feel a very great deal better. There is something about laughing with your son on level terms that cleanses the spirit.

Returning to the more conventional medium of an email, together we wrote to the Head of his school, making sure it was to his and my satisfaction. Inevitably it detailed a little of what had happened, hinting that his mother and I were splitting up but stressing that I would be the main contact – at Phil's request. He took his laptop and uninstalled my email client and user account "in case they look at it". It annoyed me that his privacy was being eroded, even at fourteen. Farewells said, he left for home, doubtless to face the music.

The rest of the evening, feeling lighter of mood than for ages, was spent thinking how to approach my employers – more than that, the leaving of my job. Ridiculously or not, my brain had not allowed me to come to a decision about it. It rebelled vigorously whenever I imagined myself entering my own office. Its reaction insisted that I was not going back to Crown Engineering.

Ridiculous? Of course. That is no way, no basis, on which to make a life-changing decision. Yet to arrive at that decision had lifted a great weight from my mind. It felt as though it had been lifted from my body too. It was a release that made me feel physically lighter and mentally almost light-headed. I cannot overstate the relief it gave.

Still in my mind was the desire to remain on sick leave for maybe another month. I thought it would be possible if played right. My manager didn't need to know of my scheming. Of immediate importance was to ensure that the nearly-due salary would be paid into the new bank account. I felt that my employers – ex-employers – should have an email telling them I was suffering from stress due to work and the family situation, and had been hospitalised. All of that was true. What hint should be given about a return date? None. Leave it open-ended. They had had their pound of flesh from me. Now, ethically or unethically, I was going to recoup some of it.

A visit from a nurse interrupted my thoughts and my cheerful greeting surprised her.

"You sound as if you're on the road to recovery, talking like that."

"I feel as if I am. My son has had a lot to do with it, and being able to make a few plans for the future."

"Don't overdo it. What you've been through can't help but leave scars, you know."

"Mental scars? Yes. I've identified where they are. One of them I've been planning to avoid from now on. Another I still have to deal with."

"It would be good if you could describe that to the doctor because he will help you deal with them – the scars, that is."

I smiled. "Maybe he can. But he can't put a marriage back together or arrange a new home for two boys and a scarred father with an unknown income, or even arrange a decent income for a scarred father."

She touched my shoulder, suddenly serious, then withdrew the hand.

"Sorry. I shouldn't have done that. But we see all sorts in here, and to find someone with the strength of mind – to use non-medical terms – to turn himself round, is rare. Rare and encouraging. I wish you well."

I found myself smiling at her. "Thank you. What you say has helped, in fact, and has encouraged me too."

As she turned, smiling, to leave the room, I thought what a pleasant woman she was. What would the boys think of her if…

Back to the days of lying in bed as a teenager and fantasising about a member of the opposite sex? I told myself off for it. Back then it had been the norm, a guilty norm maybe. But at least now I was not being disloyal or mentally two-timing the woman I was married to. Adultery, after all, was Helen's province.

I turned my mind away, and wool-gathered, ending up wondering where I had actually been over all the time I had been walking. There were images of streets. They flashed to my mind as if I were watching an old fashioned slide show, or someone's Instagram story on Phil's mobile. Some I recognised. Most I didn't. Some gave a feeling of noise and bustle and grime. Some presented peace and tranquillity, either in comparison with their opposites or because they were placid, green, and food for the soul.

The picture that stayed longest was one of a canal, maybe a dock, with those strange, colourful boats that are made to fit Birmingham's so-narrow locks and bridges. Like many inhabitants of the city, these ribbons of water with their masonry punctuations had been to me just a fact of life. I'd been aware of them, yet simultaneously dismissive. They were just present, threading their way between old buildings and new, as unremarkable as the patches of scrubland that could be found by them.

Yet dimly I realised that no other city that I'd visited had so many canals – apart from Venice. I'd never been there but knew about it, just as everyone else does.

In my memory was a basin, with boats. Colourful boats. Nobody around except for two people; a woman sitting, looking agonised, and a younger man seemingly comforting her.

My state at the time had rebelled at any hint of another human in trouble, and I remembered leaving the scene hurriedly. But now I thought that the scene itself minus the figures would be something of a tonic for my scars, as the comforting nurse had put it.

5 Escape

I woke at what was a socially reasonable time, this time feeling fraudulent at the idea of spending a day in bed or even by its side. I got up, told the newly on-duty nurses that I was having a shower, declined offers of help, and felt even better after it. Towel still in hand and still drying my hair as if I was still in my own house, I returned to my room.

Phil was there, sitting on my chair. The school laptop was with him. He looked up, and I could see the redness to the side of his face. I stopped, shocked.

"What happened?" was my greeting.

"She… she slapped me."

"Mum?

He nodded.

I was silent, yet I could feel the anger building up inside me.

"Was it last night?"

"No. All I got last night was a shouting at. I mean really shouting. Both of them. I just sat there and let it go. Then I went to check on Nat, but he wouldn't let me in. I asked him if he was all right, but all he did was tell me to go away. I tried reasoning, but he just sounded as if he was crying. There's nothing you can do if the door's locked and he won't let you in. Then I could hear *him* on the stairs so I went to my own room and locked the door."

He stopped. "But he went to Nat's room and went in. Why did Nat let him in, and not me? I know he hates *him* now. I've got to see Nat at school. It's the only time I can talk to him alone."

"Haven't you been in yet?"

"It's only eight o'clock."

"But when did she hit you?"

"I got up, and she started on at me again, telling me not to visit you. This time I told her you were my father, not *him*, and he would never be that to me, and that I was fourteen and would visit Dad when I wanted. That's when she hit me. I wanted so much to hit her back, but just couldn't. I marched out of the house and came here."

I sat on the end of the bed. Fourteen or not, I held his hand.

"Is this going to go on for long, Dad?"

I sighed. "For as short a time as I can manage. Really. I need to get out of here, even for just a few hours. It's the only way I can get my head together – no, that's not what I meant. I mean I just need to get some real, fresh air. And it'll take more than a few days to find somewhere to live – and that means sorting out the money side first."

"So we've got to put up with them for a bit?"

"For a little time, I'm afraid. You'll need to keep the peace at home as best you can. I imagine that now you've stood up for yourself she might lay off you, especially physically. You know that you have me on your side, and that you will have me on your side all the way. And yes, I can imagine how awful it is.

For you both. Please keep coming – and see if you can bring Nat in. I need to see him too. If he avoids you at school like he seems to have done at home, please tell me."

He nodded.

"And if you get any more hassle at school, phone me or get the Head to phone *me*. Not her. Please."

He nodded again.

"And I really am on your side, and will do what needs doing as soon as I possibly can. But I need to be sure that Mum and your blasted Uncle don't get an idea of what's happening behind the scenes. Oh, and I suggest you lock your bedroom door and leave the key turned in the lock. It sounds like Nat's may have been locked from outside last night. You don't want the same to happen."

He nodded again. "Ok. I will. Look, I'd better go, or I'll be late."

"Ok, Phil. Look after yourself, and Nat. I love you both."

It was a tired, thin smile that said its farewell.

The fury in me would have threatened to undo much of the benefits of the previous few days had I let myself dwell on it. Despite what I felt, I needed to concentrate on the positives, such as there were, and on making the best of them. Firstly, income. An email went to my employer's accounts department with the new account details that had finally come through, asking that they confirm without delay that the salary would be credited to it 'as the bank has been having some difficulties with the previous account'. Another work email to worry about when the reply came, but worth it.

Next, an email to my line manager, saying that I'd had an extraordinary bout of stress for various reasons including work, leading to a nervous breakdown and hospitalisation; that breakdown repairs were underway and that I needed some time to regain an even keel. All of that was, of course, true, even with slightly mixed metaphors.

A rest on the bed came next, to ensure as far as possible that my anger subsided before the doctor's visit.

The conversation with him was cordial, and he seemed pleased but told me that there was still a way to go. That was true, I supposed. My ability to think logically existed in reverse proportion to my anger. The anger that was blazing at the thought of that slap.

I proposed that a quiet walk outside would get me some much needed fresh air. He frowned.

"Are you thinking of discharging yourself? I know I can't stop you, but please don't, as there's more we can do for you to prevent it happening again."

I had nowhere else to go apart from this hospital with its free food and its free accommodation. At least for the moment.

"No," I told him. "I appreciate what you're doing, how you're helping. But I really do need some fresh air."

He thought.

"I could get one of the nurses to go with you, maybe into the park. Once you're there and you're happy that you're all right, she can come back. But could you leave your mobile number with us so we can contact you? And take our phone number so that you can ask for help if you need it? How about that?"

A half-way house arrangement. It was something and it was acceptable. An hour later I was sitting in a park with a nurse – not the more mature lady of the previous evening but a younger lass who seemed as just as glad to be in the fresh air. On the spur of the moment I asked her if there were any canal basins nearby.

"Canals?" she said, even more mystified than me. Oh well.

At last she was happy that I wouldn't collapse, and returned to the hospital. Relaxation on the open was a tonic, and I nearly fell asleep on the bench. Perhaps I still wasn't as ready for this as I thought.

The question about the canal basin was posed to anyone who passed or whom I passed later as I started walking around the park. The only person who seemed to know anything mentioned something about Soho and was dismissive when I said I wanted one in Birmingham, not a one-time seedy part of London. She waved her hand towards the hospital and gave me the impression it was beyond that.

I started walking in the general direction of her gesture, ensuring that I knew the whereabouts of the hospital which would be my home until I found somewhere for a real home for three – or when they threw me out as cured.

And then, from a main road, I saw the glint of water through a modern gate. A locked gate. A notice with an arrow said *Poppy Narrowboats – next right.*

Well, it was a chance, and the only one so far. My route continued, turned right as directed and found, near an unfriendly brick wall, a sign that advertised a rifle club and, once again, Poppy Narrowboats.

Was this the way I had stumbled all those days ago? There was nothing in my memory. Odd that it should be so close to the hospital. But maybe what they say is right, that when you're lost you actually do walk round in circles.

This long, low building must be the rifle range. And yes, there was a poppy with an arrow.

There was a bend to the right. I rounded it, and passed through some open gates. There was my memory, revealed. A quite substantial sheet of water, those odd, brightly painted boats of various lengths but a seemingly standard, narrow width – hence the name, I supposed. Of people there was no sign.

It was the oasis of peace that I had wondered about. Walking up to the end of a Victorian building I was drawn to the longest boat I'd seen so far. It seemed to be freshly painted in two shades of green, red and some yellow lining. It was un-named and looked smart and very well cared for. Others, further on, were in what appeared to be fleet colours, and as I passed one there was an expletive from it. I looked, startled. A red face looked back at me and apologised.

I laughed, and apologised back for laughing.

"'s all right," said a very Birmingham voice. "Got a problem with the engine. Another one… oh… You're not a customer, are you?"

"No," I said, "just an inquisitive type. What's wrong with the engine?"

"Won't start. We seem to get the problem in batches. They go for months, and then we get about four go down at once. It's a pain, and we're losing customers because of it."

"Going on for some time, then." I observed, my engineer's brain formulating an opinion.

"Yep."

"Tried looking at the fuel?" I asked. My recent experiences in the US, which were still a part of my mental problems, seemed balanced against the interest in engines which had been my 'thing' since school.

"I've bled it through twice," he said. "Know something about them, do you?"

"A bit," I told him, without admitting my engineering doctorate and subsequent experience.

"Want a go?"

"Well I will, but first – have you got some clear fuel pipe handy?"

He looked at me, puzzled. "Dirt in the fuel? Don't think so. New delivery a week ago."

"Still… it's worth a look for the sake of ten minutes, don't you think?"

He hauled himself out of the engine bay and headed for another, nearby Victorian building, reappearing a few minutes later with some pipe and the woman I'd seen in my casual glance all that time and a different mindset ago. I smiled at her. She seemed a bit stony faced.

"Know more about these engines than we do, do you?"

"I don't know," I said guardedly. "It depends what they are. Maybe not the make I'm used to. But I know diesels in general pretty well."

"So what are you going to do with the pipe, then?"

"Dip the tank, get a sample from it from the top of the fuel to the bottom, and then we'll see what we can see."

They both looked at me, puzzled again.

"May I?" I said with a hand on the rail. She shrugged and nodded assent.

Fortunately the end of the new pipe was straight. The fuel cap was opened and I slowly lowered the end of the pipe down until it touched bottom. The remainder of the roll was on the deck and I didn't have the reach to do what I needed.

"Could you put your finger over the other end, and keep it sealed?" I asked the man.

He frowned, but did so. Carefully I pulled the pipe from the tank, keeping it vertical. About a third of the way down the liquid turned from straw coloured diesel – cloudy – to almost clear water.

I showed them the result. "How long has the fuel been in the tank?" I asked.

"About three days. We hoped that if we left it, we could try and start the engine."

"And you say you had a delivery of fuel a week ago?"

They nodded.

"Okay. The engine won't start because the tank is feeding it water. The water is either getting in to the boat's tank or it's already in your supply. If you've been having a lot of these problems and for some time it's more likely to be in your main tank. Can we try filling a container from the main tank? A clear container?"

"What shall I do with this?" 'This' being the tube.

"Ditch it. I'm afraid it's no use. A waste oil container, perhaps?"

When at last we had a sample from the tank it was obvious from the cloudiness that they had contamination.

"When did you last run the supply tank low?" I asked.

"We never have, not even in winter," the woman replied. She was looking hopeful and really quite pleasant now that a solution was possibly in sight. Her voice matched the hope in her face.

"Then with a supply that new, I think you need to talk to your supplier. If they won't talk turkey, tell them that you've had a very experienced diesel engineer look at your supply and he has mentioned Trading Standards."

Now she looked astonished. "Would that be you, then, this engineer? Or is it just a way of getting them to roll over?"

I smiled. "It's me. I'm employed by Crown Engineering, who have sent me all over the world troubleshooting. Oddly, my last trip to the States was to troubleshoot a problem just like this. I could have told them what to check over the phone but they insisted on a visit. They had bought our engines. A bit bigger than this, though; they were powering standby generators for a large factory. Their insistence and how they treated me cost them time, accommodation and flights when all I had to do was to tell them what to check; then when they found this, to go to a more reliable fuel supplier – as I'm suggesting to you."

"They're cheap," she said guiltily.

"And they probably don't look after their stocks properly."

"Could you come to the office while I call them, please? Is that asking too much?"

I admit I was starting to feel tired after so many days of no exercise. But they were both pleasant people, and she needed help. With a bit of a struggle I lurched into the first office I'd seen for ages, discounting medical ones.

The formula of the call I had suggested seemed to result in a silence, if not an apology. She had proved quite forceful when giving her demands; an attitude I approved of, having needed such an approach many times myself.

The earpiece squawked. She looked at me. "They're asking your name and job title."

I smiled. We had them on the defensive. "Who are they?"

She told me, and I laughed quietly.

"I've had experience with them before, with a couple of local plant operators with expensive problems. Frankly, I'm surprised they're still going. Tell them it's Jack Dyer, Senior Engineering Manager for Crown Engineering, and tell them that we need the supply tank emptied and cleansed this week, and the fuel tank on each and every boat emptied as they come in. If there is any damage to the engines, repairs will be billed to them. Oh, and of course we need a full refund for the fuel they collect. You might want to remind them of the issues that they and I have had in the past and the long and expensive legal process they demanded before being proved at fault."

Her hand had come away from the phone, I noticed. She smiled at me again.

"I think you might have heard that," she said. "I want you on site tomorrow to start emptying and cleaning the supply tank so that we can get it refilled – by someone else, of course. Then you can pump out the boats that return this Saturday. Later we can arrange your payment for the boats that aren't due back in or which break down this week and which we have to attend to at some remote location."

There was more, of course, but she was insistent. After the long call she sat back and looked at me and at her employee.

"Well… and how much are you going to charge me for your expertise, Mr Dyer?"

I laughed. "On the house, Mrs… Poppy?"

She smiled back. "Two and two do indeed make four. Poppy Watson, at your service. More correctly, thanking you for your service. Ian here is an expert when it comes to just about everything else on the boats, but engines are not his forte. Don't want a part time job alongside your rather high-powered one, do you?"

"Oddly, I'm looking for a full-time job. One that's a lot less stressful. I've had enough of working all hours, and ending up at the wrong end of a flight at weekends. The amount of time I've missed with my kids is something I regret more than you can know."

"You must have a very understanding wife."

A silence grew.

"Ah. I'm sorry. I've touched a nerve."

"You don't know the half of it. But I won't burden you with my troubles."

"I've burdened you with ours."

"That's different."

"I meant what I said about a job. My last engineer left half way through the latest batch of breakdowns, and I can't say I blame him. But I'm in cloud-cuckoo land. I couldn't afford to pay you what you need."

Ian coughed, and said that he'd best be going to have a look at another boat.

"Don't worry about the engines, Ian."

He laughed and raised his hand to show agreement.

"If you really want someone, full time, I might be interested. Really. And money… well all I need is somewhere to live and enough income to feed three – the boys and me – and a little to allow us some quality time together, doing things."

Silence.

After the excitement and the unaccustomed mental activity I found my brain was once again running out of battery. It must have alarmed her.

"Are you all right?"

"So tired…" I muttered. "Sorry. Not the way to behave on a job interview."

"Can I run you home?"

"It's not far. I can walk…"

"Nonsense. After what you've just done for me. Wait there. No. You look so weak. You'll slump onto the floor and I'll never lift you. Walk with me to the car."

She helped me up. With her firmly nudging me along, we made it to an estate car with all sorts of boat related equipment in the back. She helped me into the front and I put the seat belt on automatically.

"Stay awake," she commanded in much the same tone she'd used to her fuel supplier. "Where to?"

I directed her by giving the name of the hospital.

"Oh," she said as she swung round to head to the main road. "Stress case, then. Nothing more serious."

"Stress case," I muttered, "and then some."

"Nothing dire?"

"Nothing that time and a different job and the presence of two sons won't cure."

Even after such a short journey and her efforts at engaging me I was asleep as we pulled in to the entrance. A porter had to come and help me into a wheelchair. I never even said thank you, let alone goodbye.

6 The panic

"Dad? Dad? Wake up, please!"

I was so tired; still exhausted after the mental – and physical – efforts of the morning. Perhaps I wasn't as back to normal as I thought. But the paternal imperative of Phil's pleas worked its usual magic, and I surfaced.

"Sorry," I mumbled. "Had a busy morning."

Busy! Compared with my usual – no, my previous – pace of work it was a fleabite. But it had somehow short-circuited my batteries quite radically.

"Dad, you really need to help..."

If anything is guaranteed to gain a parent's attention it is a cry for help from their child. I struggled awake.

"Hallo," I said tritely.

"Dad, it's Nat. He's disappeared."

It took a few moments, but in fairly short order I was fully awake, alert. I swore.

"What do you mean? When did he go missing?"

"He was at school first thing, I saw him and he's in the register. I tried to find him at Break but he kept moving off every time he saw me. He was trying to avoid me, Dad, I'm sure of it. And then I had another try at lunch but he'd gone. He never answered roll call, the Head says, and he's just vanished. The school's in chaos, Mum's panicking. So am I."

"Have the Police been called?" I was keeping as calm as possible.

"Yes. The school did that. They talked to me and I told them everything. They thought you're more ill than you are when they heard you were in here. But they're going to talk to uncle at his work, too. And..."

The door opened and a nurse put her head in.

"I'm sorry, Mr Dyer, but a policeman wants to talk to you."

No sooner had she said it when a uniformed officer entered, almost pushing her out of the way. He saw Phil and paused.

"I saw you at the school, didn't I?"

"Yes," said Phil shortly. "I told you he was ill, and in hospital."

"Indeed. I need to ask him some questions, so hop it, please."

I spluttered, now fully roused. "I beg your pardon? You do not order my son around. That is unacceptable to both him and me. And where is your colleague? You are required to be in pairs when you question someone are you not? In fact you are in pairs at all times."

"I am busy trying to find your son, as is my Oppo. She is just outside, asking the staff about your movements. My job is to get information from you, and as swiftly as possible. Where were you this morning?"

I told him. In graphic detail, I told him. From the corner of my eye I noticed that Phil had his phone out and seemed to be pointing it in our direction. Was he videoing this? I hoped so.

"And who was this convenient woman you apparently helped?"

"Not so much apparently, officer; actually helped. She is Mrs Poppy Watson, of Poppy Narrowboats. No doubt you'll be able to find her and check up on me."

"And you're sure you went nowhere else after the visit to her?"

"I almost flaked out in her office. As I just told you, she brought me back here."

No apology, just another question: "Tell me again why had you gone there?"

I hadn't told him, but did so now. I'm not sure if he believed me or not. He was about to ask another question when I interrupted. "Have you searched my home – my *ex*-home? Have you looked in his room? Was it locked?"

"Why do you ask?"

"Because I, too, want to find my younger son. Because he and his brother here mean more to me than they do to you. Because I am estranged from my wife as she has taken my brother to be her lover, and I have reason to believe that Nathaniel was locked in his room last night. By one of them."

Phil gasped.

"You knew this?" the officer asked Phil.

He nodded. "I told Dad that Nat wouldn't let me in, the door was locked, but that my uncle was able to get in later."

"Why would your brother be locked in?"

He shrugged his shoulders. "I don't know. I didn't know he had been, just that his door was locked."

"Had he misbehaved?"

Phil hesitated.

My turn, I thought. "Even if he had misbehaved, no balanced parent takes to imprisoning their child. And quite apart from anything else, it's a fire risk."

That made him hesitate.

"Don't go anywhere," he ordered, and left the room, radio already in his hand.

"I don't know where he thinks we're going to go," I grumbled. "I'm only just waking up… But you're not under arrest and nor am I, so he can't actually stop us going anywhere."

"Shouldn't we be out looking for him?"

"Do you think I've not thought of that? I'm worried to hell, Phil. But I know that at the moment I'd be a liability to any search. You'd have more chance of searching at home, though I'd hope that your mother already had. And where's Jonathan? Has he been contacted yet?"

"Don't know. Do you think I should go home?"

"Best wait until that policeman comes back. Look: which is nearer, school or home? You'd know any little nooks and crannies at the school, surely? Although… won't it be closed by now?"

"Should be. It's gone six, so yes."

"Then they need to get the caretaker to open it and… ah. Here he is."

This time both the original officer and his Oppo were in the room, the 'Oppo' being a sergeant who introduced them both. It was a refreshing change from the previous attitude.

"I understand you think that your son may have been locked in his room last night. If you were here, how can you know that?"

I explained what Phil had heard and what I thought could be deduced from it.

"And you're sure you were here last night?"

My eyebrows shot up. "My brother has moved in with my wife. They have changed the locks. How could I have got into the house, always assuming I could have got there in my mental state? And why would I want to? Anyway, if you're wondering if I abducted my own son, think again. He was at school this morning."

"How do you know that?"

"Phil told me."

"Ah… yes. Very well. Now…"

"Is the school being searched?" I interrupted.

"I believe so."

"Then I suggest that you ask Phil to go and help. He will know the places where pupils can make themselves scarce when they want to, the places that the staff would ignore. Also, please will you make a thorough search of their home and make sure he's not hiding or being hidden there?"

There was a pause.

"Do you think that your brother or your wife would have something to do with it?" she asked.

"Officer, I don't know. But TV dramas show enough cases where a disappearance *is* something to do with the family. I'm sure your training will tell you that."

Her colleague's radio had been making sounds during this short exchange. He spoke to her.

"A search of the school is underway. I suppose… how do you feel about helping find him? Phil, isn't it? Would you be prepared to?"

"Of course I will. He's my brother."

They left. All I could do was to lie there and worry. I considered calling Helen, but couldn't bring myself to. If she or bloody Jonathan had somehow been involved I didn't want to warn them. Eventually I got up and sat in the chair; I could be restless and tired there as well as I could by lying in bed.

It took two hours. My mobile rang: Phil.

"We've found him. He was asleep in one of the cleaners' cupboards. Dad, I'm just so…" He sounded quavery. Was my fourteen year old son about to show that he had emotions? "They want to take him home but he doesn't want to go. I can't stop them. Will you talk to them?"

"Of course. Well done, and I'm so relieved. Come back here? With him? I'll make arrangements with them if you put them on the phone."

It took me a lot of negotiating and perseverance, and reminding the officer that I was an equal partner in the parenting of both boys, and that what Nat wanted was of paramount importance. If he wanted to come and see me, that is what must happen, and I certainly wanted to see him. Reluctantly, and it seemed as if it went against every fibre of their being, they agreed he could come and make a quick visit.

I said nothing about the duration of the visit, just awaited their arrival.

It was a very quiet Nat who knocked at the door and waited for me to answer before he came in. He wouldn't look at me.

"Nat?" I said gently. "I'm not angry, really I'm not. I'm just so, so relieved you're ok."

At that he did look up. I held out my arms and he came to me like a five year old. We held each other, wordless, for a while, then I felt his grip relax.

"Confused? Hurting inside? Don't know what to think or do? Join the club. Nor did I until today. But now I've started to see what we can do."

"He was on at me last night," he said, still quavering. "Arguing. I told him to… well, he locked me in my room. I can't go back there. Not while he's there. Can't you come back? You beat him up once. Can't you do the same and send him back?"

"If I did that, I'd be the one in trouble with the Police," I told him. "But what did he say to you?"

"He was telling me that you'd gone off the rails and we wouldn't be allowed to see you any more, so I'd better get used to living at home, with him in the house. I told him that you'd be better soon, and he'd better look out then because you and Phil and me would throw him out."

"What did he say to that?"

"He laughed and said it wouldn't happen, that Mum didn't love you any more, and that you were out of the family. And I'd better get used to it. That's when I lost it and swore at him. And got locked in."

I nodded, and thought.

"He's right about just one thing, Nat; your mother doesn't love me any more. And because of what she and your uncle have done, I can't say that I love her any more either." I gave a sigh. "You know that it happens. And now you know how much it hurts. I'm hurt too, not just by that but because of the amount of time I have to spend at work and travelling.

"I can't make your mother go back to loving me, so that bit of pain, the bit that affects you and Phil as well as me, will stay. But work I can do something about, and have already started. I'm looking for a new job, one that means I'm around much more. All I need now is to find it and somewhere to live. Then, if you want, you can live there, or share your time between Mum and me."

Silence.

"He told me you wouldn't want me any more. Wouldn't be able to deal with us."

I was seething inside again.

"Then he is absolutely wrong." I was almost shouting. "*Completely* wrong. You and Phil are the best things that have happened in my life and I can't imagine life without you both. I hope you will want to live wherever I do, at least for some of the time, or permanently. Preferably permanently. But I'm not going to pressure you, or Phil."

It was his turn to sigh.

"I've been a bit of a fool, haven't I?"

"No. Someone you liked and trusted just told you lies. Radical lies. Adults can be very persuasive and can blind you to the facts sometimes. By the sound of it I'd say that you should distrust anything he says, and anything he says about me.

"As to decisions, you're of an age now where you can make up your own mind and I, for one, will respect your decision. So will Phil. And whatever anyone else says, I will fight – in the Court if necessary – to respect that decision."

Another pause.

"So Uncle Jonathan is lying."

"Yes."

"Then I hate him even more."

"He's my brother, and he's somehow gone bad. That's how I see it. Look, please can you manage to live there a few days more while I try and sort things out? Then I'll ask you and Phil again what you want to do. You can each record the conversation, so that you can play it to Mum and him, and have it available as evidence in Court if needed.

"Now I've got to tell you this: before you came in I put my phone on to record. I can send a copy of this to you if you like, so you can play it to them so that they know where I stand. But don't do it tonight, eh? Let me make arrangements, then we can surprise them and take action together. That's what I've been talking to Phil about."

"So you're not saying anything until you've got somewhere to live?"

"That, and when I've found a different job."

"Don't Mum and uncle know anything about that yet, then?"

"No. They think I'm still really ill, asleep most of the time."

He looked at me with eyes wide.

"Wow!"

"No good getting old if you don't get wise. Now, let's get Phil in as well and we can make sure we all know what's happening."

He returned with Phil and the police.

"We need to get these two back home," said the Sergeant.

He got a lift of the eyebrows from me. "I think you mean that I, as their father, need to encourage them to return. I'm very grateful for the help you all gave and am even more glad that Nat is ok. But I can arrange for them to get home, as can they. They are twelve and fourteen, when all's said and done, and very well used to making their own way around the city."

"We need to deliver them home to their parents…oh. To their mother."

"And instead you have delivered them to their father, who has discussed things with them and ensured they are both now back sailing on an even keel. Thank you, as I have said. But I will take it from here."

She sighed. "Mr Dyer, I'm not trying to argue with you or take over, or regard their mother as somehow more important. But they live with her, not here in the hospital. We have a duty to take them to where they normally live. And we can explain that Nat was confused – as he told us – and is tired. We can also ensure there are no other… circumstances around their living there. It is their welfare that concerns us. After that we shall need to have no further input into the case."

I could see the sense in a check of the two adults at their home.

"Ok guys. It looks like you have a ride in a police car coming up. Here is a twenty. Buy yourself a snack or whatever on the way – neither of you has eaten this evening yet, I guess. And Phil, how about you make sure that Nat's door can now be locked from the inside? If not, would you let him bunk in with you tonight? I don't like the idea of either of you being locked in as if you were prisoners."

They both agreed. "If you don't mind, Phil," said Nat.

"Ok by me. It'll stop him trying to brainwash you. Sounds as if that's what he's been trying to do. Don't forget, we know better. So does Dad. Night, Dad. See you tomorrow."

"Hope so." I yawned. "And I might have some news for you tomorrow too."

"Yeah?"

"Yeah. Good night for now, though."

I was just about all in, given the morning's exertions and the panic of potentially having lost a son. I climbed back into bed and that's all I knew until about ten-thirty the following morning. It was so fortunate that this hospital was attuned to valuing the power of sleep in healing the mind and that there was no hospital-type six-thirty awakening.

I felt a lot better, rose, showered and dressed, then talked to the nurse on duty.

"The doctor will be here in a moment or two. He came when you were showering, but said he'd return."

True to his word I had hardly been in the room, looking for replies to the previous day's emails, when he appeared.

"A busy day yesterday, then," he said with a smile.

"Yes. And I'll admit the morning was too much for me still. But unless I go out and walk – and get physically tired – I feel as if I'll never get back to normal."

"It's this mental tiredness that we need to bear in mind, and heal."

"Yes, and the more I do, the better it's going to get."

"Hmmm… Even if I tell you to rest, you're not going to, are you?"

"Honestly? No. I don't work that way. Not only do I need to be doing something but I have those sons of mine to find a home for."

He sighed. "But you also need to remember that the hospital has a duty to you and the rest of society as well, one that ends when you are discharged. I can accept your going out, but if you crock yourself up as you nearly did yesterday there's a limit to what I can do."

"So – be careful, or I won't help you any more, you mean," I said with a smile.

"No: be careful or I won't be *able* to help you." He was quite serious.

"Okay, doctor. I promise that I'll be careful, physically and mentally. And I'll come back at the first sign of tiredness."

"The first sign?"

I looked him in the eye. "As soon after as I possibly can."

Temporarily released, I headed straight back to Poppy Narrowboats, and the first sign of movement I saw was a tanker connected to their fuel bunker. Good. It had really worked.

Poppy noticed me and came away from the noise, smiling.

"Your name really supercharged them. They were here first thing. Their local manager appeared too. He's only just left."

"Did you tell him I was on my way?"

She laughed. "Hardly, I didn't know you were coming. He was nervous when he was here, and only escaped when he was happy their people knew exactly what they had to do."

"Maybe it was as well, after the stand-up row he engaged me in last time we actually saw each other."

I followed her into the office, sat down on one of the comfortable sofas when asked, and accepted my first non-hospital cup of tea for ages. I looked round. It was clean, plainly painted, and hung with framed photographs of countryside each of which had a ribbon of water featured in it. There was also a large map with blue lines snaking out from a central point which had been so heavily fingered that it provided the only piece of dirt in the place. Surely these can't all be canals... but my musings were interrupted.

"So what do you think?"

"What would you need me to do if I worked here?"

She looked me straight in the eye. "I can't afford you. I can't afford your expertise."

"My expertise helped put me into hospital and nearly lost me my family. Stuff a high-flying job from now on. I said yesterday that I needed something more – well, basic."

Silence. I could almost hear the cogs moving.

"Twenty engines. Look after them, change their nappies, make sure they never, ever break down. Love them, cherish them and help change them out if absolutely necessary. Get dirty. Learn about the other things in the engine compartment; batteries, calorifier, bilge pump, cooling system. You name it."

"And with my other hand?"

"Oh, help by going out to breakdowns. Every Saturday help with the fuelling, pump-out, cleaning and re-stocking. In the autumn help with drafting publicity, stuffing envelopes, taking bookings. You know, nothing major."

"And the rest of the time's my own."

"Something like that."

It would really mean getting my hands dirty, I knew that. But what was I doing at College all those years ago? What were my first few jobs like before I started with Crown? What had my first few jobs *with* Crown been like?

"Ok," I said. "I'll give it a go. But I've got to find somewhere to live nearby, somewhere inexpensive but decent, and big enough for the three of us."

"You've not even asked me what I can afford to pay you."

"I haven't, have I? And you've not asked me when I can start."

She pursed her lips, and then frowned.

"Have you heard of the concept of the tied cottage?"

My surprise showed. "Yeeees…"

"Well, how about a tied narrowboat?"

Not surprise now, but downright astonishment.

"Never been on one," I admitted.

"Are you really one of these Birmingham people who have never experienced the canals that snake to, through and sometimes under the city? Have you never seen a lock worked? Never been on an aqueduct, or through a tunnel?"

A guilty smile. "I am one such," I admitted.

"You have a lot to learn. But I need an engineer, and you have already probably saved my reputation with my hirers, and maybe you'll be able to help salvage those of them who have decided that Poppy Narrowboats are now just too unreliable. I can now contact them all with a genuine explanation. You are also overqualified, but I'm happy to accept that.

"The last piece of the equation is the accommodation. Come with me."

She led me down towards the entrance roadway and the very long boat with the superb new paint finish that I had first seen.

"I bought this to do up and sell," she said. "There was a client who said he'd pay for the refurbishments and buy the boat when she was complete. We gutted her inside, then got her repainted outside. Work on the living space started; we finished the galley and dining area, then a cabin, bathroom, then another cabin. Then the payments stopped. As a result, so did the work.

"Finally we discovered that the client had been declared bankrupt. I'm relieved there is a clause in the agreement that the boat remains our property until formally complete and handed over, so we shoved paperwork at the annoyed bailiff and insolvency people and they buggered off. Three months ago we told the client that in view of his financial difficulties we were going to have to sell the boat to recoup the money spent on it so far.

"We heard nothing. I've phoned, emailed and finally sent a solicitor's letter with a cut-off date on it, recorded delivery. Still nothing. So now I have a unique boat, attractive looking, partly finished, that I can't hire out.

"Then along you come, needing accommodation and offering to work for me for comparative peanuts, and…" She shrugged her shoulders. "Come and have a look."

7 The boat

As we'd approached the boat, walking along the length of her, I had been trying my utmost to take in her appearance. She faced onto the dockside where it made an angle with the stonework of a bank. Closer to, I could see that an uplift to the bow made her appear to have a snub nose. There was a small open space before the superstructure with seats fixed to the sides. A centre door led to the interior, and from what I could see walls – bulkheads – of light wood. The floor seemed to be wood, but only basic sheeting; ply, I assumed. Proper windows were let into the beautifully shiny sides, and looked as if they were double-glazed. Half way along a window was frosted, then two blank ones before another frosted one. Two bathrooms? Oh, she was a long boat, though obviously narrow, and I wondered at the need for the length.

I joined Poppy at the stern. This was all new ground for me.

"Semi-trad stern, as you see..."

"I beg your pardon?"

"Ahh... a traditional boatman's stern is really just a platform at the back of the doors. It gave the most room for cargo, which is what was wanted of course."

"Cargo?"

"Oh dear... yes. Boats this length, but open, were used to carry anything from rolls of steel, coal, wheat, china, oil... you name it. The Victorians developed rail freight to carry goods faster and then road freight took over in the 20th Century. Each gradually competed with the older mode of transport and eventually the carrying of goods by canal came to a reluctant end. Just about all we have now are the canals themselves, their traditions and boat designs – amended, of course, to give comfortable accommodation.

"Anyway; the stern on this is a little longer than the traditional boat stern, so your sons would be able to stand here with you as you go along."

For some reason I hadn't realised that this was potentially a *mobile* home. I swallowed. There were going to be two *very* excited boys when they saw this.

"She's got an engine, then?"

"No... a thick rubber band attached to the propeller... Of course she's got an engine, Jack..." I was surprised and pleased at being teased. "...and it's modern and powerful, a Beta 50. So it's good for rivers as well as canals."

I knew about the manufacturing company of course. Their expertise was in adapting for marine uses a tough engine that was famous for its reliability and longevity.

"Ok... I can get the boys to wind the rubber band."

A smile. "Controls are here. I can get Ian to teach you the rudiments of moving her, but you all need to go on a course, really. Come and look at the inside."

She unlocked the double doors and slid back a hatch. The smell of new wood wafted over us in welcome. As if demonstrating an aircraft's escape routes she gestured to some voids just inside.

"Heated cupboard for waterproofs on this side. On the other are electrics, windlass and pin storage…" I let that pass as I didn't understand the reason for the metal angular things and what looked like needles on steroids. The electrical panel I was more familiar with.

Down the steep central steps we went and the light wood lined walls and white ceiling caught my attention.

"Fridge, freezer, oven and grill, hob. Microwave. Washer-dryer. Food storage, more food storage. Pots and pans storage, wine rack – he was insistent on that, silly man…" I thought it was an excellent idea. "…dining table which comes off those two pillar supports and stows by the steps, then you can convert it into a double bed if you need to. Bench seats with decent backs – they extend to make the bed itself. The bench seats the other side fold up against the bulkhead when not in use. Very clever. The client found them. Storage above for glasses. With me so far?"

I nodded, dazed. Never before had I seen so much practical use in such a small place. She opened a door, shaped on the opening edge to fit the wood-lined, sloping side of the boat.

"Next right is the main bathroom. There's a toilet and a decent sized basin. The shower is a really good size; that's something else he insisted on, and this time I think he was right. It needs to have the pump on when you use it; the shower tray is so shallow it'd overflow and flood you out otherwise. That's why the pump comes on with the light over the shower."

It was a very shallow-lipped tray, so I could see what she meant.

Through another door… "Oh yes. The doors maintain privacy. Each cabin has one between it and the bathroom so that no one gets embarrassed at night. This is an airing cupboard and wardrobe combined, followed by a cabin. The double bed has storage underneath. There's more storage in that corner by the walkway, and more in the cupboards above each end of the bed.

"Storage everywhere," I said, my head spinning but loving the compactness of the space.

"There's never enough storage," said Poppy firmly. "Just you wait. Now there's another door, and the last cabin that's complete so far. There's storage again – a full height, half depth wardrobe, and cupboards in the cabin itself before you get to the bunks. They can be changed for the same arrangement as the main cabin, but that's what he asked for.

"More storage – I think he had kids too – and then we get to the unfinished bit."

The space left seemed huge in comparison with the compactness of the completed area. Just by the nearest bulkhead, incongruously and very publicly, was a toilet pedestal. Near it were some unsupported pipes. Its window was one of the frosted glass variety.

"He didn't have a lavatory fetish," Poppy told me, "not as far as I know. It's meant to have the appropriate bulkheads and door. And a basin. But you can visualise that there's space left for a state-room, a playroom, a TV room, another cabin, or whatever you want to do with it. Probably another cabin, without knowing the age of your sons."

"Still twelve and fourteen," I told her. "Yes, a similar cabin to the other one, but double beds in each, with the storage and the dividing doors. And as you say, the rest of it could be – well, anything."

"If they can make do with the bunk beds to start with, we can probably get on with the toilet and the cabin for you. It's got to be done anyway, whether you use the boat, buy it or, if you don't like the whole idea, we sell it. You'll need rugs and things, but later we'll carpet the whole boat."

I looked around the space, and thought. This part would be so good to leave as a good, big space; the sort of space that house-dwellers were more used to.

I gave a sigh. "I love it," I said. "I really do. And I think they will too. In fact I know they will. Can I bring them this afternoon, after school?"

"Better this afternoon or tomorrow than Saturday, when we're flat out turning round the boats that are due to go out again," she said. "But if you want to come and watch, do. It'll be manic, even at this time of year. I would suggest that you help with something or other, but I know you're... well, not as strong as you might be. Yet."

"I can certainly listen to engines," I said. "And – yes, if you've got a pump and a large container I can make sure they pump out the bad fuel and fill with the new, so we can make sure they stand the best chance possible."

"I've got nothing to put it into," she said, suddenly realising. "There's a lot in some of these when they get back. Would the fuel people lend us one?"

"After what they've done? If they don't provide one and actually pump each tank into it I'll want to know why. They should be able to get those flat containers – you know, the sort of thing they use at festivals to put – er – sewage in. We'll call them again. But it's all arranged with them that they do just that, isn't it?"

She thought. "Actually you're right. It was. This is going to cost them a lot of money, isn't it?"

"That's their look-out, not ours. In fact they'll probably get a fuel polisher in to clean the whole lot and get rid of the water along with any diesel bug. All they'll end up with is transport costs and egg on their faces. And a loss of our trade, I hope."

"They must have an idea they've lost that already," she said. "I was scathing with that manager this morning. And I liked the way you're using 'our'."

I smiled. "Have you arranged an emergency supply?"

"Oh yes. One of the big boys came to my rescue when I told the story. He said he'd let me have a small amount this week, then keep an eye on it for us."

"That sounds better."

"Yes. Costs more, but worth it in the end. Anyway, bring your two down later. Who knows, there may be some cake. Do they drink tea?"

I laughed. "With me, they do. With their mother, they're not allowed to. She says it's bad for them – makes them too lively. I can't see the difference."

She laughed again. "I like lively kids!"

There was a knock on the side of the boat. She hurried aft again. One of the fuel people asking how clean the main tank should be. She looked back at me.

"Cleaned of all dirty deposits, and dry of all water." I said. "Nothing less."

"Did you hear that?" she asked them. "That's Mr Dyer, of Crown Engineering."

There was a muttering, and she turned back to me. "It's like mentioning the Gestapo coming to inspect," she said, "but a kindly Gestapo – if there is such a thing."

It was my turn to laugh. "I've been called many things in my time, but not the Gestapo." I stretched out my arm in the time-honoured way, only to bark my knuckles on the door frame. "Ow! Serves me right, I suppose."

We climbed back onto dry land.

"I'll explain about the rest of the boat when your lads are here. Three memories are better than one."

I nodded. Though I was still elated, the excitement of seeing what would be my new home was now receding and I could feel a tiredness creeping back. Damn.

"I'd better get back," I said. "I don't want to flake out like I did yesterday."

"Ok, or you can always rest on the boat. But if you need to get back for your boys, no problem. Let's just agree a salary, can we?"

I nodded, suddenly aware that this really mattered as much as the tied cottage-cum-boat. She mentioned a figure. "That includes an amount for the boat, and it's a stab in the dark, really."

I thought. No mortgage. Possibly Council tax, electricity, insurance and so on. Food… It was a lot less than I'd been earning up to then, naturally. But was it do-able?

"I need to do some sums," I said. "It might be possible. I suppose, though, I could do some consultancy work on the side, couldn't I?"

"Of course," she agreed readily. "And if there's repair work that you can refer our way, I don't see why there shouldn't be some sort of commission. My turn to do some sums."

We shook hands, smiling at each other. Once you really looked at her, the character shone through and she was a really pleasant person. Someone I could work with. And for.

By the time I reached the hospital I was beginning to feel a tiredness, but nothing like the level of the previous day. I grinned at the porter in the hall. "No wheelchair today, thanks. And I'm sorry about yesterday."

"That's not a problem, boss. You're welcome."

A cold lunch had been left in my room along with a note. *Really, Mr Dyer, we do expect our patients to be home for meals. Hope you're feeling ok.*

I smiled, and ate, then lay fully clothed on the bed. I had to be back and un-tired for the appearance of two sons later on.

"Dad? Dad… Oh, he's asleep. Did we tire him out yesterday?"

"Did *you* tire him out yesterday, you mean."

"Phil…"

"Ok, ok, I'm sorry. But…well…"

"I'm sorry too," Nat said. "I never thought I'd sleep for such a long time, especially when it was so uncomfortable."

"Ok. No more said, all right?"

Where did Phil get his compassion from, I wondered. I opened my eyes as if I'd just woken, and stretched.

"Hallo, guys. How are things? Are you ready?"

"Ok. Ready for what?"

"I've been busy."

"Is that why you're tired?"

"It's why I *was* tired, Nat," I told him. "Now I need you to come with me and look at something."

"Have you found somewhere we can live?"

"Ah well, that would be telling, wouldn't it? I've found a job, anyway."

"You *have?* Does it pay a lot?"

I laughed, swinging my feet onto the floor. "Nothing like what I was getting at Crown. But then… well, I'll go through that later."

We headed off. "I'll be back in an hour, nurse. Honest. And I've got two excellent support staff who also have my interests at heart, just like you do."

I steered them towards the basin's access road, fielding questions about what they were going to see, and telling them nothing.

"Poppy Narrowboats!" Nat exclaimed when he saw the sign. "If the engines sound like that, they certainly need you, Dad."

I laughed. Why hadn't I thought that way about the name?

We walked by the rifle club, just as I had done that first time, and they were fascinated at the idea of joining. We turned the corner at the end, and there were all the boats, with "my" seventy-footer nearest to us.

"Is that where we'll be living?" asked Phil, pointing at the Victorian workshops. He was wearing a dubious expression.

I smiled again. "That is where I'll be working," I told him. "I just want to find my prospective governor."

"Is he very strict?" asked Nat as we approached the office door, which was open.

"Terribly," said a severe voice, Poppy's voice, from inside. "Come in and let's have a look at you."

Nat hesitated. Phil had a grin on his face and entered first, with me second and Nat a still doubtful third.

Poppy couldn't keep a straight face for long, not with my grinning at her. "You told me you had two children, Jack. These aren't children, they're young men. You're all very welcome. And no, I'm not strict. I'm only grumpy with people who don't do what they said they'd do, like fuel companies."

"They haven't messed you about again, have they?" I asked.

"No, they're falling over themselves to be helpful. The latest is that they're bringing their own bowser on site early on Saturday to pump out every boat that comes in, and then do the same for the rest that are here already. The manager says that he hopes by doing this he'll avoid any more mentions in the trade press like last time."

"Does he now? Well, we shall have to see what happens on the financial side, won't we?"

"Would you really do that, Jack?"

"If it means warning others, yes. Don't forget that we both have history with the company, and they don't seem to have learnt from last time. I have to ask how many others are having breakdowns."

"And speaking of money, I need to talk to you about that," Poppy offered.

"Ok… more, or less?"

"Oh, more. About ten per cent more."

"Done," I said.

"What – just like that?"

"Yes. With a bit of consultancy, I can cope. Can't we, guys?"

"Yes!" said Nat excitedly, no doubt relieved that she was not strict at all.

"If you say so," said Phil, more cautiously.

"And there would be some money in it for anyone who was to help, unofficially, on Saturday mornings, when the boats come back. Later, when you know about it, we have to go out with new hirers in the afternoon, too. I can't employ anyone until they're sixteen, but now and again an envelope might be delivered to those people, just as a gift."

That made their eyes open wide.

"Now that your father has a job, the only thing he needs – you need – is somewhere to live."

The faces dropped. But Poppy laughed. "I may have found somewhere, but you might not like it. Your father knows, so how would it be if he took you to have a look?

"Dad… you never said!"

"No, I didn't, did I? You might not like it, though. In which case I'll have to look again."

Nat was hopping from foot to foot. Had he been eight he would have been jumping up and down.

We walked back down past the boats whose engines were apparently now in my care. As we came to the left hand bend in the dockside road out of the yard to the official highway the boys started to follow it. I walked straight on, towards the bow of "my" boat.

"Where are you going?" asked Phil.

"To have a look at a place we might live." I watched their faces change from the puzzled to the amazed.

"On a *boat!"* Nat voiced it first. Phil just looked from it to me, back to it again.

"Only if you want to," I said.

This time Nat did jump up and down. I walked up to the stern and made them wait there while I explained about the good, powerful engine.

"Wait, you mean we can *move?*" It was Phil's turn to be amazed. Nat just looked for the answer, eyes sparkling.

"It's what boats are for," I told them.

"Yes, but… but… oh, wow."

I opened the doors. We toured the kitchen and dining area, then I told them about the possibility of converting it to a bed.

"Who's sleeping there?" asked Nat. "They'll be going to bed latest!"

"And getting up first to put the kettle on," I told him.

"Oh."

"Nobody will be sleeping there, unless one of us invites visitors. No, we all sleep through here."

I gave them the tour of the boat, ending at the bunk equipped bedroom.

"Now, here is a bit of a problem," I started. "When they were building the inside, this is as far as they went. What you see here is where I hope you two could sleep until the next two cabins have been done."

Then I opened the far door, and they both laughed at the very public toilet.

"Well, I *suppose* we could use it at night," said Nat.

"Without curtains? I don't think so," his brother retorted.

"That'll be partitioned off and a basin installed. On the other side the partition of it will be a room like the one with the bunks. That'll have a double bed, or maybe a sofa-bed and a table. In fact we could do the same with each of them."

"That'd be better," said Phil, "then we'd each have a room. Like at the moment."

I nodded. "And the rest of the space – well, we can do what we like. It could be a proper living room with TV and all."

"I like having a big space," said Nat. "Then we could have a really big TV in it."

"If you can afford it."

"If *I* can afford it?"

"Well, I won't have anything like the income I've got now. So unless you want to starve so we can have a big telly…"

"We could bring the one from home."

"I really don't think that would be a good idea. It's a bit like stealing."

"But *you* bought it."

"But with money from the joint account. No, we need a TV and it'd better be one that can work on a battery."

"Battery?"

"Well yes. I don't know what the boat runs on, but it won't be mains electricity."

"But you said it had an engine," said Phil.

"It does. I don't mean that the boat has an electric motor that makes it move, I mean that all the lights and the fridge and freezer – and the TV – will be either 12 volts like a car or 24 volts like a truck."

There were disappointed expressions from both.

"I'll see what we can do. Anyway, what do you think about it? Will you come and visit? Or will you come and live? Or do you need time to think?"

They looked at each other. No words passed. I saw the flicker of a smile start on Nat's face, and it was echoed on Phil's. He was the first to break the silence.

"Can we go back through the boat, Dad, and have another look?"

We walked back to the cabin with the bunks, with its light wood walls and white ceiling. They looked at it.

"Are you sure we can make another one like this? And can it have any more space? And can there be a TV in it?" Phil was used to a normal size room.

I thought. How do you design rooms in so small a space? "There must be a way of using a collapsible bed," I mused, "but one that can have the duvet on even when it's used as a chair, or a sofa. I know – what about those Japanese things? A futon? Or a sofa-bed with storage underneath? We could have a fold-down table above it that comes down during the day if you need a desk. And maybe a fold-down bench the other side as a guest seat."

Phil looked interested. "USB sockets? Mains sockets? Look, Dad; there are mains sockets already here."

They must have been there on my first visit with Poppy, but I'd missed them. with Poppy. I'd even missed it going through with the boys. So there was mains on board. But how?

"I need to talk to Poppy…"

"Who?"

"Oh, she's the lady you met, the owner of the marina and the hire boat business. And of this boat, at the moment. She'll be my boss. Poppy Watson is her name."

"Oh. What a funny name."

"Think of it as being from a flower, Nat, not coming from the sound of a sick diesel engine."

"Oh – yes, a poppy. Like Remembrance Day."

"And like the really nice wild flowers that you see in fields sometimes," I reminded him.

"So you really think we could have all that?" Phil, this time.

"If I can imagine it in a few minutes, I'm sure it can be done. If not, I'll resurrect my old woodworking skills and make something. Or Ian can."

"Ian? Who's Ian?"

"Ian works for Poppy around the marina. At least, I think that's it. There may be more. But we have a lot of questions to ask."

"Ok. But I think we have a question for you." Phil looked at his brother again and raised his eyebrows. It provoked a positive nod.

"When do we move in?"

8 Money and the move

"So you like the idea of living on a boat? Despite the small rooms? There are a lot of people who agree with you. So what do we do now? When do you want to move in? Should we wait until your Dad is fully back to health and can start working for me? That'll give me a chance to get the guys to finish off the inside."

The boys looked at me and I laughed. "There are a lot of questions there! But we do need to think about the remainder of the layout. You see, the cabin that's got the bunks at the moment, we think that'd be better with a sofa-bed or futon, and a table, maybe hinged to provide a desk." I went through what we had discussed, and said that there would need to be an identical cabin the other side of the small bathroom so that they could have one each.

Poppy thought. "Seeing the age of these two gentlemen I agree completely. Why don't you sketch a plan, we can talk about it and then get it done? I realise I'm going far too fast, and effectively spending money on you when I don't know whether you're going to stay. But I'm looking at it this way: firstly the boat needs to be completed, and secondly if you have a comfortable home you're more likely to stay. I hope."

"How about it, guys?" I asked hopefully. "Does that sound as good to you as it does to me?"

"Yay!" Nat, at least, was enthusiastic.

"Sounds really good." Phil agreed. "Do you really want us on Saturday?"

"If you can arrive by eight o'clock in the morning…" Phil looked shocked "…then you'll be very welcome, if you work hard," Poppy said. "How about your Dad, though? He's not fully recovered yet."

"I can listen to engines. I can bleed the new fuel through and make sure they start and sound right. You've got tools to be able to replace fuel pumps, have you? Just in case?"

"Well… we have, but we've always had someone visit to do that. But if you think you can… what am I saying? Yes, is the answer."

"How about we come back at the same time tomorrow?" I asked. "Then you can talk us through the non-engine part of our boat – if you have the time. We're all but ignorant of how things work. We can show you what design we'd like, so you can tell us it can't be done."

"We can do most things, and I think futons might be a really good idea even if they might be a little low for use at a desk. But we can look at that as well as separate, fold-down seating. The best of both worlds. Yes, come back tomorrow and we'll go through it in more detail."

"We'd best go home from here," Phil said. "they told us again not to come and see you, so we'll be in for a shouting when we get back – if we tell them."

"Best that you don't," I told him, once again internally seething. "But if they really are unbearable, phone me."

They caught a bus. Tired but very happy I walked back to the hospital.

"You've done it again!" said my favourite nurse, accusingly. "There's a meal in there for you, and the doctor says that he must see you tomorrow, and not to go out until he has."

I pacified her, ate, checked that the joint bank accounts hadn't been tampered with, and checked emails. Work wanted me to sign an electronic authority form for the account payment, my manager said he hoped I was getting on all right and that he looked forward to seeing me "when I was ready", and that was that.

I doodled some drawings for the boys' bedrooms, included a decent amount of storage and all the things they'd mentioned, and it really started looking liveable-in. The TV issue was one thing that bothered me until I realised that if we were in the marina there was going to be mains, and a decent set would work. If we were out, we might be able to find somewhere that had mains that we could run in. I'd need to ask Poppy. And not just about that!

At about nine o'clock that evening my phone buzzed. Phil, messaging me on WhatsApp which I'd set to retain messages at my end. "*Row. Hit hard by uncle. Locked in. Won't come back. Need to live on boat.*"

My fists clenched. One day he would meet my fists, but not now.

"*If any danger, call Police and me. Will talk Poppy tomoz and move in. Nat ok?*"

"*Locked in room. Can hear him crying. Not sure what happened.*"

"*Don't hesitate call Police if needed.*"

I waited for more, but nothing happened. I made a decision.

The joint bank accounts were in their usual healthy state. I transferred half of the balance of each of them to my new account, knowing that she couldn't access it. That made it look very healthy indeed.

Helen and Jonathan had jobs which meant they were away from home all day. There was an opportunity to get the boys' clothes and other things away from the house if they could get me in at lunch time. There were one or two things of mine that I wanted, too, apart from clothes.

Another message to Phil: "*Make sure you leave back kitchen window unlatched. Hide it with a plant. N can get in there. Go home at lunch and I'll meet you both there. Sort all else out later. Tell me if you can't.*"

There was a long delay. I started wondering about calling the Police myself. Then:

"*He was in here apologising. 2 late. Will do. CU tomoz.*"

Phew. A minute thread of decency from my no-longer-beloved brother. But, as my astute son had said: too late. At least I felt that I could sleep now.

The following morning I met with the doctor. He asked me the usual questions and hummed and hawed a little, then asked me how I felt about being discharged and becoming a day patient.

"I think I can cope," I told him. "I've managed to find somewhere to live, somewhere the boys can live too. And there are other arrangements I'm going to make today."

"And you have no ill effects after yesterday? Not exhausted?"

"No – oh, I was tired, yes, but I'm significantly less so as each day passes."

We agreed that I'd switch to day-patient-hood the next morning, and I asked what that really meant.

"We want to see you once a week for a bit," he said, "so come in to the clinic on Monday and I'll just make sure you're coping. But if there's a major problem, come in at any time and talk to whoever's on duty."

I was early at the house at lunchtime. The garage lock hadn't been changed, so I got the car out and put quite a lot of tools in the boot before parking it in the driveway and locking the garage again. The boys arrived eventually; their journey was as long as mine had been. Phil's face was bruised, and once again my fists itched to mete out the same treatment to the bully that my brother had become.

Nat made short work of getting in; fortunately the entry point backed on to the garden. The front door readily unlocked from inside. His first words were "I'm sorry, Dad, but I knocked that plant onto the floor in the kitchen. It's a mess."

To his astonishment I laughed. "I think that just about serves them right, don't you?" I photographed the broken pot and the earth on the floor anyway, along with the size of the window, in case of false accusations later. And I photographed Phil's face, with his permission.

Suitcases were packed with clothes and other personal items belonging to the boys and to me. The car's boot was looking very full. I was nervous, and I think the boys were too; Helen wasn't due to return until about four-fifteen, the time they usually returned from school. Still neither of them had been given keys to their own home – amazingly – so I didn't think she'd be late. And if she was early there might be a show-down, though at least Jonathan wouldn't be there.

What none of us reckoned with was the school. Phil's phone had beeped a couple of times, and to give him his due he had ignored it because we were so busy. So when a too-familiar voice shrieked at us from the pavement we froze.

"What the *fuck* is happening? What are you doing with my sons?"

After the first shock the boys, unsurprisingly, looked anywhere else but at her. As calmly as I could I closed the car boot and looked at her, then at the two lads.

"That's the lot, you two. Hop in, and I'll deal with this."

They hesitantly climbed into the car, one in the front and one at the back. I turned to face her and drew breath. She was glaring at me, her face twisted in outrage.

"Get out of the car, you two, *now!*"

I waited, my back to them, watching her, hoping against hope that the boys would make a stand and not be obedient. A door opened. My heart sank.

Nathaniel, bless him: "Mum, we are going to live with Dad. Uncle Jonathan hits us. You hit Phil. We don't want to live with him. We've decided."

This time her yell was tinged with fear as well as anger. "I said 'get out of that car!'"

It was my turn. I was calm and quiet.

"We never used the language you used in front of them and I'm sad you've changed so much that you have now. They have independently decided that they want to live with me, not here where you and your boyfriend can hit them and lock them in their rooms. I imagine that if you want, they will verify that themselves, in writing. For myself, I have good accommodation for us all, and they have seen it and approve of it."

She started talking in that loud, voice she had sometimes used later in our relationship when things weren't going her way between us. "You can't do this. They are my children."

"They are my children as well," I said quietly. "Never, ever forget that. You and your live-in lover have mistreated them to the extent where a call to Social Services would mean that they would be placed on an 'at risk' register at the very least. Get that into your head. Nat and Phil are coming – they have decided – to live with me and that is an end to it… no, shut up. I said SHUT UP!"

I never talk like that, not to anyone. She stopped in shock. Instinctively I continued in a hard, loud voice.

"It is you who have made the choice that led to this, you and him. So know this: you will find that my salary will no longer be paid into the joint account, and that half of the balance on each joint account is now with me.

"Also, you will sell this house and I will take half the proceeds; a solicitor will oversee it and act as referee. Alternatively your boyfriend can sell his flat and I will take all the proceeds providing it equals or exceeds half the residual value of this house. That way, when we die, it can be willed to the boys. I will write to you with all this and give you an address."

I said all this at top speed so that she had no chance to interrupt, and as I was doing so I was opening the driver's door. Finished, I started the car and moved out of the drive, narrowly missing her.

The boys looked back. I couldn't. Didn't want to.

"She's crying," said Nat uncertainly. Phil was silent.

"Like I cried when I had hit your uncle and went walking around the city," I told him. "Men have emotions too, and they cry too, you know. And there was no one looking back at me to see if I was all right."

"There was," said a deeper voice, the one sitting next to me. "But I had no idea what to do. I thought you'd be back soon."

I sighed, the mental turmoil now starting to calm down and to leave me with the empty, shaky feeling that comes at the end of an adrenalin-fuelled episode.

We drove for some time. My general direction was the marina, but as I settled down more I thought that they should really return to school. I broached the subject.

"Not this afternoon, Dad. Please."

I sighed. "I suppose not to stay, there's been too much going on for either of you to be able to absorb lessons. But please, can we go and talk to the Head and tell her what has happened? I'm surprised she hasn't mentioned your bruising to you, Phil."

"She did. She said I should come and see her at lunch, but I didn't."

"Then that's even more of a reason," I told them. "We'll go there and make our peace, and tell them you'll be back on Monday. All right?"

Reluctant agreement was voiced. I changed course.

"We are required to call Social Services if a pupil is being assaulted."

I think I remember that the argument had gone round in circles twice already. This would be the third time. It had started quite pleasantly with "My sons are now living with me because they have asked to and because my wife's lover is mistreating them." Perhaps I should have insisted the boys were with me in the interview because I would have rephrased some of the things that the still-present anger were making me say. I tried a different tack.

"And what good will that do?"

She looked at me as if I was stupid. "I will alert them to the possibility of child cruelty. Really, Mr Dyer..."

"No, you didn't answer my question. I have removed them from an actual cruelty, not just a possibility. And I have done so as soon as I knew about it and at their request. So while they are with me, they are not in danger."

"We only have your word for that, and they might return to visit or decide to return home."

"*What?*" I swallowed hard, hoping my anger at her comment would vanish with the saliva. "You've only had my word for their safety for the last three years we have been associated with the school. You were happy enough about that. They now have the possibility of cruelty at their old home, and I have removed them from that, at their request and because I care about their safety and how they are brought up. If they return to their mother and her boyfriend, *I* will call Social Services, because I care about them and will not accept their being put into danger by anyone."

I think it may have been third time lucky. She finally understood what I was saying.

"So you are absolutely certain that if they return to their mother and... and... to live, or even to stay overnight, Social Services will be called?"

"If the danger is there at the time, yes."

"By danger, you mean your brother."

I gritted my teeth. "Yes, I do. If he is there, they won't be."

Silence.

"And by the way," I added into the pause, "their home is the new address that I have given you, not the old one you have on file. That is their mother's only. For the moment."

"What happens if they return home, though?"

"I hope they do, because home is that address..." I pointed to the paper "...the address I just gave to you. Not the one you've had all this time. If that changes, then as I keep on saying, Social Services and you will know about it. Immediately. Good heavens, do families never split up, and the children move away with one of the parents? I'd have thought it happened all the time. Sadly."

Her look was as if she was annoyed, not pleased that she wouldn't have the unnecessary work of engaging officialdom. It seemed to me that I had wrung all the common sense that I could from the situation and let it drip into her brain.

"Our regulations say that when a pupil has been assaulted by a parent, immediate contact must be made with Social Services," she said in exasperation. "I'm sorry, Mr Dyer…

"Just a minute," I interrupted, "you said 'by a parent', didn't you?"

"Well, of course."

"I have been telling you that Phil's bruising was caused by my wife's lover, not by a parent."

"Parent or carer – it makes no difference."

"He is absolutely *not* a carer. I have not agreed to his being a carer, and I am one of the two parents. Has my wife informed you that he is a carer?"

"That makes no difference…"

"Yes, it *does* make a difference. My brother has been at my old address less time than a visitor, a house guest, might spend with a family. No one registers their guests as carers. They don't even register babysitters. It's a ridiculous notion. He has not been registered anywhere as a carer, and I would never agree to it. Nor, incidentally, would Phil. And no, he is not sixteen and therefore cannot decide for himself legally, but he is very intelligent and decisive.

"My wife's new lover is not a carer for my children, therefore Phil was not assaulted by a carer, therefore you have no duty to report this.

"Look, I am very tired and so are they. We will be going now, going home – to the address I just gave you. And if I find that you have involved Social Services it will be to the detriment of my children, against their and my wishes. If my situation ends up in a divorce court you will find that needlessly having called them will rebound on you or whoever made the decision. That is all I'm going to say now. You will see them both on Monday morning.

"Last thing, and please take careful note of this: neither my wife nor my brother is to be permitted to collect my sons for any reason. That is where the problem lies. If that is allowed to happen I have to warn you that there really will be trouble."

I stood and headed out, ignoring her bleating behind me. A letter would be coming her way by Monday, stressing the last point and summarising what we had said. Wordlessly I beckoned to the boys and headed back out to the fresh air. In the car I sat for a moment, unwinding.

"Are you all right, Dad?"

I nodded to Phil. "I think they call it a meaningful discussion, or a discussion without coffee. I've just had a chat with your Head who wanted to call Social Services because you were hit by one of your carers. I had to explain that the man who hit you was not a carer, and it seemed to confuse her."

"He's not a carer. Not any more. I used to like him, but…" he shrugged "…not any more. Bully."

I nodded, and started the car. "Does that go for you as well, Nat? And apart from the occasional babysitting years ago, he never *was* a carer."

"Yes. Definitely. You only heard the half of what he's done."

My head swivelled. "What do you mean?" Now he had alarmed me.

"Oh, the shouting and the locking in. And the way we weren't even allowed keys. No, he changed."

I had wondered if he had meant something far more unpleasant, but it seemed not, to my relief. I drove to the Marina and surprised Poppy by turning up with a full car and two sons during school hours.

"I am a refugee," I told her. "In fact we all are. Phil was hit by my brother last night and locked in his room. They wanted out, I wanted them out, so we've been round there and collected everything with us. May we sleep on the boat, please? I've been discharged."

9 The first night's sleep : the first day's work

She took another look at us all, and the laden car. "The first thing that's going to happen, Jack Dyer, is that you're all coming into the office for a cup of tea and a piece of cake and to sit down. After that we will all help you move stuff onto the boat and see about getting some food in for you. No arguments."

She chivvied us in and sat us down in the sofas, arranged in an L shape and unusual in a workaday office, and went to put the kettle on. The boys looked round again, properly, and took in the calmness that seeped from the way it had been set out and decorated.

Armed with a tray of mugs and cake, she sat too. We told her the full story and I could see she was horrified.

"And this… it is your brother who has done this? Surely you must have seen it coming. There must have been some sign that he was like that?"

"There was no sign that he was going to start making love to my wife, or that they would change the locks on our house while I was in the USA at work, let alone that he would start bullying and assaulting my sons."

"He has no family of his own, then?"

"No. His wife left him after three years. Actually, I may still have her details. Maybe I should tell her what's happened and ask if she knows any more about him. I can't get over the idea that my trusted brother has done all this. We used to be really close. And it was only recently…"

That visit to him, I thought. The visit where I opened up about Helen and my drifting apart. He must have been laughing up his sleeve at me, but was such a good actor that I never realised he was telling the biggest lie of his life.

Again, my fists clenched.

I told them about the visit. It shocked all of them. The boys were speechless.

After a silence, Phil summed it up for all four of us.

"What an arsehole."

Poppy looked him. "Hmm… Probably not the language to be used in front of adults normally, but I agree with you. Except that arseholes have a use and nobody can manage without one."

Phil looked at her gravely for a moment, then I saw the smile start. He chuckled. "I thought that someone would bawl me out for that, but he is. I don't know what else to call him. Not here"

"I think that's up to you and your brother, Poppy said. "Your father probably has some names for him too. Maybe they're something you can share. Usually when I'm really, really angry with someone I write two emails or letters to them. One is what I really think, and one is the socially acceptable version without the swear words. I have to be very careful not to send the wrong one, though."

Poppy had surreptitiously lightened the mood. Now she became businesslike. "You'll understand that we haven't had a chance of doing anything to the boat yet, so there are still only the two cabins. I'll get our carpenters in on Monday to make a start, but you'll need to bear with me while it's done."

"Thank you. Of course. I've been thinking about the futon idea – I can buy those..."

She interrupted. "We can make those, though. It'd be cheaper – have you seen the price of them online? And if my people build them they'll incorporate storage as well. We need to make use of every inch for you, especially as you're living on her. It might take a bit longer, but the result will be worth it, trust me. We have two experts we call in – they're as good with wood as you are with engines."

I laughed. "You've got scant evidence of that so far..."

"But I have got some very caustic comments from the boss of my old fuel supply firm. He complained that you were unrelenting when you had dealings with them before. Apparently you presented evidence about what was going on inside the fuel pump and engine because of his fuel."

"Good," I told her, "That was the intention. The next action was in the courts because he was so pig-headed that he wouldn't see sense. It involved the company at national level, not just his division, but they never fired him. He must have had his fortune told, though. The whole thing didn't have a great lasting effect on the company. It's too big, I suppose. Your experience shows that they have enough emergency funds to throw at a problem."

"Indeed. That's why I'm so glad you're available to be on his case and fight our corner. So – to return to the carpenters, you'll perhaps understand their standard a little better now."

"Please, Mrs... Mrs Poppy, how long will it take them? You see, Phil snores." Nat was impressed by her sincerity.

"Oy, you!" Phil was affronted.

"Forget it for the moment, please, you two."

"I don't know yet. I shan't until I've talked to them. In fact you probably all need to talk to them. And I'm Poppy. Everyone calls me that, except people I don't like or am having an argument with – like fuel suppliers."

Nat grinned.

"Actually, it might all happen sooner rather than later. I think they bought a lot of the wood for the work and had to store it when we told them to stop as the money wasn't coming in. In fact..."

She reached for the phone.

There was quite a long discussion, but at last she started to look hopeful.

"Here's the deal," she started. "They'll pop in on Monday on their way home and have a look at what you want, then measure up. They can make what you want in their workshops, between commitments. The bulkhead work might need them on site for half a day or a day, so they might not do that for another month, but when they and the materials are here they could get on with it quite quickly, he says.

"How are you with plumbing and electrics?"

I blinked. Back to College days and pipework and cabling...

"My copper pipe bending skills are a long time ago," I admitted. "But running cables shouldn't be a problem. That's a normal adjunct to engines for me."

"You'll have 12 and 240 volts to run, don't forget."

"Will I? Oh... well, they're all wires..."

"Yes, but... Let's go down to the boat, shall we? I'll do that technical tour for you, then you'll understand."

Leaving the car still loaded, we boarded the boat. Poppy lifted the floorboards.

"You get 230v mains from the shore – here's the cable. I'll need to put a meter on it because it's on our supply. We'll pass on the cost at the rates we pay. Please – make sure you unplug it before you move, or there will be an almighty spark as it breaks, and everyone else's power will go off and they'll be grumpy, as will I.

"The battery also provides mains if you switch over to it. It's done from the batteries via this inverter. But it will deplete your batteries very quickly indeed, so if you need it when you're not plugged to the mains, run the engine."

There was puzzlement on the boys' faces. "It'd be like connecting ten phones up to the same remote charger. It wouldn't last long," I said. That was their language, but I made a mental note to go through the physics of it some time. I couldn't face it then – I was still only a day from needing frequent rests on a hospital bed, and the stress of the day was beginning to tell.

"The other power you have, which does lighting, fridge, freezer, cooker ignition and radio and TV, is 12 volts. Like a car. It has car sockets, but we also put USBs in with them. Are you all right?"

This was to me, because I was swaying.

"Not really," I mumbled. "It's been a bit of a day. Look, can I just get my head down for a bit? I'll be all right soon."

"I should have thought of that. We should have thought. Look, how would it be if Phil, Nat and I went back to the office and made a list of food and stuff, then it'll be ready for when you feel you can go shopping."

By this time I was feeling decidedly woozy. All Poppy got was a nod from me before I stumbled off to lie on the double bunk. I heard someone close the door on me, and that was the last I knew.

Not for the first time, my alarm clock's tune was "Dad? Dad? Wake up!"

I did, and felt better. "Hallo Nat," I said to the open door.

"Oh good. Poppy's taking us out to dinner so no one has to cook. Are you ready to come now?"

"Oh... Oh Nat. I'm so sorry. What's the time?"

"Seven, I think. The table's booked for half past."

"Oh..." I cautiously stood, found that I was ok, and smiled at the face that was looking at me in some concern. "I'm ok, really. And yes, I think we could all do with a meal."

"Yeah... Poppy's marvellous. She's..." he paused, then continued lamely: "She's booked at a restaurant she knows."

I wondered what he had been going to say.

"Ok. Let's go, then."

He looked down. "Dad! You had your shoes on! On the bed!"

I smiled, and chased him up to the cockpit.

"Hallo Jack," "Hallo Dad." The two welcomes made me smile. No censure for sleeping away the late afternoon, then.

Poppy led on. To my surprise she took us past the old office and into an alleyway. At the end of it was a modern gate, which she unlocked.

"You'll get a key for that, all of you. It opens all the other gates which we lock when there's nobody around."

Phil marvelled. "We weren't given a key to our own home, and now we're getting keys to a Marina!"

"And be careful who you let in!" said Poppy, mock severely.

A turning off the main road, a turning off that turning, and an old street of what must have been council housing until recently. Half way down there was a pub sign. We wouldn't have found it in a hundred years, or if we had we would have discounted it.

"It's very local," she said. "*The Navvy* started life as *The Navigation Inn*. About fifty years ago it bent to custom and changed its name to what everyone called it anyway. About ten years ago it started doing food, and found that local people really valued the way they did things. It's a small menu, but everything is fresh, and cooked fresh too."

I had crossed to the bar and looked round at her and the boys. "What are you all having?"

"I'm doing this."

"No you're not – you've helped us out of a hole and have done so much already."

"But you have saved me more than five hundred pounds worth of fuel, and you'll be saving the business in due course."

It was one of the first of two friendly arguments that evening, both about who would pay for what.

We were sitting with drinks and menus when a thunderbolt of a memory hit me. Expletive suppressed, I turned to the others.

"We've got no bedclothes!" It had been something we had all forgotten when collecting as many of our possessions from the house as we could.

Two grins broke out.

"Dad, while you were snoring away, Poppy took us to a superstore," Phil said. "Most importantly we bought some bread and milk and cereals and stuff for breakfast. Then Poppy said that there were no saucepans or stuff like that on the boat, so we bought them too. Then she thought of things like toilet paper and tea and towels and…" He thought.

Nat chipped in: "Tetrahedrons and tassels and t…" He ran out.

"And probably other stuff starting with T as well," Phil returned to the fray. "So we got that. Then we thought of bedclothes and she said it be better to buy double sizes of everything because that's what we'd need. So we spent an awful lot of money."

"Attiteration." Nat was trying to carry on the joke but realised a moment later what he had said. Poppy dissolved into laughter.

"Sorry," he said, for once blushing, "alliteration."

Poppy noticed my expression. "Don't worry. It caused a laugh, as it was meant to."

"I really am so grateful," I told her. "When I realised just now that there was so much we hadn't brought with us, I thought we would have to rush off and buy stuff tonight before everything shut."

"Fortunately there's a twenty-four hour store fairly close. So you'd have been all right even if we hadn't had a shopping expedition."

"But to use your money – that really isn't fair."

"I told them it's their allowances for the next ten years," she said, "but they didn't seem to believe me. You settle up when you can, there's no hurry. The important thing now is that we eat, then get your gear on the boat before it's too dark, and then you can have an early night. I'm really hoping that you are all still ready for tomorrow. It'd really be a help. It's an early start; eight o'clock briefing, then we wait with dusters at the ready for the first one in."

"Dusters?" I think we repeated the word simultaneously.

"Well, not in Jack's case. Dusters and engines don't mix. What you two end up doing depends on where we can fit you in. It could be anything from filling fresh water tanks, cleaning windows, cleaning toilets, dusting or cleaning surfaces… all with someone else guiding – at least the first time." This was said with a look at me with raised eyebrows.

I don't think they had done any housework in their lives, those two. On one hand it was something new they were being trusted to do, but on the other the idea of cleaning a house might be not so welcome.

"How about it, guys?" I asked.

"Fine by me, so long as you get me up in time," Phil said. "I don't mind what I do."

"Me too," Nat said with only a little less certainty.

It was getting quite late when we returned to the marina; conversation had flowed during the consumption of a really pleasing dinner; Poppy had been right about its quality.

"If you'll let me, I'll make the beds," said Poppy. "I'm so used to doing them on the hire fleet that I'll be quickest. I suggest you stow things in the galley, then we can keep out of each other's way. Anything not needed tonight could be taken on at the bow and stowed inside the empty part."

"You're being so kind to us," I said, really thankful that an expert was in charge.

"We help each other out on the canals," Poppy told me, quite severely for her. "Never forget it."

I shut up. Poppy disappeared with duvets, covers, sheets and pillows, helped by Phil. Nat and I started with the food and equipment for the kitchen.

It must have been a record for a family of three moving into a new home. Poppy wished us a good night's sleep after about an hour, and about half an hour after that I chivvied two yawning sons off to fight over the bunks. Eventually the arguments became so prolonged that I marched in and told Phil he was on the top and Nat below. "You can swap over in a week," I ended up. "Good night!"

I set an alarm and retired to bed.

A seven o'clock call was easy for me, even after my problems. Nat was up shortly afterwards. Phil just groaned each time I called him and only emerged when I told him that he'd get no allowance from me this week now that he could earn it unofficially by working. The threat of missing breakfast may have had something to do with it too. As always, he was fine once he had prised himself from out of the covers, had a pee and a cursory wash.

Using the taps reminded me that I had no idea where the water came from or what we had to do about it – if anything. One of the boys' potential jobs returned to mind; if they were required to fill water tanks on Poppy's boats for half the day they would soon be experts and could be left to sort out our arrangements. I told them so. There was no adverse reaction.

We emerged and headed to the office, where we were greeted by a surprising number of people, with an approving grin from Ian and a smile – tinged with relief, I thought – from Poppy. She introduced me, making much of my working background. There was a surprised murmur at the mention of my employer. She remembered, just in time, that I hadn't resigned yet, and swore everyone to secrecy.

The main information concerned the fuel, the fact that there was a supply arriving for the newly drained tank from a different company and that the old supplier would be pumping out every last drop from each boat. That produced a groan.

"How are we going to get through them all, Missus?" someone asked.

"We have two young gentlemen here who have volunteered to help. I think it's probably best if one of them sorts out the water tanks – that had better be Nat – and Phil fills the diesel… oh, sorry."

There was a general chuckle with which Phil joined in, I was glad to note.

"Phil the fill," he said in as sonorous a Welsh accent as he could manage, and caused another laugh. Good. I'd never really seen before how he behaved in front of an adult group. For some it might have been daunting, but he obviously felt at ease.

"It's essential they're filled to the brim, Phil. Someone can show you…"

"I can do that," I volunteered.

"Thanks… and the amount you put in *must* be entered on the sheet by the pump. Don't let anyone interrupt you doing that, please. Same with you, Nat, or you'll be wasting water. Your efforts only need a tick by the side of the boat's name on a check list once it's done. I'll give you a key, show you where the filling point is and where the hoses are. You can fill two at a time. But it'll become clearer when you do the first two.

"That'll release others to help inside. So actually we should make it all happen on time."

There was a little more, but we were interrupted by the sound of a truck engine. A general stir interrupted Poppy, who just said "Here we go…"

It was the fuel delivery; the company I'd recommended had got it right. The new delivery was almost complete when another tanker appeared, and stopped in the middle of the approach road. I looked at Poppy.

"Shall I?"

"Please. If you need reinforcements, just shout. Don't pee him off, though. We need him." The thought had occurred to me too. I went to see him and introduced myself – in a friendly manner. After all, not only was he an innocent employee but we needed him on side. He must have been warned, because he turned quickly from being a slightly sullen, defensive type to being very helpful. Given that there would be boats in shortly, and clients' cars moving, he readily parked the tanker outside and walked in to the office for a tea and a piece of the seemingly ever-present cake, even if was only just past breakfast time. Poppy had seen me escort him there, and soon came in herself, all smiles.

"I'd been told I'd be unpopular," he admitted between bites of cake.

"Ah, you're popular. You're helping to make today possible," Poppy told him. "Our complaint isn't against you, just against whoever let water into your tanks at the depot which infected our supply here and from that infected our boats, making them unreliable."

I felt sorry for him. He'd only been given half the story. When he'd heard the number of breakdowns Poppy had suffered he was sorry for us.

I explained what we were having to do, and he was enthusiastic about helping. "You've gone over to the other firm for fuel, then?" he asked when we had finished.

"Yes," Poppy told him. "Mr Dyer recommended them."

"Maybe I'd better ask them for a job!"

On one of the boats that hadn't been hired out Poppy had shown Nat what the water tank fillers looked like, and where they were. He was standing near a double tap, hose at the ready, trying not to look proud carrying his badge of office, a brass key with a long, thick screwdriver blade on it.

An engine was heard at the entrance to the channel that ended at the Marina basin, and the first of the returning boats came into sight. The steerer was welcomed by Poppy as we helped with the mooring. She asked, as we were to learn was her custom, whether there had been any problems or breakages, and then asked if we might please deal with the engine, empty the loo tank and fill the water tank while they packed.

That was the start of what was to be a hectic morning for us all and a baptism of fire for Nat, Phil and me. So far as I was concerned Jacky, the tanker driver, helped make things easy, working with me as I started on each boat. Phil unlocked the fuel cap, I lifted the engine cover boards. Jacky gave Phil the hose and he stuck it down to the bottom of the tank. Jacky started the pump, then we all waited.

Once each tank was empty I could replace the fuel filter and run off the fuel pipes into a container, to be emptied later into a bucket on land. Once the pipes were reconnected I signalled to Phil who was by then ready with the filler from the new supply. While the tank was filling I bled the new fuel through, then tried starting the engine. Fortunately these are good tempered engines after a fuel interruption and each started after very few attempts.

We were lucky. None of the engines seemed to be suffering. My dubious skills at changing an injector pump that was half way down the side of an engine that would be partly obscured by a boat's hull weren't needed. I was immensely relieved.

A few delays occurred because of the time taken to empty and refill each tank completely. That delayed each boat's move further up or down the jetty, or to another row of boats alongside. In one or two cases it made life awkward for the returned hirers to carry their luggage out at the bows, encountering a twelve year old with a live water hose as they did so. All but one of them accepted it in good faith, and I think Poppy pacified the impatient ones with a bottle or two of wine. To be fair to them, the impatience was down to having a long drive ahead of them. They just wanted to get on with it.

By about two in the afternoon all the boats were back, emptied, fuelled, watered, toilet tanks emptied and the inevitable scratches hurriedly painted. I was aching from so much bending in confined spaces; I had one son who, despite his best efforts, smelt of diesel but was smiling, and another who was wet through, happy and smiling. Phil was sent off to shower and change – I know what diesel can do on skin if left – and Nat told to get a towel, dry himself and change.

All that was left now was for the interior cleaners to finish, for the preparers to follow after them with the courtesy tea, coffee, milk and biscuits, the bedding, a final check and some flowers. Then we would be ready for the first of the new hirers. I waited until I had one non-smelling and one dry son back, and was released from duty. "I can't ask you to help showing hirers where everything is, or take them out through a lock," Poppy told us. "Not until you have the knowledge yourselves."

"I wish we could," complained Nat. "I'd love to have a go."

She smiled. "There's always tomorrow."

I think he'd have hugged her if he'd known her better.

'Our' boat's galley, even in its non-homely mode of having been recently moved into, was something of an oasis. I started making tea. The boys sat, and in the Pavlovian reaction of the young, dug their phones out.

Almost immediately there was a reaction from each of them along the lines of "I've got twenty-four missed calls!" Their phones had been switched off since school the previous day; mine had been on silent since the meal the previous evening (apart from the alarm, which over-rode everything).

"It's Mum," they said, and started looking through the messages that had also piled up.

Phil looked up first, and I could see the anger in his eyes. "She's saying that you've kidnapped us, that if we don't come home she's calling the Police. She sent a lot of messages saying she's sorry and it won't happen again and would we call her urgently."

Nat looked up too. I could see he was just unhappy. "She's saying the same to me too. Dad, I've got to answer her. Tell her something. I can't just... just..."

I could see the tears start to form.

"There are going to be a lot worse messages on my phone, I'm sure. When we left, I told her what was happening, so there is no reason for her to accuse me of kidnap or to call the Police. You each decided to live here, too."

I couldn't leave it like that. God knows I wanted them living with me, in safety. But I had to be fair to them, and I had to make sure there was no compulsion or brain-washing that could give rise to accusations later. I gathered my thoughts.

"Yes, you decided. But you still have free will and can change your minds. If either of you want to do that and return, I will respect that decision and take you back, either one of you or both. And I will still love you.

"I won't deny that it would hurt me like hell… no, that's not fair. It's like blackmail. The trouble is that just as I want you here, she will want you there. As far as I'm concerned each of you is an intelligent person who can decide on his own, now or later. Neither she nor I have the right to insist. The law takes a different view though, at least until you're sixteen. I don't know what a Court would decide. Maybe it wouldn't decide the way you want, and that would cause you a lot of distress.

"How about you each go into a separate cabin and reply to her? Then I can't influence what you say. I'll see what she's said to me and do the same. Oh damn…"

The kettle had boiled. I made tea. They sat quietly, reading the messages again, straight-faced. There was a period for brewing and stirring and thought. I plonked a mug in front of each of them.

"Don't spill it on my bunk, please. Or on your own. I love you, each of you, separately and together. Never forget that."

Nat jogged the table as he rose and slopped tea over the edge. I smiled at him and threw him a cloth. He mopped up and threw it back; there was the vestige of a smile at his lips and I wondered what it meant.

With each of them dealing with their messages in their own spaces I looked at my phone, and almost immediately wished I hadn't. Apparently Helen had been trying to call me and was upset that I'd never picked up and how dare I take the boys away from here when they were her sons. And Jonathan… Jonathan was accusing me of causing Helen so much upset she was nearly hysterical and telling me to bring the boys back immediately. *He* of all people was telling me to bring them back.

I sent one message back to the pair of them. It told them that my sons had each decided they wanted to come with me, to live with me, and had left their old home with no pressure whatsoever from me. "*As I write this they are replying to Helen's messages, again with my not knowing what they are saying. I will respect their decisions, whatever they may be.*" As a parting shot I told them my view about my brother's sly, underhand action, listening to my marital problems whilst worming his way into my wife's arms. And I left them in no doubt about my reactions to each of them hitting and imprisoning my sons. Especially my brother.

It took a long time, and was probably the longest text message I have ever composed. I checked it and paused with my finger over "Send". This was one of those times when going back would not be an option. Indeed, already it was not an option for me. I knew I couldn't return to live with Helen, not even if she dumped my traitorous brother. Love had started to evaporate before he came onto the scene. His weaselling in to Helen's affections constituted the removal of any feeling and trust that remained with me.

I pressed the button, then sat, staring into space.

It was quite a few minutes later that the boys returned, straight faced. They came to sit one each side of me. For once their expressions – or lack of them – held no clue.

"Do you want to go first, Nat?" asked Phil.

The younger boy gulped and nodded. He held out his phone for me to look at.

"I don't need to read it, Nat. It's between you and her, but I will if you want to."

He nodded. I looked. "*I didn't want to choose but you've made me. I'm living with Dad and want to come and see you but when uncle's not there. Love Nat.*"

I gave him a hug that nearly squeezed the breath from him.

Phil hesitated. "I told her that I thought she'd been a cow to do what she's done and I wasn't going anywhere near her whilst he's there," he told us. "I said I was staying here and was happy at the idea."

It was his turn for a hug, and I resumed staring into space. I had to: there was a depth of such relief in my mind that it was bringing tears to my eyes.

"Now what do we do?" Nat asked.

"Just a minute," I sniffed, trying to calm down, and aware they were both watching me gravely. An arm went round my shoulder: Nat's arm. Phil saw, and did the same.

"Us against the world, eh?" I said when I could.

"Us and Poppy," Phil said. "She's been marvellous."

"I wonder... can we go shopping again and get something for a meal for four tonight? Then we could invite her... oh." They looked me. "She's never mentioned a husband, but I suppose she's married and we should invite him."

"He never came to the pub last night," Phil said.

"Her husband's dead," Nat announced. "I asked her last night when Phil had gone for a pee."

"Nat! That's not tactful."

"Why?"

I thought. "It's personal."

"She knows about... about what Mum's done. And getting together with *him*. That's personal.

A surge of surprise washed over me at the sudden, quick fall from grace of a previously beloved uncle. It was an echo of, but independent from, my own dismay and disgust at his underhandedness. The thoughts that I had put into the earlier message to them returned to mind. I wondered how they had thought of him before, so carefully phrased the question.

Nat thought. "He was okay, and we got on well. But…"

I waited.

"There was always something… not quite right?" It was Phil, now. "You felt he never quite meant what he said? That he was only saying it because he thought it was the right thing to say, not because he *felt* it. I don't know. It's just how I felt."

"Is that it, Nat?" I asked.

He nodded. "It was fun being with him but when you were back home you always wondered what he *really* felt."

I gave a sigh. "Living with him for so long, I must have been blinded to that. Or if it developed over time, I just never noticed. He's a year younger than me and for years we were inseparable – like you two are. I hope to God you'll remain so. And always be completely honest with each other. Don't change like he seems to have done. Sometimes telling the truth hurts, but as we're discovering now, not telling the truth hurts a lot, lot worse."

Between us we cut sandwiches for lunch, using the limited supplies that Poppy had organised for us to tide us over. Leaving the small amount of washing up we emerged into the light, to find our now-tamed tanker driver wandering aimlessly about. All around the marina the contents of cars were being carried into boats by hirers – clients; helped at times by the staff who appeared unexpectedly smarter than during the morning's rush.

"I suppose I should be getting back, really," said Jacky reluctantly. "But I've never seen anything like this. It's so well organised. And anyway, as soon as I think I'm going to be able to get out, another car comes in."

I thought for a moment. "Has anyone talked to you about the boats that aren't going out?" I asked him.

"What do you mean?"

"All of them will have full tanks, and probably the fuel's contaminated."

He looked horrified. "If I don't do them all, I'll get Mrs… Mrs… "

"Mrs Watson."

"… Mrs Watson will have my guts for garters."

"How about it, chaps?" I asked my two. "Feel like doing a bit more? We'd better check with Poppy first, though."

Interrupting her thoughts between two groups of hirers registering, I put the suggestion to her.

"Oh, yes *please*! We must. I'm surprised that his boss didn't tell him – no, actually I'm not surprised. It's those five over there. I've not stopped since you went to lunch and I was hoping that Jacky wouldn't go until we released him. I'll leave you to deal with him, shall I?"

Our boat provided a pack of rubber washing-up gloves, an item that Poppy felt would be no doubt essential for domestic use. I had never used them for dishwashing, but they proved their worth for supporting the wide dieselly hose between Jacky's tanker and the five side-by-side boats. Jacky operated the machinery, Nat and Phil provided support to the hose as it was manoeuvred from boat to boat, and I did the actual hoovering out of each tank. The remaining maintenance could be done during the week.

Given that the tanks on each boat were full to start with, the job was quite time-consuming. Almost as soon as we had started emptying the first of the tanks my phone had started ringing, but knowing who it was likely to be I ignored it.

We finally finished over an hour later, by which time the hirers' cars were all parked neatly and staff were just awaiting the nod from all the less experienced hirers who needed induction to the boats, and training on steering and locks. Just as we did, I thought.

Finally we bid our farewells to Jacky, who stopped at the gate and ran back.

"I suppose you wouldn't be prepared to speak for me if I went for another job, sir? It'd really mean a lot."

"You suppose wrong, Jacky. I *would* be prepared to give you a reference, but one obviously based just on today. You've been more than helpful, especially given the awkward circumstances which could have cast a dark shadow on everything. As it is, I'm grateful to you – and so is Poppy Watson – for how you've worked with us. Yes, please give the marina's address, and my name, and I'll talk to Poppy about it too. And good luck."

Poppy was hovering by one of the boats. I told her of progress and what I'd said. She was enthusiastic. "That could have been really awkward, couldn't it? But what a nice man."

"He could be a candidate for turn round days too, I imagine – if you need someone else. He seemed very interested in everything."

"It's a thought, certainly. Now, what about you…?"

"We're just going to get a few more things for the cupboards and then I'm going to start cooking dinner for four. Cocktails at six-thirty, dinner at seven or seven-thirty or later depending how my sous-chefs and I get on."

"Who's the fourth?" she asked.

"You, I hope. Otherwise the three of us will be stuffing ourselves."

She laughed. "It would be rude to decline, and I would hate any of you to over-eat on my account. Thank you, I'd love to join you. Pardon? Oh, excuse me." She had been called away to the group on the hire boat as they were ready for their tutorial.

10 Instruction

I remembered the ringing of my phone. Yes: It was Helen. Helen demanding to come and see me. Tonight.

"Has either of you had a reply from Mum?" I asked the others. They dug out their phones, looked and shook their heads. "Well, I have. She wants to come and see me tonight. So... I can either tell her that we're busy entertaining; or I can tell Poppy it's off for tonight and tell Mum where we are and she can find her way here."

They looked at each other. Nat shook his head.

"I vote we tell her we're entertaining," said Phil. This time Nat nodded.

"Ok," I said, "I'll tell her that. She'll probably want to see us tomorrow or Monday. Shall I tell her a day?"

"Not tomorrow," Nat said to my surprise. "Let's enjoy the rest of the weekend, and see her on Monday."

If ever a son was to censure his mother, that was perhaps one of the most tactful but devastating ways of doing it. The quote didn't appear in my reply to Helen, though. I would leave it to Nat to communicate his own feelings directly.

I told her to leave her boyfriend at home on Monday evening, to arrive with us at eight o'clock after we had eaten, and that the address would come in a text that afternoon. I had no wish to have her turning up before we were ready for her. And I had no wish to make her welcome by inviting her to a meal.

Almost immediately she responded. "*That's not good enough. It must be tonight, or tomorrow night.*"

I said a rude word, out loud, to the boys' astonishment, and showed them the text.

"Bloody cheek!" Nat exclaimed.

His brother nodded. "She can't tell you what to do."

"She can't tell *us* what to do," I responded. "What would you like me to tell her?"

"Just say 'No, Monday'. Then if she whinges, tell her it's tough. Oh, and tell her that she and uncle have put all of us through enough." Phil seemed to be quite angry at her attitude, as was I.

"How about this: 'None of us likes the tone of your last message. The boys and I have decided that Monday is the date and 8.00 pm the time. You will get the address at 7.30 that night.'"

They nodded, and I got busy on the phone. "Sure?" I asked, before hitting the 'send' key. They nodded: I pressed it.

"Now for shopping. What are we going to give her to eat?"

"I thought you said she wasn't coming until Monday," Nat complained.

"I was talking about Poppy, and tonight."

"Oh. Oh, that's all right." He was obviously not looking forward to his mother's visit. Was it because of dislike, or the likelihood of unwelcome confrontation? I couldn't imagine that it was going to be fun, but I was nevertheless determined that the boys should be there when we talked. They were the reason I was here, living on a boat, and not still in a hospital or in a dire bedsit somewhere.

"What can you cook?" asked Phil.

"Why me? Why not: "what can *we* cook?""

"I can't cook. Don't have a clue."

"Nat?"

A grin and a shrug of the shoulders.

"Then we need a cookery book, make a choice of something in it that's dead easy, and get the ingredients."

My phone buzzed again. Damn the woman.

"How dare you talk to me like that. And don't involve the boys in this. I'm furious but if it's got to be Monday then it will have to be."

Again I showed it to Phil and Nat. "What?" Phil exclaimed. "But we *are* involved. We're her sons. How dare *she* want us out of it!"

"Agreed," I said. "I vote that we don't respond, just leave her to stew."

"She's not being very nice, is she?" Nat commented sadly.

We went shopping.

The mood lightened with the picking up of a cookery book entitled *An Engineer's Recipe Book* with the subtitle *Basic Cooking for Reluctant Cooks*. I looked at some of the recipes, and laughed. It was really lightly written, with quips, hints and really easy instructions. Most cook books I'd seen were either very verbose or assumed you were a cookery expert, had done it for years, or at the very least that you knew the basics. I always confuse tsp with tbsp and so on, so was glad when I saw all the measurements were metric. I'm very used to metric. Engineers' language.

We decided on a roast-in-the-bag spicy chicken, with instant gravy and a couple of veg. No trimmings to confuse me, unless you counted two bottles of a quite good white wine as a trimmings. The boys thought they could cope with making a fruit salad.

"I should hope so!" I told them. "Time at the stove? Zero. You've got it easy."

"With cream," said Nat, ignoring me.

"And ice cream," Phil added.

"Did you get any kitchen knives yesterday?" I asked, not having looked at the drawer where they should have been stored.

It seemed not. We bought a few more kitchen things too that I thought we'd need. "As we find things we're short of, we need to write them on a board," I said.

"Then we'll need a whiteboard," said Nat. "This is like being at school. Can we run to a computer and a projector to go with it?"

I confess to buying some decent beers, spirits and mixers too, and some lager-type stuff which I knew was alcohol free but the boys didn't.

We made the dining area look quite good, I thought. It was mainly their ideas and, better still, their preparation. I was working back from what the engineers' cook book described as T (the time the meal should be ready) and deciding when the first important step should take place: the ceremonial Turning On the Oven.

"Right," I said as I did so, "that's the countdown started."

Poppy arrived, we all chatted and sat or cooked as necessary, and at T minus zero I started dishing up. The first thing I discovered was that there's not enough room to dish up properly. The second was that the chicken, despite the science of the book, was overdone. We all said we liked crisp skin and meat that fell off the bones, so it was all right. Maybe a bit dry, but the gravy sorted that out.

There was a feeling of accomplishment. My part in the day's engineering – the boat type, not the cooking – had gone well. Poppy, and more importantly her hirers, her customers, were happy. The boys and I – and Poppy – seemed happy to chat, a fact that she remarked on.

The only trouble was that as the evening wore on I could feel that I was getting more and more tired. Despite having consumed only a single glass of wine I could feel myself feeling 'out of it' and eventually Phil noticed.

"Should you go and lie down, Dad? You look all in."

I apologised to them all, especially our guest, saying that if I didn't go, I'd fall over. In fact I nearly did on the way to the cabin. Once there, I think I must have gone out like a light. Again.

I woke eventually and looked at the time. Damn. Ten o'clock. By the lack of light behind the curtains it must be evening still; not morning. As I felt better, I stood and cautiously opened the connecting door to the galley.

Two boys, one in mid-yawn, looking at their phones. No change there. I looked over at the kitchen area, then frowned and looked again.

Clear. Clean. Nothing left out. Tidy. They noticed my intake of breath.

"We've done it all. Poppy and us. She went about… about twenty minutes ago."

A feeling of intense relief washed over me. The pile of used pans, plates, utensils and dishes had been one of the sights that had added to my exhaustion and not to have to face it was a tonic.

"You're wonderful, the pair of you. The three of you. Thank you."

"It's easier than cooking," Nat told me.

"But not as rewarding… well, actually it is when it's all done and tidy, like that."

"Will you be ready by ten tomorrow morning, Dad? That's when Poppy and Ian are coming."

I raised my eyebrows in lieu of a question.

"We're going to take her out. They're going to teach us how to steer and do locks," Nat said gleefully.

"Are they? Well, I'd better make sure I'm ready, then. As had you two. Nat looks as if he could drop off at any minute. Phil no doubt wouldn't want to miss the start of it by clinging to his bed, so might it be an idea to start the going to bed process now? Then I can get back to healing sleep without the risk of a shower user wandering through my cabin in boxers."

To my surprise they got up and went. Phil had showered once already – the anti-diesel-smell shower – but Nat elected to have one. We all got to bed at a reasonable time. I assume they slept; it was quiet down that end of the boat. Thanks to my two hours of sleep it took me ages to drop off again.

"It's your turn."

"No, it's yours. Dad did it yesterday."

"He's nearer. He could do it again."

"He's still not well."

"He'll be fine."

"But he's not yet."

I suppose it was better than the "Daaaad…" alarm call that usually meant problems.

"Thank you for your concern, gentlemen, but I'm better every day," I called through the thin bulkhead. "And whose turn is it to do what? Then I'll know what I'm meant to be doing."

A short silence. "Putting the kettle on," said Phil's sleepy voice.

"Oh – is that all. Perhaps I should hold my head in my hands and groan theatrically to gain your sympathy. But no; I'll go and do it, and even get up properly. But there's no such thing here as tea in bed, by the way. The boat's too small. So it'll either be hot and fresh tea, or stewed tea, depending on your arrival time in the kitchen."

I looked at my watch. Nine o'clock, and Poppy and Ian were due at ten. How could I have slept so late?

"We've got an hour," I added. There were suitable thumps from their cabin which probably meant that Nat was getting up first, as usual. I followed suit and had just filled the kettle when he appeared, tousle-headed.

"Hi Dad." He looked cheerful.

"Hallo you. All right? Hairbrush wandered off in the night?"

"Can't find it."

"Bathroom? And it must be well sound-insulated, because I didn't hear the taps in use between you getting up and coming in here."

He was about to make an instant comment, but instead hesitated. "And *I* didn't hear them when *you* used them, either."

Caught.

"The priority is the kettle. I was going in after that."

"So was I."

"I'll beat you to it."

He was nearer the door, so won easily. Good strategy, I thought. Advantage: Jack.

By the time Poppy knocked on the side of the boat we had breakfasted and made a pot of tea for her and Ian. The boys were fizzing and I was quite eagerly anticipating what was about to happen. We gathered outside, in the small area by the stern; the semi-trad bit.

"What's the first thing to do?" Poppy asked.

"Untie the ropes." Said Nat.

"So that as you drift away, the mains cable separates with a flash and a bang?"

"Oh. Surely no one forgets that?"

"Would you have remembered?"

He thought. "*May*be…"

"Your job, then, Nat," I told him.

Poppy called to him: "Take it off the land side first, or you could drop a live lead into the water."

We watched him. "How does it work?" He shouted. "I can't shift it."

Ian clambered ashore. Even he had difficulty, it was so stiff. "Better do something about that," he muttered. Eventually we managed to separate it from its socket at both ends and were told that, just this time, we could leave it uncoiled on the quay. Nat and I untied the ropes from the rings on the coping stones.

"So now we're afloat, what happens?" asked Poppy,

"That's what we want to know," Phil told her with a cheeky grin.

He received a severe look. "The first thing that happens, before you even take off the mains lead, is to engage common sense. That needs no tuition from anyone."

He was taken aback, as was I. She was right, of course.

"The second thing you do is to be aware of what's going on and what's about to happen. If you think someone has missed something, you ask them. If it's urgent, call out the question in a loud voice. The first thing we should have done is to start the engine and let it settle down. It means you have control of the boat once the land has lost its grip."

I frowned. That should have been my province. But she was absolutely right. I bent to the key, then hesitated.

"A bit of throttle for the first few seconds? How about pre-heat?"

"That's better…"

She talked us through the starting procedure and told us that she had checked the engine's oil and coolant levels the Friday before. Again, that should have been mine or ours to do.

"Daily?" I asked.

"Yes. The engine is pretty new, so it should be fine. Best to check, though. We need this rope coiled or we'll trip on it. Does anyone know the right way of doing that?"

There were right and wrong ways to coil a rope? We all looked puzzled.

"I'll do it, you watch, and we'll have some rope lessons later."

Ian took the tiller and steered for the basin exit. "Watch how the boat doesn't so much steer as swing round a central point," he told us.

The basin was walled all round, having started life as a small inland port where the boats of old would deliver or tranship goods. Opposite Poppy's Marina base now were some residential looking boats, and occasionally people would appear on them and wave cheerfully to anyone watching. Indeed, Ian lived on one.

All eyes were on Ian as he straightened up, travelled the short distance to the end of the short arm from the old basin and turned right.

Here, the canal proper was a magic contrast. It was if we were in the countryside, not still deep in the vast City of Birmingham. It seemed that my home city still had some surprises for me. The water below us was gin clear; lily leaves floated on it, dipping a little as we passed. I recollected the few canals I'd spotted from bridges in the past. The water in them always looked grey, murky, unhealthy. But this had life in it.

The boys were taken aback too, the more so when a grey shape started walking along the bank away from us, looking back as it were with annoyance before spreading a pair of huge grey wings and slowly taking to the air. With their calls of amazement from the boat ringing in its ears it gained height and wheeled round above the trees, then swooped back down to another vantage point ahead of us.

"Heron," said Poppy. "When you're steering, don't keep watching it or you'll go into the bank, sure as eggs is eggs."

"Heron's eggs?" Nat asked.

"Quite possibly," she grinned. "So now we're going in a fairly straight line, who's going to steer?"

To my surprise Nat didn't shout out first. Phil volunteered.

So started a period of constant concentration from him. He reported later that if he took his eyes off the bow for a second, the boat imperceptibly veered off course. In contrast, when there was a gentle bend in the canal that he had to follow, to make a change of course took forever.

"She won't fit under there!" he exclaimed as the first bridge came into view.

"She will, you know," said Poppy. "Just aim for the middle of the channel, not the middle of the arch. There's a towpath on the right that means the channel's not central. Reduce speed a bit if you want but don't drift or you'll have no steerage."

My phone rang. I ignored it.

The concentration level on Phil's face sharpened still further. I couldn't tell if he was enjoying this or not. My pleasure was multi-faceted. Firstly I was moving slowly and, it seemed, in a countryside whose green-ness was completely unexpected; secondly I was with people I had quickly come to like and could relax with, and thirdly both my sons were engaged with learning a new skill, one which could have real, adult-sized consequences if things went wrong.

Phil's breath must have been pent up since he started engaging with the bridge, because as we emerged unscathed from its arch he let it out.

"Phew! Made it. Wait – is that another one?"

A much wider bridge spanned the water ahead. As if in emphasis, there was a bus on it.

"Was there a bridge there?" Phil asked, looking at the bank to our right. "Under that raised bit?"

"No, it was a wharf," Ian told him. "They unloaded stores for the prison there."

"Prison?" Nat asked. "Is that what it is?"

"It is. Winson Green Prison at your service should you need it, and I hope you never will. My brother did, silly man, and he didn't enjoy it a bit."

A revelation like that requires questions not to be asked. But…

"What did he do?" asked Nat innocently. I was about to tell him not to be rude but Ian answered.

"We both enjoyed a pint when we were just a bit older than you. Booze affects people differently: I would get quieter and quieter when I'd had a few, but Stan would start arguing, then fighting. One day he hit a man so hard it really did some damage. The Police were called, he went to Court and ended up in there for six months."

Phil steered under the road bridge.

Ian's family history should be a moral tale for my two, I thought, and I hoped they'd latched on to it. To be fair, they were not combative types and I hope they never would be.

"Is that the railway?" Phil asked as yet another bridge appeared around a bend.

"It is," Poppy told him, "And you need to slow right down past it because there's a turning just after, and we turn right."

"Ok… shouldn't be a problem. I've done bends already."

"No. When I say a turning, I mean like the turning we made onto the main canal from our basin," she chided. I remembered how sharp and awkward that had been.

"Somebody else had better take her," Phil said doubtfully.

"Not likely!" Ian told him. "You're doing fine, and anyway how are you going to manage when you're on your own?"

"Dad'll take her."

"Far as I see it, Phil, you're the most experienced of the three of you so far, so it'll be you teaching him later."

Phil risked a quick glance in Ian's direction. Imperceptibly the bow swung off course so he frowned and corrected it before slowing the engine.

The railway bridge was awkward. Although wide, it was built on the skew, so the canal had to bend as it entered. After that the foliage returned before another bridge crossed. Immediately after it the canal seemed to end.

"Slow now, and steer for the middle. No, slower than that. Stop her swinging round – use the tiller. That's it."

Now I could see what they had meant by the boat pivoting round a central point. Under Ian's direction Phil managed to have her heading in a straight line before the next instruction came.

"Get into reverse and slow her. Anyone want to go down the bows and look both ways? If there's something coming, cross your arms, then point to where it's coming from. If it's clear, one arm up – like a thumbs up, but bigger."

Nat bolted down the steps. It seemed that I was redundant. Phil pulled the lever back to engage reverse. What had Poppy said… ah yes.

"Phil, next time could you pause a second in neutral when you do that? You'll put a strain on the gearbox, going straight from ahead to reverse."

He nodded to me, but intent now on what was happening ahead. The bow must have been just emerging from the bridge. From the stern we could just see that to the left, past a substantial house, the canal came in at an obtuse angle. It should make the turn easier, I thought. Nat's head appeared above the cabin and an arm shot up into the air.

"Good," said Ian. "Keep her at this speed and make a gentle turn… a bit more… good. Keep her like that…"

We started to approach the left bank, but the bow was turning right into the main canal.

"Into neutral now, then let her drift round." Phil reacted as he'd been told, and waited.

We were slowly making the turn, but to me it seemed we wouldn't be able to get the angle right to complete it. Ian was watching the bank to our left. Once the stern was nearly clear he called out again. "Now reverse. Quite a bit of it."

Phil pulled on the lever. "What do I do with this?" he asked, his hand hesitating on the tiller.

"Just hold it there and wait."

Gradually forward movement stopped, but the bow continued its swing.

"Enough! Now into forward, quite fast revs, and pull the tiller further round the way it is."

Phil did. The boat had all but stopped its forward movement, and now seemed to be turning on its own axis. Its bow continued its pivot to the right, so clearing the further bank, and the stern was being pushed to the left to position us straight down the channel. Instinctively, at what I supposed was the right time, Phil straightened up, then looked aghast at what looked like two extremely narrow squeezes either side of a central island.

"Bit fast now, lad," Ian warned him.

"But what do I do?" he said in a panicky tone.

"Pick a side and steer so you're flat against the bank before you get there." Ian reduced the revs and put his hand on the tiller. "Right hand one." Phil removed his hand. "You're still steering, Phil. I'm just helping you get straight."

The hand returned.

Between the two of them they just about got her straight in time to fit through a channel that seemed only a very few inches wider than its hull.

"Why?" asked Nat, having rejoined us. I was wondering too.

"There used to be a toll booth on the island," said Ian, "Back in the day a company owned one particular canal, or a group of them. Charging tolls was how they made their income."

"I'm glad it's free now," said Nat.

"You'd best ask Poppy about that! The Canal and River Trust are in charge of the whole shooting match now. They have a licence fee for every boat on their water, and it's not cheap."

"But they do have a lot of work to do," Poppy reminded them. "Even if they do waste it occasionally in silly corporate schemes."

"How about Nat or Dad having a go?" Phil asked. "It's exhausting!"

"You carry on a bit," Ian told him to my surprise. "Get it really inside your head. The you can sleep on it, and tomorrow it'll be easy."

"Tomorrow? I'm back at school."

"Well... whenever you can. Maybe your brother won't be as good as you are at it. And perhaps you'll be out somewhere and your Dad needs a sleep."

"I hope not!" I told him vehemently. "I hope that that period is over."

"Well, you carry on a bit anyway, then you can swap over. You've got to get into a lock yet."

So this would be the lock we'd go through, it seemed. Would it be that difficult?

Phil continued. His line along the canal was a little wavy, but seemed to improve as he got to grips with steering. He complained that it took more concentration than he thought he possessed, but seemed to be enjoying the experience. Parkland and bushes had given way to brick walls and industry, often graffiti-decorated. I was reminded of the canals I'd glimpsed fleetingly so many times whilst travelling around the City.

"You want to bear right in a minute," Ian told Phil. "It's a gentle turn, but best slow down a bit for it."

A slight left bend and a road bridge; then a graceful, white balustraded iron bridge crossed over us, leading to a widening of the water. A twin of the bridge crossed a branch leading off to our right. Phil pulled the tiller over and was about to increase the speed again when he paused.

"What's that?" he asked, pointing ahead to a bridge which seemed to be blocked off at its further end.

"That's your lock," Poppy told us. "You need to slow right down and stop on the left, past that tree that's sticking out."

Ian nodded agreement.

11 Boats are meant to move

To give him his due, and with some pride, Phil stopped exactly where he'd been asked. The drawback was that we were still about five feet from dry land.

"You didn't say how close," he complained when this was pointed out, "or that you wanted to go ashore."

Ian laughed, Poppy just looked at Phil, and I didn't say a word. I'd probably have done the same as him. After all, I'd heard of lock-keepers, so who was I to comment?

"So how do we sort this out?" Ian asked. "We send a jet of water out to the middle of the canal. That'll start her stern pivoting towards the bank. If she starts going forward, give her a touch in reverse. Then get that rope…" he pointed to one whose free end was near us, coiled up, but which was attached to the boat at her centre "…hop ashore and pull her in. Then make fast."

Phil's weren't the only eyes to glaze over. Ian explained again, and Phil managed the first bit. The stern was approaching the bank. He jumped off.

"What about the rope? You'll not do much without." Poppy reached for it and threw it ashore, hitting Phi on the head as it landed. He caught it before it slithered into the water. Pulling on it brought the boat to the bank. Very slowly.

We made fast, walked under the bridge and up well-worn steps. All of we Dyers had glimpsed locks before, of course, as they peppered the Birmingham street scene, and we even knew what they were there for. None of us had a clue how to work one.

We soon did.

We learnt that the square windey things are called paddle gear, that they raised or lowered underground paddles which let water in or out of the lock, that they're operated using a windlass, and that they're hard work. Particularly if you're twelve. Even if you're forty-ish.

"You wait 'til you meet wide locks," said Poppy. "They're really hard work. Even some of the deeper narrow ones can be difficult."

Working that first lock brought forth so many safety instructions I started to wonder if this was such a good idea for the inexperienced. But stepping back from the paddle gear ("Take the windlass off the spindle! If the ratchet goes it'll fly off and brain someone. Or it'll fall in the water, which is more of a nuisance") and listening to the water rushing out of the chamber… It gave an unexpected sense of satisfaction. As did opening the lock gate, done so slowly as to be almost ridiculous, but impossible to do fast. And to see your elder son, with a scant hour's experience, vanish with his mentor to bring the boat in to the lock… Is it surprising there was a smile on my face?

Poppy noticed it. "You're getting the bug. Already. And you've hardly even started."

She was smiling at me. Why should that increase my enjoyment of the moment?

Between them, I suppose, Ian and Phil lined the boat up to the lock, and as the bows came into view I gasped as I saw the clearance between the boat and the masonry. I should say, really, the lack of clearance. I've seen boats approach docks when we've been on holiday…

A sudden remembrance, unlooked for. Family holidays in foreign climes, the resorts of the wealthy. Those out-of-reach expensive power boats that approached the side, carefully cocooned by fenders, as if they were floating Ming vases. The intakes of breath should one of those vast, dilated white plastic scratch-preventers be squashed enough between boat and stone that it protested with a squawk. The hidden grins on our faces, we family of four, as we heard the minions on board being berated by a haughty voice from above.

My smile vanished. Good times, but no longer for us.

Here we were, with a narrow steel hulled boat being steered by a fourteen year old – with help – into a-nearly-as-narrow gap. In Birmingham.

It didn't bear comparison.

Did it?

Then I thought of the smiles on the boys' faces – and mine up to that moment. I thought of the ready willingness, happiness, of my employer and her… what was he? Staff member? Another employee? Or was there something else there? But no: Poppy was middle-aged. Ian was over sixty, to judge by his appearance.

Whatever he was, his readiness and Poppy's to spend a rare late spring day, a day of rest, to teach canal ways to a man and his family whom they'd only recently met. Was that friendship? By the feel of it, by the growing ease between us all, I felt it must be. There was none of the walking on eggshells feeling that had been increasing over the last three family holidays with Helen.

"Are you going to close that gate, Jack, or sit on it looking glum?" Poppy was getting at me, but nicely. I jumped up, my glum thoughts interrupted (a good word, glum, and she was right).

The big, lower gate closed, we walked to the other end. I awaited instructions. None came, so I watched what Poppy was doing and copied her in winding the spindle in the approved manner. Yes, she had insisted that I ensure the locking pawl was on the rack to prevent it dropping. I saw that Nat had taken over after the first few turns, and was winding for all he was worth to prove his strength to anyone watching. He was actually doing well, I thought. Poppy said something to him, he nodded, and she crossed over to my side.

"Now you seen how it works, you can open the gate, make sure the paddles are lowered and close the gate after the boat's left, can't you? I'll go and prepare the next lock." It was, after all, only about a hundred yards away.

"Ok," I said, only a little apprehensive at being in charge. I need not have been. Each of us did what had we had been taught. Phil steered out of the lock and slowly towards the next one. I shut the gate and watched anxiously as Nat picked his way across the massive, handrail-equipped squared-off tree trunk that was the gate's operating lever.

A disturbance of water was spreading from the next gate. I looked up at Poppy who was getting the last few inches of height from her paddle gear.

"You head up to the top gate," she called to me when we were at the same level and could hear, "and Nat and I will sort these out. Ok, Nat?"

He nodded, no doubt pleased to be trusted with the gear and the gate on his own. I wandered up to my next workbench, the top gate, and sat on the beam, marvelling at its size and wondering how heavy it was. With one eye on what was happening at the other gate I nevertheless took in my surroundings. It seemed odd to have come in just half a mile from housing and heavy industry to a quite pleasant residential area, with wild flowers blooming with spring growth from every crevice. There were signs of the earlier industry still though, over to my right. I didn't climb the little wall to investigate it.

It seemed so much more wholesome than being either in a stuffy office, on a plane, in someone else's plant room or engine hall. It seemed so much freer, dare I say it, than being at home in an increasingly strained atmosphere.

My daydreams were interrupted by a jolt and a creak and I nearly fell off my wooden perch. A bow had nudged the gate with a little too much gusto and I looked indignantly toward the other end where a conversation was in progress. Above them, Nat was straining at the beam and was slowly closing the gate. I wondered when to start winding.

"Slowly up," came a voice to my left. Poppy started on her paddle gear and I followed suit. She paused, looked back, called "Ok" and wound the rest of the way. The boat started rising.

We must have been quick learners. That and the third lock were dealt with, and no more bumps were caused by the steerer. It was at the third lock that Poppy took us up the bank and showed us that the canal we had turned off was running parallel.

"Beyond that is yet another canal," she told us. "It's actually a dead end, or an arm. It's the Engine House Arm and just up ahead of us it crosses the New Main Line by an aqueduct and joins this one where that bridge is." She pointed to a brick bridge another boat's length beyond our lock. "This is the Old Main Line. The new one was opened quite recently, in 1827."

The boys' heads snapped round.

"*Recent?*" Phil exclaimed.

"Well, the old one was built around the 1770s. It's all relative."

"Wow."

"So are the gates and things that old?" Phil asked.

"The gates only last about twenty-five years, though some seem to get forgotten and are older. Probably some of the ironwork we've been using, the paddle gear, might be original. Difficult to say."

We looked under the bridge at the Engine House Arm as we passed. It seemed very narrow, too narrow for us, though Poppy and Ian told us it was fine. "Turning left down there might test you a bit, but it's do-able. After all, seventy-footers did it to take on cargo or discharge it."

It was shortly after this that Nat relieved Phil at the tiller. Being shorter, he had some difficulty in seeing over the roof to steer, but Poppy had spirited away a folding step which he happily perched on.

If anything he did better than Phil. He seemed more in tune with how the boat pivoted when steered, though it may have been that he had been watching his brother's efforts and listening to Ian. It was therefore Nat who steered us under Galton's mini-tunnel, where Telford Way crosses over the canal. Soon after, we entered what looked like deep countryside.

"You'll be soon be going into one of the most peculiar parts of any canal, anywhere in the country," Poppy told us. "You'll know it when you see it. It's distinctive, not pretty."

A motorway bridge, I thought, as we approached some massive, tubular legs. The road deck roofed the canal, then both changed course to head in the same direction, both canal and the motorway, so we were in an echoing, noisy world where conversation was carried on at the shout.

It seemed the ancient and the modern transport links were intent on weaving themselves into one. The water road swung from side to side of its concrete roof; the noise from the motor road never abated. And then, even more bizarrely, a junction appeared just where there seemed to be a wide canal ahead, leading into the open air and away from the long pit of snarling traffic noise.

Our path, it seemed, was the narrow, constricted way through the concrete forest.

"Spon Lane Junction," Ian announced above the sound effects. "Now we're going over the New Main Line. This is the old one."

'The old one' appeared just as happy to be intimate with its modern partner, even to the extent of throwing another semi-subterranean junction at us. The left turning was even signposted: "Titford." We turned right.

It was really quite surreal. Emerging around the next bend from the dimness and noise was a release from a stress that I'd felt since first we experienced it. The more distance we put between us and that road – the M5 as I discovered later – the better I felt. In conversations later the boys said they felt the same.

More factories, a few brown-field sites and a welcome increase in peace. "Look up to your right," said Poppy, "and you'll see the Gower Street Branch. That heads up to the route we could have taken out from the motorway. We'll be passing the other end of that on the way back. And in a minute we'll stop on an aqueduct, and I'll show you something else."

Ian said something quietly to Nat, who reduced the revs. Ahead of us were low walls, one each side of the towpath. The co-steerers stopped us by the left hand wall, Ian took the rope and we congregated on the towpath. Poppy pointed below us and away.

"The aqueduct supports are on one of those toll islands," she said, "and down there is the northern entrance to Netherton Tunnel. Yes, it's a canal tunnel and it goes under Oakham and comes out at Bumble Hole. It's about a mile and three-quarters long."

I was pretty certain that one, if not both of my two young gentlemen would chuckle at the name but they were so taken aback by the tunnel's length that they were wide eyed.

"You mean, boats go *through* that?" Nat asked.

"They do. It's the way down to the River Severn at Stourport."

"But..." Nat didn't finish his sentence. A light had appeared at the dark entrance to the tunnel, to be followed by the rest of a boat. The light snapped off, and doubtless the crew were blinking in the sudden light.

"How long does it take to get through," I asked.

"About forty-five minutes, I think. It's best if you don't go too slow. That way the water that the boat displaces cushions you from hitting the sides. It's two way though, so if you have to pass someone it can get interesting."

"Is there room for that?" Phil asked.

"Oh yes, it's over fourteen feet wide. Most boats are just under seven, so they fit alongside each other."

We watched as the cruiser passed under us, the steerer acknowledging us. We waved back.

"Any minute now, we can have lunch, if you'd like to stop. There's an old basin along here where we can go if there's not a fishing match going on. They like boats in there because they disturb the mud and cut the reeds. It's quite shallow, so boats in there help keep it open for fishing."

We entered an area of pleasant, modern houses. Not far along was a gap, and Nat steered cautiously towards it. Remembering what he had heard at the previous junctions, he came almost to a halt before swivelling the boat to face it. Once again, the canal water was clear. Inside the basin it was indeed completely lily strewn, and the boat made the leaves dip and submerge as it nosed carefully through the entrance.

Beyond was a lagoon, boat-deserted, surrounded by railings. They were friendly, three-bar railings designed to stop cars driving into the water but without stopping pedestrians accessing it if they wanted. All round it more of the houses were planted, semi-detached and small apartment blocks. Every bit of the wide block-paved area by the water had mooring rings set into it.

Under Ian's tuition Nat swung the boat round. There was so little actual forward and backwards movement that we seemed to be turning on the pivot that Poppy and Ian had been telling us about. It was not so much a sixpence we were turning on: sixpences aren't seventy-feet long. But it was an impressive manoeuvre. We moored, facing the entrance. A pleasant, if urban outlook faced us. The kettle was on. All was well.

At last I remembered that my phone had rung earlier. I dug it out and looked: Helen. And a voicemail. I listened to it: *"We found the address and are outside the gate of this horrible basin. Come and let us in."*

"Bloody cheek!" I said out loud. Four pairs of eyes swivelled my way. "How the hell did she get the address? And I told her to come on Monday, not today."

"Mum?" asked Nat. I nodded.

"And bloody Jonathan."

"Oh. I'm glad we're not there then."

"Not half as glad as I am," I admitted.

"Do you need to get back?" asked Poppy gently.

"Not likely! We're having a day away from our troubles and I'm not going to let her spoil it." A little frantic thinking on my part. "I'll text her, tell her we're not there today and would see her tomorrow. Without Jonathan."

It took me a few moments to concoct a response, insisting that my brother must not be there if she wanted to see anyone at all.

It had hardly gone when the phone rang. Helen.

"Did you get my message just now?" I said in lieu of a greeting.

"I'm not taking that from you. Wherever you are, come back now."

"No. Not only because we don't want to, but because you have your boyfriend with you. Also, we can't. We will expect you on your own tomorrow at eight in the evening."

A pause. Then Jonathan's voice. "Jack, you're not being reasonable. Helen wants to see her sons."

I jabbed at the screen to cut the connection, then looked up. The eight eyes watching me were now grave.

"Just a moment," I asked.

Hurriedly I composed another message: *Tell him that I will not speak to him and remind him that a child cruelty case can still come his way. You are not welcome until tomorrow, and then alone, and not really welcome then.*

I told the boys what I was about to send and looked enquiringly at them.

"Er..."

Nat wasn't sure.

"I don't like the last bit, Dad."

"What? Alone, or not welcome?"

"Not welcome," he said in a small voice.

Divided loyalties: inevitable, and I should have foreseen them. Poor old Nat. Not only was he the younger but he had not been on the end of a slap from her. He was feeling the same attachment as he always had, even if it may have been diluted by recent events. Even if the attachment was weaker it would be unfair on him to make her think she wasn't welcome. I nodded and deleted those words.

"Sorry. I was thinking about my own feelings, not yours. I've taken out that last sentence. Ok now?"

"I think you should insist that uncle doesn't come," said Phil. "Say it from me. From both of us."

I added to the message what he had said and told her it came from the boys, as well as from me. They agreed it and I pressed the send button before looking up at Poppy and Ian.

"I'm really so sorry about having to do that," I told them. "It should have been done in private, but she just surprised me by saying that she was at the Marina. Turning up like that! I can't imagine how she got the address."

Poppy shook her head. "Well, there's no way of getting in, not without being seen by the cameras. Look, it's good to have support, and you can rely on me. On Ian too. In fact I wonder if there's some work that needs doing in the marina tomorrow evening that would need a couple of useful guys to be there around eight o'clock."

"We have to be there to see Mum," Phil said quickly.

She smiled. "This time I wasn't thinking of you two. I was thinking about friends of mine whose presence might be a support if anyone turned up who was unwelcome."

"You mean Uncle Jonathan?" Nat said wonderingly. "Could they push him in the water?"

Poppy laughed. "If he did turn up and they were to separate him from your mother, I'd hope that they would be professional about ejecting an unwanted intruder from private property. If he were to trip on something and fall in, that would be unfortunate, wouldn't it? We should have a witness there too."

A grim smile from me. "I don't want to cause anyone trouble over this. But a security guard, even an unofficial one, would be a comfort to me – to us – and a warning to him."

"I think we can do that, Ian, can't we? After what Jack's done for us already I think it's probably the least we can do."

"I guess one or two of the others would be happy to nip back and do that little bit of unpaid overtime. And if Seppe and Ifor are coming in to do a more accurate measuring up for the cabin arrangements, well, that's half an army. They'd be the first on the scene if there's any unpleasantness."

"Do you mean…" I started. Yes, they did. The interior woodwork designers could probably be there in case of a problem, and quick to react to one. The others would be 'around'. And it sounded like Poppy would be there as a witness.

"How about it, guys?" I asked the boys. "Does that sound safe to you? Is it too much?"

"So long as they keep Uncle out, it'll be enough." Phil was positive about that. Nat nodded sadly, and I made a mental note to chat quietly later and get an idea of what he was really thinking.

It was my turn to face the scrutiny of an instructor, an employer and two sons as I took the tiller after lunch. The left turn once through the entrance to the lagoon was accompanied by so many instructions from all but Poppy, who just laughed, that I was totally confused and nearly drifted onto the opposite bank.

"Not so easy, Dad, is it?" Nat laughed as Ian helped extricate us.

"I've only been at it for thirty seconds, Mr Expert," I told him without talking my eyes off the pleasantly wide canal ahead. The first part of my stint was quite easy, once I had acclimatised to the vagaries of the steering, or as Nat put it, the swivelling. It was a pleasant area. For some reason I expected Dudley – of all places – to be totally industrial even outside the town centre, but here was this clean canal (mainly), passing the back gardens of people's homes.

And then the canal seemed to come to an end by two large grain silos.

As the vista opened up I was relieved to see that it was a junction, although it did mean that I would have to take a sharp bend. I started to slow, to the approval of Ian who was watching.

"We turn right up there," he said. "Left takes you to the Black Country Museum and the old Dudley Tunnel. You can't get through that with a diesel engine – there's no ventilation. And you'd get lost. There's big caverns in there and it's complicated. The only way through is to book a tow. It's free, but I've never done it."

It occurred to me that although we were a Birmingham family, we'd never visited the museum, although of course I knew of it. I should put that right. It would pass a wet afternoon, or if it was as large-scale as Blists Hill in the Ironbridge Gorge it would pass a good deal more time. How odd that I should know more about a museum in Staffordshire than in my own city.

Remembering what Phil and Nat had been taught I did my best with the bend. Maybe the best verdict was Phil's comment. "Nice zigzags, Dad."

Mine was a more twisty canal than the boys' had been and included a very narrow, cavernous bridge under a main road. And then, once again, the canal seemed to end.

"Now what?" I asked.

"Left under the bridge to Wolverhampton, or right to start heading back, which is what we need to do," Poppy said. "Once you get up towards Wolverhampton there are a lot of locks, and that's probably something you'd want to do over a weekend. Though midweek in school holidays would be better as it avoids Saturdays."

Saturdays! The change-over day. Of course, I'd be needed for that, and the boys would want to earn their money.

"It's an awkward turn here," Ian told me. "Try and come to a stop with your bow pointing towards the bridge 'ole..." It wasn't an expression we'd heard up to then but I knew exactly what he meant without explanation "...then shove the stern round with a blast ahead and left rudder."

Well, I tried.

The canal we were aiming for was at more of an acute angle than I expected. Despite my best efforts and Ian's running-commentary instructions, I found myself heading for the bank. And that after he had told me to give that 'blast ahead'. The residual forward motion was a bit too much for comfort and I found Ian putting the engine back into reverse – at some revs – to avoid us connecting with concrete too violently.

"Bit of an awkward turn," he grunted when we were pointing in the right direction again. "Needs practice."

Almost immediately there was a lock. My first, and the first downhill lock for my two. The boys watched with scorn at my attempts to bring the boat in once they had opened the top gate, so I reminded Phil that at least I'd managed to get to the side for them to go ashore and not stop five feet away. He ignored me.

There were three locks there, and gradually I realised that softly, softly catchee monkey applies to a beginner on a narrowboat as well as to Ghanaian simian hunting. The third of the locks was entered without touching the sides – even if the boat was moving very slowly. I was given a sarcastic round of applause when the front fender finally touched the end gate.

After that and a bend, the canal was as straight as a die. It was really quite boring, though I managed quite a few more dog-legs as my attention wandered. Two of the crew kept a tally of them but Poppy and Ian were far too polite. I managed to squeeze through the aqueduct over a major road and also managed not to be startled by the occasional train running parallel to us.

"That's the branch down to the Netherton Tunnel," Poppy told us as we approached a pair of the cast iron footbridges that seemed such a feature of the trip. There was even a finger-post to the right to prove it, though the canal itself was apparently featureless. A short distance further and a similar channel branched off right at ninety degrees. I was told it was the Gower Branch and I'd seen the other end of it earlier.

I needed to buy a map.

We continued. Phil took the tiller again, and now proved he could be quite an accurate steerer, though he did nearly become intimate with the bank when he tried to look back up the Walsall Canal as we passed its junction.

"At last!" he announced soon after, having ignored our jibes. "There's a bend!" In fact there were two, and a junction to the left leading straight into a lock.

"Don't turn left," Ian said. "That'd take you back under the motorway where we were this morning, at the first junction."

"What's that then, Ian?" Phil asked, pointing ahead.

"Oh, that's just a motorway bridge, nothing like this morning's horrors." So he didn't like them either, I thought. "This is a boring bit really. It's in a ditch so you can't see a lot from it. The water's inclined to be mucky. All you've got is the higher level on the left which is the Old Main Line where we were this morning. We're on the New, and then the Engine Arm crosses a bit later."

It was as he said. The aqueduct carrying the Engine Arm was a punctuation of interest, and Phil was almost too busy looking up at it to notice another of the toll islands ahead. He wiggled the boat through somehow.

"Lucky," I chided when we were clear of it.

"All planned," he lied.

Another bend. "This is where we turned off this morning," Poppy said. You're on home turf now."

Nat took over again, just to experience some junctions.

"I'm not very good at this," he complained as the boat threatened to drift sideways as we took the turning back towards the prison. Ian sorted him out. Past All Saints' Park again, where I had taken my first tentative steps on day release from hospital, and there was the junction to the marina. This time Nat slowed right down and carefully threaded the boat's seventy feet under the bridge as if he'd been doing it all of his twelve years.

Ian took over, and with a complicated manoeuvre turned the boat in the confines of the basin. It looked as if it was a continuation of the moves we had been practising at junctions, but I wasn't going to try. The boys, too, were quite glad not to be given the responsibility.

We moored. "Kettle!" I said, and went below to wrangle it whilst the others moored and reconnected the electricity.

12 Engines

"Well, Poppy, Ian? How did we do?"

"Weeel…" Ian started.

"A damn sight better than many of our first-time hirers," Poppy interrupted. "I'm going to give you one of our printed lists of dos and don'ts and you can each come out with a separate boat next Saturday to see what we cover. There's still a bit to learn, but we'll soon get you to the standard where you can introduce hirers to the boat, then teach steering and locks to someone."

"But it'll take some time before we're that good, surely," I said, surprised.

"*You* don't need to be, Jack. You'll be wanted here for checks and servicing. But there's nothing to stop Phil and Nat from taking people out." Phil's face took on a smug look.

"I can't teach adults how to do things," Nat complained. "They won't take any notice."

"They jolly well will. If you start showing them – what – how to fill the water tank and where to put the key afterwards, then work your way up the boat, and do it with the conviction of experience, they will. All we've got to do is to give you the experience. A few trips with our staff when they do it and you'll know. And if you show round some of the older hirers they'll think you're cute and hang on to every word. I promise I won't tell them the truth."

"Do you think… Hang on! What d'you mean 'the truth'?" Poppy was watching him with a cheeky smile on her face, the same expression as he himself used when he'd said something outrageous. "I am cute!"

"Well, that's a first for me," I said. "I've never heard Nat admit to being cute before." I winced theatrically at the look he gave me.

"Sorry, Nat," Poppy told him, "I couldn't resist a tease. Trust me, you'll know all there is to know about the boats then, and in any case everyone has a list to follow, a script, if you like. That makes it impossible to forget something. And another thing: next week, you could take the boat down to Gas Street Basin, turn there or further on at the Mailbox, and explore some of the other loops. I'll give you a map so you don't get lost. No locks, unless you *try* to lose yourselves."

"Would you trust us with her on our own?"

"Why not? We all have to start somewhere."

When they had left us, after copious thanks and having said how much we had enjoyed the day, we settled down with a small, borrowed TV from the Marina's spares. Soon we were all saying that we really had to invest in a decent set. And soon.

"We need to see what space we've got once our carpenters have started," I insisted. "It'd be silly to buy something now that we have to sell later at a loss – when we find there's room for something bigger."

That shut them up, and we continued squinting at the set we had. It was a lazy evening, the only real punctuation being the need to cobble together some food. It was very basic indeed. The engineers' cook book was ignored completely.

We had a fairly early night and they were ready to leave on time for school the following day. With the two gone, and the shortest commute in the world ahead of me, I looked forward to half an hour's unheard of peace before leaving for work. The boys knew how to reach school by bus from the Marina, and were just about to leave with my formal letter notifying the school of our new address when Poppy hurried across.

"You need one of these each," she said. "I'm glad I caught you. You could have had difficulty getting back in otherwise." 'These' were keys for the Marina gates. "And I hope it goes well today, guys. I promise we won't overwork this one." She indicated me.

They had been such good company over the weekend that I was sorry to see the grey-trousered, blue-jacketed pair walk away. Was this what Helen had been used to? Or had she been so keen to get to her own work that it meant nothing to her?

Work for me consisted of getting to know how things operated, where things were kept, who did what. By far the most important knowledge was getting to grips with the rota of engine services, and to discover what my predecessor believed had to be done as part of each. And without mincing words – and I hope he doesn't see this – it was rubbish. It was completely disorganised. It was part of the reason that breakdowns had been happening, even given that the main problem was fuel quality.

I looked heavenwards, retrieved the engine manuals and started from scratch, concocting a spreadsheet for the records, knowing that I knew I could automate it later. Seeing that a candidate for an engine service was actually in the marina I clambered over to it and lifted the covers.

How anyone could actually service an engine in that condition beat me completely. It was filthy. Just about everything was covered in oil and grease. Ok, I had been mainly a test-bed engineer and a large-installation engineer, but I knew the importance of making sure that an engine is as clean as possible. This one was gunk-ridden. Quite apart from the judgement that any customer would arrive at about standards, it's more pleasant to work with. It's also the only way you can see any leaks and other problems.

Poppy was surprised, but supportive. The marina possessed a vacuum pump and a bowser big enough to store the results of using a degreaser – which of course produced liquids that couldn't be dumped in the water. All it needed was the boat to be brought over to the wharf side. Hmmm. One day's experience. I powered down the boat's bilge pump so it wouldn't try and pump out anything into the water and fetched the keys.

No one actually laughed, but my efforts weren't pretty despite the previous day's practising. Heads kept appearing and disappearing from moored boats opposite and from our own fleet, but nobody offered help or criticism. That pleased me. At last the boat was adjacent to the concrete and moored.

Our boats' engines are green. I discovered that fact only after a blast of power wash and solvent. Pumping the results out of the bilge was a mucky business, but essential. I didn't stint, and rinsed the whole thing off with more water.

One previously invisible fuel leak, a worn drive belt and a full service later, I started the engine and listened to it with engineer's ears. Lovely. Regular as clockwork and no unpleasant noises. I had earned a tea. Presenting myself, still filthy, at the office I was welcomed by a grin and a mug already poured.

"Bathroom's in there," said Poppy, still smiling. "Need some personal de-greaser?"

I grinned back and went to wash.

"Can I ask about your previous engine guy?" I started when I had by now-cleaner hands circling the mug. "Was he… well, tell me about him."

She sighed. "He was with us for two years. There were issues, I won't deny it, but he was a really nice guy. It wasn't until the breakdowns started getting ridiculously frequent that we started to have arguments. Then he just walked out – just as my son was visiting from Canada."

It flashed back at me, that tableau that I had glimpsed on my long, disturbed walk. A woman, sitting in front of an old building, head in hands, being comforted by a younger man.

"And you were sitting on the bench outside one evening, your son with his arm around you, comforting you."

Her head snapped up and she looked at me directly. "How do you know?"

"Because I was on my mad walkabout. I must have come in at the main gate and saw you both. It looked almost as unhappy as I was, so I went again. But it's what brought me back."

She gave a long sigh. "It was the last straw, the straw that almost broke the camel's back. I spent the next week wondering how to tell the staff that we were going to have to close, that I was giving up the business after so many years and that I'd failed it."

"Was it really that bad?"

"Have you ever been somewhere where, no matter what you do, your circumstances just slide down from bad to worse? That they reach rock bottom and you can take no more? Oh – Oh, I'm sorry."

We had each been on a similar journey, but for very different reasons. Hers was business and mine personal.

My smile must have been grim. She apologised again.

"It's ok," I told her. "I think we're both on the up by now."

"I do hope so. At least you have a home and your two lads want to live in it, and I have an over-qualified engineer with some new ideas on how things should be done, and who's already started to solve problems. It's just that the two circumstances are hardly equally important."

She was right. The solution to her problem was reliable engines and therefore me. The solution to my problem was…

What?

For Helen and me to get back together with the boys and carry on as if nothing had happened? Maybe, but it wouldn't be happening. She was out of love with me and, with recent events in mind, I was out of love with her. No solution.

For me to leave, for the boys to stay with her and my brother and for them all to live together as a happy family? Over my dead body, with the way that the brother had treated the boys. In fact with the way they had both treated the boys. And the boys didn't want to live with Jonathan in the house either. No solution.

For me to involve the authorities about the mistreatment of the boys and run the risk of their being removed from both of us? Over my dead body. No solution.

For the boys to live with me here, in straitened circumstances but in safety? It would leave Helen and her boyfriend to make a go of it together, if they managed to. I recollected his first wife's leaving him again, and wondered why it had happened. Separation from their mother would cause the boys unhappiness, but they would be suffering that whatever happened, alas. And they could see Helen when they wanted to – if she was on her own. I wondered what separation from me would mean to them, but found myself rebelling against even considering that.

This was my scenario, the way my mind had been working all along once it had again become capable of working in a straight line. It was the only logical solution.

"Penny for them?"

I gave a start, which slopped still-hot tea over my right hand.

"Ow!"

"Sorry. It looked as though you'd just come to a conclusion."

A nod. I shook my hand to start it drying. "I have. At least, I've finally worked through the logic of how I reached that conclusion."

The thought processes, put into words, cemented the solution in my mind.

"What about the boys' choices, Jack? Don't you think they should hear all that?"

That, of course, was the fly in the ointment, the rusty bar in the concrete. Would I be able to go against the boys' wishes if they changed their minds?

"They have, more or less," I confirmed to her. "You know that they really matter to me. And it would hurt me a lot if they chose differently. They've already said what they want, though. Nat might need a prod, but I think the prod is Jonathan. When we eat tonight I need to repeat what I've just said to you, and make sure they accept it, in line with what they've decided so far. And I mean what I say about their visiting Helen. It may be that she has to come here, though she'd probably want to meet them on neutral territory. But if it's somewhere else, without a chaperone, it would mean that Jonathan could meet them too."

"I'm not sure I'd want her to have a key to the Marina, even if it puts a barrier between her and the boys," said Poppy.

"I don't want her to have one!" I told her vehemently. "If they want to see her, they will let her in, or I will. Those gates are very, very useful barriers."

Another engine, lunch, and an afternoon developing the spreadsheet and creating a better, more detailed, more friendly and more helpful engine record system. It was encouraging to have added the details of the two I'd dealt with and see an immediate reminder automatically flash up for their next service.

I was done for the day. My two were in the boat, standing at the kitchen work surface with snacks, when I joined them.

"Been here long?" I asked.

"Hours!" complained Nat.

"About forty-five minutes," Phil corrected. "We were going to come and find you but weren't sure if it was the right thing to do."

"This is the sort of environment where you'd be very welcome to do so," I grinned at them. "In fact if it wasn't I'd not be as happy to work here."

"A good day, then?" asked Phil.

"I thought that's what parents are meant to ask their children," I laughed. "But yes, thanks. Very rewarding. How about you?"

"Oh, we had a lecture from the Head. She told me I was to talk to her if ever we were unhappy." Phil was non-committal about it.

"Did she now? I hope you told her that that is what parents are for?"

He hesitated. "Not quite, but I did say that we always talk to you and you would sort it out."

I paused before responding, a silly thing to do because I could feel an emotion start to take hold of me. Such trust! I hoped I deserved it. But then sorting things out *was* what parents are for – one of the many things. It's one of the many responsibilities that have to be learned early on in parenthood, but a responsibility which so many parents never do learn.

I had to look out of the window and get my breathing going properly again.

"So I will," I told them both in as serious a voice as they had ever heard from me. "So I will, even when you have wives or husbands and children of your own. The older you get, the more difficult the unhappinesses are likely to be, but I can always talk things through.

"And that brings something else up…" What a way to lead into the subject. Thanks, Headmistress. "I've got some things a little clearer in my mind. Can I just repeat my thought processes to you to see if you think I'm right, wrong or have missed something?"

They continued looking at me, which is often the way of the youngster to give agreement.

I outlined my thoughts of the morning when talking to Poppy. When I'd run out of words there was silence, which was broken by Nat.

"So we could really see Mum when we wanted to?"

"Well yes," I said, surprised. "Did you think there would be any doubt about it?"

"Yes," he said. "I thought it would be only now and again. You know, a special outing or something."

Was that the reason for his hesitations when we had talked it over before? Had it just been his brother's more positive reaction to their being with me that had persuaded him?

I pushed between the two of them and put an arm round each pair of shoulders, one narrow and one most definitely widening.

"You two are as free as safety allows, with only school and homework – and food, and maybe a bit of company for your poor old father – getting in the way," I said quietly. "Oh, we can each make commitments to be places, and if it means the other two going as well, or just one of us, or neither of us, then we talk about it beforehand. But once committed, that's a commitment. We don't break them unless something dire gets in the way."

"Like being called to go to the States," Phil observed. I winced.

"Won't happen again, promise."

"Not even if a hirer takes a boat over there?" Nat, speaking in a happier voice.

"Not even then. I give one of these an hour at sea and it'll be lifeboat time."

"Dad," Phil complained, wriggling from my hug, "you're nearly being soppy."

"Guilty," I told him, drawing him back in. "I love my sons and I want them with me and to see them happy and become useful men. Now, when Helen comes don't forget you have a free choice. I've told you what I want, she will tell you what she wants. Whether you change your mind is up to you. If you need time out, say so and I will make sure she respects it, as will I."

We decided on fish and chips as a meal. They love them, I tolerate them and Helen hated them and the smell that lingered in the house. These were very good, being produced by one of the few old fashioned chippies still left. We – and I mean we – had washed up, the wrappings were in the bin so as to continue to provide a pleasant atmosphere for Helen. We were ready. As ready as we could be, though all a little jittery.

Why should that be? Helen was hardly an ogre. But she was potentially a threat to the life that I had, maybe hurriedly, planned out for us.

A knock at the side of the boat: I looked at my watch. It was only seven. Nat was nearest and went up. Two men, strangers, both large...

... both smiling. They introduced themselves as the carpenters who had been fitting out the boat, and my heart settled down. So did my jitters, a little.

"We're Losardo Brothers," one of them said. "I'm Guiseppe but I'm just called Seppe, and my brother is Ifor."

Their accents intrigued me but it was Nat the irrepressible who asked them where they came from.

"Italia," said Seppe, "then 'ockley." The difference in the pronunciation of the country and the Birmingham suburb made us all laugh. It reduced the jitters still further.

"It was our parents who came from Italy," Ifor told us. "They wanted an English name for me and found a Welsh one by mistake." We welcomed them in and offered tea, which they declined on grounds of time.

The five of us looked at the layout of the boat and the two of them heard again what I'd dreamed up. Poppy had given them a good idea, so we were talking from a good base of knowledge.

"How big do you want the bathroom to be here?" Seppe asked.

"Only big enough for the toilet and a small basin," I told him. "But if you can get any more storage in there without making use of the toilet awkward for an adult, that would be great."

"Can't we have another shower in there, Dad? It'd mean we don't have to queue as we do now."

"If we did, it'd mean a smaller cabin next to it, or a smaller TV room. And that means a smaller TV," I told him. The last would be the consideration that would change his mind, I was sure, although a smaller cabin for him could also do it.

"I could have a bigger cabin and an en-suite shower," he said happily. "Then I could have a really good soak every time."

"And get through the hot water in one go, you mean; not to mention having to nip out in mid shower and fill the water tank," I said. "And if you do that, could you give the entire marina notice, please, so they can avert their eyes?"

"Ok, ok," he said without missing a beat. "I know when I'm done."

Seppe and Ifor laughed at the exchange. "We heard that you were going through some problems," Ifor said, "so we thought we'd find you depressed. It doesn't sound as if you are."

I told him something of our problems and the fact that the boys' mother was due to visit us any minute.

"We'd been told," said Seppe. "We thought we'd do a bit of measuring and a bit of thinking and drawing, then when you were free again we could go. Or talk to you again. Whichever was more… more tactful."

"Thank you," I laughed. "It's good to know there are so many people on our side."

We agreed to leave them to it and closed the doors between the dinette and where they were measuring.

"I suppose I'd better go and see if she's there," I said eventually.

"I'll come with you," Phil offered. Nat nodded.

There were still ten minutes to go before the witching hour.

13 Helen

We could see a car at the gate as we walked towards it. From the shadows behind us two figures appeared. I checked behind me and recognised one of the regular staff who so far I'd seen just at a distance, and one of the change-over, Saturday, staff. They kept out of the line of sight from the gate, but kept pace with us.

I readied my key, then thought to look through the gates. There were two in the car. Jonathan was the passenger.

"You're uncle's here too," I said in neutral tones, but in a voice loud enough for our unofficial security guards to hear. No one moved. I didn't unlock the padlock.

Helen realised eventually that we were not going to allow the car in. She opened the driver's door.

"Are you going to let us in?" She demanded, haughtily.

"You know the answer to that. I made it very clear in texts and on the phone."

"Don't be childish. Let me come in and park."

"Certainly. When your lover has left the car and walked a hundred yards away."

"Really, Jack..."

"Yes, really, Helen. I told you what the conditions were to your coming here."

"What do you think Jonathan is going to do? Fight you?"

"Good luck to him if he tries. I don't want him to cause the boys any further hurt with his damaging antics."

"For goodness sake. He can sit in the car if I park it inside this... this place, can't he? Do you really mistrust him that much?"

"I trusted him all his life. I even told him about our relationship difficulties. And look how he repaid my trust. No Helen, I don't trust him in the slightest. Nor do Phil and Nat."

"How can you say that? You have no idea..."

"Phil's bruised and cut face said all I need to," I told her slowly, emphasising the words, "and it will just take one call to the Police to dump him so deeply in the shit that he'll wish he never came near them. Or you."

The passenger door opened. He emerged.

"Jack..."

"Walk away. Walk away from the car NOW. Then I will let the car in. Without you. It's only Helen, the boys and I who are going to talk."

"I need to talk as well, you know. I'm in this too, whether you like it or not."

I almost ground my teeth.

"You bastard, I don't like it, in fact only a complete ..." I couldn't find the word. Well, I could, but I wasn't going to use it in front of an audience. "You've jumped into my marriage. You've sh... made love to my wife. For months. And you expect me to be reasonable? You have ended my marriage. I will say this again because you've proved yourself too stupid or too insensitive to have understood so far: you are not going to try to influence what my sons want to do."

"Be reason…"

"We don't want you near us," Phil shouted suddenly. "Go away, like Dad says. You're not part of this family any more."

Jonathan froze. Maybe he heard the venom in Phil's suddenly-treble-again voice.

"I don't want to talk to you either," Nat's quieter voice said from my side. "Go away."

The two by the car said something to each other. Jonathan closed the door and stood back; Helen got in the car and started the engine.

"Walk," I called to Jonathan. He turned his back and did so. I unlocked the gate and the boys pulled them open. We watched the back of the car to judge when we could close it again, but just as Nat was struggling with his side there were running footsteps and Jonathan dodged through the gap.

Phil, with quick reactions, put a foot out to try and trip him up, but he avoided that, looked over his shoulder in triumph, and ran straight into the two unofficial security types. They struggled with him a moment until he realised that they meant business, then sagged to a halt.

The success of our little piece of insurance calmed me. I walked over to the three of them.

"The boys thought it would be a shame if you tripped over something and fell in the dock," I told him. "They're not yet of adult enough size to make that happen, and of course as their father I would deprecate such an accident happening. But they and I would laugh if it did, because it would be payback for the imprisonment in their rooms and for the injury you caused Phil."

He would not meet my eyes.

"The boys and I are going to talk to Helen now," I said to the two holding him. "If he does fall in, he'll probably want to drive home." I looked around. Helen was watching, speechless. "I suggest you give him the keys. He might need them. Put the car outside the gates first, though."

"I'll do no such thing..."

"Then he'll have to walk. No taxi will take him, nor a bus, not if he's that wet."

"What do you mean wet?"

I had moved away from the water: she was watching me. The boys were moving towards the boat.

There was a shout, and a splashing.

"Probably best if you take the car out. He'll need it," I said to Helen.

"You made them throw him in!"

"Looks to me as if they're fishing him out," I said, pointing to the two pulling at the arms of my spluttering brother. "They're saving his life after a trip."

There was the flash of a camera from the direction of the office. Poppy, taking a photo.

"I am the Marina owner," she said pleasantly to Helen. "So unfortunate that he tripped but I'm glad my employees managed to save his life. Perhaps we should send his photo to the papers. They might get the RLSS medal. What do you think?"

Helen looked at Poppy, speechless, with daggers in her eyes.

With some manoeuvring the car was taken outside the gates. Helen was inside them. Jonathan crossed wordlessly to her and snatched the keys. The gates were firmly locked behind him.

"Well saved, gentlemen," I said to the two "security" men as if they had been goalkeepers. "Thank you so much , and I owe you."

"I'd like to say 'any time', said the regular man. "But it might get a bit suspicious."

I laughed, wished them all good night and thanked them again, and joined Helen who was standing, furious, by the gate, as the car sped away. Phil and Nat were keeping their distance, I was glad to see. Whether they were laughing or not I *couldn't* see.

We led her towards the boat, to her surprise.

"That was an evil thing to do," she said quietly. It was the tone of voice she would use to the boys when there was really going to be some trouble coming. It had happened to me, too, in the past. Now, I recognised it and didn't care. In fact I really enjoyed not caring.

"He fell in," I told her. "Tripped over something. It's a Victorian quayside and there are hazards there. He's lucky he didn't crack his head, being so careless. But then he knows about hitting heads, doesn't he? He practises on his elder nephew. Doesn't he?"

She glared at me.

"I thought you might at least take me to where you were living," she complained, changing the subject as we climbed aboard.

"We are taking you there," I told her. "This is our home."

"What? Here? On this…?"

"Yes, we live on a boat."

She gasped, but followed us down to the dinette and watched as we sat around the table. She joined us. The boys were silent. No one put the kettle on.

"This is a put-up job, isn't it?" she started. "You intended to throw Jonathan in, didn't you?"

"I had nothing to do with it," I said, conscious that the voice recorder on Phil's and my phone were both running. "I told you just now that he must have tripped over, and it was nothing to do with any of us. In any case, each one of us told you that we didn't want him here and that he wasn't to come. It wasn't just me, it was Phil, Nat and me. He has no place in any arrangements we make with you – or any arrangements that we choose not to make. Don't forget that he gate-crashed into the Marina, almost literally, and as such was a trespasser. What happened to him was his own fault."

My mind floated back to the desperation I felt when I was lying in hospital, trying to get the energy together even to remove my share of the joint bank accounts. What a difference between then and now; maybe I now had the upper hand.

"Well?" she asked, when nobody else volunteered to speak.

"Well indeed," I responded. "You asked to come and see me, I think it was about the boys. I insisted on their behalf that they should be here as well as it's their life and…"

"They're children," she interrupted. "We decide what is best for them. They can't decide anything like this until they're eighteen."

"Wrong," I told her. "At sixteen someone can decide where they will live. But any parent who won't listen to what their children want when they – the parent – has let them down isn't much of a parent."

She gasped. "How dare you say that?"

"How dare you stand by when Phil was hit? How dare you not stop your lover from locking them in their rooms? How dare you hit Phil yourself?"

We glared at each other in silence. What she was waiting for I didn't know. I was waiting for the next verbal fusillade.

Phil cleared his throat. "Just so you know, Mum, we are staying here, living with Dad. Uncle Jonathan isn't safe to be with. He makes us both uncomfortable. And he – and you – have hit me. Maybe he's hit Nat – I don't know, but uncle went into Nat's room that night. Nat said that he was trying to persuade him that Dad didn't want us, that he had gone loopy, and that he wasn't part of the family any more."

"That's not true," she said.

"It IS! It IS true." Nat suddenly shouted at her in frustration. "It was my bloody room. I was there. I hated him even more for what he said. When we visited Dad in hospital he said he loved us and wanted us with him. I told uncle that, and he said it was just Dad trying to be nice. But he was lying. Uncle was lying. I hate him now and I'm not living where he is. Nor is Phil. We've made up our minds."

"You'll live where we decide you live."

"I won't." He glared at her.

"No, we won't," said Phil hotly, before I had a chance to say anything. Perhaps it was as well that I didn't, for the moment. "If you order us back there, we won't go, and if you kidnap us – either of us – we'll go to the Headmistress or Social Services or Childline and play them the recordings we've got."

Helen's eyes widened. "Don't be stupid. Recordings? What recordings?"

I thought it was now my turn. "I think you must realise that with intelligent children like ours, they know to collect evidence when there is potential trouble ahead," I told her. "When they have been talking about their experiences with your boyfriend and complaining to me about him, I have recorded their accusations. It's been done with their knowledge and approval, naturally. They too have recorded those conversations and, I hope, other unpleasant conversations at their… their *old* home." I stressed the word. "I'm quite sure Nat will have recorded the lies that Jonathan spouted about me, and I'm surprised you didn't know about them, anyway. Or perhaps you did. Perhaps you planted the idea in his mind.

"Anyway, the sum total of those recordings is evidence enough to convince any Social Service person – or the Police, or the Court if it comes to that – that there is a case of cruelty, and that my sons and I are convinced it would happen again if they were to return to live with Jonathan present."

"My family will not be dragged into dealing with Social Services," she told me, looking daggers again.

"At last we are in agreement. It would do no one any good if it can be avoided. But I tell you now, that that is what will happen if you try and take these two away from here against their wishes and mine, and try and force them to live back at their *old* home. Coercion will affect them even more than they currently are affected. More than that, it will result in a Police case against Jonathan, of that I am sure. The recordings will guarantee that the evidence sticks, and I will ensure that they are taken seriously."

We let that sink in.

"We're both going to stay here, Mum," Phil said, quietly now. "We've talked about it, we've told Dad, we've each recorded our decisions, and recorded ourselves telling him, too."

Silence.

"Quite the little spies, aren't you?" she said bitterly.

"We all need to be sure of where we are, and able to prove our discussions to any official enquiry," I told her. "So now we can take it as read that the boys will be living here with me, I hope. There is to be no attempt by you or my brother to force them, or to try brainwashing them into going back there."

"Neither of us would ever try and brainwash them," she protested.

"Too late. You've already heard that Jonathan lied to Nat in an attempt to do just that. So perhaps he's not the angel you doubtless hold him to be. After all, what angel climbs into his brother's marital bed before it's even cold?"

"Jack!"

"Unpleasant, isn't it? Perhaps you'll start to understand how I feel, then."

"I didn't mean that. I meant that it's not a suitable thing to say in front of these two."

"But in his and your eyes it was an acceptable thing for him to *do* in front of these two."

"They never saw…"

"Whoah… They're not stupid, nor innocent, and they have good hearing and astute perception. You don't see that they are really no longer the little boys you believe them to be."

"I realise that by the language they used to Jonathan. And to me."

"Well, surprise, surprise. They are at school. They learn words like that from their friends and acquaintances, and how they're used. Usually they choose not to use them, especially to their parents or other adults, because they're well brought up. But *in extremis* they will, just as I find myself doing. As have you. Remember?"

Another silence. I felt that a lot of points had been made and that she had no argument against them. I continued, in quieter, gentler tones.

"They have said… no, best that they tell you themselves what they want. About visiting your mother," I added for their benefit, turning to them. "Do you want me to go down the other end so you can talk to her alone? Then she'll know that these are your choices, not mine foisted on you."

Nat frowned. "What's 'foisted' mean, Dad? Is it the same as 'forced'?"

"In this context, yes, Nat."

"Oh, that's all right," said my forthright son. "We know *you* wouldn't do that. Mum, Dad says we can visit you somewhere when we want to, so long as uncle isn't with you."

"He did, did he? Big of him. How about when *I* want you to?"

"Yes," he said surprised and a little dismayed, "So long as it's safe, not in school time and we're not… *committed* … to be somewhere else."

Phil nodded. "Applies to me too. Neither of us want to… to… not to see you."

This time the silence was extended.

"But if you won't see me when Jonathan's around it means I'm hardly going to see you," she said as plaintively as she could manage. Then to me: "That's not right. I'm their mother."

All that time in the hospital listening to what the boys had told me meant that my answer was ready and obvious.

"And if it had all gone to plan, and you and he had managed to keep hold of them by saying that I was round the bend, didn't want them and wasn't part of the family any more, how often would they have been able to see me? Not at all, I imagine."

"I'm their mother."

"And I'm their father. We are equally their parents and you forget that at your peril. They know that I am very far from being 'round the bend' as my brother so kindly put it, and that I want them with me just as much as you may possibly do. It's Jonathan who's no longer a part of my family so far as I'm concerned, except by blood. So whilst he's living with you, they can get together with you whenever you want and they agree, on the express condition that he's not present when you meet. As I keep on saying, he's not safe in the way he treats them and I don't want him anywhere near them. I think you'll find they say the same."

"I don't want to see him," Nat said. He was quite vehement about it, and I wondered why. He'd been lied to, but that was all – well, it was enough. But that *was* all, wasn't it?

"How about you, Phil?"

A shake of the head. There was still a fading cut there. "No. He used to be like… well, the favourite uncle, but he's changed. He's…" He paused and touched his scar. "I don't want to see him again."

"So that's that, "I said brightly. "Now all we need to do is to sort out finances. I told you what was going to happen. You'll either sell the house and pay off the mortgage, and I take half the proceeds, or you can sell Jonathan's flat and pay off *its* mortgage and I take the same amount from that if it's more than half the value of the house."

"I can't just..."

"You can't just make decisions like that, you mean? I think you can. To sell the house you need authority from me and it'll be done through a properly briefed solicitor. If you choose to sell his place it's not my business except that I expect half the expected residual value of our house. Your choice."

"And where are you and they going to live? You can't live on a boat."

"Well yes, actually we can. And we are. And we all like it."

"I need to check it for myself."

"*What?* Don't be so damn intrusive. You're not welcome to. I was hoping to have a letter to hand to you tonight, summarising what I've said, but I haven't had time to compose it. You'll get it in a day or two, by recorded delivery.

"And of course there's the contribution you need to be making to the boys' welfare. What I'll do is sort out a spreadsheet which will separate out your contribution of the food bills, half their clothing and other bills and so on. That'll be emailed to you once a month and I'd like quick settlement of it, please, say within three days."

She gasped. "So not only are you taking my sons away..."

"I'm not. They are choosing to live with me."

"Irrelevant. You're depriving me of my sons and you expect me to pay for the privilege? Think again. You'll get nothing from me."

"Oh do *listen!* The boys have decided. I haven't deprived you of them. Anyway, are you saying that you don't care enough about their well-being to contribute to the expense of it?"

"I'm saying that since you have them, you support them."

I rolled my eyes to the ceiling. "That's not how it works, and it's not how it looks to them. You are a parent still. You have responsibilities."

"You left the home."

I gave a bitter laugh. "I *left* the home? If you remember, you successfully excluded me from it by changing the locks. You even deprived Nat and Phil of a key so they couldn't come and go as they want. No, any court would rubbish a claim that I deserted the family and would tell you that you had to help support your sons." I thought a moment. "If I had voluntarily left home and the boys stayed with you and your lover, I would be expected to pay upkeep for them – if not for you. As we are, the boot is actually on the other foot. So you will need to contribute."

"You earn enough to pay for their upkeep three times over."

"My finances don't come in to it. In fact, since it's your actions and my work that caused me to react to the stress at last by having a breakdown, I may be leaving Crown. So it's very likely that the less demanding job I get will pay nothing like as much."

"I can't help that. I don't earn enough to pay maintenance, and that's the end of it."

"Then you'll have to make arrangements. Perhaps when the house is sold and you're living somewhere cheaper it'll be easier for you. By the way, did I say that I won't be making mortgage payments any more? Don't forget that you've excluded me from enjoying my own property so I see no reason to contribute to it if I'm not allowed to live in it."

"You want it every way you can, don't you? Do you think that's reasonable?"

"I didn't want it this way at all," I told her bitterly. "If I'd not been cuckolded by my brother, been locked out of my house, nearly had my sons brainwashed into thinking I was mad, and then discovering that they were the victims of child cruelty at your lover's hands, you wouldn't now be in this situation. So I'll do as I say and summarise this in writing, properly witnessed, and you'll get it as soon as I can arrange it.

"Now, I don't think we need to delay you any further. Anything you want to say, guys?"

I'd been so intent on negotiating with Helen that I'd not seen the effect it was having on the boys. They looked numb, shocked.

"Bye, Mum," said Nat, sadly.

All Phil managed was a wave of the hand.

She glared at me, barely acknowledged them and stormed out of the boat as quickly as she could, leaving the door open. There was silence when she had disappeared.

14 Aftermath

Both sets of eyes were downcast. I went to the clear part of the kitchen area and stood facing them, arms spread wide.

"I need some comfort, Phil, Nat. Can you help me, please?"

First Nat, then Phil came and allowed a hug.

"I'm really, really sorry you had to witness that," I said softly. "Now perhaps you realise I am determined that nothing in this family is going to be held secret from you, not even its finances. All I ask is that you don't discuss our money situation with anyone else, not the Head at your school, not friends, nobody apart from me."

Slowly, they nodded agreement. "What about the money we get from Poppy for Saturdays, Dad? Should we give you that?" Phil's question floored me.

"Phil... no. That is yours, earned by your own efforts. And it won't continue much beyond the summer anyway because there are fewer hirers in the winter."

He looked relieved, but continued. "It just seems that you and Mum are earning too, and spending it on us. So we should do the same, but in reverse."

I gave him an extra squeeze. "But you see, Phil: we 'had' each of you, twelve and fourteen years ago. You didn't 'have' us. When you have a child you know that they are dependent on you until they become legally independent at eighteen. And even then, a parent who can do so will still offer support. If you decide a university is for you we will continue to support you. You are ours, and we are yours, but the onus is on us to help bring you to adulthood. And to let go when you need your independence."

The look of relief was still there. Perhaps I had convinced him. I was about to say something else when the boat lurched and the door from the stern opened. Helen, looking even more angry than when she had left.

"Are you going to let me out so I can get in the car when it arrives?" I wondered what she thought about the tableau we presented; a father with his arms round the shoulders of his sons.

We had forgotten the locked gate. I made a move to oblige, and looked at the other two.

"Coming?" They nodded, straight-faced again and made ready to follow. As they did so the communicating door to the cabins opened and a face looked in. Ifor.

"Oh, sorry," he said. "I thought you were free."

"Nearly," I told him. "We have to go and open the gate to let... my wife out."

He looked at the angry and now astonished face.

"Ah," he said uncomfortably. "I'm sorry. We were just measuring something and the boat rocked. We thought you'd finished, then the boat rocked again so we weren't sure what was happening."

"And just who are you?" Helen demanded. "More intrusive security?"

"Whoa...miss. Er, Missus. We're not security, we're carpenters measuring up, as I said. But if there are intruders in the Marina we can certainly help eject them."

She looked at him with distaste and turned. I flashed Ifor a smile and a wink. He gave me a thumbs up and disappeared into the cabin area again.

At the gate there was no sign of Jonathan. Helen looked impatient and dug out her mobile.

"Where are you?" she asked into it.

I was glad not to be able to hear my brother's voice.

"How long are you going to be?"

Faint sounds from the other phone.

"Half an *hour?*"

"What am I meant to do, then?"

"Yes, yes; all right. Perhaps they'll give me a cup of tea."

"What do you mean too pally? It's not a question of pally. It's a question of having to wait for you."

It seemed that all was not sweetness and light between those two either. I looked back to the boat. Two shadows disappeared back onto the bow and ducked into the end cabin again. I smiled to myself. The 'intrusive security' were doing their job.

I made the obligatory cup of tea. Even I couldn't bring myself to make her wait outside in the semi-dark. We sat uncomfortably in near silence. At one time she started to bring up the money situation again but I very quickly butted in.

"We're not starting that again, Helen. I've told you what you need to do and why. And it was unpleasant having to do so in front of these two. But I'm determined they understood what was happening, where the law stood, and most importantly what was fair and equitable between us."

"What about Jonathan?"

"As my father would have said: Hang Jonathan. He can decide what he wants to do – after all, he's done so already, damn him."

"Dad…"

"I know, Phil; I'm sorry. It's distasteful. We'll say no more."

And, give or take a slightly forced, slightly insincere questions about their school experiences, we said no more. At last her phone bleeped.

"He's here," she said having looked at it. "He says he wants to talk to you."

"Then he can carry on wanting. I don't want any direct communication with him except in writing. You can pass on what we've… agreed and he can read it himself when the papers arrive."

"He says he must…"

"And I say he mustn't. I'll let you out. Perhaps it would be good if our friendly carpenters could be on hand to make sure there's no attempt at trespassing again. I'll call them."

She started saying something but I ignored her and opened the connecting door again. "Ifor? Seppe? I wonder if you could give us a hand, please?"

My brother was waiting at the gate when the six of us reached it. Almost immediately he started talking.

"Shut up," I told him in a voice that, I hoped, was enough to squash him.

"I've said what I have to say to my wife. She will pass it on to you and I will confirm it in writing, as we've agreed. Step away from the gate."

"Jack…"

"I said step away. These two gentlemen here are happy to prevent trespassers, just like the security guards are. Step back."

"Here you are, guv," said the large and imposing looking Seppe. "I've got a key so I can open it and make sure nothing happens."

I looked at him gratefully. Helen started to bluster.

"Good night," I said to her, and walked away. The boys echoed me, sadness in their voices, and it wrung at my heart.

They followed me to the boat's bows and we turned. Once again my hands went to their backs and I confess it was not just to offer comfort but to demonstrate solidarity to Helen and Jonathan. It pleased me that they accepted it and didn't do the usual wriggling away, so perhaps they appreciated it. Its ulterior motive made me feel guilty.

Seppe's and Ifor's presence was a comfort as it took our attention away from the hurts of the previous hour. The five us settled down in the dinette to talk beds, cabins, toilets, TVs and carpentry. I broke out some beers, including the remaining non-alcohol bottles from Saturday night.

"We've been here a long time," Seppe started, "because we were designing what I hope you wanted. Let's make sure we're right. We were talking about a fold-out futon, three parts. As a seat it'd need to be at normal sitting height, so we need to mount it on a box that would house a drawer for storage. In front of that, attached to the side of the boat, would be a fold-down table the same width as the seat or bed. Folded up, it'd reach to the ceiling. We might need to adjust the bulkheads so that the window doesn't get in the way.

"That gives us a study, with a wide seat like a sofa, and a desk. To use it as a bed, fold up the table and secure it, then release the sofa's back and roll the end support out. The middle legs drop by gravity and the end is a solid sheet for stability. With wheels.

"Then to make it a seat again, lift the first fold and pull up, then push the end support. It rolls back on the wheels, the other legs fold up automatically, and bingo, you've got a sofa again. The rake of the back could be adjustable.

"And the other thing was a fold-down bench seat hinged to the opposite bulkhead. If we get it right it could be a headboard, if you want to sleep that way round."

My engineering speciality deals with large, hot, reciprocating, noisy lumps of metal. It doesn't deal with things that are easily saw-able or which don't need years of R&D before a cautious prototype is built. Despite my draughting and technical background it took me some concentration to visualise the details of the workings of the bed, or sofa, or whatever it was. The boys' eyes had glazed over. Seppe put a piece of paper on the table and went over it again for us.

"So it'd do what Dad said at the start?" Nat asked hopefully, trying to make sense of the maze of lines, figures and arrows.

"It will," said Seppe happily. "But the mattresses will need to be bought and

I don't think they're cheap. I'll get you some prices. How tall are you going to grow?"

Nat looked at him, then at me with a question in his eyes.

"My height," I said decidedly. "And then a couple of inches more."

"We'd better get a longer boat, Ifor," Seppe teased. "Two metres, or he'll have to sleep like a banana."

"What is all this likely to cost?" I asked, bringing the conversation back to normal.

"We'll have to see how we get on first," Ifor said. "If you're really going to be our guinea-pigs and give us the chance of developing a piece of furniture to sell, we can maybe charge a bit less. But let's see, first."

"And can you price the other woodwork too, please?" I asked. "We don't know whether the Marina is paying for all this, or me. Us."

Seppe grinned and nodded. "Poppy's our client," he said. "She'd decide if she thinks it's value and if it's acceptable to you, and she'll pay. How she sorts it out with you…" he gave an expressive Italian shrug.

"How about the TV?" asked Nat.

"Sorry, we don't build them."

The expression on Nat's face was comical, then he grinned. "A wooden TV! Can't you make one, really?"

Seppe grinned at him. "You can have whatever size of TV you want. It all depends on what you want in the front there and whether you want a low-mounted TV so you don't have to crane your neck, or a high mounted one that doesn't get hit by furniture or people kicking it."

"And how big the remaining space is," I added. "No good having a big screen if it's only a couple of feet in front of us."

"You should have about ten feet – that's just over three metres to you two."

"We three. I work in metric too," I told him.

"We work in anything. We're happy buying three metre lengths of 4x2 inch timber, for example; it seems logical to us. But you should have a good space down there, especially as you'll have the full width of the boat to play with."

"Best we leave any decisions until we see the placement of the final bulkhead, I should think. Is that all right with you two? Can we manage with the small screen for the moment?"

"S'pose we'd better," Phil said reluctantly. "It's not for ever, anyway."

"No, it's not," I confirmed, looking at Nat's disappointed face. "Just as soon as the last bulkhead's in place, we'll make plans and talk to Seppe and Ifor. Then buy a cinema to go in."

Nat's head jerked up. "What? Really?"

"No, not really. Although… let's see what we can find and what we can afford, shall we?"

"We'll get on with it as soon as we can," Ifor told me, still laughing at Nat's reaction to the cinema idea. "Your spec for the futons has got me interested and I want to see how we can make them work, so I want to have a play with that first." He looked thoughtful. "I'll make up one of the sides out of some scrap wood first and test it out. If it really does work we could offer it for sale as a piece of made furniture."

"I've never been a guinea-pig before," said Nat suddenly. Phil gave a theatrical squeak, then coughed, causing a general chuckle.

"That means a treadmill somewhere, doesn't it?" I said innocently. "It could go at the end, instead of a TV."

They left eventually, and we were on our own. "I like them," said Nat. "They're good fun."

I hoped that the interlude would have lightened the mood from Helen's visit. As we were about to gravitate to the TV something occurred to me.

"Anyone got any homework they have to do?"

Two groans gave me the answer and they were banished to the dinette.

The remainder of that week saw a complete lack of mechanical or any other breakdowns, an achievement that drew a remark from Poppy as I was about to leave work on Friday afternoon. "So you won't want me any more," I said mock-morosely.

"Not after tomorrow's change-over, no," she responded. I looked up, half ready to believe her. "Not until Monday morning, anyway."

I was tempted to put out my tongue, but didn't. She smiled.

"How about you, Jack? Are you ready to make this a permanent post, or is it too early to say? And have you resigned from Crown yet? I can't in all conscience pay your salary until you have. It wouldn't stand up to scrutiny." The comment brought me up short.

Resignation from a long-standing, very responsible and very high paying job. A job that was a career. A job that used my training and abilities to the full. The plus side.

A job that had helped to cost me my marriage, although the more I considered it the more I knew that it had never been the main reason. A job that had taken me away for long periods and deprived me of experiencing the development of my own children and of the fun we could have had over the years – as demonstrated by the fun we'd had even over the last week. A job that had given me that breakdown… The very, very minus side.

I drew in a breath and let it out in a rush.

"Yes," I said, "Yes, I need to resign from Crown. And I need to take up your offer of a job formally, if you're offering me a job, formally."

"You've only had a week," she almost protested.

"Yes. A week that started and has continued with the fun of having my two around, along with new colleagues who treat me as an equal, not as some untouchable, exalted engineering demi-god, and who are friendly. Genuinely friendly, not friendly because they want something. Work that takes me back to my youth when I was a proper engineer dealing with engines that aren't also exalted and mounted on plinths to do their work."

I paused, thinking hard.

"Being called on to give a hand with someone else who needs it. Getting help from colleagues in the same way. Having a boss who knows what she wants and is direct about it, but who will bend over backwards to help when it's needed. And a boss who comes to a meal on a boat when it's offered. Are you free on Saturday night?"

A real laugh. "Jack, really! Yes, I'd love to. But really it's my turn to cook for you three."

"I think your Saturday is full enough without cooking as well. At least I get over half a day free as I can't take hirers out yet. It won't be a very exotic meal, probably just a salad as it's getting warmer now."

"And I suppose you want some more tuition on the Sunday, do you?"

"Hah! I wasn't angling for that. But if you're offering, why not?"

"Of course, there is a possibility…"

I waited.

"Ah – not this weekend because we've got Jacky coming back to pump out the last two boats. But then… once we've got the last of them out of the Marina we could go off for the remains of Saturday and all of Sunday, perhaps even get back on the Monday."

"Don't forget school."

"Of course. Bother. But an overnighter, anyway. I could sleep in the dinette and we could get a bit further. As it is we'd probably only get down the Northern Stratford a bit…"

"Stratford? You mean Stratford on Avon?"

"Well, yes. That's where the Stratford Canal goes. Look…"

There was a map in the office, at the customer side of it. I'd noticed it that first time, and subsequently on my way in and out, but never looked at it properly. There was a smudge just above the centre of Birmingham. "That's where we are," she said. "I must get a new map. This is getting dirty."

I looked. The number of blue lines in the city, showing canals, was still surprising. Poppy's finger traced one south.

"We could go down past the University and Bourneville, then turn left at Kings Norton Junction. That's the Northern Strat. There are places to turn down there, so we should get to about Earlswood Reservoir, I should think. Maybe to the Blue Bell. That's nice. They do good food, too, and it's a friendly pub. We can turn near there and come back. No locks, but a tunnel, so that'd be an experience."

"We must go down to Stratford itself some day," I said. "Oh, they've been, as have I, but it's not the same as arriving by canal, is it?"

She smiled. "No, that certainly adds something. Getting into Stratford Basin is a bit bendy; you have to go slow. But there's usually mooring there, and as you say, it's well worth it."

"But that's more than a couple of days?"

There was a shadow at the door: my two, still in uniform from school.

"We thought you'd fallen in, Dad. You're late."

"Sorry," said Poppy. We've been planning some more trips out for you."

The accusing looks vanished and smiles appeared.

"Where are we going?" Nat.

"We thought you could go down to the Thames at Oxford, follow it down through London, then come back up the Grand Union," Poppy teased.

"How long would that take?"

"Would we miss any school?"

"Three weeks or more. So yes, you'd miss school and that's why it can't happen yet. It's a marathon. Give yourselves a chance. But one day, why not?"

"So where were you thinking of?" asked Phil.

"Down the Northern Stratford Canal to a pub, turn round and come back. No locks, but a tunnel and some countryside. That's for Saturday evening and Sunday. And then later, in school holidays, further down the Stratford."

"Wow... To be, or not to be... Shakespeare, you know." Phil, showing that he paid attention occasionally in Literature lessons.

"I know that," Nat told him. "How long does that take?"

"The play?" asked Phil innocently, "oh about..."

"Shut up. How long, Poppy?"

"It's about a week," Poppy told him. "It does depend how many hours you do a day. You'd leave on a Saturday after changeover and get back by the following Friday. Please!"

I laughed. "That sounds really good. We'll talk about that."

"Are you coming too?" asked Nat.

"I am tomorrow," she laughed, "and bringing a sleeping bag."

"How about when we go on the Stratford?"

She paused. "Ah well, that depends."

"What on?" Irrepressible is Nat, when he gets going.

"All sorts of things. How many boats we have out, how many breakdowns we have. You know, that sort of thing."

He thought for a moment. "It'd be nice if you could."

He got a smile form her that he didn't expect.

15 Jonathan

The weather was wet for Saturday's change-over. It made life unpleasant but we soldiered on and did what we had to. Nat was even wetter than before as he wielded water-tank filling hoses. After dealing with the two remaining boats which still had bad fuel in their tanks I managed to service two more that were due, according to my predecessor's records. Fortunately they weren't as gunge-ridden as the first one I'd encountered.

Phil nearly went in the water at one point. He slipped on the smooth, wet decking and only saved himself by grabbing onto the tiller arm and scrambling back, red faced, having somehow clung on to the fuel hose's nozzle. I just looked at him and raised my eyebrows. He ignored me.

Between filling the boats he really made himself useful by fetching filters from the stores, and passing me tools as I needed them. In fact, without him I couldn't have managed to do all that I did. The only job that was impossible in the time was cleaning the engines off properly, so I hoped there were no undetected leaks under the little grime remaining. By the time we had finished I almost envied Poppy in her dry office and the crews doing the interior cleaning. They were dry too, and warm. We were not: it was mid-June and should have been warmer.

We were finished. I sent the boys to the boat to shower and change and went, dripping, to the office to record details of the two serviced boats on my new system. Poppy grinned at me.

"Still like working here?"

"Leaving on Monday," I said. "Do we get this often?"

"Not too regularly. And usually not this bad when we do. This is October weather."

"Tell me about it," I said, dripping onto the keyboard.

"Should we scrub today's trip?" she asked suddenly. "It's not much fun steering through this."

"Let me look at the forecast when I've done this," I said after some thought. "And I'll ask the other two."

"They're good lads," she said suddenly. "A lot of kids would have skived off once they got as wet as those two. They stuck to it, though."

"Good parenting," I said without thinking.

She looked at me quizzically and smiled. I wondered what was in her mind.

It wasn't until later, in the shower, that my mind wandered back to that look. It hit me then: I had been away so often that most of their parenting had been done by Helen.

Had she instilled dependability into them? Maybe: from a quite young age they had been trusted to reach school by public bus service on their own. It had been remarked on by some of the other parents on the rare occasions I'd been present with Helen at plays or sports events. I had always smiled sagely and told them that both Helen's and my parents had done the same with us all those years ago, and we had been safe.

"But it was all so much safer in those days," I had been told. "You didn't get the weirdos then that you do now."

Well, we did get them, but so rarely as to be negligible. We met one, Jonathan and I, when we were eleven and twelve or so. We'd just laughed at him and run, and he never bothered us again. Helen and I had discussed it, of course, and decided that independence and responsibility on a daily basis were more important than the unlikely event of our two being alone with someone who had unhealthy tendencies towards them. Certainly not on the journey to school that they had to take so regularly, since there were always others around.

The boys had never reported any problems, we saw no sudden changes to their behaviour, and they responded so well to the trust we showed them that all four of us benefitted.

Trust: Helen, Jonathan. Huh!

"Will you be long, Dad? I need a pee." Nat. Damn.

"Use the other one," I said without thinking.

"In daylight? No thanks." I'd forgotten we had neither bolts on the door nor curtains at the windows there.

"Use the office one. I'm still showering."

"Ok."

"Nat back?" I asked Phil later after I'd dried and was dressing.

"No. He went to the office so I should think he's talking to Poppy."

That seemed logical. But then a thought spring into my mind. It was Saturday afternoon. New hirers were coming in. Poppy would be talking to them, jollying them along, waiting for their boats to be ready. I frowned.

"That was ages ago, and she's busy."

"Oh…"

Something worried me. I emerged from the shower, still half clad.

He looked up and met my eyes. "Should I go and find him?"

"Would you? I'll start cooking something."

He went. Once dressed I busied myself with tins and rice and anything else I could find. The rice was about to boil when the door opened fast and Phil's worried voice interrupted my thoughts. "Dad – he's missing. He used the toilet and came back here. Except that he didn't." I looked, then flung open the connecting doors in the rest of the boat. Empty.

I swore. Was this Helen and Jonathan again? Do I phone Helen? I rushed out of the boat, nearly tripped onto the quayside and headed for the gate which was wide open as it always was in working hours. Nothing. I headed down to the end of the rifle club building; a car was parked half way along it. It looked like Jonathan's.

I'm heavy for sprinting, especially nowadays. But I found I was having to think about my feet and how to make sure I didn't trip over, or over-run on my headlong dash towards that car.

It was Jonathan's. I wrenched at the door. A face snapped round and saw me, reached down and fumbled, probably with the keys. A door opened at the other side.

"Open this door, or I call the Police," I yelled with all the force I could muster after that sprint. The engine started. I hit the car with all my force as it jerked forward and away, and narrowly missed having my foot run over by the rear wheel. I dug my phone from my pocket and was about to hit the nine three times when a scared voice called out.

"Dad!"

I looked up at Nat and stared, then found myself collapsing to the pavement with relief and the release of the stress of the previous few minutes. He crossed to me and sat beside me. I hid my tears from him by holding my head in my hands.

"It's all right now. I got out when you came to his door."

Careless of who might see us I flung my arm round his shoulders until I had calmed down and stopped sobbing like a... well, like a twelve year old. Him? He seemed fine, totally unphased. I was drawing strength from him, just as I had hinted would happen way back when I was in the hospital bed and talking to Phil.

Phil, whose running footsteps were approaching. He flung himself down the other side of Nat and put his arm round him too, an arm that was impatiently shrugged off.

"It's Dad who needs the hug, not me. I'm fine."

The comment made me almost want to smile. A few deep breaths more; I let out a sigh, hugged them both and turned to Nat.

"What did he do?"

He looked embarrassed. "I'd just come out of the office and there he was. Nobody was near him, and he was just looking around. Then he saw me and said he needed to talk to me. I said I didn't want to and he just said it was ok, but I'd left something important at home when we left and he'd got it in the car, and would I come and fetch it to save him coming back. So I followed him down here. He unlocked the car and shoved me inside, then went round to the driver's side."

I nearly said something at that point but stopped myself.

"He told me Mum was really missing me and he was going to take me home for a visit, so I told him that we were going out this afternoon and I'd call her. He said it wouldn't take long and I'd be back before you missed me. So I asked him what it was that I'd left at home."

He gulped. "He said that wasn't it, it was just to get me to come to the car, and did I realise how much Mum and he were missing me. And he put a hand on my back – you know, just round it so it felt like he was holding me in the seat."

"I didn't know what to say, but he left his hand there while he talked more, but I didn't really listen. It just felt so... so wrong. He was still talking when you tried to get in. That stopped him and I managed to unlock the door and get out."

By this time I had frozen. *Had* Jonathan been about to kidnap him? What was in his mind? Surely he wouldn't have dared to? He must have realised that the first, most obvious thing I would do was to call the Police. After all, kidnap of a minor is an offence which no one takes lightly.

"Do you think he'd have driven off with you if I hadn't come along?"

"I don't know," he admitted, after a pause. "He was really just talking."

I needed to talk to someone else. Poppy. No, she was busy with hirers. It wouldn't be fair. I had to decide. But…

I reached for my phone. "I'm going to call the Police," I said.

"No, Dad, please!" Nat said. "It'll just make Mum even more angry. I just want him not to come here any more."

"But the only way I can stop that is to get the Police to tell him, and to back it up with a Court order," I told him.

"But…" Now he *was* upset.

"Nat…" It was Phil's turn. "Nat, he's right. And Mum should have stopped him. She knows we don't want him here."

"But…"

There were approaching footsteps and we all looked up. Ian had heard that Nat seemed to be missing and had seen Phil and me rush out of the Marina. He had seen us all from the corner, apparently collapsed against the wall, and was worried. He explained all that as we struggled to our feet.

We walked slowly back to the Marina, explaining as we went.

"It's not obvious that he was going to take Nat away," he said after some thought, "though the Police might think so. And if he wasn't, and can somehow prove it he wasn't, they might think you're trying to get your own back. No…" He held up his hands as we all tried to interrupt, "no that's *not* what I think, but it might be what they think. If he'd actually driven off with Nat then that's different. I'd be calling them myself and telling them to go to your old address."

"But I can't just let him get away with it!" I said hotly.

"Why not call your wife and tell her what's happened, and tell her if he ever comes near them again you *will* call the Police?"

"I've already done that in the last few weeks. And I've told the Head of their school I would, too."

"But did you tell your wife that? Why not give her a call and tell her that it will be an accusation of attempted kidnap if he comes here again? And let's have the details of the car so that if anyone sees it they can warn you."

We were now back at the Marina. Ian apologised and said he had to rush off but that he'd be back. By that time I'd made up my mind to call Helen and give her what for. We entered the boat to the horrendous smell of burnt rice, burnt plastic saucepan handle and a cloud of steam that would have graced a sauna. The flame was out, but there was this other smell. How long…?

"Get out!" I shouted to the boys. "Quick!" I lunged forward and turned the gas dial back to off, and went outside myself. It had been cold; all the windows were shut. I ran to the bow and thrust open the doors, held my breath and flung open all the doors on the corridor to get a through draught.

They were hovering by the rear doors, still on the boat. "Come away," I said hurriedly. "If there's a spark in there at the moment it could blow up. Go into the office... no, better than that, stay by the roadway and stop anybody else coming near. And tell anyone smoking to go well away because of gas. I'll go to the office."

Serious-faced, as well they might be, they hopped off and hurried back to the roadway. I ran to the office, had to hop from one foot to another while she continued her welcome to some new hirers, and then was able to outline what had happened.

"Is everyone all right?" she asked, calmly.

I assured her we are and told her the boys were keeping people away.

"Which way is the wind blowing?"

I didn't have a clue. She walked outside to the water's edge. "Ok… get the big fan from my office and go into the front. Don't do anything if you can smell gas near the floor. If you can't, plug the fan in and leave it at the next door, pointing towards the stern. Keep people away while it's getting clear. When the next cabin smells clear move the fan up. Keep doing that but don't switch it off. Here's an extension reel. Plug that in first up in the bows, undo it all and use the cable as you go up. If it's ok up to the galley, leave it blowing air through that and out the stern doors.

"I'll get there once I've got… Oh, *good* afternoon. I recognise you – you've been with us before, haven't you?"

I escaped with the fan and the lead.

It was actually not as bad as it could have been. There was no smell at the bow doors and only a little as I approached the dinette. There it was a lot less than when we first came in, probably due to the southerly breeze encouraging the gas out of the stern. I stood for some time with the fan, directing it down to the floor and up to the open door as if sweeping up cotton wool.

The boys were still on guard duty, with some anxious looks over towards the boat when Poppy marched past them with a concerned smile and followed me up the boat from the bows.

"It's not too bad," she said, sniffing. "I think you've got it out, haven't you? If it was bad to start with we might need to raise a trap to the bilge. If you go back beyond the door, we'll have a sniff and see what's what."

I was so relieved to have someone there who knew what they were doing. With the fan off and the doors closed we snuffled the air at head height, waist height and then for completeness, at floor level, like dogs. First she, then I, got a fit of the giggles and we both sat on the floor laughing.

"Are you sure we're not releasing Entonox into the dinette?" she asked.

"Entonox? What's that?"

"Nitrous oxide - laughing gas. It's used in medicine for pain relief."

"Not unless we've also been boiling the kettle with it," I assured her.

She scrabbled about under the rear steps and removed a circle of the flooring. I'd never noticed it was there. She put her nose to the hole she'd exposed and again sniffed.

"Nothing," she said, replacing the disc. "It's all gone, but I should leave everything open and avoid using the cooker for a bit. We'll need to get it serviced. It should never stay on once there's no flame."

"Cold lunch, then."

"'fraid so. I'd better get back."

"Thanks for being a joint truffle hound."

She grinned widely. "I've done some strange things in this Marina, but nothing that strange before."

"Hope you don't have to again. Not on my account, anyway."

She left and I beckoned the boys in. "Smell anything?" I asked, having shut the door on the rain which was once again falling. It was their turn to sniff.

"Poppy's perfume," Nat observed.

"No gas? Nothing unpleasant?"

Phil came and sniffed at my left armpit. "Well, now you mention it…"

I dug him in the ribs.

"I need to phone Helen," I said, serious suddenly, having remembered what had started all this.

"Then can we have lunch?" Phil asked.

"How about you two get it ready? No gas to be used, no sparks or naked flame, just in case of any gas left."

"What do we do if we smell anything?" asked Nat.

"Call me and get out."

I vanished down to the unfinished cabin and sat on the very exposed toilet – with its cover safely down. Fortunately Helen answered my call and her first words accused me of scaring Jonathan. "You know you're bigger than him, and you've hit him once before."

"Like he – and you – hit Phil, you mean?" I countered. "Please listen while I tell you why I'm phoning."

The story of the events kept her quiet, and when I added the saga of the gas and its potential danger to the boys I think she was silenced. There was no response from her end, anyway.

"What I need you to do is this: tell my brother that the next time he comes near the boys, they or I will call the Police. We shall accuse him of attempted kidnap, giving details of what he did today and what he's done in the past. Had he not been my brother he would now be the subject of a massive Police paedophile hunt and that is what will happen if he ever comes near them again."

She had found her voice. "That's overkill, and you know it."

I laughed. "Not at all. In my book he tried to kidnap Nat today. Neither of the boys trust him or like him any more – his splitting their parents apart might up have something to do with that. And what I've just said is not just a threat. The boys or I *will* call the Police. He will be in more trouble than he can ever imagine. He will be in a Police cell whilst they investigate and from what I understand they don't like nonces. So tell him that, from me. That's all I have to say. Goodbye."

I gave her no chance to reply.

We had a cold lunch. Even I drank squash.

During the washing up, Ian knocked at the door. "I've got a gas sniffer," he announced. "If I set it up for you, you can check in the bilge and the engine compartment and make sure there's nothing left there. I know you and Poppy have had a sniff round, but this thing's even more sensitive than your noses."

He showed us how it worked and what to look for. "Every cabin has a trap down into the bilge," he told us, "so your job is to find them and test underneath. I'm sure you won't find any, but it's best to make certain. When you've done and we have some time, I'll come and sort out that stove."

We thanked him. He rushed off to take the next hirers for their instruction cruise.

"Well, that's this afternoon sorted," I told the boys.

"Aren't we going out with Poppy?" asked Nat.

"I thought that the weather would be against us. Although we've got waterproofs there's no need to get wet when we've got a better day tomorrow and can do a shorter cruise in the dry. And we need to be sure about this gas. There's next week. I don't think the Marina's got so many boats out then, so turn-round might be easier. We could get away earlier."

"Awww…" Nat.

"Didn't think you liked the rain."

"I don't. But it'd be nice to have another trip. With Poppy."

"Yes," I admitted, "it would. And we will, but not such a long one, perhaps."

Fortunately we found no more gas traces anywhere on the boat. What we did discover were the almost hidden traps in the floor which, Poppy told us later, were the last thing most boat owners got to know about. She joined us in the late afternoon, soaking wet, and begged a shower. I put the water heater on again, then quietly started cooking some braised chops which I'd bought for our trip. It was one of the few recipes that had stuck in my head from the engineers' cook book.

There was a hot drink and a Monopoly board waiting for her when she reappeared, wet haired and changed into dry clothes. She accepted gratefully, then started sniffing.

"It's not gas," she said, puzzled, "but I don't know what it is."

"Ahh," I said. "It's a great shame but I seem to have over-catered again. It'll take an hour or two, apparently."

"He never even said anything to us either," Phil complained, sitting at the table and getting the Monopoly set out of its box.

It was one of those understated, happy evenings. You can't say that it was anything but low key and ordinary. But we all laughed and ate, and drank a little, and played card games after the Monopoly. It was ten thirty before I noticed the time and exclaimed.

"I wondered when you'd notice the time!" Nat said gleefully. Phil just grinned.

"And I must go," Poppy said. "I've really enjoyed tonight. It's a shame we couldn't make a move, but the weather was awful and your problems with the boat put the kibosh on it. Oh, and the other issue."

I'd almost forgotten the 'other issue' in the fun of the evening.

"How about tomorrow?" she asked suddenly. "Shall we try another trip if the weather's fine? The forecast is better."

A quite early start was agreed, though I could see a look of comic dismay on Phil's face at its early-ness. We all walked Poppy home. I felt the boys needed some blood moving after such a long time sitting. She lived in a quite ordinary semi-detached house near the Marina, in fact just by the end of its approach road.

"Convenient," I said.

"Too convenient sometimes. I'm nearest if anything goes wrong."

"It won't now. I'm looking after the engines."

"You'd be surprised how stupid some people can be," she said. "You may have tamed the engines, and thank you for continuing to do so, but nobody can tame people."

We bid our good nights and went back to the boat.

16 Gas Street and more Helen

Even Nat said that Phil looked a complete wreck when he dragged him off the bunk the next morning. Theatrical groans were still to be heard from the bathroom when Poppy knocked on the door.

"Is he ill?" she asked, concerned.

"Just an attack of teenage-itis. It's been getting worse over the months, and now he's… oh, hallo Phil." I was glad for his sake that he was dressed, even if only from the waist down. "Are you all right?"

"Tea," he croaked, still theatrically. "Quick. Hallo Poppy." He was off again, and hopefully not back to bed. Nat passed him with an expression of fully-adult resignation, then grinned. He was, I noted, fully dressed and tidy and I was about to comment when I thought that it would be condescending. I handed him Phil's mug of tea instead.

Phil joined us soon afterwards. His engagements with us started with the rust of monosyllabic conversation, but changed slowly to a more polysyllabic nature as the tea lubricated him.

My phone rang. Helen. Damn.

"Can I see the boys today? It's the only chance I'll get this week."

There go our plans, I thought. I wasn't going to stand in their way though. "I'll ask them, although we'd got a voyage planned."

"You don't actually move that thing, do you?"

I looked at the phone in disbelief. "Well, naturally," I told her in a surprised tone. "It's in the nature of boats to move. It's part of their DNA." I hesitated. "I'd invite you to come and join us, but you might find it be too uncomfortable for us all. Hang on, I'll ask the question."

A look round to them all, then I put the phone on mute.

"She wants to see you today," I said to them. "You heard what I said to her. What do you think about her coming as well? Or… or meeting us somewhere? Perhaps you could go off with her for a meal, or something."

I could almost see the cogs turning.

"If she came," Phil started, "Are we sure that *he* wouldn't be with her?"

"I'd make absolutely sure of that," I said. "Wherever she met us we can make sure he's nowhere near."

"Could she… could she come with us?" asked Nat. "From here?"

"I'll ask her, shall I?"

"What about you, Dad? Don't you mind?"

I hesitated. I did mind, really, but I'd rather the boys saw their mother. Besides if I told her a flat 'no', even on their behalf, it could easily be turned against me by bloody Jonathan.

"Do you mind, Poppy?" I asked.

"No, of course not. There's plenty I can do at home."

"Oh, I didn't mean that. I mean did you mind her coming too? With you and us?"

"I wasn't expecting that," she said after a surprised pause. "Do you think it's a good idea?"

"I think it's an excellent idea," said Phil.

"I agree," I told her. "It will stop either of us starting a row. I hope."

"Hmm... if that's the reason, I'm not sure..."

"And we want you anyway. Don't we?" this was to the boys, who both nodded vigorously. I hit the mute button again.

"We'd all like you to come with us. How soon can you get to the Marina? Without Jonathan, of course."

"I'm not coming on your damn boat! I just want the boys to come and see me."

"I think it'd be best if I put this on speaker so they can talk to you direct," I said, as serenely as I could despite my annoyance at her attitude. "You're asking them to choose between a voyage on their home, learning about it and how to use it, and seeing you somewhere you've not mentioned."

"That's not fair," said her suddenly amplified voice. "I just want you to take them somewhere and I'll pick them up."

"Mum... please come with us."

The tone of Nat's voice was definitely one of pleading. There was no guile in it, just a plea that he wanted his mother to engage with him in something he liked doing.

This time the silence was deafening.

"It'd be good if you did," Phil added when there had been no reply for a few moments.

A sigh could be heard over the phone.

"All right," she said, and I could hear the reluctance in her voice. "I will, but I don't know why you prefer the dirty canals round the city to a nice day out in a park."

Nat let out a single "Yay!" Phil was a little quieter. "Good. That's good. And we prefer to do things like locks and steer the boat because we're not kids any more, Mum."

"You are to me."

"How soon can you get here?" I asked, ignoring that comment.

"I need to get a few things, and I suppose I'd better bring sandwiches and a drink, hadn't I?"

"Helen, we *live* on the boat. That means cooking on it. We can do better than that."

"You never even made tea for me the other night until... until there was a delay."

"That was different. If you set off now you should be here in about twenty minutes, I suppose. We'll let you in at the gate."

"All right."

It was, I thought, an ungracious farewell, but then she had been persuaded to make a visit to the boys that maybe she wouldn't enjoy very much. I hardened my heart. It was the boys who wanted her here, not me.

"Are you sure you want me here?" Poppy asked when the call was over.

My mouth was about to open when they both chimed in with variations on "yes". It pleased her, I could tell. The mood lifted. This was going to be an interesting day, and I hoped that it wouldn't be interesting for the wrong reasons.

As I talked the boys through the very simple engine checks, Poppy unplugged the shore electrics. At about the right time we manned the gate, key in hand, and waited for the car to arrive. Late. I checked for passengers and was relieved to see she was alone. We opened the gates and let her in. She apologised for taking a long time, saying that she had to persuade Jonathan that he would be more than unwelcome.

"Didn't you tell him what I said after yesterday morning?" I sked angrily.

She hesitated. "It wouldn't have been the right time."

"Then I'm going to write to him tonight and press the matter once and for all," I said. "He's got to realise that none of us trust him and that I will most certainly call the Police if he comes anywhere near them again."

"Jack, please may we leave it there? I don't want to spoil the time with the boys."

Well, this was a different attitude, and refreshing. I wondered at it.

After the pleading from Nat that she should come, and the agreement from Phil, the welcome she actually received seemed a little muted. There were smiles, and they both submitted to a kiss, but after such an absence and an absence for such reasons… well I was assuming there would be a welcoming hug.

Never assume, they say.

They led her back to the boat. As she boarded, Poppy's face appeared from below. Helen's moth gaped.

"Helen, this is Poppy Watson," I called in some alarm. I didn't want her to jump to the wrong conclusion that Poppy was anything but what she was. "You met her. She's the owner of the business and today she's going to be our instructor."

A smile supplanted the shocked expression and Helen and Poppy shook hands.

"The kettle's just boiled," said Poppy.

The table looked crowded with Poppy and Helen sitting at it with the boys, so I stood in the doorway like an umpire, ready to ensure fair play.

Nat prevented any iciness to the atmosphere by describing what we intended to do. "Poppy says we go into the City centre, then take a right past Bourneville, through a tunnel and stop at a pub.

She pulled a face to show she was impressed, though whether it was genuine or she was just humouring Nat – or Poppy – I didn't know.

"So what do I have to do in all this?" she asked.

Nat looked at her, and the rest of us maintained the silence.

"Just be with us."

Emotions hit hardest when you're not expecting them. I felt my throat start to constrict and knew it was an emotion caused by his comment, and for him;

not for her. With difficulty the realisation came that this was why she was here; because the boys wanted her and because she wanted and needed to see them. She was their mother, after all.

I started the engine. Nat untied the bows and pushed. Phil did the same at the stern. We were away. I gave way to Phil at the controls, mainly to let him show his prowess. It was not lost on Helen, who looked at me quizzically.

"He's better at it than I am," I told her.

This time, at the bottom of the short arm from the Marina we turned left. Phil had indeed learnt well, pivoting the boat round so that we were in no danger of nearing a bank. He did the same about fifteen minutes later, having been warned, as we emerged from an imaginatively graffitied brick wall canyon and passed under a bridge. Opposite us was another of the old cast iron bridges, this one as heavily decorated with graffiti as the brick canyon. It formed a crossroads of canals.

"Left," Poppy said quietly.

The surroundings after the turn seemed similar to those we had encountered the previous week. A shallow cutting, part brick walled and partly vegetation lined, and broad. "Is this the New Main Line?" I asked Poppy, and was glad when she confirmed it. Another canal turning, heading obliquely back on our right. "Where does that go?" I asked in desperation at ever learning where this labyrinth started or ended.

"Icknield Port Loop," said Poppy. "You could have got to that if we'd gone straight across that junction where we turned left."

We snaked past building sites, blocks of gardened flats, bridges. To our right a glimpse through an oblique bridge of moored boats on a wide basin tantalised me.

"Another Marina?" I asked.

Poppy laughed. "The Old Main Line again. It comes out again just up there, opposite Legoland." Legoland is stuck between the huge Arena and the canal we were on, and I wondered if Poppy had mentioned it for Nat's sake.

Nat was looking wistfully at me, then more doubtfully at Helen. One of the major things he'd had to leave at the house was a large, ageing and now only occasionally used Lego collection. He had been to Birmingham's Lego Centre in the past and it always resulted in a lot of expensive (on the Parents' part) pleasure, a pleasure that we'd detected to be secretly shared by Phil. We'd not visited it for a couple of years and Helen and I had thought – hoped – he'd been weaned off the love of the sharp-edged bricks that were so painful an encounter to bare feet. Helen must have encountered them more frequently than I, given our old rule of no outdoor shoes in the house. She hated Lego.

Reading his thoughts, I said quietly: "A visit on a wet winter Saturday, I should think." It was worth it to see his face change from surprise at hearing his thoughts read to a sudden grin of pleasure at the idea. I really hoped I'd not rekindled a love of the wretched things; if so it could lead to a few expensive purchases and a plea to bring The Collection onto what was, after all, a small boat. A narrow boat.

Here, the feeling of ignored canal had been banished. Modern developments with their imaginative and imposing architecture jostled with the functional red brick or cast iron canal bridges and surfaces. It was and is a contrast which should jar on the aesthetic nerves but somehow fails to do so. History has been partly swept away in favour of letting in light and modern life, but the elegance of the historic functional designs still shines through.

We must have passed the Old Main Line's other entrance, but our attention was drawn to a wide area, a basin. Not a particularly different sight to any of us except Helen, perhaps, as our Marina is a basin. The difference here was an oddity: offset to the left was what appeared to be an island. A roundabout in the canals. Even Helen, who had been mainly quiet up to then, exclaimed.

"An odd thing, isn't it," Poppy said to her. "They say it was only put there in the last war so that the canals could be dammed off if they were bombed. Underneath it is a railway tunnel and they had to protect it from possible flooding. Straight on here."

It was fortunate she added that because poor Phil was looking all round him with panic on his face. "Do I go round the roundabout?" he asked suddenly, knowing that it would be too late to do so without a lot of reversing.

Poppy laughed. "No. It's not a road and the Highway Code doesn't apply." He relaxed again and headed straight for the bridges ahead.

"Down to the left there is the Farmer's Bridge flight. I was going to take you down there to give you some more lock practice. A *lot* more lock practice seeing that there are about a dozen of them. But it's not very pretty, even if it's interesting."

"How long would that have taken us?" Helen asked. It was almost the first attempt at conversation she had made since we left and I had been nursing a feeling of unease that this was all going to go disastrously wrong. At least if she was engaging in conversation I could start to feel a bit better about the atmosphere.

"It's about ten minutes a lock, with a good crew and without any waiting for boats coming the other way," Poppy told her. "I suppose two hours plus, and the same up again. Probably best encountered when you're going somewhere. When they get to spend a little more time on the move than just a day, they could go down the Grand Union – which is what it leads to – and come back a different way."

"So where do these all go, these canals?"

Poppy laughed. "Turn right once down there and follow your nose, and you'll get to London. Turn left eventually and you'll get to Yorkshire and Lancashire. Go the way we're going and you could get to Worcester, or Stratford, or Oxford – or join up with the Grand Union again and reach London."

"Good heavens," Helen said, now totally surprised. "I had no idea."

"Nor had I – we," I confirmed, taking the blank expression on Nat's face as confirmation. Phil was preoccupied, having seen the next bridge blocked by an approaching boat.

"Which side do I go?" he asked in urgent tones.

"Steer to the right. Boats always pass left side to left side."

"Port to port," Nat muttered.

Poppy laughed again. "Yes indeed. Odd how on the canals port and starboard are hardly ever used. I suppose it's because the old boats were usually steered by men off the land, not sailors."

The boat passed us safely. We were heading to a low tunnel-like obstruction ahead, an obstruction with daylight at the other end.

"Broad Street crosses there, and it has buildings on the bridge," Poppy continued, "that's why it's so wide." We all knew Broad Street from the top, but not from canal level. "Beyond that is Gas Street Basin. It used to be a dingy area and not particularly pleasant. The only way you could get to it was down a dark alleyway. Now it's a favourite place to sit at the water's edge and drink. Best to slow down a bit, Phil; there are lots of boats moored in the basins beyond."

For some reason we'd never been there, nor did we even know about it. Maybe it was because, with two growing kids, Helen and I had stuck to the pubs and eating places near the house. Venturing further afield was something done only when on holiday.

Emerging from the bridge-cum-tunnel was a revelation. The contrast between old and new was all round us. To our left a small lake, with moored boats, extended to what looked like a terminus. On the right were the old buildings repurposed as bars and restaurants which appeared to converse across the waterway with the modern offices and flats opposite. Straight on, the canal seemed to end at a pair of modern blocks, one of which proclaimed itself as The Mailbox. The other was a landmark I knew – but from the roads in the area. The Cube.

"Sharp right at the end, unless you want the boat to visit the pubs," Poppy told Phil. He smiled and steered. And then suddenly we were out of the touristy, revamped City centre. The change made me blink. At a stroke it had changed from the attractive environment to the severely mundane, with a stone wall both sides of the water and towpath, and no view over the cityscape at all. A slight relief further on was the approach of the railway, visible now through a set of railings, which gave us something of interest to look at. As the next few miles of canal - and Cadbury World – passed, there was a little more of interest. Phil thought it was time he had a rest, and gave way to Nat to steer, much to Helen's alarm.

"Don't you think he's a bit young to be in charge of a big boat like this?" she asked me in Nat's hearing. It annoyed me.

"No. Not at all. Quite apart from wanting him to have the opportunity, he's already done stints on the tiller and we all know that he's very capable." All quite true, and mainly for Nat's ears. I went down into the dinette to put the kettle on, caught Helen's eye and beckoned her down.

"Do you think that was the right thing to do, to question his abilities in front of everyone? He's not stupid and he's twelve. Thirteen soon. Didn't it occur to you that he's been out before on the boat and that if Poppy wasn't happy with what he could do, experienced as she is in teaching hirers, she would have said something?"

"I still think that he's too young."

"And I don't, and I know he's not because he's proved himself capable. You've not seen him…"

"That's not the point. He's too young for that sort of responsibility."

"No. I can't agree. If he had reacted differently last time, I'd now be asking Poppy to give him more lessons – which she will do if he makes any mistakes. It's not as if he was on his own up there, is it?"

"I just said, it's not the point. He doesn't know what to do in an emergency. He doesn't have the experience."

"And this is the way he'll get it – they both will. I will. Don't you see…"

"I see very well. It's the experience of life that I'm talking about."

"How does that affect learning to steer a narrowboat? If he gets into trouble, one of us will help."

"I really didn't expect you to be this dogmatic." She was now angry.

"Nor did I expect you to be so oblivious to what he's being asked to do – *under controlled circumstances*," I answered her. "Poppy's the expert. If she thought either of them was too young or couldn't cope, she'd say so."

"Oh *damn* Poppy!"

I wasn't sure what to say to her in response. So I just looked her in the eyes and lifted my own eyelids.

"Is tea ready yet?"

We both looked round. Phil was looking hopeful. "And why Damn Poppy?"

"This is a private conversation…" Helen started.

"This is a conversation about whether your brother should be allowed to steer the boat or whether he's too young," I said to counter her comment with the truth. I'd have continued, but he jumped back in.

"He's as good as I am. Nearly. And he does what he's told, and Poppy or you or I are there, so…" he shrugged his shoulders. "And Poppy says that the old boaters' kids used to start steering the boats when they were about nine."

"There you are," I said, turning back to the kettle.

"Anyway, you're not allowed tea," Helen said, I suppose in some attempt to regain control.

"Mum, I like tea. I've had it for years, just not…" He omitted the phrase "when you're around."

"Has he?" she asked me, as if he was expected to have lied.

"Yes, he has. He just said so. Why would he lie to you? And Nat has too. He's decided that he likes it."

"They're too young."

"Really? In whose opinion?"

"It's just known."

"Plainly not. Show me medical evidence and I'll apologise and explain to them why they can't have tea any more."

She looked at us both, then flounced back up to the deck.

Phil looked at me. "Is it true?"

"What?"

"That tea's bad for us?"

"All I can tell you is that I drank tea from about eight onwards and I don't think it's damaged me. I'll say to you what I said to... to Mum: if you can find some medical evidence that tea is bad until you're – what? Thirty? – then you can stop making it."

He looked at the kettle.

"Mum's changed," he said quietly, as if talking to it. There was no helpful answer I could give. I knew she had, not least because she and I had been out of love for so long, but because he was right. I just gave him a hug, which he didn't wriggle out of, and turned to climb up again.

"Am I making it?" he asked my back.

"Do you want to?"

"Don't mind."

"Shall *we* make it?"

He looked round suddenly and the smile was back on his face. He just nodded.

The kettle had just boiled when Nat came down, looking angry.

"She's turfed me off steering," he said before I had a chance to ask.

"Who? Mum?"

He nodded, still angry. "I told her I'd done it before and she said she didn't care and I was too young. She made me give it to Poppy."

"What's she saying to Poppy?"

"Dunno. I came down here."

"Stay there, please, both of you."

Why, oh why did she have to spoil things?

I went up to the deck in time to hear Helen tell Poppy that she hoped she didn't mind but that they were her kids.

"Wrong. They are our kids," I told her. "I'm sorry, Poppy. This shouldn't have rebounded on you. Do you mind going down and help make tea – for all of us, please?"

I took over the tiller and waited until she was out of sight.

"Helen, that was unnecessary and rude. Besides... No, let me talk... Besides, this is the boys' and my home. You don't have the right to tell me what I do on it. I've told you that both Phil and Nat are good at steering and I know better than you on this one. This is our boat, not yours and I will allow Nat to gain the experience of steering it, with one of us standing by if I see fit. You don't have the experience of the boat, the canals, or what he and his brother can do. So I'm going to call Nat up again and he will steer, with me standing by."

"You will not. It's not safe. He's too young."

"You never argued round in circles when we were together. What's changed?"

"Nothing. I just know what's best for my own sons."

"You just demonstrated that you don't, and they're *our* sons, not just yours. And they have chosen to live with me. Look, don't you realise that when next we go out, you won't be here, and both boys will be steering and operating locks? And as they prove they're competent they can be left to have all the responsibility of making the thing go?"

"They are not to. It'd be irresponsible of you."

"It'd be irresponsible not to. For goodness sake, don't you care that they are being educated by doing this?"

"Don't be stupid. Education happens in school, not on a boat."

I gritted my teeth.

"Helen, that's one of the most stupid things I've heard you or anyone say. Education starts with babies and therefore patently *not* in schools. All through family life kids get education from parents – how else does sociable behaviour get passed on? How do all sorts of things get passed on? It's all education."

"I'm not talking about that…"

"That's the trouble. You're not. But I am. Here they are, learning an old craft; one that Victorian and early twentieth century kids learnt, complete with its discomforts, its potential problems. They're learning social history, industrial archaeology, modern design versus Victorian design and technology – you name it. But whatever you say about it, it's going to continue, and continue now." I opened the hatch and doorway which I'd partly closed to keep us private and called down into the dinette. "Nat, your turn again. It's all right now."

Before he came up I received such a look from her that, had it happened before things started to go astray in our marriage, would have told me I was on very thin ice indeed. At my stage now, with two sons who seemed to be on my side, it made little impression.

Nat came up. She went down.

"What have you said to Mum?" Phil asked when he followed Poppy up again. "She's sitting in the dinette, staring out of the window, not talking to anyone."

"I've told her that you, Nat and I know more about boats than she does, and that I have faith in your abilities which I'm afraid she seems not to. I told her, I'm afraid, that this is our home and that I decide what goes on, which people do what. It's not strictly true, of course, because we're all under tuition from Poppy still. Other than that, more or less everything else we decide, we decide as a team. But when it comes to…"

I was about to use the word 'outsiders' but it didn't seem tactful.

"…people who know even less than us telling us what to do, it's not something I believe that we should accept."

There was a silence which extended as we all realised there was little that anyone could say that would be helpful to the situation.

17 Lunch and the journey home

We continued, somewhat silently; the mood was reduced, if not depressed. Having delivered a mug of tea to Helen and the remainder of the mugs to those of us not sulking, we left her alone in the dinette where she seemed happiest, despite having wanted to visit the boys.

At last Poppy pointed out the canal junction.

"That's the Northern part of the Stratford Canal. Guess where that goes? We'll carry on for a bit, then there's a tunnel, Wast Hills tunnel. It's a bit special. It's over a mile and a half long."

"You'd better take her," Nat told Poppy, "or Dad. Or Phil. Don't think I should."

"Nonsense," Poppy told him firmly. "You're as capable as any of the rest of us. Reduce speed if you're happier that way, but with the lights on in the boat and the headlight at the front you'll be fine. Anyway, I'll be up here."

"I'll go down and switch on the lights, shall I?" Phil offered.

"No need yet," Poppy said. "There's another mile to go."

"I'll go and warn Mum anyway," he said. "Tell me when we're getting close, will you?" I wondered if he wanted to try and talk sense to her, to try and re-ice the cake – or maybe paper over the cracks.

"Tunnel coming up!" I shouted through the hatch about a quarter of an hour later.

"What am I meant to do about it?" asked a cold-toned voice.

"Where's Phil?"

"Gone down the front, sulking."

I climbed down to talk to her, to keep the conversation more private.

"Why sulking? What have you said to him?"

"I told him what I told you. Nat's too young to steer this boat. In fact I'm not sure Phil's old enough either. I told him that too."

"So you started a row."

She looked daggers at me again. "I told him what is the truth. Just because you don't see it, it doesn't mean it's untrue. They are both too young. I can just accept that Phil can steer, under supervision, but Nat is too young."

"It's rubbish that you're talking," I told her angrily. "Absolute rubbish. If you knew anything about boats… no. We've been through this and I'm…" It was getting darker and my mind was subconsciously saying 'rain' to me when it there was a long blast on a horn and it went completely dark. I had been going to add "…not going to say it all again" but instead just said "Damn. Tunnel," and started fumbling for the light switches. In the joint confusion I encountered Helen, who had also stood up either in alarm or to find a switch, and for a moment found I was touching her quite intimately.

She was very aware of the location of my face, as I discovered when it encountered the flat of her hand.

"Don't touch me, you pervert!" she screamed at me. I stepped back in shock and hit my head hard on what felt like the corner of a cupboard. The door to the bathroom opened and allowed light to flood in past a young figure, his face fortunately hidden.

"What the *hell* is going on?" asked Phil, its owner. "Can't you two behave? It's really bad of you, in front of Poppy and all." He must have found a dinette light switch because we all finally managed to see each other in a tableau of anger and unhappiness.

"He tried to fondle me!" Helen said angrily.

"Well, you're married. It's what couples do. Though not when they're as old as you."

That scathing, innocent comment pulled us both up short. "In fact I was trying to find a light switch," I said, aware of a wet feeling at the back of my head. "Instead I found your mother's breast and she took exception and hit me. She seems fond of doing that to people she's meant to love."

It was perhaps a silly thing to say, but when I started saying it I was so intent on keeping my voice level despite a probably bleeding head that I just let the words flow.

She drew in her breath but was interrupted before she could speak.

"I know," said Phil, bitterly, and walked back towards his shared cabin again.

I'm glad to say that his words took the wind completely out of her sails. In the silence I glared at her and followed Phil. In their cabin there was one chair, placed there temporarily so there was somewhere other than the floor for clothes. He was sitting on it, looking down. When I appeared he looked up briefly.

"Cow," he said.

"It's not going well, is it?"

"Does she have to come back with us?" he asked. "Can't... *he* come and get her from the pub, or whatever it is?"

"He could, but what about Nat? He'll probably want to be with her for a bit."

"Not sure. Maybe not after what she said. He's angry too. Your face is red."

"It's not that that hurts," I told him. "It's where I hit my head on the cupboard."

"Let me see."

How are the tables turned, I thought. My elder son, and he's tending to my hurts.

He asked where the first aid kit was and went to fetch it, returning with Helen. In the cabin he turned to her. "This is my room, Mine and Nat's. It's private."

"I'm your mother."

"It's still private." He stared at her; a challenge and another mini-tableau.

She turned eventually and stalked back to the dinette (as far as it's possible to stalk in a narrowboat corridor).

Water was applied to what he described as a small gash to my head, with the comment that there was nothing to worry about. He seemed to dry it too, even to the extent of wiping down my collar. There had been this Red Cross first aid course, I now remembered. Faced with the increase in knife crimes around the city he had elected to attend it in preference to the self-defence course that the school had recommended. He'd just turned thirteen at the time and had said that he'd only gone because one of the girls in his year was going and he hoped he could practise on her. Later he'd admitted that she left after the first two weeks – hopefully not because of his attentions – but he had continued to the end and taken the exam.

"Thank you, Dr Dyer," I said.

"Don't do it again." It was said in a serious voice. I looked round in surprise. "It's bad enough you two splitting up, but when you fight like that it's..."

He looked away, and I could tell just how upset he was. "Sorry, Phil," I said contritely, as if I was him apologising for having been caught at some misdemeanour. "It really didn't start off as a fight. And trust me, the last thing on my mind when it all went dark in there was to start... well, you know."

"I suppose so," he sighed. "But it's horrible."

I nodded. "Forgive me?" I asked.

"It sounds like her fault," he said with a shrug of his shoulders. "So can we get her to leave us at the pub?"

"I'll try. Let me talk to Nat."

"I... I don't know," Nat told me when I'd got him on his own later in their cabin. "She wasn't nice when she told me I couldn't steer, when I'd been doing it last Sunday. I told her that, and she said she didn't care."

"Well, Phil would like her to leave when we get to the pub," I told him. "He knows it's a decision you need to make for yourself. No one is going to ask her to go if one of us wants her not to."

Silence.

"Shall I leave you to think?" I asked him gently.

"No. I'll come up with you now and...and see how it goes."

But Helen was in the dinette. "I'm being collected at the pub," she told me, ignoring Nat. "If you can't be with me without arguing then there's not much point my being here, is there? I'm better off at home."

I said nothing, just wondered if Nat would. He looked at me, and raised his eyebrows.

"It's up to Phil and Nat," I said. "You'll know that you're here because you wanted to see them and they wanted to see you. And, for the record, the arguments were started by you, as both of them know – as does Poppy. I won't argue with you if you want to get off; whether they want you to leave us is their decision."

"I've made up my mind, thank you. I've phoned Jonathan and he will come and pick me up."

"Very well," I said, though watching Nat's face. Was the relieved expression because he wanted her off the boat or because he wouldn't have to make a choice?

We had just emerged, mole-like, from the tunnel by this time. Helen remained in the dinette. Poppy told Phil to look out for the winding hole.

"What's it look like?" he asked.

"Just an indent in the side," she said. "It'll be obvious – and you've seen them before."

"Is that it?" we all called, more or less simultaneously. Phil put the boat in neutral.

For the next few minutes the air was thick with instructions from Poppy, trying both to direct operations and to explain why things happened. "It's like making a tight turn," Phil muttered, "one that doesn't actually go anywhere. You just push at the bank as if you're trying to open them up."

"Not that hard!" Poppy exclaimed. "Just use the bank to stop the bow from swinging, then the stern's *got* to swing round and point you the other way."

We made it and moored. I called Helen up and told her we had arrived and had turned – and couldn't help adding that Phil had made the turn.

"Where's the pub?" She asked, having ignored the comment. "I'll come to the… the *marina…* and collect the car later."

Poppy pointed to the bridge about a hundred yards distant. "Through the bridge, up some steps and you're more or less in the car park."

It looked as if she was about to ignore Poppy, not to thank her. Instead she levelled her eyes at her.

"Well, I hope you're very happy together," she said.

Poppy looked questioningly. "You make it sound as if we're attached in some way, not that it is a business arrangement."

"Oh, so he's paying you, is he?"

Poppy gasped. "Are you insinuating what I think you're insinuating? Because if you are, you'll let me correct you. I am here as Jack's prospective employer, and I'm teaching him and his sons how to steer a narrowboat. Any implied suggestion otherwise is disgraceful."

She laughed bitterly. "I think I know otherwise."

"Really? Then your thinking is a hundred and eighty degrees off the mark. Think again before you start making actionable accusations. Especially as it seems that currently you are the expert in the infidelity stakes."

If looks could kill… Helen appeared about to explode. Phil, now tying up, just shouted "Mum!" She looked at him, stepped onto the bank and walked up towards the bridge.

"She never even said goodbye," Nat said sadly.

We kept glancing at her figure until she had disappeared under the bridge.

"I'm really sorry," I said to Poppy – and to the boys. "She really has changed dramatically. I know she is strong minded, and in fact I probably wouldn't have been so attracted to her had she been otherwise. But what we just witnessed was just way beyond any reasonable behaviour."

"I think she's met her match in you three," Poppy said. "You won't let her walk over you, Jack, and neither will Nat and Phil. It must be so hard for you all and… well, I'm on your side, that's all."

We tidied up mugs and made sure the boat was secure. I swallowed hard and texted Helen: *Have you both left the pub yet?*

Five minutes later there had still been no answer. We decided to take a chance and walked the short distance along the towpath, up the steps and into the bar.

No one remotely Helen-shaped could be seen, to my relief. We all (I think it was all) breathed a sigh of relief and bagged a table for four. Gradually over a leisurely – and by then necessary – lunch our mood lifted from the downright depressed to the pleasantly relaxed. We were easy in each other's company again. The need to continue walking on eggshells to avoid unpleasant reactions had passed.

I couldn't help still feeling sorry for the boys, though, as it had been their chance to see their mother. Particularly at Nat's age and still at Phil's, it should be essential to maintain a regular contact. The circumstances Helen was manufacturing would threaten to make them unwilling to risk a visit.

I paid the bill before Poppy had a chance and interrupted her protestation with the simple reason that she was teaching us free of charge, and that I needed to apologise for a morning which I euphemistically described as difficult.

On the journey home, after some banter from Phil about not turning the boat again, I was told that steering was now my job and that they would stand with me and criticise. Steering through a long tunnel is an odd, slightly unnerving experience. It seemed that the more I was sure that I was steering straight, the more likely it was that one or other of the tunnel walls was too near the hull. Straightening up, in my case, meant over-straightening, so that progress was more zig-clang-zag than a straight line.

It was late by the time we returned to the Marina. For the last few miles I had been wondering if there was such a thing as a canal-side fish and chip shop that would cost less than the king's ransom that the exotic bars would doubtless charge. Poppy had the solution.

"Simple: before we started I rigged up a barbecue near the office. It's only a gas one, but it'll be quicker. In the office are some bits of salad and rolls – even a box of matches. You provide the plates, I start cooking, and then we can enjoy the evening."

"We've got some beers too, so we can bring those," I said.

I texted Helen, and twenty minutes later she appeared at the marina gates. Having checked for signs of Jonathan and found none, I let her in; wordlessly she collected the car and drove away.

The boys watched her, sadly. She never even acknowledged them.

In the near-centre of Britain's second city, by a waterside, there took place a barbecue. It was manned by four tired, increasingly contented people. Cooking, laughing, occasionally incinerating burgers and sausages, they watched the day's light change its character as it slipped off the bright suit of day and donned the shadows of night.

We slept well.

Only one of the hire fleet needed my attentions the next day, Monday. By late morning I felt oddly redundant. Swept to the back of my mind by a new kind of more practical work at the Marina there was still the small matter of a resignation letter to Crown. Even more importantly there were formal letters to write to Jonathan and Helen, letters which needed careful drafting and despatch by secure means. Poppy was looking at me as I pondered in front of a computer.

"Are you doing what I think you might be thinking of doing?" she asked. I worked out the English.

"If you mean the resignation letter, yes," I responded. "And the letters to Helen and my brother. If you don't mind, that is. There's nothing I can do at the moment until we get one of the other boats in, or you post me onto something else."

"It'd be good to be able to get the situation regularised," she said. "That comes first, really. But I think you need to get a solicitor to look over the drafts of the other two letters."

I pulled a face. "It's the cost, really. That and not wanting to let solicitors get their mucky paws on my situation."

"But you do need Helen and... and your brother to realise that you're serious, surely? They're more likely to take it seriously if it has a solicitor's name attached, I'd have thought. How about..." She broke off, thinking. "I use a solicitor occasionally, and they're good and not too expensive. How would it be if you asked them to take a look and make suggestions if necessary? Then you could say on them that copies are being lodged with your solicitors, and give them their details."

"What happens if Helen and Jonathan reply to the solicitor?"

"You can ask them to send the replies on to you. It's not as if you're dim, and unable to decide matters or compose letters. They'd realise that."

"I suppose it'd show that I wasn't just wasting paper and ink. Would they do that, do you think?"

"What – waste paper and ink? Ok, ok... No, I think they'd play ball. It may be they'd hope that if it went wrong, they'd get the opportunity to take the case on professionally. If it did, I imagine you'd short-circuit them and just go to court. How about trying them, anyway? Would you like me to sound them out?"

Each of us wrote. Poppy's offering was an email, mine an email and two draft letters.

"That was quick!" Poppy exclaimed later when I'd finished my drafts. "They've responded already and are happy to play ball. Tell when you're ready and I'll give you the address."

"Now, please."

That was easy. I sent the drafts together with some introductory paragraphs and an explanation.

Now to polish the draft resignation email, I thought. It was half way through that I started considering the reaction of the person receiving it, my immediate line manager, otherwise known as Mark, the technical director. We normally rubbed along together very well and it seemed somehow crass just to drop him a resignation out of the blue. A phone call would break the ice, at the very least. With some trepidation I called him on my mobile. The reaction was friendly.

"Jack! I was wondering when you would call. I've heard quite a bit from your wife, you know."

"Really?" I said after what I hoped had been an inaudible intake of breath. "And what did she have to say about me?"

"Well… before I answer that, how are you now? Have you been able to work through the stress?"

"The mental breakdown, you mean. That's what my email to you said, and it's true. I'm sure it matches what Helen told you."

"Well… not exactly."

"So you mean that it doesn't? I see. I'll tell you what happened from the start then, shall I? Then you can tell me just what Helen's version was."

I gave him the account from the beginning, omitting only the parts of the story that were unlikely to have been hinted at by Helen. When I described where I was now living there was a single interjection.

"Wow!"

I paused, and gave the usual line back: "Yes, we live on a boat. You sound as if you're impressed."

"I am – I think. We're talking about a narrowboat, I suppose?"

"We are. She's seventy feet long, currently has a kitchen and dining room combined…"

"You mean a dinette."

"Yes." He had surprised me. "You know something about these boats, then?"

"We've been on holiday on the canals many times. Last one was from a firm called Poppy Narrowboats, right in the centre of the city. I can't recommend them, though. We had trouble with the engine twice, and they had to come out to us. But go on."

Should I tell him? No. I decided to keep that to myself for the moment. "Then there's a bathroom and shower, two cabins, and room for more when the carpenters have finished. She's being fitted out, more or less to our design, but it's a long story."

"Hmm. And there's a lot more to it than your wife has told us. She never mentioned… er… another man, just that you'd separated from her and were going off the rails in hospital."

I laughed humourlessly. "How kind of her. Yes, there was a lot more, wasn't there? I'm so lucky to have two sons who have helped me enormously. It's largely thanks to them that I've recovered as quickly as I have."

"So you're back to normal, then?"

"Well, mentally yes. Probably. But…" I swallowed, not wanting to say what I knew must be said to make sense of all this preparation. If ever there was a time in my life when I was conscious of holding a blowtorch against the bridge of my life, this was it.

I prepared myself. "Mark, I'm really sorry about this, but I'm going to have to resign."

There was an intake of breath, then a long drawn out sigh. "I've been worried that you were going to say that ever since I answered the call." Another sigh. "I suppose we've been managing without you, but it's not been easy. You seem to have details at your fingertips of almost every engine installation we've ever had dealings with, and although it's all on record, it's a lot of work having to research information. It's even more verbiage for someone fresh to think their way through to reach possible solutions."

"I know," I said as contritely as I could. "It's probably that element of always having to duck and dive between problems that contributed to the stress. Not to mention the sudden trips to far flung parts of the world." I shuddered, mentally.

"Yes, I was going to catch up with you about that U.S. trip. You weren't exactly tactful with them, were you?"

"I wasn't," I told him firmly, "and when I tell you it was down to their dirty fuel you'll understand why. I hope they've installed better filters and have dealt with whatever problem their suppliers were wishing on them. I strongly suggest you amend their service contract to reflect the need for the rectification to come from that end."

"They've complained about another failure since," he told me. "I asked if it could be the same problem as previously and he didn't know. I was thinking I'd have to make a visit myself. Instead I'll get them to check."

"It'll be expensive for them if they don't," I confirmed, now feeling decidedly peculiar. A sort of unease was creeping over me, almost as if he was going to ask me to go and visit them again myself. No amount of telling myself that I wasn't going and didn't have to go would make it any better.

"Mark, I'm going to have to go," I said suddenly. "I'm feeling rotten again. Just the talking about… about Crown engines is doing it. I'll call you later, or tomorrow. But I am resigning. I'll confirm by email."

18 Work starts

Without waiting for an answer I replaced the phone and supported myself on the desk with both arms. A stir in the air beside me proved to be Poppy, and an arm was going round my shoulders. It was so surprising that I nearly gave a start, but found I had no energy. Along with the surprise I felt a comfort, a yielding softness that I hadn't felt for a year or more.

Very gradually, over several minutes, the weird feeling left me. I started to feel better, and to enjoy the closeness, the presence, the care of… Of my employer. Damn. This mustn't happen. I looked up at her and saw the look of concern. Was there something else too? Or was it my wishful thinking? Wishful thinking? What? She was my employer. She was a friend too by now, certainly, but nothing else.

That really brought me back to earth; good solid, sensible earth. Poppy was just being her usual pleasant, helpful self. That was enough. She didn't want me to flake out in the office as had happened before, all that time ago.

All that time ago - it had been only about three weeks, but now I could see myself nowhere else but here. Here was low key. Here was stuff that was easy, non-demanding. The stuff of my apprenticeship. The high-powered, globe-trotting, never-stopping Jack Dyer had drawn in his powerful horns and was now a younger, far more placid and less demanding animal.

"Phew," I said quietly.

"Better?"

"Probably. Talking work – old work - or even just mentioning Crown Engineering installations and problems just sent me off again, threatened to derail me I suppose, to use Helen's so-kind analogy."

Poppy's arm left me. Damn. Why did I think the 'damn'?

"I'm so sorry," I said to her. "Once I get this email off to Mark it will draw a line under my time at Crown, and the stress – I hope. Although I like him, I don't know if I would like a visit from him. We'd just talk engines and Crown, and I'd derail yet again, I suppose. It's a pity; we got on quite well and he's just told me he's holidayed on the canals. As a client of yours, in fact."

"Really? What's his surname?" It was almost as if she was glad to change the subject from the presence of her arm around my back.

"Pinter."

"Rings a bell." She crossed to her computer. "Yes, two years ago. Oh." A face was pulled. "We had to go out to them twice with fuel problems. No wonder he's not come back. He's one of the ones we'll need to write to over the winter to tell them what's happened."

"Probably one I'd better write," I offered. "In fact… no, I'll leave him in ignorance at the moment, I think. Then once the sting's gone out of my having suddenly resigned I'll be able to kid him on a bit, perhaps get him back to do another holiday with us. Just so long as he doesn't talk Crown or big engines to me."

"Ok, I'll leave him to you. Telling people will be a massive job and will probably need quite a lot of phone calls by way of hand-holding. Many of those will come your way."

"I can cope with that." It was something I was certain about. "If anyone has doubts I can happily quote science and experience at them, and of course what we've done to solve the problem."

"Good. We'll call it team work, then."

Standing up made me aware that I was not completely back to normal. Lunchtime took me back to the boat and instead of eating, I laid on the bed to have a rest. Waking later, I saw a very Phil-like shape looking down at me.

"Problem?" I asked, my voice thick with tiredness still.

"Only you. Are you all right?"

"Yes, but it's only lunchtime. I just laid down for a rest."

"Dad, it's half past four and we're back from school."

With a struggle I sat up. "What? But…"

"Have you been overdoing it, Dad? We thought you'd recovered."

I told him about the phone call and to the best of my ability how I'd felt.

"You need to go back to the hospital. Aren't you a day patient, or something? What is that, anyway?"

I explained. "Well, you need to go to one of their sessions and tell them what's happened," he told me in the same severe tone I had used on them both over the years – when I'd been home which, I now knew, had been far too infrequently.

"Yes, Phil," I said meekly.

Nat appeared, also looking anxious. "Poppy said that you were out for the count."

"I have been. I had to phone Crown before lunch and it made me go all silly again."

"Are you all right now?"

"I think so, but Phil's persuading me to go to the next Hospital day surgery."

"You should, so long as they don't keep you in."

"If they need to keep him in, he must do what he's told," Phil told his brother equally severely. He got a surprised look in return. Oddly, they hardly ever argued, though there were some meaningful discussions sometimes. I tried sitting up and was pleased that it seemed to work. Standing seemed to be similarly effective.

"Well, if you're up, I suppose you want a tea," Phil offered. "I'll put the kettle on. You'd better come into the dinette where we can keep an eye on you."

I gave him what I think is known as an old-fashioned look, but nevertheless meekly followed them into the dinette. A knock at the door admitted Poppy, who looked at me with something like relief.

"I'm still sane," I told her with a grin, "and have been told I have to attend Hospital as a day patient next week. Phil's in charge of the kettle and I have to sit here to make sure that I'm not going to flake out again."

"Quite right too," she said. "I came and knocked after lunch and when there was no reply I came in. You were so peacefully asleep that I just left you there." She cleared her throat. "I was concerned, so I did the same at about three. You were still asleep. I didn't know what to do, so – well, I did nothing."

"It's very kind of you," I said. "I'm really sorry about this afternoon. I'm not much use to you, am I?"

"Have we had any call-outs?" she asked. "You did everything that first Saturday – and last Saturday too. We can afford to honour sick leave, you know."

"Yes, but…"

"Yes but nothing, The mind is a strange thing…"

"…Especially Dad's," Nat put in.

"…And you ignore its problems at your peril. You look after yourself, Jack Dyer, and don't come back to work until you're sure you're better, Yes, I'd love a tea, please."

It seemed as though I had been told off by both my employer and my elder son. It was comforting to know that I was being looked after, since most of the time working for Crown was spent living on my own wits and caring for my own needs. Usually it worked, though there were times when site visits and the associated work became so intense that meals would pass me by. It had been explained to me when in hospital that this was asking for a troubled digestion and a disturbed biological clock.

Phil and Nat served tea, taking it on as old hands even to the extent of shooing Poppy back to her seat when she offered to help. They even found the remains of a cake and offered it round, just as Poppy did from her office when we were there.

I'm so lucky with those two, even if I'd not been round for a lot of their growing up. A lot of the credit needed to be given to Helen.

I gave a start at the sound of a knock on the side of the boat. A mock-Italian accent with a cross between Birmingham and Welsh colouring it announced our two friendly carpenters-cum-security men.

"Can-a-we come and… Oh, hallo Poppy. Can we come and beg a cup of tea and then start work on some partitions? Then we may have something to show you." We all expressed amazement that this should be so soon after the measuring, given that Poppy had expected there to be a month's delay.

With their influence and cheerfulness the remainder of the concern about my grip on reality vanished into thin air. There was increasing hilarity of some of the stories of the Losardos' exploits when working for their more eccentric clients and the ache-inducing laughter was a tonic. These two were obviously at home with Poppy, and now by association, with us. I felt pleased and somehow honoured to have them as friends as well as knowing they would be working on our home. We'd all seen the work they'd done on the fleet boats, and especially liked the little flourishes they added, the unexpected carvings. If anything would help make Poppy a sought-after holiday provider again their little touches should. Once, that is, the engine reliability was seen to have improved. No: more than improved, I vowed. Solved to 99.9% reliability.

At last Seppe nudged his brother and suggested a start might be a good idea, was answered with a grin, and the two vanished. We were still talking about them when large expanses of panelling started to move outside, seemingly on their own, down towards the bows. (We had elected to moor stern on; it made access quicker.) There was some rocking, some noises off, and they passed outside the dinette again, no doubt returning for more. We couldn't help but notice what appeared to be a great deal of wood which was destined for us.

"They seem to have started a lot earlier than you thought they could," I remarked.

"I think they were impressed by your engagement and the quick designs you gave them," Poppy suggested. "And they're Italian at heart, and don't like seeing that *bambini* don't have a fully functional home."

"What's a *bambini?*" Nat asked.

"Small children, in Italian," I instructed. "A child is "*bambino.*"

"I'm not a *bambino*," Phil protested.

"Shh," I said. "Just pretend. It's acting in our favour." He was still unhappy about the epithet, but subsided.

"I'd better get back to the office," Poppy said. "I've got to finish off and lock up soon, and there are things to be done. Good luck with those two – they'll be pretty quick, knowing them."

"I need to start cooking, or these two will deafen me with their rumblings." Phil and Nat assumed hurt expressions, but still managed to appear famished.

It's amazing what can be done quickly nowadays with frozen chicken. Our freezer seemed to be overflowing with it, particularly when the boys had had anything to do with laying in stores. I made a note to remove from supermarket trolleys in future anything that hinted at being chicken burgers, and to add more fresh vegetables. At least we were well out of the brussels sprout season, so reducing the number of times when noses were likely to be upturned at my culinary efforts.

I was cooking, with help, when a knock came at the door to the cabins. It was Seppe, and he had an embarrassed expression; I countered it with a quizzical look.

"We smelled the cooking," he almost mumbled, a contrast with the strident telling of anecdotes earlier. "We wondered if… if you might…"

"You're hungry," I grinned at him. "Join us. One of us will tell you when it's ready. Anything you don't like?"

"We're Italian… well, when we want a change from Birmingham," he said, perking up. "We eat anything. And sorry for asking. And thank you."

He disappeared again. I coated some more chicken in my *Engineers' Cook-Book* instructed, special seasoned breadcrumbs and added them to the pan.

When Nat, technically the only one of us remotely to be regarded as *bambino* went to tell them that it was ready, he was presented with a closed door again. Thumps emanated from behind it. He tried to open it; there was an exclamation and it was nearly slammed in his face.

"Dinner's ready," he called. There was more muttering, the door opened about twelve inches and Ifor's head appeared horizontally in the gap.

"Sorry. We don't want you to see this until we've finished," he said in a sideways voice. "We'll be with you in a moment. Thanks." And the door closed again. Thumps continued from inside and Nat returned to recount his experiences.

I dished up. Sounds of washing came from the bathroom after a while and they appeared, grinning.

We had eaten, they had returned to work and we had washed up. The boys were doing homework. I was reading as best I could despite the interruptions from one or other asking for academic help. They know I almost always referred them to a book or the internet, so there was the usual amount of groaning, page turning and keyboard operation. Very occasionally in their studies there came a problem that really interested or infuriated me, and I became more involved with solving it. Always, when this happened, I insisted that my help was mentioned so it was seen not to be all their own work.

The door opened: we looked up. A wide grin surrounded by Seppe's head.

"Come, *vi prego*,"

We stopped, mid-sentence, mid-question or mid-essay and jostled to be first, knowing that a surprise had been brewing since they arrived. Seppe was waiting for us at the door to where they had been working.

"We need you to be honest," he said. "We have been able to do what we think you want and it's assembled here. Before we fix it finally we need your verdict." He stepped out of the way and allowed us entry.

Not only had they apparently installed two bulkheads but there was the carcase, to my design, of a double futon base against the further one.

"Is this what you mean?" he asked.

Cautiously I looked, but Phil was ahead of me. With a sort of yelp he flung himself on it and laid flat.

"It works," he announced. "Give it a mattress and it'll be lovely. And big."

"How about as a seat?" I asked, half annoyed at the cavalier approach and half laughing at him.

"Seat? Oh…" He jumped up and looked at it wonderingly.

Seppe leant forward and gripped a bar, an extension of the part of the bed nearest the bulkhead. He pulled. Obediently the hinge between two sections rose, the base rolled behind it. There was a click and amazingly there was an non-upholstered sofa in front of us.

"Wow," said Phil as he more cautiously lowered himself on it. "It works at that, too. Wow."

"So you approve of my design and their adaptation of it?" I asked so as to try and gain some filial approval.

"It's not bad," he said. "In fact it's more than that. It's pretty ace."

"There's good storage underneath," Seppe told him. "You get to it through this –" he swung open a cupboard by the gangway. "We thought the best thing to use there would be individual boxes. Left as one space it's be too deep and you'd lose things in it."

This time Phil did look him in the eye. "You've thought of everything."

"Not quite everything, but we're working on it. If that works for you and your brother we can design the table…"

"That's easy," said Phil. "Four legs and a top."

"And how do you fold it away when it's a bed or you want floor space?" I asked.

"That's why we're working on it," Ifor said. "It's giving us headaches. If it's hoisted up when you want to sleep, it won't fit under the roof. If we hinge it at the side it rises in front of the window and blocks it. And we can't just move the bulkheads to suit – it won't fit properly."

"Flat on the floor, flat on the ceiling, a separate table that stows away, a telescope table that comes out from the side, an inflatable table…" It seemed that Nat had found his voice and was looking at the less obvious ways of achieving it.

"Inflatable table," Phil scoffed.

"Where are your ideas?" Nat countered. Phil was silent.

I cleared my throat. "I came up with the design for the bed. Whether it's floor, ceiling or separate completely… I don't know. It's difficult."

Ifor's turn. "Ceiling's dangerous in case of failure. Separate – yes, but nicer if it was easier to stow. Floor – possible, I suppose, but it'd need a full extra layer of wood or you get a ledge. I wonder if it would work…"

"You mean a table that rises out of the floor? How would that work?" I asked rhetorically. I was trying to think of ways of arranging a magical table raised on pistons that would need to be sunk into…. Into the floor, through the hull, into the water below. Stupid boy, Pike. Be logical.

We stood, looking at the floor. Nat broke the silence. "This side could be on legs – no, a solid sheet – that folded inwards as it went down."

"That'd need a double thickness of wood to avoid a ledge," mused Ifor, now completely back from Italian to Birmingham. "Could be done, though. It'd need small rollers to avoid scraping the surface."

Nat nodded. None of us said a word; it seemed we had none to contribute.

Nat again: "Is there room at the other side for a hidden channel? Could there be a weight in it, like an old-fashioned sash window?"

Where on earth did a twelve year-old get to hear about something that obscure? School? With us somewhere? I knew Nat was quite practical, thank goodness, but it takes something a bit special to apply learning to a problem so early in life.

Ifor looked at him, then at the wall and the futon, then back again. Seppe was doing the same.

"It'd sink back as soon as you lent on it…"

"Catches," said Nat.

Once again a look, and this time a grin.

"You're really with this, aren't you?" Ifor said to him. "A counterweight system in metal channels is a good solution. Catches – I don't know what sort, but with metal you can have curves and there should be a way of letting it drop into a slot when it's up. And when it's down, come to that. Let's see what we can come up with."

"Can I help? Please?" Nat had the bit between his teeth.

Seppe and Ifor looked each other, and a nod passed between them. "It'd mean coming to our workshop," Seppe told him, including me in the conversation. I looked at Nat, who had seen the glances and was now looking at me pleadingly.

"I suppose so, if you two think he could help," I agreed.

"Whether he helps or not, if he has – if you have an interest in design and problem solving we need to help with that, I think," Ifor told us both. "We'll be stopping early again tomorrow, so that'd be an opportunity, if you're both happy with the idea."

Nat nodded. After a moment's thought, so did I. He might be bored there, or he might find ideas that suited what seemed to be an inventive, practical brain. They gave us the address of their nearby workshop along with their mobile numbers, and arranged a time.

Of course, the day clinic at the hospital was on a Monday. I had missed it. There was no residual problem the next morning so I went to the office and caused Poppy to frown. I was all right, I assured her, and started work. About an hour later there was a phone call. Poppy's tone changed, first to one of concern and later, as the conversation continued, then to one that was professionally non-committal.

She looked at me. "Engine breakdown, I'm afraid. They say that there's a peculiar smell. It sounds like overheating to me, but there's no way of knowing why. They have no clue about engines. Can you go out with Ian? Take some clean water and tools and see what you can do. I hope it's not too expensive."

"So do I. Is it a boat I've serviced recently?"

She gave me the name: *Cowslip*. I checked while she went to find Ian. No, she'd not been serviced by me. The paper record showed a reasonably recent service date; I noted the engine hours he'd recorded.

Poppy Narrowboats had a van, I discovered. Everything I thought I'd need was loaded, along with a good supply of water, and we set off.

19 The best hirers...

"They're only at Kingswood junction," Ian explained. "they've not got very far in three days, but it's their holiday, not ours."

"A lot of pub visits, I imagine," I suggested. "Late nights and late morning starts."

"Lucky things. That's what holidays do for you."

It was a fairly short journey, even given Birmingham's traffic. We arrived at a car park. Ian dialled the hirers' mobile and asked for their exact location, telling them that we were in a car park at Lapworth.

"Oh, we've gone on since then," said the remote voice on loudspeaker. "It still smells, but it's not stopped."

I gave a gasp. Ian looked furious. "You need to stop *now*, please. Not in five minutes, but *now*. The chances are that if that engine doesn't stop immediately you will have destroyed it."

"Oh, we're happy to take that chance."

"But we – the hire company – aren't. An engine costs about nine grand, fitted, and if you deliberately destroy it... well, you can imagine what that will do to your deposit."

The phone went quiet.

"All right, we'll stop," said the voice in a sulky tone. "But hurry so we can get on, will you?"

I could see Ian's teeth gritting. So this was what a bad client was like on the canals, was it?

"If you can tell me where you actually are," my colleague said in artificially patient tones, "we will get to you as soon as we can. Which direction are you heading?"

"We're on the Stratford Canal."

"Ok. Heading toward Stratford or towards Birmingham."

The question was repeated. Something was said in the background.

"We're not sure."

Both sets of eyes in the van lifted heavenwards. "Are you going up locks or down them, and how many have you done?" Ian asked, still as patiently as possible.

It seemed that they were going downhill, and they thought they had been through two locks.

"Have you stopped yet?" asked Ian.

"Just mooring now."

"Good. It's a fairly long walk from the car park to you, but we'll get there with our tools as soon as we can. They are heavy, though, so it'll take about twenty minutes."

There was a squawk on the phone.

"No, we can't run with the stuff. Just stay there and we'll be with you."

"Get them to boil a lot of water," I urged.

He looked at me, then raised his eyebrows and passed on the message.

To my relief the van contained a collapsible sack trolley. The big toolbox was secured to it. I looked at the water.

"No," said Ian, "we'll use theirs. They can damn well fill up again. They'll have to turn tomorrow anyway."

Dragging a toolbox on wheels on corrugated land is an annoying occupation; annoying and noisy. Despite being secured the toolbox kept trying to escape. We arrived at the boat to be welcomed by a man and a woman standing on the stern with pint glasses in their hands and a smell of hot water and steam drifting away from them. Our greeting to them was cool, and became cooler when the man referred to his watch. Neither of them moved.

"I need to get to the engine hatches that you're standing on, so please will you come onto the bank where it's safe." It was an instruction, not a request. "Then I'll see what's made the engine overheat." Even Ian, the non-engine man, could tell what the smell was.

Reluctantly they complied.

Lifting those boards released a further cloud of steam to the atmosphere, and the smell of hot coolant, hot metal and oil was almost overpowering. I looked round the side of the boat.

"Did you check the water this morning?"

"Yes. We were told to do it every day, though I don't know why. I don't with my car." I let that pass.

"And did you smell this yesterday? Or before?"

He shook his head, taking a leisurely bite at his lager as he did so.

By now the engine's coating of steam was clearing. I looked down at the green lump of an engine. It was one I'd not had a chance to clean as yet. There was a lot of water in the bottom of the boat so I checked it for oil floating. Some, but not enough to indicate real damage. Then a double take.

I looked round the side again at the two hirers who seemed not to have a care in the world. "When you checked the water, did you replace the filler cap?"

The man looked up, casually. "Can't remember."

Subconsciously I slipped into Crown Engineering senior trouble-shooter mode. "Please will you try? You see, your security deposit depends on the co-operation you offer at this moment as we discover whether the overheating is down to you, or to the company. Can I ask whoever performed the check this morning to get back on board, carefully, please." It was neither a suggestion nor a request, but a demand.

Reluctantly the man came over, still with pint glass in hand.

"Put that down, please, and get into a position where you can observe." I'd spoken to old-style headmasters in my time and subconsciously the tone of voice had entered my armoury for use at need. This was such a time. I waited while his eyes opened in shock at my tone. The glass was put on the rooftop with a bang and he stood looking at the engine and me.

"The cap goes on there." I pointed. "Correction: the cap is *meant* to be on there whenever you are not checking or refilling the coolant. I ask again: do you remember or do you not remember replacing the cap when you had checked it this morning?"

"I think I did."

"Did it need any water adding?"

"Don't think so."

I sighed. "Mr… what was your name?"

"Mr Smith."

"Smith. I have to be plain; you need to be certain if you want your deposit back. Did you add any water?"

"What's all this about a security deposit? We always get it back."

"Do you always leave the water filler cap off and continue to run the engine despite the temperature gauge telling you it's well over-heating?"

He shrugged his shoulders.

"Ian," I called, "how much is the security deposit nowadays?"

He looked over to me in surprise. "Five hundred, I think."

"Can you afford to lose five hundred pounds?"

"They wouldn't do that!"

"Ah, but they would if the engine is damaged because of your carelessness, especially if you decline to engage with me when I ask you what has happened. So I'll ask again: did the engine need water this morning, and did you fill it?"

This time at least there was a silence while he appeared to be thinking back. "I didn't put anything in it."

"Did it appear low? We ask you to add water if there is no water visible through the filler hole."

"No, it was fine."

"So what did you do then?"

He frowned. "Ah – I remember, the cap wouldn't go on properly the first time. It felt a bit flimsy."

"Flimsy. Could it have been held on only at one side when you turned it?"

"Turned it? Are you meant to turn it? I just put it on and pushed it down. That's what we were told to do."

"That's what you were asked to do with the oil filler. That's over there. This is the water filler which has to be turned to engage it with the lugs there."

"I don't know anything about lugs."

"They're there to be seen – look. And there's a matching set on the filler cap. The two engage."

"First I've heard about it."

"But they're there, in front of you. Plain to see. What's happened when you didn't put the cap back is that the pressure of water has washed it off into the bilge and the coolant has followed it." I looked up. "Ian? Can you switch the bilge pump on, please?"

"We can do that as we go along," said the hirer.

"This boat is not going anywhere until we know that the engine is undamaged and safe to use," I told him shortly. "It will take time to find the cap that you lost, to check it, fill the system with hot water and make sure there are no leaks.

Then I have to run the engine to temperature and check it's not blowing water out of anywhere."

I really wish the engine had been cleaned so that detecting any water leaks from it would be easy.

We were watching in the bilge, Ian and I, for signs of the water cap in the hot water that had collected below the engine when a face appeared from the boat. A girl, about twelve, her pasty face almost untouched by sun or anything to do with the outdoors. She blinked at us in surprise.

"Hallo," I said. No reply, but she stood looking at us.

"Are we nearly ready to go?" she asked in a lazy voice a few moments later.

"Not even nearly," I said, and then thought on. "Can you tell me if the water's boiling yet?"

"What water?" she asked, puzzled.

"The water we asked to be heated so we could refill the engine."

She looked behind her. "There's nothing on the stove."

I could see this developing into a longer job than we thought and called up to Ian. "She says there's no water on the stove heating so that we can fill the engine."

"I'll ask." He disappeared to ask the two still drinking clients. I heard voices.

"They thought you were joking," he said shortly, "so they've done nothing about it." My eyes rolled heavenwards. "Will the engine have cooled enough by the time we've found the cap for us to fill from their hot tap? It's been nearly an hour since we told them to stop the engine."

I confess I'd omitted to think about the engine-heated domestic supply in its tank. With an overheating engine it was going to be very hot indeed. We settled on that.

The level in the bilge was diminishing. Since the water in it was as clean as any engine coolant can be, I was relieved when a circular shape could be dimly seen, smiling at us from an inch below the surface. It was fished out. I handed it to the girl. "Could you wash this in the sink, please, to get rid of any gunge on it?"

She took it from me as if it would bite her. There were some swishing about noises in the sink and she wordlessly handed it back. I tried it: it fitted and secured perfectly. So that settled where the fault lay.

Operator error. Really more like operator damn carelessness.

Cautiously I felt the engine temperature. Lower, but still not ready for cold water. I called back down the boat to the girl. No response. For goodness sake… The two on the bank were talking to each other.

"I need water from the hot tap," I called without waiting for them to stop. "Lots of it. Can you fill a big jug, please, and hand it to me? I'll need a lot of them."

"Can't you do it?"

Once again I gritted my teeth. "Yes, I can. However… let's look at this a bit differently, shall we? If I do it on my own, it will add very considerably to the time it takes to get you on your way again – assuming that we can. That means that my colleague and I will spend longer putting right a problem that was caused by the loss of a filler cap that is entirely down to you. We have retrieved it, it secures properly. As I explained, you didn't fit it properly. The whole length of time we spend will be chargeable to you as it's... well, frankly, your carelessness."

"I take exception to your attitude and the way you're treating us."

"I see," I told him slowly. "And I take exception to your attitude to me and to the engine on this boat which I look after, and which has to get you back to your car by Saturday at ten in the morning. Now, are you going to waste your and my time and your money, or are you going to get me the hot water I need to get you on your way?"

It seemed that I was fast becoming a "Looks could kill" magnet. However, they vanished down to the front and before too long the first jug of hot water was being thrust, none too gently, into my hands.

"Please could you be a little more careful?" I asked in measured tones. "If one of us is scalded by this it will delay things, especially if it's me and I have to go to hospital."

Slowly, I filled the cooling system with about four jugsful of hot water, then bled the air from the skin tank and refilled. Oh: I also replaced the filler cap. Ian provided a lot of absorbent paper and I cleaned and wiped dry every bit of the engine I could reach. There were no immediate leaks evident once the procedure was complete, to my relief. A check of the oil level and a look and a sniff inside the oil filler cap told me the oil was burnt but untainted with water. It would need changing, but could wait until the following Saturday.

I climbed out of the compartment and started the engine, registered that the temperature gauge was amazingly normal, and ran the engine up to a fast idle.

Had we got away with it? The exhaust looked normal.

I climbed off the stern and stretched my legs. Ian looked at me quizzically. "Too early to say," I told him. "It'll take another ten minutes or so before any problems can be seen, though we may smell it first."

Two heads popped over the coaming to look at us. They must be standing on very little, I thought, seeing that the engine covers were on the grass next to us.

"So can we go yet?" asked the woman, the first words she had said to us.

Ian answered her, thank goodness. "We need to make sure that there are no leaks when the engine's thoroughly hot. That'll take about fifteen minutes. If there are leaks, we take you back to the Marina with us and return here to tow the boat back because it wouldn't be safe to let you continue. If there aren't any engine leaks, you can be on your way."

"We're tired of it here, though," she said haughtily.

"And if you leave now you would have nothing to stand on, and we would have further to walk back to the van with our tools." I was so glad it was Ian dealing with her attitude. He was probably thinking that I would explode if I'd had to give an answer, and he was probably right.

"How about you spend the time making us a cup of tea?" I suggested, almost with my teeth still gritted. "One sugar for me, and none for Ian."

When you talk to people who are some metres away over the sound of an engine running, you have to speak loudly. I was conscious of another figure in the offing. A tall man, scruffily dressed but somehow tidy and with an air of authority to him.

"Forgive my intrusion," he said to all four of us in a cultured, southern accent, "but is there anything I can do to help?"

We were all waiting for the engine to show a leak or not, so there was time to explain the situation. When we had finished he nodded. "I've been listening to proceedings," he told Ian and me quietly. "I'm sorry for you. We're just making tea so we'd be happy if you'd join us. Or better still, we'll come and chat to you as you doubtless need to keep an eye on the boat."

"Thank you, sir," said Ian, responding naturally to the air of authority. I echoed the thanks, though just as instinctively omitted the honorific.

"Good," he said with a smile. "Give us two minutes."

"It's all right about the tea," I told the two hirers who had vanished back inside the boat. "One of the other boat owners has offered us a cup, so please don't bother yourselves." The tone was as sarcastic as I could make it. I'm not sure if they even heard me, as there was no response.

The mugs of tea, brought over with a plate of cakes and biscuits soon after, were very welcome. Joined by our sudden host and his wife – a stately looking lady who had a wicked glint in her eye – we sat, without ceremony on the grass by the towpath.

"I imagine they are your best ever customers," said the wife in as innocent a tone as you could wish for.

Ian laughed. "There are very few that unpleasant. And we only see them once."

"We're going to invite them back next year, free of charge," I replied to her just as innocently. "I imagine Poppy has an old metal bathtub with oars she'll give them."

Before long we were all deep in conversation, swapping stories. It turned out that he was a headmaster of a quite well-known public school and this was their preferred means of winding down to normal speeds of living. There is a charm about even urban canals which forces the pace of life to slow; probably it has a lot to do with the three miles an hour at which most canal cruising happens.

"You've broken up early," I remarked.

"We do. The campus is taken over by a language school and to be honest I keep out of the way as much as possible." He sighed. "The last day of term is the most depressing of any in the school year. All our exam-takers leak away from the school in batches as their last exam finishes. They return for the last day because there are so many things happening to engage them, as well as friends to greet for what may be the last time. In the case of the sixth form, all the staff have got to know them so well over the years and have seen their attitude to us change as they've grown up. They are almost like friends, and some of them become just that. They are, after all, adults by that time, albeit young adults. Treat them as children at your peril.

"To have to bid what may be last farewells is a bittersweet endurance test. One is genuinely sad to see them go, maybe for the last time. But equally one wishes them so, so well for their future, and hope that the school has equipped them for it. It certainly isn't for the want of trying."

"He should retire, really," his wife said, pricking the balloon of dignity. "But the school is his life. Our lives," she added has he looked reproachfully at her. "Yes, Mack. I love them too. Most of them."

"It gets to be a way of life," he admitted.

"As do engines," I admitted, and told him a little of my story.

"And now you're looking after a fleet of narrowboats."

"Only their engines. Ian's the expert on everything else, and keeps them all spick and span. And safe."

"And you're based in – where is it?"

I told him.

"I suppose there isn't room in your marina for another boat, is there? And would you take on another engine? And Ian, would you be prepared to look after the rest of her when we're not there, in term time?"

Ian and I exchanged glances. Ian spoke first. "I'm not sure if there are any spaces in the marina at the moment. You see, Poppy doesn't own it; she rents our area from the Canal and River Trust. So you'd need to get a mooring from them, I suppose. We'd need to put the idea to Poppy, see what she says."

"Should we come up and see the marina?" Mack asked. "Then we could talk to Poppy – she's the owner, I take it – and she could satisfy herself that neither of us has two heads."

We both laughed. "She'd take our word on that," Ian said, "but you'd need to see where we are and make sure you like it. It's certainly secure."

'Our' hirers were approaching, looking annoyed – as usual. Their expression had hardly changed since we first met them. "It's gone fifteen minutes," said Mr Smith. "Can we get going yet? It's very noisy without the boards on the engine."

"Indeed," I told him in a level tone. "And all this time I've been listening to that noise, that engine, so see if it's making any untoward noises. I've heard none so far, so in a minute we'll go over and look for any leaks. I'll join you there." Another way of telling him to go away.

"Ian, have you got a business card of the marina, or something with the contact details on it? If we give you that, Mr…" I laughed. "You know us as Ian and Jack, but we don't even know your names."

"I was called Mack when I first became Head. They thought I didn't know, but we all get to know these things and it doesn't surprise me since I was blessed with McTavish as a Christian name. This is Georgie, and together we're the Attwoods. We'll be in touch – maybe bring the boat up some time."

"That would be good," said Ian, "but please not on a Saturday because it's our hirers' changeover day and we're flat out, and not Sunday because we all try to have a rest at home. Any other day and we'll give you coffee and cake, and talk boats and moorings."

We said our thanks and farewells, then headed off back to the boat. One thing

I'd not done was to sniff at *Cowslip's* exhaust, so I rectified that and could smell nothing too awful. It also looked normal, and even when I reduced the revs to tickover it was colourless. Phew.

Back down in the engine bay, standing on its supports I looked all round for signs of leaks, either steaming or black – or, worse, blowing something from a cylinder. Nothing. Phew again.

Again I climbed out, this time with a nod to Ian. We replaced the engine covers and delighted in the sudden relief from the noise. I stopped the engine and waited.

Nothing happened. Two or three times I knocked on the side, but still no one appeared. Now exasperated I entered the boat and walked down to find someone, calling "hallo?" as I went. I found them at last. They were on the bed. Let's just say that they were hugging each other, with two pairs of trousers on the floor beside them. I didn't wait to examine the situation, just ducked outside the cabin again and knocked hard on the side. "Would you come with me please? Now? We have to return."

There was a start from the bed, and a pair of bare legs reached for the floor. I retreated to the cockpit so as to distance myself from the unwanted experience. Eventually the man came up, suitably re-trousered, I'm glad to say.

"Well?"

It wasn't a good rejoinder.

"You're very lucky," I told him. "Your carelessness could have cooked the engine, and your continuing when we had asked you to moor and stop – well, it could have finished the engine for good. As it is, somehow, the engine has survived, though it will need a very full service this Saturday to get rid of the fluids you've overheated and for me to check it over thoroughly once again.

"From now on it needs to be checked – *you* need to check it – very carefully, and any overheating on the gauge needs you to stop, wait at least half an hour, and refill with *hot* water. I repeat that. If you don't, you run the risk of the same thing happening again, and that will most certainly lose your deposit for you. Will you do that?"

Again, a look of daggers. Then: "all right."

I turned my back, gained the bank and walked back to the Attwoods' boat (suitably called *Forest*) without turning. Ian joined me.

"Poppy will tell them to get stuffed if they ever try booking with us again," he said as if to offer comfort.

"I damn well hope so. I can't remember meeting anyone as rude as that, not ever. And I've met a few whose managerial style has come pretty close to being objectionable."

"Like Poppy, you mean?"

I looked at him, and saw the grin threatening to take over. "Exactly like Poppy," I laughed. "Though, to be fair, she can speak her mind when needed, I'm sure."

"She can. She's had to. One or two of the Saturday helpers in the past have turned out to be worse than useless and she's told them off well and truly before telling them to walk. She speaks her mind all right."

My memory returned to Helen's semi-accusation the previous Sunday and Poppy's bluff response. I nodded.

Again we said our farewells to the Attwoods and dragged the redundant toolbox on its reluctant wheels back to the van.

20 ...leave things behind

Poppy was incensed when she heard our story. Without my having to deliver a plea about not hiring to them again she pronounced that very decision. "I am going to write to all the other hire boat operators in this area and warn them too," she said. "I'll use it as an opportunity to tell the companies about the problems we had too, despite the information having unofficially reached them already. What they don't know is that we have a solution, and that he's called Jack Dyer. And I'll tell them about the fuel supply change. I can introduce you. It might gain you some useful consultancy work."

Financially, for us, it was early days. I was aware that the boys and I should eventually have the proceeds to half a house – less half a mortgage settlement. That relied on The Opposition seeing sense as dictated by my letters which the solicitors had backed up and annotated for free. Thank you, Poppy. Yes, a slowly growing amount of consultancy would be helpful if it didn't mean travelling and staying away overnight.

She heard about the Attwoods. "We might be able to get more spaces here," she said. "It's not something I'd thought seriously about, acting as a marina too. It's most certainly a good idea to take on boats that need nursemaiding – if you're prepared to sort out the mechanics, Jack. It might give some of our Saturday people some more work too, or it could happen on a Friday; in fact it wouldn't matter what day it was done so long as we met the owners' requested frequency."

"I'll do the admin for it," I said, "unless Ian would rather it was him. After all, you've been here longer by quite a bit!"

Ian shook his head. "You've shown me the record system for your engines, and you can beat me into a cocked hat with that sort of thing. I'm happy doing it and recording when I've done something, so it's over to you on that one, with Poppy's say-so."

"All yours, Jack. Perhaps we can advertise in the magazines once CRT have released some more spaces to us. Or the boats that are already here might appreciate the service. We've been approached for engine matters in the past – and for fuel, but I'm not licensed to sell it. If we get a lot of requests, though... who knows?"

Lunch. A sit down. A long time astride an engine, leaning over, is enough to give anyone a backache, and I had one. I even lay on the bed for a bit, but this time was careful to set my watch so as not to repeat the episode of a few days previously, though this day's circumstances were different.

I found Poppy on the phone when I returned. It seemed a long affair, talking about costs, space and the possibility of expansion. She was certainly quick off the mark if this was to the Canal and River Trust. In sign language I asked if she wanted me to stay out, but she beckoned me in.

At last it was over and she sat there, looking annoyed. I raised my eyebrows.

"A lack of decision making ability," was her verdict. "We have to put together a business plan. It's almost as if they don't want a guaranteed, regular income but are happy to put up with the hassle of defaulting owners, the sort we occasionally get here. I know there's one boat over on the other side which hasn't moved or seen its owner for over a year. Whether its licence is valid or its mooring fees paid I have no way of knowing. There's nothing valid in the windows."

"So if the Attwoods were to ask for a space, could we help them?"

"They couldn't mix in with our fleet. There's too much potential for damage as we shift ours around. I can moor them against your boat. But then it's unfair on you when you want to go out – or when they do. All the other owners here are liveaboards like you; they work in the city and the boats don't move, but at least they're here legally. There's not really a prospect of offering a cleaning service to them, or a nursemaiding service for their boat because they come back after work and are here at weekends."

I thought. "If the Attwoods' boat – thinking for a moment just about theirs – were moored between ours and the stonework, that would mean it was even more secure. We wouldn't mind that, so long as they didn't mind our clambering over theirs as we got on or off."

"I can take that," she said thoughtfully. "It would start a precedent that we might build on if any other boats leave their moorings. It'd be a good way of building up a client base gradually. Let's see what they say when they see it, and go from there."

"Changing the subject," I started, "do you want me in the interview with the Smiths when they leave *Cowslip*? Or would you want me to leave it to you?"

"The engine needs a service, you said."

"Yes." I grimaced. "It does. An engine wash, a change of filters, oil and coolant, and a run up to speed again to make sure I can hear everything that's going on inside it."

"Cost?"

"Roundly £50 if I use decent engine oil, which I want to. Plus time."

"Crown Engineering rates or Poppy Narrowboat rates?" she asked with the first smile I'd seen since I'd started talking.

I laughed ruefully. "Charge Crown rates, and it'll take up most of the rest of their deposit."

"Better make it ours, then. There's also your and Ian's time for attending the breakdown. Sounds expensive for them. I wonder how they'll leave the boat."

"So do I. I doubt if the kettle will have been used much, they seem only to drink lager. All day. I feel sorry for their daughter. She's such a pale little thing – I'm sure she's not enjoying the holiday."

"Daughter? Was there a daughter?"

"Yes – I assume she was the daughter, anyway. She just appeared at the stern door when I was down with the engine. She didn't say much. I couldn't help contrasting her with Nat. They're about the same age."

"Your two have been properly brought up. There's the difference, I guess. I didn't notice a daughter when we handed the boat over."

"Maybe they picked her up somewhere else."

"I hope she actually is theirs."

"She wasn't disturbed or anything, just – well, quiet."

Poppy nodded. There was nothing we could do about that, anyway.

I gave the boys a quick sandwich when they arrived from school. Nat was due to go for his conference with Seppe and Ifor – as I reminded him – and there was a noticeable look of importance on his face as I came out with the term.

"You going too, Dad?" asked Phil.

"Do you want company?" I asked Nat. He shook his head scornfully. I was happy about his going alone. He was twelve plus, it wasn't far away and goodness knows the two of them bussed around the city without a qualm. He phoned Seppe and was told they would be about half an hour, so they had time to eat and sit down for a few moments. I promised the meal would be ready soon after he returned.

It had completely escaped any of the three of us to put some sort of time limit on the visit. Nat had left the Yard just after five, and the meal was ready at seven-thirty. When he still hadn't returned by eight, I phoned Seppe's number, suddenly worried. A Jonathan-shaped worry.

Seppe immediately sounded contrite. "I didn't realise how late it is, Jack. Really sorry. I'll bring him back now." He ended the call without giving me the chance to say anything. He was as good as his word, and the two of them appeared ten minutes later, Seppe flustered and apologetic and Nat bursting with enthusiasm, wood chippings in his hair and on his clothes.

His school clothes. Damn.

"I don't know where the time went, Jack," Seppe grovelled. "He's got a brain like a sponge, this one, and a lot of ideas. We managed to teach him a lot, too. But now Ifor and I must close the workshop and go home. We will not be popular with wives."

"He's not popular with me," I said mock-severely. "He has a watch, and he should have known better than to have kept you both so long."

Seppe looked astonished. "No – he has been a tonic. We both enjoyed it and we want him to come back – if he wants to. But now I must go. Sorry again, and good night."

He was gone. Nat was still grinning, Cheshire cat like.

I brushed him down outside, to his disgust, and told him to brush his hair or he'd end up eating wood dandruff with his food. At that he suddenly remembered he was hungry and rushed off to the bathroom. (I was reminded about young boys later when visiting it myself barefoot, before bed, wondering what the grit was beneath my feet).

Of course we heard all about it as we settled down to eat – and for a long time after. It seems the workshop was an Aladdin's cave for him, and best of all if he made a suggestion Seppe and Ifor actually listened to him and thought before replying. He'd been told that some of what he had dreamed up could be used for the collapsible table, and had told him the drawbacks with some of his other ideas. He'd learnt a lot in a short time.

"You've been working on one of the machines, haven't you?" asked Phil suddenly.

Nat paused, and looked at me doubtfully. "Yeees…" he started. "But it was with one of them watching and telling me what to do. And I had to wear goggles."

"Good for you," I said, surprising him. "What did they get you to use?"

"Mainly the lathe," he said hesitantly. "Bits go all over the place, but it's such fun."

"I saw earlier what you mean by bits," I told him. "Next time, can you brush yourself off there, and not bring them back here?"

"I can go again?" he asked with a face so enthusiastic that I could tell this was important to him. At the moment, anyway.

"If they'll have you. Don't forget that they're busy, though, and it won't be a regular occurrence. And please let me know if you're going there beforehand so I know that you haven't just disappeared courtesy of your uncle."

A look of astonished distaste. "He wouldn't dare!"

"He's tried once," I told him.

"Yeah, but… he wouldn't. But ok, I'll tell you when I'm going,"

"And if he tries it with me he'll get hit," Phil added. "He's hit me once, so it's fair game now. And it wouldn't be his face that I'd hit."

That comment was better ignored, I thought to myself.

There were no further call-outs that week. Nat became a little quieter by Friday and I wondered what had happened, whether he was missing Helen. Phil had gone off for some emergency shopping at my request, and I was able to ask him.

"No," he started hesitantly. "Well, yes, but no. I mean I know she's there and we can fix up to see her when we want. But I hoped that I might get another visit to the workshop and they haven't asked me."

"Is that why you've been a bit quiet?"

He shrugged his shoulders. "Have I?"

"Yes. But have you phoned Seppe? It's his number you've got, isn't it?"

"Do you think I should have?"

"Maybe they're wondering if you were really interested, and were disappointed that you'd not made contact. It works both ways, you know."

"Do you think that's it?" he asked, wide eyed. "I could just have phoned them?"

"Well yes. But don't forget it's only two nights ago and they're busy. Also, it's Friday, they might have gone out with their wives, and anyway we have an early start again tomorrow."

Changeover day provided the usual challenges. My priority was *Cowslip*, of course, though I was glad to keep out of the way of the Smiths and only start work on the boat when they were in the office, being talked to by Poppy. One of the cleaners was shifting gear on at the bows just as I had started. I heard an exclamation from the kitchen and poked my head up to look in.

"Poppy's going to be furious," she said in response to my question. "They've broken the teapot, some of the plates, and haven't bothered to wash up for at least a couple of days, I imagine."

I thought for a moment. "Can you take a photo of the damage and the grot?" I asked, "and take it over to Poppy now? She's talking to them at the moment."

The girl, quite a young girl, about eighteen, I supposed, looked worried. "I don't think…"

"Please, take the photos. I'll go over with your phone, if you trust me, and show her. Then we can download them later."

"Should I email them to her instead?" she offered.

"That's even better; good idea. I'll go over when they're on their way and make sure she looks at them before the hirers go."

She set to. "Were these the people you had to go out to?" she asked in mid-photograph.

"They certainly were, and a more unpleasant trio I've not met. Their deposit is already being bitten into, and the mess you've found will do more."

She was quick, and now warned of potential problems started to look at the rest of the boat. I called after her. "Can you send the first ones to Poppy now? I'll go over and tell her."

"Ok," she called back.

A rag disposed of most of the dirt from my gloves. I emerged from the engine and made my way over to the office where loud voices were to be heard. Not standing on ceremony I went straight in. There was indeed an argument in process.

Mr Smith turned to me. "Don't you knock before you invade your employer's office when there's an interview taking place?" At that point he recognised me. "Oh, it's you."

"It is indeed," I said as pleasantly as I could. "Once again you've made a mistake. Mrs Watson is not my employer. Even if she were, when there is something she needs to know urgently I would react in exactly the same way to bring it to her attention. And so far as I'm aware this is her office, not yours, and you don't get to decide what goes on in it."

"If she's not your employer, what are you doing here?"

"Continuing my report on your antics on the hired boat you have abused for the last week. Poppy, could you look at some photos of *Cowslip's* interior that have just been taken? They've been emailed to you."

"We don't have time for this," said Mr Smith to his partner. "Come on, let's get out of here."

"One moment, please," said Poppy. Fortunately I was standing in the way of the door, and moved backwards a little to block it. Also fortunately I'm quite broad, so it didn't need much blocking. There was a gasp from the desk. Poppy looked up.

"So you have broken quite a lot of china. No ordinary washing up has been done and the sink is filthy. What else is there you have left in a mess?"

"You employ cleaners at the end of the hire. That's their job."

"Just as it's your job to respect someone else's property that you're hiring, and not to live like…" She paused. "Oh, good God…"

With some difficulty she turned the screen round. A new email had appeared, this time showing the bedding.

Without a break the man started. "Accidents happen. Look, we need to go."

"Just now you were trying to argue the toss with me and were prepared to continue doing so despite all the evidence. Now, in the presence of someone who has seen that evidence, both on Wednesday and now, you suddenly need to leave in a hurry. There has been no genuine explanation, no apology. Your attitude to my colleagues and to me has been appalling, and the state of the bedding you have been using is absolutely disgusting."

He started to speak again but Poppy overspoke him. "No. Listen to me for once without interrupting. I will evaluate every bit of damage that you have caused on that boat. It will be countered against your deposit – that is what the deposit is for. If there is a balance due to you, it will be paid. If you need to pay more I will pursue it with you and through the Court system if necessary. Further, I will share all this information with every other hire boat operator around the waterways, since patently you are not to be trusted with over a hundred grands' worth of narrowboat. In fact I wouldn't trust you with a matchbox."

A line of sparks formed between the two sets of eyes… no, not really, but it was as if it had. The Smiths turned and pushed past me, went out and slammed the door. Poppy and I were left staring at each other. I'd just opened my mouth to ask if she was all right when the door opened again.

"You spread this round and we shall sue for defamation of character."

I imagine we were each about to retort that a defamation case can't be based on the truth when the door slammed again. This time I did manage to ask Poppy if she was all right.

"Yes," she said regretfully, "except that I lost my temper with them. And that meant losing the argument, in my mind. And then you came in and thank God interrupted us all." She paused, obviously still angry. "How can anybody, *anybody*, be such arseholes?"

"Not many bother," I said briefly, wondering the same myself. "Look, I'd better get on with that engine. Your young lass on *Cowslip* is having to deal with god knows what horrors."

Poppy swore. I knew her well enough by then that it didn't faze me; after all, it didn't form part of her normal vocabulary.

"I'm going to have to switch the next hirer to another boat. I can't have them taking over something that's been treated like that. Stop Helena trying to do anything, would you? We'll leave *Cowslip* on one side and fumigate her during the week."

The door opened again to admit the first of the next week's hirers. Poppy engaged 'welcome' mode and told them that they were very early and would they like to visit a local restaurant or pub and have lunch as the boats were never ready until two thirty at the earliest. They took the hint and disappeared.

I returned to *Cowslip's* engine, told Helena the news and watched her thankfully leave the horrors and go to another boat. My eyes drifted across towards the entrance. Two small figures were sitting against a wall. I frowned.

Nat and a girl. Both were looking straight ahead.

I hauled myself off the boat again and crossed to them, frowning again as I recognised the girl.

The Smiths' daughter. Something was wrong, obviously. I squatted in front of them. Nat looked at me very seriously.

"Maisie's been left behind by her parents," he said bluntly.

"How did it happen?" I asked her.

She said nothing. Nat spoke instead. "She was meant to be in the car but it was too hot, so she got out for some air and went to look at what was happening. Her parents must have come back and just got in the car and driven off."

"Have you tried phoning them?" I asked her.

This time she did speak, after a shake of the head. "I don't have their number. I don't have a phone."

This wasn't the time to ask why either should come about. "I'll get their number from the office and call them on my mobile," I told her. "We'll get them back in a jiffy. Or better: Nat could you keep trying them once we have the number? Then Maisie can talk to them herself."

He nodded. I got up, then heard Maisie speak again. "I wish I was back at school."

"Where do you go?" asked Nat. "We haven't broken up yet."

I left them to it. Returning with the number I saw that Nat's face was serious again. "Ok?" I asked. If ever there was a comment to a youngster that will only ever receive the answer "yes" despite what the youngster was thinking, that is it. All Nat did was to nod.

"That's the number." I gave Nat the piece of paper. He dug out his phone and punched out the number, then automatically put the phone to his ear.

"It should be Maisie who answers it," I reminded him, and he handed it to the girl. She took it, gingerly, and held it as if it were a bomb.

It squawked. "It's…it's Maisie," she answered. "I'm still at the boatyard."

There was a torrent of talk from the phone, inaudible to us, but the girl's face looked more and more downcast. "When, then?" she asked. There was more from the other end. "So what do I do?"

The phone was still squawking when I held out my hand for it. Maisie gave it to me as if it was a hot potato. I listened and was immediately horrified and disgusted at the invective that I heard – this was from the woman, presumably Maisie's mother.

"Hallo," I said as pleasantly as I could. "We've met. I'm with Maisie at the marina. When, within the next hour, are you coming to fetch her? And please don't use the sort of language I just heard to me as I will not accept it."

The line went quiet. Then: "Who the f… who are you?"

"You know me as the engineer who came out to you when you let the engine on the boat overheat."

"We can't fetch that little…wretch at the moment. She'll have to look after herself until we can get there."

"And when will that be?"

"We'll get there when we can."

"Not good enough. Don't worry, though, I'll make a phone call. We'll get someone who can take care of her."

"Do what you like."

"Oh, I shall do what the law requires me to do."

"What?" I could hear a change in the tone at the mention of the law.

"If there are youngsters whose parents deliberately leave them somewhere there are procedures to follow. You should know that."

After a pause: "we can't come back for the moment."

I frowned. "You just re-entered the discussion where it started, at the beginning. A circular argument gets nobody anywhere. Either you come back now or we contact Social Services to come and look after Maisie until you deign to come and do what you should be doing."

"How dare you…"

"Easily," I interrupted. "I'm a parent and my sons' welfare is my priority, just as it should be. I know bad parenting when I see it – and hear it, in this case – and I imagine Social Services will too. But the choice is yours."

"I haven't got access to a car at the moment."

"Ok."

There was a pause. "What do you mean?"

"I'm waiting for you to give me a time when you'll be here."

It's pointless reporting what the next string of words were. Swearing adds nothing to the main story of why we live on a boat. I clamped the phone to my ear so that it was inaudible to the two youngsters. When it stopped I just said: "Social services, then. Bye."

21 Maisie

Mrs Smith started again, and the words in the tinny speaker on my mobile carried as far as Nat, who is known for picking up language from school and occasionally using it in front of me accidentally (as did Phil), and even his face registered astonishment. Maisie, on the other hand, remained unsurprised and downcast.

"They're not my parents," she protested as I ended the call. "They're my aunt and uncle."

"Parents?" I asked, briefly.

"Soldiers. Abroad somewhere."

"Can you contact them?"

She shook her head. "Secret."

"Can your aunt and uncle contact them?"

Again a shake of the head.

"Are they like those two?" asked Nat, finding his voice.

"No! nothing like that!"

It was so vehement that I found a lot more sympathy for her than I had up to then.

"How long are they away for?" I asked.

Again the shoulders told the story. I carried on looking at her. Gradually she looked up.

"I hate them. She teaches me at home and it's boring. I used to go to a boarding school but they stopped that ages ago, just after I went to them."

"Do you think your parents know about that?"

The inevitable shrug.

"How far away do these people of yours live?" I asked.

This time she actually thought. "We left at midday to get here to get the boat."

That would have been about two in the afternoon. Two hours away would mean a big area of town and country. But then… they had left the marina only about fifteen minutes previously. They couldn't have got very far away in that time; they could even be still in the city.

"Where are you living at the moment?" I asked.

"It's near Wakefield," she said. "A tiny village where nothing happens and there's nothing to do."

"I've got to go and fill that boat," Nat said suddenly, aware of Poppy looking reproachfully in his direction, then frowning as she noticed the girl. Nat rushed off. I noticed that Maisie was watching as he walked purposefully over to the boat, trailing a hose, undo the filler cap and poke the hose in; all done in a very businesslike way.

"Is it his job?" Maisie asked.

"No. We just do it to help out. You see…" How much do I tell her? "We live in the boat over there, and soon I'll be working for the marina. So it's a sort of 'thank you' for the use of the boat."

"I hated being on the boat," she said suddenly.

"Not enough to do?" I remembered her complaint about the village where she lived.

"Nothing happened. I was told to keep out of the way in case I fell off." She was unbending at last.

"That's a shame. We love living on ours, and when we take her out the boys steer and work the locks."

"I wish I could help him," she said, looking at Nat who was leaping over the bows of a number of boats on his way to turn the tap on again.

"You could, if you don't mind manning the tap,"

For the first time, she looked animated. It took Nat a few minutes to gather what she was trying to do for him, but it seemed to be working and I went back to finish off *Cowslip's* engine. At last I finished and was about to start it and see what I could detect when Phil called me.

"Odd smell from this engine, Dad."

Unfortunately it wasn't odd for me. It was another overheat victim, but at least I could detect the problem easily. Hot water was dripping into the bilge from a split hose.

By the time that was dealt with and I'd helped Phil, we were nearing the time when all boats due out that afternoon were ready except for clean sheets and other linens. That always happened last, after a quick lunch. Nat brought Maisie with him, to Phil's surprise. I left them to it and grabbed Poppy, telling her the story. She was immediately appalled.

"I can't believe the parents would be completely incommunicado," she said. "What about her school?"

I explained about the home schooling and that they weren't her parents.

"The school she was at, then. But for now we need to give her something to eat, with us, and I'll take her back with me later if the relatives haven't bothered to appear by then, I really think, though, that this is a job for Social Services, even if you don't like involving them."

"I've got nothing against them as such," I protested. "But if I can solve my own problems without them I'd rather. The two cases are very different."

She held up her hands. "I know, I know. But in this case they may be able to use official means to contact the parents in the services and ask what their intentions were. It wouldn't surprise me if they didn't know she no longer went to school and that the relatives are free to pocket the money intended for her school fees."

The idea had wandered across my mind. To hear Poppy voice it made it more likely to be the truth. Well, I'd promised that I would call Social Services. With a deep breath I looked up the number.

Pillar to post, post back to pillar. It was a Saturday and no one was present in any of the various offices. At last I found a woman who, once she had got over the initial suspicion of me and my possible motives for making a report, was helpful. It seemed that a caution flag had already been raised about the family, as it had been noticed that she was only ever seen with one of her relatives, and on what appeared to be a short leash at that. She never seemed to smile, and never spoke. In fact she presented all the signs that I had seen when she'd appeared on the boat.

Presented with the change to home schooling when she had arrived in the village, the attitude became even more interested.

"The uncle and aunt are meant to be returning to the marina to pick her up, when they can be bothered to," I told them, and was immediately asked to go over the details again of how she had been left behind.

"I need to refer this to someone," she said.

"May I have your number, and can you tell me your name again, please?" I asked. "I've spoken to so many people before you in the last two hours that I stopped making notes."

She told me readily enough. "I'm Nina Rowley. Can you find out which school it was she attended?"

"Hold on, I'll go and ask her."

I sought her out. She was on our boat, playing cards with Nat at the table and, praise be, looking almost animated. "I've had an idea," I lied. "Can you tell me the name of the school you used to go to?"

I got a name and returned to my mobile in the office to pass on the information. She obviously knew the school's name – as did I since it was so well known – and told me she would call back as soon as she had made some sort of contact.

"What happens if they arrive to pick her up?" I asked.

"You'll have to let her go with them. If there's any sort of physical abuse or anything, call the Police. Once they've dealt with the adults, please would you give them my details, and we'll confer."

"We can put her up here overnight if necessary," I told her. "My younger son is her age and they've sort of hit it off, it seems."

"I'll have to look at that, of course," I was told. "But don't say anything to her about it until I've called you back. It's best if we can make firm arrangements and then tell her."

"She's twelve, don't forget, and needs to be consulted."

"But she's a minor, and we know what's best for her."

This was exactly the attitude which I was afraid of if it ever became necessary to call Social Services to deal with our own issues and I was more determined than ever to keep them out of our life.

"I don't agree that's the best approach," I told her, "not at twelve. Her wishes need to be respected."

"We deal with this all the time, Mr Dyer, and you need to trust us to know best."

"The people who know best are parents," I countered. "Are you a parent? Because I am, and I have a twelve year old who is very self-aware and decisive. And reliable. I'd put his wishes first."

"Good. But Maisie is neither of those things, so we have to do what we see is best for her. I will call you back."

It was almost a cut-off, certainly a dismissal. She had a point, but I wondered what Maisie would be like had she been allowed to blossom normally over the year, and not be enclosed in the cellar of mental control that seemed to have been her lot.

Poppy was checking over the boats that had been made ready. I had no idea what Phil was doing but he was still intrigued by the complexity of the operation and anxious to take a part in it, to be useful and to be seen to be useful. I had a flashback to myself at fourteen, when I had latched on to a back-street garage and started to do simple jobs for the boss on a Saturday morning, probably much to the amusement of the staff. It nurtured the seed of the engineer in me, I suppose. At the very least it had rendered me unafraid of dirtying my hands or, to my parents dismay, anything I was wearing.

On the dockside was the party of hirers who had appeared earlier that morning when it had been too early to start loading their possessions onto their boat. It was still too early, so I invited them into the office and put the kettle on before checking the boat they had been allocated. Whilst they nursed mugs of coffee I located the boat, then Poppy.

"Give me ten minutes," she said, "then I'll come over and you can show them round the boat – and the engine! – and let them load. Don't give them the keys, though, or they might try and set off before we've done the induction."

They proved to be a pleasant couple and quite canal-experienced, so much of what I was going to tell them would prove to be to grandmothers about eggs. We were still talking over the engine when my phone rang, so I excused myself and told them they could load as soon as they liked and someone would be with them to show them the ropes, but that they should explain their experience level again.

The call was Nina from Social Services, thank goodness, and the first thing she asked was whether the relatives had reappeared. "Not as far as I've seen," I told her, "and they'd not know where she was if they had."

"Where is she?"

"Playing cards with my younger son in our boat."

"Good. We've discovered something and I'm coming to intervene, with a colleague. We'll see you in about half an hour. Please don't let the girl go if the relatives do appear. Tell them we're on our way and will talk to them. Please don't let her appear when they are there; we don't want them to see her."

"I'll ask Maisie to stay in our boat." Referring to her as "the girl" had stung me.

I visited Nat and Maisie. They were still sitting at the table, this time sharing music from Nat's phone. They both smiled at me when I looked in, so it seemed that Nat had a sort of magic with her. He was possibly one of the few people her own age she'd seen for a long time. Poor girl.

I went in search of Phil, who was looking for Poppy. He listened as I gave a shortened version of events and asked him not to tell his brother or Maisie and risk destroying Maisie's happiness. Poppy appeared and asked Phil if he could possibly help on another of the boats; this day there was an odd number of staff, so he was genuinely being a great help, not just making up numbers or being humoured.

Briefly I told Poppy what was happening. She nodded. "Probably the best thing," she commented, then rushed off to see the next arrival of hirers. I hung about like a spare part, ready to be a receptionist, do what I was asked, or fend off Maisie's toxic relatives. Nothing happened that I could usefully do until a smart couple drove into the marina and walked towards the office. They received the normal friendly welcome.

"We're not here for a boat," the woman said in a voice that was dimly familiar. "We need to see Mr Dyer, please."

"Oh?" I asked cautiously, "who shall I say it is?"

"Nina Rowley and Frank Pope." I recognised her name and introduced myself.

"You'll want to meet Maisie," I said. "She's at home with my lad Nat. I'll go in and explain it all to her."

"You don't know what we have to say to her yet." Frank Pope spoke for the first time. "We've done more than a little research into this and – well, there's a surprise for both you and for Maisie. We've traced her parents and managed to speak to them. We don't know where they are, though; the call was connected by the Ministry and put through to us."

My sense of relief was tremendous.

"The parents are horrified at what's happened, and want her out of the care of the relatives immediately. We have no details, but normally the family lives in a gated community, and for security the girl goes to a remote boarding school, as you know. In the summer they all go quietly abroad for long holidays at a remote location. It's all very secret. Apparently if it wasn't the whole family could be in danger from extremists.

"We told her about you, and as they see it you've rescued her, and they're very grateful. As to what happens next, the problem is that it'll take the parents a week to return safely, so we have to find somewhere safe for her to live until then."

It sounded very high powered stuff, and I wondered what on earth we had unwittingly got ourselves involved in. "How much of all this do the relatives know?" I asked them.

"That's what has galvanised the Ministry. The relatives think that the parents are overseas and in the military services. The daughter thinks the same. We're guessing, as you must be, that there's a great deal more to it than that; we're thinking MI5 or something along those lines. For her sake we don't want her to know our guesses, otherwise she might worry even more about them. If the parents want to level with her they can, but we shouldn't relay our own guesses.

"Even more, the relatives must be left completely in the dark. The Ministry have made up their minds from what's happened that they're unreliable."

"Unreliable!" I exclaimed. "I'll say they're unreliable. Unhinged would be a better word. But which Ministry are we talking about? Can you tell us that?"

They exchanged a glance. "I imagine that if we *did* know they wouldn't allow us to tell you," Nina said. "Our line managers referred it up, I suppose phone calls happened somewhere at a high level and there was enough concern about her to make a contact necessary."

"So what is going to happen?"

"We're going to talk to her first and get the full story about her treatment direct from her."

"You'll find her reluctant to talk."

"We have our methods."

"That sounds ominous."

"What I meant was; we are trained in talking to children and getting answers."

I reflected for a moment before agreeing. "Very well. I'll go and talk to her and..."

I was immediately interrupted by Pope. "We can't allow that. We've got to be seen to have prevented any attempt to lead her answers. I know from speaking to you that you would try not to, but we have to be seen to be squeaky clean."

Even with that comment to sweeten what had been said I remained annoyed, not least of all because Nat had befriended her and it seemed disloyal to him, and offensive to me.

"What you forget," I started, "is that you want to enter *my* boat, *our* home, so as to talk to her. So what is going to happen is that I will go and talk to *my* son and his friend, and ask if they are happy with two strangers talking to them. You also forget that my son has befriended Maisie and she has opened up to him, and through him to me. Without him, she would still be a prisoner of her relatives."

"Mr Dyer, I hoped you would be reasonable. We must talk to her on our terms." Frank Pope sounded alarmed.

"You can talk to her, but on neutral terms that guarantee that she will be swayed by neither you nor us, in our home."

"Your boat," Pope said.

"Our *home*. We live on a boat: it is our home. And I too want to make sure she is treated well."

With bad grace, and after a few more exchanges, they agreed. Perhaps I could have been accused of kidnapping Maisie, but her parents would hardly have allowed an accusation of that to hold any weight. After all, they regarded us as her rescuers, not her abductors.

My entry to the boat was greeted by a peal of happy laughter. It sounded as if Nat and she were hitting it off. And when I saw Maisie I could hardly believe that this was the rather unappealing, straight-faced girl who had wandered up the boat earlier. Her hair, which had previously been severely tied back into a band, now hung loose, and although needing to grow a bit, it accentuated her face and made her look normal.

When she saw me her expression changed and it seemed that it was to Nat that she looked for help.

"Hi, Dad," he said in his usual, happy way. "We've been swapping stories about parents and – well – *others* who come in to a family."

Had they, now. Well, it appeared not to have been a traumatic discussion on either side, as might have been expected.

I took my lead from him. "I'm glad about that because just like us, Maisie has been through trying times. We have a chance of helping her out of them, so I think we should, don't you?"

They both looked hopeful.

"Does that mean that Aunt and Uncle won't be looking after me any more?" she asked.

"I really hope so, and so do Social Services who have done a lot of digging. They're so concerned that they want to talk to you about what's happened, and when it happened, Maisie. Would that be all right? I can be here as well, or maybe you'd prefer it just to be Nat. We won't say anything, but just be here to – well, be a presence, a support, if you needed one."

"Will they take me away?"

That was what I didn't know, though I supposed so. Nothing had been said about where she was going to live if not with her relatives. I was honest with her, and told her it was best if the two who were waiting outside – with mounting impatience, no doubt – told her everything.

The interview went fairly well. Given the previous exchange I was surprised and relieved to be allowed to stay, and with Nat. Indeed, Maisie was surprisingly positive that if we didn't stay she would say nothing. I made sure that my phone was recording the exchanges, just as Nina and Frank probably did. Maisie was now relaxed enough to be able to recount the details of the past year of her life. Although her experiences were not anywhere near as traumatic as so many others one hears about, it was plain that neither her education nor her life had been remotely on a par with her parents' expectations.

Maisie's main worries were where she would live until her parents returned, whether her parents would be angry to be brought back into England to see her, and what would happen if her relatives returned. Nina and Frank didn't know where she would stay yet as arrangements still had to be made. They and we told her that her parents would love her just as much as they always had, and not to worry about her relatives as they would be dealt with by Social Services.

"You mean *you*," she asked the other two, surprised.

"Yes, "said Pope, "and if there's any trouble we get the Police here too. So you need not appear when they do show up. In fact it would be best if you didn't"

At last they were gone, though only as far as the dockside to await the Smiths. By this time all but one of the week's hires had left the marina and Poppy was the only one left to run through the boat with its hirers and to take them out for their tuition. I asked Maisie and Nat to stay in the boat and went to find Phil, who was wondering where every one of his family had vanished, and asked him to join the other two and make sure they didn't reappear on the quayside until it was all settled.

It took four hours for the errant relatives to return. By that time most of the crews who had travelled to the next locks with their hirers to instruct were back. They were in the office with Poppy for the usual de-brief when an approaching car was heard. The Social Services pair had been invited into the office too, out of courtesy, for tea and the never-ending cake. All knew the situation and guessed this was the end-game, so to speak.

Poppy, Nina, Frank and I bore down on the car. A nondescript looking, young member of staff happened to walk past as we stopped by it, and closed the Marina's main gates as we had arranged.

Mr Smith's face appeared at the driver's window. "We've come to fetch Maisie." This was addressed to me but it was Pope who answered.

"I am Frank Pope and this is Nina Rowley. We are the Social Services' case officers appointed for Maisie's well-being. Please will you stop the engine and both leave the car so that we may discuss the situation?"

"Just get the girl and stop messing about. We don't need Social Services."

I looked at Nina, who seemed the more senior of the two. She straightened up and smiled.

"I'm sure you don't want us, but from your attitude and from what we have heard from Maisie and from the hire company staff, you certainly need help. More importantly Maisie needs our help, as do her parents. We want this to happen without fuss but we need to hold a discussion with you both about her care and about her parents' required schooling arrangements which have apparently been ignored."

There was a renewed spate of swearing, which we all ignored. The group of us just stood by the side of the car. I learnt later that Maisie and Nat were listening at an opened, curtained window in the boat and were laughing at the words as they emerged. I asked them later how many they already knew. Nat went quiet: Maisie told me quite innocently that she had heard her aunt and uncle use them in front to her regularly.

After a while Smith lost patience.

"Oh, for fuck's sake..."

Without warning, he shot the car forward and made an attempt at a three-point turn. We all scattered so as not to be run over. The young lad who had closed the marina's gates snapped the lock shut and walked to the comparative safety of the water's edge near our boat where he was protected by some serious looking, ancient steel bollards. Frank Pope was already on the phone, calling the Police.

For the next ten minutes or so there was a lot of shouting and bad language from the car, all of which we ignored. Eventually sirens were heard and blue flashes were reflected from windows nearby. The gates were unlocked again and blue uniforms announced the beginning of the end of the Smiths' freedom.

We – Maisie, Nat and I – were able to persuade the two officials that we could look after Maisie for the night, or for the week until her parents' arrival. Their agreement came as a complete surprise to me as I thought they were more than fussy about who they took on as foster parents, even temporarily. We were on no lists, nor did we have any vetting or training. But it seemed that Nina was quite senior and had checked on us well before they came to pay us the visit. It was a source of comfort to me that no one had seen fit to flag us up as a potential problem family, despite the breakdown I had suffered or my brother's efforts to discredit me.

Nat and Maisie were still engrossed with a game of some sort when I reappeared, so I beckoned to Phil and we went outside.

"Are you sure you're happy with her staying with us for a week?" I asked him, knowing that he would be honest but that it had already been arranged.

"I'm just annoyed that my kid brother has pulled before I could," he said. The face was straight, but despite the changes that happen so quickly over puberty I could still detect the child-smile in his eyes.

"Twit," I said, with my usual come-down. "You know it can't be anything like that. They're the same age, she's in trouble and just like you he's a natural helper of people in distress."

"I just think he's just been on the pull," he persisted. This time the grin was open. "Has she got an older sister?"

"You didn't answer the question," I told him. "Are you happy with her staying with us?"

"Of course I am. I'd have to think harder if it was to be a more permanent thing, but a week is nothing."

"He's happy about it, I suppose?" I persisted, "Or haven't you had a chance to ask?"

"Happy? Looked like it just now, didn't it?"

"Phil, you know what I mean."

He grinned. "What do you think? Yeah, he's happy about it."

Thank goodness for grounded kids.

Poppy returned, knocked at the side of the boat and we told her it was all arranged. As it was late and we were tired I took all of them to the pub she had introduced us to. Over the meal we told Maisie the pattern of our life. Back at the marina, late, we sorted out bedding for Maisie in my cabin; I would be sleeping in the dinette so as to act as a sort of buffer between Maisie and the outside world.

Sleep came easily that night.

22 Parents

It turned out to be a weird week. Although there was work to do I found that I was constantly calling into the boat to make sure Maisie was ok. To start with she was happy reading, explaining that much of her time with the Smiths had been spent doing just that. Later, she came to watch what I was doing, or to talk shyly to some of the others as they worked. When someone mentioned helping to tidy and check one of the boats her eyes lit up and after that there was no stopping her. Poor lass; she had been deprived of the company of ordinary, decent people for so long that she found conversation to be a tonic.

Nat took possession of her when he returned, of course. He succeeded the first day, but after that she told him that she wanted to finish off her work on whatever boat it was she was working on. He gave in and came to help her. Maybe to hinder.

The next Saturday was an eye-opener for her, just as our first experience of change-over day had been. We'd told her what had to happen and immediately she asked if she could help. Poppy agreed, and put her with one of the teams of two. They would be doing the quick, thorough check of the boat, then its cleaning job, before the prep team came on board in the afternoon to redo beds, renew the other linens and put the finishing touches to the living spaces.

She came out of the last boat, tired but beaming happily, and was in time to see an anonymous car enter the marina. It disgorged two people and her eyes lit up.

"Mummy! Daddy!"

She rushed along the marina as if rehearsing for the final scene of *The Railway Children* to which, in its way, I suppose, it was the equivalent. There were soft Birmingham coos of "Awww..." from all around me, and I confess to feeling a lump form at the back of my own throat.

It was a long embrace, but soon Maisie was leading the doubtless bemused, smiling parents down to where we were watching them. They stopped and there was a brief, embarrassed pause before Maisie realised she needed to make some introductions.

Inge and Carl Parish were of a kind that I'd not encountered before. With their daughter they were normal, welcoming, loving people. With other people there was this all-but-hidden reserve. Maybe with my week's-worth of being *in loco parentis* I had developed a shell of protectiveness very quickly and was hypersensitive about Maisie's well-being. I felt as if I was being held at bay, very carefully, almost imperceptibly, by the parents. Maisie's reaction to everyone was much more human, and her parents included Nat in their smiles when Maisie had showed as only youngsters can that he was a real friend. The Parishes smiled at the antics she described and seemed to pay close attention to her describing her horror that I should have given up my cabin to her. "He said it was so that nobody could come past him to...to..." she faltered.

For once I received a look from both parents, almost simultaneously, that spoke louder than their previous, pleasantly correct, words had done. Was I being over sensitive, or was the next smile in my direction more honest?

"Under the circumstances," I said, "where a disastrous couple had been so dishonest and careless about a child, wouldn't you want to protect them against any possible attempt at recapture?"

Mr Parish smiled, a little thinly I thought. "One of those two is my step-brother."

Damn. I'd forgotten. But then, wasn't I the victim of a brother, a real brother who should have been on my side?

"What you don't know is that I too have a brother who is *persona non grata* as I imagine yours must be now," I told him. "All those years of brotherhood and trust went out of the window when mine engaged himself with my wife, and then tried to capture my sons and take them back to their old home – the place where he is now living with my wife. And this despite my sons having declared that they didn't trust him and that they wanted to live with me. So unfortunately I have experience of toxic brotherhood.

"Perhaps you'll understand now that if there is a possible danger to a child for whom I am responsible I will do everything in my power to protect them. As I have for my sons. As I was prepared to do for Maisie. It doesn't matter to me whether a possible danger comes from a friend or relation."

I think I must have been unconsciously using public meeting mode, as all the youngsters looked surprised. Maisie was the first to recover, gave a shy smile and came, for the first time, to offer me a hug.

"Thank you," she said, looking up. I smiled, and my irritation went off the boil. I hugged her back and looked up at the Parishes.

"Is it true what we have been told?" Inge asked, "Did my brother-in-law really take Maisie from school and try to home-school her?"

"You'd best ask Maisie herself about that. It's certainly what she told us and I'm sure she's not spinning a yarn."

"You said so just now, didn't you," Carl said to Maisie, "and I could scarcely believe it."

"Well..." I had been going to retort that all he had to do was to phone the school but I decided they were intelligent enough for that to be more than obvious. He nodded.

We had been so engrossed in the reunion and the nuances behind our first exchanges that none of us had noticed the arrival of the Social Services duo who were walking towards us. Introductions made, they confirmed that what Maisie had said about her schooling was true. The Smiths were now formally "under investigation" with the Police for fraud and attempted assault with a car – or some such. The information floored the Parish parents. Given their guessed-at background, not knowing what to say was a new experience for them. Inge hugged her daughter again, so perhaps that was the only comment necessary.

We retired to the office for the inevitable cup of coffee and cake. Again the Parishes were surprised at seeing so many welcoming faces, and hearing so many guileless comments about how lovely a girl Maisie was. "And she doesn't shirk at getting her hands dirty, or anything," said one deep Birmingham accent. A look of surprise crossed the parents' faces, but no censure was offered. Maisie was, after all, looking radiantly happy and at ease with all these people.

Gradually the temporary and the few permanent staff started drifting home after their long day. Discussions had been taking place between the Parishes with Nina and Frank, papers were completed, examined and signed, and the latter two left.

"I suppose you'll be taking Maisie home now," Poppy made the comment that the boys and I had been avoiding, and that Maisie was also not willing to ask.

"Not home," Inge sighed. "That will be a long way off. At the moment home is a hotel, and is likely to be for a while until we have decided what best to do." She hesitated and looked at her husband.

The attitudes had changed radically over the last hour. They had been persuaded by all that had happened that these people were genuine, that the boys and I were genuine, and that we were normal and could be trusted.

He smiled. "I'm sorry we had to start off by being – well, a little distant. A bit cautious. We have to be very careful what we say and do. When we were first contacted by – by our employers about our daughter's safety we naturally reacted with horror. We had to look yet again at how we've lived our lives and what our priorities should be. Given what's happened and with the confirmation that you, Maisie and Social Services have given us we've decided that we need to – well, to adjust. To start living a normal life and be with Maisie as proper parents at last."

He looked at his wife, who smiled back. "Yes, enough is enough," she said quietly, mainly to Maisie, "and really we should have done this before."

She looked at the rest of us. "In our case adjusting means all sorts of practical changes, not the least being that we have to find somewhere to live. And quickly."

"Does that mean you're going to live in England?" Maisie asked, a glint of hope in her eye.

"No," Carl said with a smile, "it means that *we're* going to live in England. It means that your Dad is going to be an ordinary Dad like Mr Dyer, and your Mother will be a real mother. And we'll all live together. No more boarding school, unless you want to, and proper friends who can come round at any time."

He looked at Nat, then at Phil who had just joined us and was trying to catch up. Nat grinned; Phil looked non-committal. He had had far less to do with Maisie than Nat, unsurprisingly as he was two years older.

Maisie spoke for the first time since hearing all the news. "Can I come here and help on Saturday mornings, please? I've had such fun today."

Once again they appeared floored. Inge sighed. "We need to think of the security risks, darling. But if we can get over that hurdle, then yes, I don't see why not. And there may be times when we need to take you shopping, don't forget."

"But that can happen on Sundays," she retorted hopefully.

"I think," said Carl, changing the subject, "that we need to take all the Dyers and... and Poppy? Have I got the name right?"

Poppy confirmed it.

"We need to take you out to say thank you for looking after Maisie so well until we could get here." The girl smiled widely.

"Well... really there's no need." There wasn't. My hesitation was because we were due to go out for our usual post-Saturday-changeover meal.

"I think there is," Carl said, "and unless anyone tells me not to in the next five seconds I'm going to book a table for seven at the hotel we're staying at."

There was a precise five second gap and he pulled a mobile from his pocket. A table for seven was booked, as he had threatened, and a room number given.

"We only have a five seater car," he announced, "so perhaps if we take Maisie and Nat – if that's all right, Mr Dyer?"

"Jack," I announced, "and if it's all right with Nat it's all right with me."

"Thanks, Jack; and we're Inge and Carl. Are you happy to take Poppy and Phil?"

"Of course," I said. "But where are we going?"

"Oh, silly of me. To our hotel. We're staying at the Grand."

To the boys, this meant nothing. To Poppy and me it meant five well-earned stars, visits from many local-ish celebrities, and exceptionally high prices.

"Oh now, look…" I started.

Carl held up his hand. "We're being accommodated by our employers. You've probably learnt enough about our situation to realise that our employers are the British Government, so effectively your income tax is paying for it, if you stretch your imagination a bit. But what you have all done for us means that we want to and we shall entertain you tonight. If that means an overnight stay because it gets late, so well and good. You are our guests, and that is the least we can do to thank you."

Poppy and I were almost open mouthed – fortunately only figuratively – at the idea of a meal at a five-star hotel, let alone the prospect of staying there overnight. For Phil it would be something to crow about to his friends on Monday, no doubt. To Nat it was a matter of surprise but little else. Neither of them had much of an idea about the hotel rating system, but we were all about to discover more.

The Saturday's efforts were all done. Only we seven were still at the Marina. The Parishes came on board our boat to collect Maisie's belongings, both frowning when they saw how poorly she had been dressed. "They took most of my other clothes back when they left the boat," she said. "But there wasn't much. Jack bought me a few things to tide me over." They said nothing, but I could see the anger in their expressions.

The boat intrigued them. The second toilet, still making its point in the last cabin-to-be, made them laugh. I explained the situation and explained that the furniture was being designed and made by our two Anglo-Italian carpenters. "And by Nat," I said with some pride, "although he's not been to see them this last week. He's had other things on his mind."

For the first time I saw my younger son's face turn red. Maisie was nearby and was the only one to notice, and she quietly slipped an arm round his shoulders, an arm he didn't shrug off. My brain made a swift recalculation: he was nearly thirteen. I remembered some of the sudden, visceral attractions I'd suffered at about that age. This, at least, was to someone his own age and not the young, attractive and far too old Year Elevens and teachers who had formed my mental wallpaper.

"Had we better change?" I said, conscious that despite my best efforts with Swarfega my nails were still darkly decorated, and the boys were in old, over-worn clothes.

Carl hesitated. "Hotels aren't as regimented as they once were, but maybe 'smart casual' would avoid any ruffling of feathers. We've only just arrived in the city so haven't tested the water, but nowadays I think they're just pleased to get trade."

I smiled. "No shorts and T-shirts, then."

Maisie looked uncertain. "What should I wear?" she asked.

"We'll sort that out on the way there," Inge told her. "In fact, if we left now we could find something in a shop for you, then book in and see our rooms. Would you mind, Jack? And Nat, of course?"

"We'll see you there in about an hour," I told them. "Nat, you need to get some school type stuff, I suppose, and perhaps you could shower and change at the hotel."

They left. It was odd seeing Nat go off with them, but I reminded myself again that he *was* almost thirteen…

"He'll be sharing a room with her," the irreverent, maybe jealous, Phil said as soon as they were out of earshot. "I wonder if they'll be showering together?"

"Phil! Shut up and have a shower yourself. And be quick. None of your usual thirty minute voyages of exploration."

It was his turn for a red face, which he probably didn't think I noticed. Serves him right for his own comment.

We met up with Poppy outside. A very attractively dressed Poppy who looked elegant in a simple dress with a belt and a loosely tied scarf. I'd never seen her except in jeans and some sort of top before, so this apparition made me blink in surprise and to smile at her.

"You look fantastic." They were the first words that came to mind and I realised with a shock that the comment might not be welcomed.

But she smiled and quietly said "Thank you." Then, looking behind me: "It's not that much of a surprise is it, Phil?"

I turned too. He was just standing and staring, and I could almost see the "Wow" thought bubble over his head."

"Phil!" I called, torn between wanting to stop him being rude to Poppy and not wanting to bawl him out in front of someone else.

He shook his head and was gracious enough to apologise. "It's just that – well, Dad's right. You really do look awesome."

That increased her smile. "Then thank you, too," she said. "And you don't look too shabby yourselves. No, that's wrong. You both look ready for a five-star hotel and I'm proud to accompany you both."

We must all have been presentable, since on arrival the car doors were opened by a concierge who smiled, before another of them drove the car away to be parked, somewhat to my alarm. Inside we met more smiles, no sniffy expressions, and were shown up to the Parishes' rooms as they had arranged. Maisie looked so different we wondered if she was the same girl. Even Phil was taken aback. Nat looked smart – surely someone had pressed his trousers so that, for once, they were uncreased apart from where they were meant to be?

That evening was an experience. It was just so different from any hotel the boys and I had ever been in, but there was none of the stuffiness that top-notch hotels are accused of by those without experience of them. Yet everything was quietly efficient without being embarrassingly servile or over-attentive. We found we were enjoying the company as well as the food; even Phil of the hollow legs was at last seen to be happily replete.

Though the Parishes had checked that rooms would be available we had decided not to stay overnight. It just seemed too much generosity to accept. Very late, when all three youngsters were seen yawning, we took our leave – after ensuring that we would keep in touch, of course. Indeed, Maisie and Nat, even if only just approaching their thirteenth birthdays, would have been most upset had there not been the promise of visits to each other.

Without ceremony I rushed Phil and Nat off to their beds as soon as we arrived in the marina; I'd left Poppy at her front door. It took me a few minutes to realise I no longer had to adapt the dinette to sleep in and thankfully regained my own cabin. That was all I was conscious of, until the disgraceful hour of ten-thirty the following morning. For once Nat was following the same student hours as his brother: all was silent. For reasons connected with the previous night the idea of breakfast held no interest for me. I hoped the other two wouldn't be clamouring for it like two reproachful fledglings.

When I next looked at a clock it was eleven and I felt as if I could just stretch and carry on mouldering there as I had at university all those years previously. When eventually there were sounds of movement I decided that I'd better show willing and started the waking up process properly.

It was raining and dismal. We read books most of the day, despite it being summer.

"Huh," said Phil when reminded. Nat was deep in a book and probably hadn't heard us.

"Last two weeks of school," I reminded them later that evening.

"Poppy's not been round," Phil mentioned as a complete *non sequitur*. He was right. She hadn't. It was odd. We seemed to have been with her just about every day since we claimed asylum – my term, coined as a result of my mental issues – with her.

Phil retired to his cabin and was back ten minutes later. "She's not well," he said.

My eyebrows shot skywards. "You *phoned* her?"

“No, I sent a pigeon. Of course I did. I told her you were here and pining for her.”

Had my eyebrows been capable of further ascension, they would probably have done me some harm. “Phil, I hope you didn’t.”

The voice was, for a change, entirely serious, and Phil knew the tone, as did Nat. Phil had the grace to look serious too. “No, I didn’t. But your reaction tells me that she means a bit more to you than just being your boss.”

Blast the boy. Damn and blast the sudden perspicacity of the young family member. The search through my memory for giveaway signs came up with nothing.

“You have no idea what you’re talking about. And I’d be glad if you didn’t assume. You know what I’ve told you about that, and there’s a defining line between assumption and deduction.”

“He doth protest too much, methinks” Phil said, pushing his luck. Damn Hamlet and GCSEs. I looked unblinkingly at him, a look which in the past had never failed to quell. It didn’t this time either.

“Oops,” he said with a hastily suppressed smile. “But she’s not well. Says she ate too much last night and had indigestion, and has felt under the weather all day.”

“Anything else?” I asked, keen to give nothing away.

“She’s better now, and thinks she can face cooking.”

“I hope you told her that she’s welcome here and that you’re going to cook for her.”

Finally his expression seemed to be on the verge of contrition. “Should I have?”

“Of course. You’re asking after her health, not me. And when she mentions facing the cooking of a meal, a gentleman offers help of some sort. You’re the knight in shining armour. Phone her back, then cook.”

“What?”

“Ask her, not me.”

“I mean, what have we got?”

“I don’t think the kitchen cupboards are locked.”

“You’re no help.”

“You dug the hole. It’s up to you to get out of it.”

The lowest common denominator of Phil’s cooking ability and our supplies was the simple omelette. With additions. He called Poppy back, this time with me – and possibly Nat – listening, though the book in which Nat’s nose was buried never wavered.

Actually, it seems, he had rescued her and our evening. Except that my omelette was burnt.

23 Emerson

Nat received a summons on Monday after school to the Losardo brothers' carpentry workshop. He was gone some time and at nine o'clock I was starting to worry when he reappeared. Criticisms were about to be made when his smug expression opened into an outright, pleased smile.

"It's tomorrow," he said.

"What?"

"They're coming round to build … things."

"Good. Do I get to know what 'things' these are?"

"No. Secret until tomorrow when they're built."

Tomorrow came bringing, in order, the boys back from school, a large van, the Losardos and what looked like wood panels, and Birmingham's best quality summer rain. Nat was hopping from one foot to the other, waiting for a chance to help, and soon the three of them vanished into the boat and started. Phil and I left them to it for a while until the marina's closing time, then cautiously entered the boat.

There were some noises off, so to speak, including some cursing in two low voices and one higher one. During a lull I knocked at the door, opened it and revealed a scene of apparent devastation which started just past my own cabin.

A door closed to hide it, and Nat appeared, dusty and with a scratch to his face.

"Hallo, Dad," he said innocently.

"What do we do about food?" I asked, ignoring the pleasantries.

"I'll ask," he said, and dodged back behind the closed door. It reopened a moment later.

"They've brought sandwiches. They say they'll eat them as they go, but tea would be very welcome."

"And are you joining them with sandwiches?"

He assumed a shocked expression. "Well, I *could...*"

"But you'd rather not. Shall I call you when it's ready? Or would you prefer a plaster on that cut first?"

"What cut?"

"On your face."

"Oh – is it bleeding? No, it's ok. Give me a call, would you?" He was gone before I could protest.

He appeared about five minutes after the second announcement that food was ready, and sat down still looking smug. And dirty.

"Unless you really want to practise being a louse and eating wood, I suggest a wash of face and hands first, please."

He didn't argue, but went to the kitchen sink, doubtless depositing his washing water into the pans stacked there.

We had completed the washing up and Phil was doing homework by the time the door opened again and he reappeared, once again looking grubby and this time with the red mark of a potential bruise to accompany the cut.

"Ok, you can come down now," he announced, unbearably smugly. We went, leaving footprints in a layer of sawdust.

The bunks had been stripped out of the boys' cabin. In their place against the opposite bulkhead was a very comfortable looking bed, already complete with mattress. Against the nearer bulkhead was a folded-up panel with what looked like upholstery inside it.

"Now watch," he said in triumph. The bar on the futon was pulled, as before. The bed deck developed a hinge and pulled up to form a seat back with the lowest part rolling back and up to form the seat itself. Nat went to tread on a panel in the floor. It magically rose about fifty centimetres, then was lifted into position and pushed into the wall, apparently thereby securing it. Supporting legs had unfolded from underneath as it rose. He sat on the bench and put his weight on the table which seemed as solid as a rock.

"Now let that seat down," he said. Phil, nearest to it, did so. Again, legs, connected by a bar, swung out to slot into the floor to support it.

"That's really clever," I said, and I wasn't joking. Phil looked pleased too and agreed, I think wondering how much of this was the brothers' design and how much was *his* brother's.

"I think it's ace," Nat said. "This is yours, Phil."

That brought a smile to his face. "Why mine?" he asked.

"Mine's not ready yet, so I've got a mattress on the floor. But we've got the other toilet ready now. Come and see."

Seppe and Ifor were standing, grinning by the tiny bathroom's open door. It took me a moment before I realised that the presence of a door was new, along with the bulkhead it hung from. I looked in. For the first time the very public toilet pedestal was no longer public, and sported a tiny washbasin and storage unit, splashback and mirror, and a tiny cupboard above it.

"It looks fantastic," I told them all. "Is it Nat-at-twelve size or Dad-at-45 size?"

"It's just about Seppe size," said Seppe with a grin. "Perfectly useable, though I haven't."

"You can't use the basin yet, Dad, because the plumbing has to go through the hull." Nat turned on the tap. Nothing happened.

"None of the plumbing's been done yet," Ifor told me. "But we can get on with that tomorrow unless Nat instructs us to finish his cabin first."

"I hope Nat isn't instructing anyone," I said. "I hope he's asking."

"He's given us a lot of ideas," Seppe said with an indulgent smile. "And we've looked at every one of them. Quite a lot of the design of the table mechanism is his. All we had to do was the measuring and the calculations of the weights and forces."

I suppose Nat was right to look smug. He had shown some of his inventiveness when we had first looked at designs, and I was pleased he'd been able to see some of those ideas come to life. By the look of his grin, so was he.

They did indeed finish the bathroom from early the following day, and continued with Nat's room so he would get a surprise on his return from school. There remained a serviceable lounge space whose arrangements I decided to leave until we'd all had a better chance to think.

Nat and Phil looked pleased when I found them later. Phil was in full flow with homework on his new desk and tried to look impatient at being interrupted, but I could tell how pleased he was with it.

"Why have you swapped with Nat?" I asked. "Have you agreed it with him?"

"Of course. I just wanted… wanted a bit more privacy." The sort of privacy that also required thirty minute showers, I thought.

"It needs a phone and one of those Newton's Cradle things with swinging balls to make it look really good," he muttered.

"Try your pockets," I said, thinking of the phone. His completely astonished look took me by surprise and I thought back to what I'd just said before bursting out into laughter. Fortunately he joined me.

"Dad!"

"It was an entirely innocent comment until you looked so surprised at it. Then I had to think."

"You're not meant to… I mean… *well!*"

"You forget that I too have been fourteen and male," I said carefully. "You may think that you're the only one, but I was there first."

"You mean…?"

"What do you think?"

There was a knocking on the boat. Nat was in the galley and must have answered it, as there were voices. I went to see, and to my surprise found Inge, Maisie and Carl there looking very serious. Nat's smile glowed when he saw Maisie, but quickly vanished when he saw how upset she was.

"What's happened?" I asked.

"We can't say too much," Carl started, "but investigators have followed a terrorist cell to us and have told us to vanish until they've discovered what's been happening. We called a taxi to escape from the hotel, and then wondered where we *should* go, and if it would be safe for Maisie. To cut a long discussion short, we wondered if here would be a good place for Maisie, if you would take her on again? We can look after ourselves."

I thought for all of a second. "Of course she can stay. In fact you all could. We've got room now that they've finished off the cabins."

His face almost cracked into a smile. "I really appreciate that, more than you can know. But for Maisie's safety we need her to be separate from us for a time – a very short time – until at least the people concerned are behind bars. We're probably going to be in a small guest house somewhere, then a rented cottage if we can find one quickly."

It sounded like the stuff of nightmares, of a film plot. Maisie was looking alternately proud and scared. I noticed that Nat had reached for her hand and that once again she had allowed it.

"How long do you think it will be?" I asked. "Not that Maisie isn't welcome

– she is. Very. But it'd be good to know when she can stop worrying. When we can stop worrying on her behalf. And..." This had only just occurred to me. I swallowed. "... are my family at any risk?"

Inge grimaced. "Until we know more about what's been happening, who has seen and said what, we just don't know. That will be one of the first things that we hope that the investigation will discover. In the meantime I suggest you just go about as normal, but if you see anything amiss like the same stranger cropping up more than twice, for example, I'd like you to call a number and give information, then do as you're asked for as long as you're asked."

A silence fell, and it lasted a long time. All of us were now thinking hard.

Carl was the first to speak. "I hate the idea that we have unwittingly brought this on you. Neither we nor... nor the people we've been working for had any idea that this cell was in existence until one of its members was careless. Then the... our employers moved fast, but not before this target was able to track us down. And all that happened in spite of all the efforts everyone had used to keep us from being noticed. The whole reason we were sent to the Grand was to throw anyone off the scent. It seemed to them to be a better bet than one of the usual miscellaneous safe houses where a target might expect us to be. Our lot are as angry as we are that it didn't work, especially as a five-star hotel is such an unusual place to be sent. We – and they – regarded it as entirely safe to be normal and to invite people to join us there. I'm just sorry we didn't go to a normal pub for a meal and not involve you at all.

"In a way, so do I," I confirmed grimly. "We didn't have any idea of the danger we were being put into. If we had, we'd just have said our farewells and got on with life."

"I realise that," Carl sighed. "I really do; and I'm more sorry than I can say. It's entirely unforeseen."

There was another silence.

"At least you won't have to move rooms again, Dad," Phil said. "I'll use the mattress in the front and Maisie can have my cabin." He had broken the bubble of concern. We started talking contact methods and the practicalities.

"Was the taxi you used secure?" I asked Inge quietly, thinking about the spy novels I'd read where a taxi is waiting for their particular target.

"We used a hire company known to... to our employers," she answered equally quietly, "and told them to come to the hotel's garage which one of the concierges had scanned for us first. It's as safe as it can be. And we made sure no one followed it, and that no one was around here when we arrived."

"How are you leaving?"

"We'll ask the same company," she said. "They're used to this sort of thing."

Were they indeed! A good company to know, no doubt. I wondered who vetted their drivers.

We were again in deep conversation when there was another knock at the side of the boat. There was immediate silence. Phil, sitting nearest the connecting door, beckoned all three of the Parishes down to the cabin spaces. Once they had vanished I opened up the main door which Carl had closed behind on their arrival.

Poppy.

The tingle of anxiety that had taken my whole body subsided. I sagged. Poppy's eyes opened wider. "What's the matter?"

Wordlessly I made room for her, closing the hatch and door again and causing her to look even more concerned. The Parishes had heard Poppy being greeted, and returned to the dinette.

We explained the situation to her. Quite naturally she was horrified. "It's like a spy novel," she said, "But now the danger is real. Could be real. Is it any help if you stayed with me? I'm just at the end of the approach road here. You'd be very welcome and I have room."

Inge and Carl explained once again that they needed to be more remote from Maisie, whilst still near enough to grab her and go if the need arose. "It's very kind of you," Inge said, "but we have to take directions from our employers. They will make arrangements for us, but living here on the boat would be wonderful for Maisie as it's a gated community and so far as we know it's not known about."

"When will you be told where you're going to be?" she asked.

"We don't even know that," she replied. "They will phone us when arrangements have been made. It could be any time."

"You can stay here until they phone," I told them.

"And if they don't phone by whatever time, well, you can stay a night at mine." Poppy again.

Phil and I made teas and coffees. Up at the end of the galley area he looked at me and spoke quietly. "Are we really in any danger, do you think? Is it as bad as they say?"

"It's one of those situations where neither you nor I have any experience, Phil. The books you read are fiction, and who knows how true to life they are? We have no way of knowing, not really."

What more could I tell him? It was indeed all foreign territory to us. And that prompted a question for the Parishes.

"Excuse me, but are you able to tell us what country is involved in all this? Is there a particular nationality we should be wary of? Or is there any clue where the danger might come from?"

Inge and Carl looked at each other. I noticed a brief raising of eyebrows.

"No," Carl said. "That's one of the problems. We would be very wrong to mention any nationality. What… what we've been involved in goes across borders so it wouldn't help. All I can say is that the cells in Britain are few, small and isolated. It's unknown how they have learnt about our return here. To look out for any particular nationality wouldn't be helpful in protecting any of us."

'Any of us'… those three words put us all on the same level as the Parishes and brought it home that we were all apparently at risk. It increased the level of alarm I felt.

"So what do we do?" I asked, thinking it was a rhetorical question.

"Carry on as normal, as I said. Go to work; go to school. Be aware of any new people who want to come into your lives. We shall be on an encrypted email and will give you all the address. We'll also send you a software patch for your phones and laptops that'll encrypt any message you send to us and permanently delete it after sending. That will protect you all. In fact I'll do that now."

Silence reigned as he got busy, then was broken by a series of chimes and other noises from every device we had on board. It was nearly amusing and prompted a general smile.

"The first thing you do when you want to message us is to use your normal email, type the address I'll give you in a minute, then add another word after the address: *Emerson*. That name won't appear on the screen at all. If you don't use it we'll know it's not you and we shouldn't trust it, but we'll get people to where you are who will… help."

This was real spy story stuff and I could see the boys' mood was lightening at the thought of using it.

"Do we have to use it to contact Maisie, too?" Nat asked. I should have realised that the two would have swapped addresses before. Inge and Carl exchanged glances.

"Best not to message each other for the moment, please, though it's a very remote chance that either of you are on their radar. Maisie now has the means to contact us, so we can pass on anything securely, if needed."

"Does that mean phoning too?" Nat asked plaintively.

"Yes. But you'll see each other each afternoon, don't forget."

The conversation became more general. Nat went to show Maisie how his and Phil's cabins worked and eventually we heard laughter from the front of the boat. It was perhaps half an hour later that Inge's phone coughed politely. She answered it and asked if she could use my cabin to talk. With two doors between her and us, and hopefully similar soundproofing between her and the younger ones, the conversation was private.

She returned and looked at her husband.

"We have an address. They said that a car would collect us but – well, something occurred to me about how we were discovered. Let's just say that I think we'd be better off in an ordinary taxi."

Carl returned her look, eyes wide.

"Or I could take you," I offered.

"If we were seen, that would trace you back to here as well as to us. What you could do is… no. More secure than asking you... Poppy: please could you use your land line to book a taxi for us? We'll catch it near the main road."

"I'll use the office line. That's used a lot at all times of the day and night. And I'll use the taxi company we always use for customers."

Carl nodded. "Good. Thank you."

She and I went to the office, carefully looking round to ensure that there was no one else around – no one who shouldn't have been there. The only person we saw was Ian on his boat, filling his water tank. We exchanged waves.

Poppy made the call and was promised a taxi on Lodge Road thirty minutes later. They knew her well enough to accept that even if she was unable to give a destination apart from the city centre.

Back at the boat leisurely farewells were said and, with Poppy and Maisie, they walked up the path to the road to be let through its gate onto the road to coincide with the half hour specified for the taxi. Apparently Poppy was to emerge from the gate alone whilst the others waited out of sight. The taxi came, Poppy crossed to make sure she recognised the driver, hugs were exchanged behind the gate, and the Parish parents were on their way.

It was only half an hour later that a message came through on Maisie's email, with *Emerson* in the subject, to say they had arrived and were safe. No further details, unsurprisingly.

Monday… back to the real life of work and school. I had an engine service to tackle. My mind was wandering over the events of the weekend and how much, if at all, any of us was in danger from these unspecified people.

To change the oil in a canal boat engine, you have to pump the old oil out. Getting a container under its sump to drain it as you do with a car or one of Crown's engines is out of the question – there is zero clearance below it. What you're meant to do is to arrange a container by the pump outlet to collect the waste oil as you operate the pump. So intent was I on our problems that I omitted the basic step of placing a container there, and pumped vigorously whilst looking around the Marina. The oil spread itself over my trouser leg and foot before joining the water in the bilge.

The bilge pump empties fluid in the bilge into the canal when it reaches a certain level.

When sanity kicked back in, I hurriedly tugged at the bilge pump's connection so that it didn't start automatically pumping and so pollute the marina. All I could do was to stand on the engine mounts, dripping oil and cursing, wondering what to do next.

By the time I'd rigged up a pump and a container, cleared the bilge, cleaned everything, wiped up the oily footprints after stopping anyone else from treading in them and spreading the misery (or slipping off the boat into the water) I had wasted an hour. And I still had an engine that was now low on oil. I stood astride the engine, ready to start again. Poppy and Ian were visiting a supplier, Maisie was helping Helena on one of the other boats. Angela, one of our Saturday staff, had been called in, with toddler, to man the phone.

Four men walked in from the approach road. They paused, looking at the boats, from ours near the entrance along to the remaining hire fleet side by side and parallel with the quay, and at the few residential boats opposite. It was so unusual that even had I not had a raised awareness of danger I should have been concerned.

At the time I was still waist deep in the engine bay, making ready with the pump again and, this time, an old oil drum. I was filthy, and probably only my head would have been visible above the boat's hull. The four sauntered down to the office, which has a sign advertising itself as Reception. By this time my phone was in my hand and I was emailing Inge and Carl's address, plus *Emerson*, with the details.

That done I looked around again and there was no sign of anyone; presumably they were all in the office. I hauled myself from the engine bay and carefully found my way to where Maisie and Helena were deep cleaning a boat.

"Maisie, there are four strangers who have gone into the office. Something doesn't look right so I've emailed mum and dad. If anyone calls, stay here. Helena, if they do, you come out and you tell anyone you've been cleaning the boat. If they ask, you've been working on your own. Maisie – if anyone else gets on the boat, hide. Stay there until you hear one of us call *Emerson.*"

Wide eyed, she nodded. "Where do I hide?"

Helena is one of the level headed ones. "Down the front there's the bedding storage. Get in there – it's cramped because the spare bedding's there – and make sure the cushions fall back into place on the lid. No one will know."

I emerged from the boat, to find the four men plus our phone handler and her small daughter looking straight at me. Unhurriedly, because I wanted to play for time and because my boots were still inclined to be slippery from the oil, I crossed over the backs of the boats to the one whose engine I had been working on, then climbed down into the bilge again as if nothing had happened. I even started pumping out the oil again.

There was a lurch as someone climbed onto the boat next to it. I looked up, hoping my expression didn't betray my jangling nerves. A man appeared, looking entirely normal.

"Mr Parish." He said. It was a statement, not a question. Fortunately there was a hint of doubt in the voice.

"Never 'eard of 'im."

I had lived very close to Dudley as a child and teenager, and knew enough of its people to be able to take on board the local accent as it had been spoken back then. I could pass as proper Dudley when I wanted to. It's useful, because if you have any of the older Dudley generation talking together, conversation can be incomprehensible to anyone from outside the Midlands. I had used it as a trick before when two of us as young teenagers had been grilled by people we didn't like.

My response to the man's question was in an accent which was as deep Dudley as I could manage. It took him a moment to realise even what those four words meant.

"He visited here on Saturday afternoon. Maybe afterwards. Have you seen a stranger?"

"Wouldn't notice on a Saturday," drawled my Dudley self. "We're all hare-arsing about, fettling the boats, like."

This time it took him longer. Ahh… the power of dialect.

"But you must have done. Him and his wife, and a little girl."

"I don't deal with the hirers. That's a Poppy job."

"A what?"

"A Poppy job. The boss's job."

"Ah. But they wouldn't be hirers. Visitors."

I just shrugged, said "Haven't seen them," and carried on pumping the oil. He watched, irritated, possibly wondering what to say. There was a shout from the shore. He called back.

"He says he's not seen them. He says he's too busy on Saturdays to notice. Obviously he's not him, and he can't be one of the people who were at the hotel."

"Go to that other boat," came the call from the shore, "the one he walked back from. They're probably on that."

I had finished pumping the oil. What he didn't see whilst he was watching his partner on shore was that I'd used some of it on a horribly oily rag to grease the top of the gunwale between him and the next boats either side of me. He would have to step on each of them to be able to get across the open engine bay and pass over my head.

He looked back. "Which boat were you on?"

Damn. Now what?

"The one Helena's on." With the long, very specific vowels of any variant of Birmingham patois this must take some unravelling by a stranger so the "What?" I heard next hardly surprised me.

"What boat?" he repeated.

"Didn't see a name. It's the boat Helena's cleaning."

"What – over there?" He pointed over my head.

"One of them. But you'll never get across here."

"You underestimate me."

Before I could explain what I meant in my best Dudley-ese he had balanced a foot on my gunwale's oil patch and planted the other one beside it. His next step would have been on the stern gunwale had not his left foot slipped. There was a cry and he fell backwards, hitting his back and head on the side of the boat he'd just left, then collapsing in a heap in the water.

There was a shout from the shore. An arm extended in my direction and, fearing the worst, I crouched down into the boat. There was a pop, the sound I recognised from films as being a silenced gun being fired, and an immediate clang from the bulkhead of the boat. Something fell into the water.

24 Aftermath

I had never been shot at before, nor have I been shot at since. I'm not a hero, even when there might be an unconscious person drowning in the water next to me – not when my own life is in danger. I stayed crouched in that bilge, hoping that something would happen before the man rushed to fire another shot at me from nearer. To my mounting horror footsteps were approaching, climbing from boat to boat from the quayside towards me. I tried to gauge how far they had reached; I tried to think what I could do to save my own life. It seemed inevitable that I was in danger and, incarcerated in an engine bay, unable to escape quickly enough.

I also heard a car engine at speed, the squeal of a skid. There was a shout.

Then to my horror there were two more shots, followed by a cry and a splash that was so close that water reached the bilge were I was. More shouting followed, including "Get on the ground! Now!" in the commanding, slightly panicking tone that you hear in Police dramas and on bodycam footage that's played on the news.

There were no more sounds apart from talk at more normal volume from the land. I raised my head up. A figure saw me, crouched and extended an arm, then saw my oiled up state and, no doubt, my complexion under the oil on a shocked, scared face.

In the hope that I was right and that these were security men, I called out that there was also one in the water who had hit his head. There was considerable relief that surged up me when the call was almost casually returned by an unconcerned "Ok," One of them came over and looked down to the water.

"Hard, these boats, aren't they?" he asked.

My response didn't engage in casual conversation about metallurgy but it did tell him not to use my boat as a step as there was oil on it.

"Thanks." Then a call to the bank. "Get the woman and girl in the office and tell them to stay there while we fish these two out." Then to me: "Is there a boat hook anywhere?"

"On the roof of that boat," I said, pointing to the one he was on.

He looked, climbed on the side to retrieve it and returned to the stern, near me, then fished down for the man who had fallen on the oil. I looked to where he was aiming, to where the man was floating. Now I could see the damage to the skull. I could also see the grey-white matter visible underneath it. It had started seeping into the marina's dirty water. I retched, and not just the once, jettisoning my breakfast over the boat's stern. I subsided into the bilge again and sat on the engine in shock. Even in that condition it came to mind that I was thankful to have vomited into the canal, not the boat, so saving having to embark on an even more horrible pump-out.

About fifteen minutes later the same man came back to replace the boathook and looked over at me. "Are you all right?"

"No," I said, thankfully reverting back to my normal speech mode. "I feel dreadful."

"Not a pleasant sight. I'm pleased he fell in before he got a chance to take a shot at you. Fortunate for you, if not for him. Unfortunate for the other one who we had to stop in his tracks before he shot you. We've covered them up now, so it's safe, though their friends are still handcuffed and ready to be removed. So maybe if they don't see you it would be safer, just in case. We're just waiting for the Police who now have to be involved, unfortunately. Once the others are out of the way we can get you out. Where's Maisie?"

Once you know you are meant to mistrust strangers it's quite difficult to engage normal trust again. I thought, hard.

"Who contacted you?" I asked, ignoring the question.

"Mr and Mrs Parish. Where's Maisie? Is she safe?"

That was better. Still feeling ill I managed to stick to my guns.

"What's the word in the email subject?"

He looked at me and laughed shortly, then nodded. "Well done. You know what you're about. '*Emerson.*'"

I nodded, suddenly deflated, relieved.

"She's in one of the boats up there with one of the cleaners. I think she'll be in hiding. She won't come out without my voice and the safe word."

This time there was a look of surprised respect in the face that was still watching me like a hawk.

"Do you feel like going to reassure her? And the others in the boats over there who are looking a bit worried? We've got the main four, and we know that's all there are apart from a couple of underlings, a driver and another one, but they'll find life unpleasant very soon. So if Maisie stays out of sight until the two on the quay have gone, she's safe. Don't forget that there's oil on the gunwales."

This was when I was hauling myself to my feet and starting to climb out of my place of safety. I looked at him with a sudden thankful smile and very carefully cleaned off the shiny surface I was about to walk on.

Helena looked at me cautiously as I appeared on the boat. "It's all right, Helena," I said, now weary. "It'll be all over when the two they've handcuffed have been removed. Is Maisie all right?"

"She's hiding, like you said."

I nodded, then looked up at the owners of the residential boats opposite. "It's all over," I called. "I imagine Poppy will tell you what's happened as soon as she can."

They had no time to respond as Helena and I walked through the boat to the front cabin. As I approached I called. "Maisie. *Emerson. Emerson.*"

A muffled exclamation and the lid of the storage under the bunk lifted a little. "Thank goodness. It's horrible in here. Have they gone?"

"Yes." I lifted the lid and Helena helped the cramped girl from the cocoon of duvets and pillows. "They've…gone. Two are waiting to be taken away as soon as the Police arrive."

"How many were there?"

"Four."

"Where are the others?"

I hesitated. "It's a long story."

"They're dead, aren't they?"

I couldn't lie. Helena's hand came up to cover her mouth. Maisie just nodded.

"I'm glad they're getting out of it. Mum and Dad."

"So am I," I said fervently. "So am I."

"I'll be back for you as soon as the coast's clear. Helena, could you stay with her, please?"

With some caution I returned to my engine and looked at the quayside. Two bundles were lying, dripping and covered, by the water's edge. Two more figures were sitting, facing the wall, by the old store where we still kept our spares. At their back was a motionless figure. I saw no reason to show myself should they turn, so carried on replacing the oil in the engine. The smell of the new oil, so familiar to me in each of my occupations since college, reassured me, made me feel better.

With the engine full, and checked, I decided to start it. Mainly this was the usual check so I could listen to it running, but this time I wanted to turn the propeller and disperse what my horror had caused me to deposit into the still water. It worked. And the engine sounded normal. A quick check of the coolant and I climbed out to replace the boards over the engine. Immediately there was comparative quiet. The gunwales received another good scrubbing to remove the remainder of my hastily concocted trap which had proved so disastrously effective.

On the quay a Police van had appeared, together with two smart looking cars, one marked and one not. Of the two sitting on the quay there was no sign. Presumably they were in the van.

I collected Maisie and Helena and went to join the officials and face the music.

"I'm glad it wasn't a Saturday." Poppy's first words struck me with a blow. What on earth could have happened in the controlled chaos that Saturdays brought, and which could only become busier once schools had actually broken up. My mind rebelled at the idea. Too much chaos.

We had explained why there were Police and unmarked people around on what should have been the quietest day of the week and she was appalled, quite naturally. I found her looking at me in an odd way, a way I couldn't read. It was almost as if… No. She was my boss, my employer.

"How did you make them think you weren't anything to do with it?" she asked.

I had to go over my schoolboy error with the engine oil pump and suddenly she laughed. In fact for a moment I thought she was going to lose control; her laughter seemed uncontrolled. But she calmed down and let me explain my use of the old, thick Dudley accent I could recall at will. "With that, and the fact that I must have looked like a piece of cotton waste that's seen better days, they thought I was a junior staff member."

The question session was interrupted by Inge and Carl whose first action was to hug Maisie. It was some time before they could bring themselves to meet my eyes or Poppy's. When they did there was a silence before Carl made the simple comment.

"I really don't know how we can ever apologise to you enough for what we landed you with. Nor can we thank you enough for taking the actions you did. Nothing we can say can express it, nor can we do anything to make it up to you."

I thought. They were right. It wasn't their fault, but because of them, or the relatives, we had had to be a part of it. It wasn't fair, but nor is terrorism. I decided to be bold.

"You can look after Maisie. You can make sure that none of the other cells of your terrorist organisation ever find you or her, or us, in the future. That would be enough."

Did that constitute a put down? I didn't really know. Like most I'm not used to having gratitude or grovelling apologies heaped on me. It's uncomfortable.

"Oh, we'll be doing that, most certainly," Inge responded. "I should say that so far as the terrorists are concerned others will be doing so. This has just reinforced again our decision that Maisie should come first in our lives and we are kicking ourselves for ever having given priority to our careers." She grimaced, and paused. "Jack, despite all this I hope that Nat and Maisie can still remain friends."

"I doubt if either of us could stop them even if there was a reason for doing so," I said, uncomfortably surprised that there should be a doubt about it. "They're young, and over time it may fizzle out. Or it may grow stronger. I don't intend to try and interfere unless Nat is unhappy, just as you'd do the same with Maisie."

"We would. We shall. And I hope that once this has had a chance to become 'experience', we can still visit you and you us – when we've moved somewhere it's possible to visit. At the moment we still have – er – security to consider. But that consideration will vanish in a few days unless something goes wrong. But that's not likely once we have the… once *they* have the other two out of the way."

I'd forgotten the driver and the A.N. Other. Something else occurred to me. "Do you want Maisie to stay with us for the moment? I suppose so, as there are those two to consider."

"Yes please," Carl put in. "And best not to mention any of this to anyone else for the moment, including Maisie and your two. We'll ask the others not to. Then once it's safe we can perhaps pitch up at a less public hotel, Maisie can join us and then we can look for a real home."

"Maybe once the hires have settled down we can take a week out and go for a trip, all of us," I offered. "And you, Poppy, of course."

She smiled. "I think you might find that accommodation could be a problem there, Jack. Even on a seventy-footer."

I thought. "Shouldn't be. It'd be a squash, certainly, but if the boys shared, Maisie has one of their cabins, Inge and Carl have the front one… Oh." I felt a rush of blood to my face. That would have meant that the only double left would have to be shared by Poppy and me.

"Oh..." she echoed, smiling; whether it was at the thought or at my blush I didn't know.

"Perhaps Maisie could sleep on the floor in the front," I muttered.

Inge looked from Poppy to me and back again. "It'd be lovely if we could," she said. "We could see a little of our own country for the first time in years. All those years..."

How exactly I dug myself out of that trench of embarrassment of my own making I now can't remember. Gradually the quayside cleared of the Police and whoever the Parishes' protectors were. Inge and Carl said their farewells too leaving Poppy, Maisie and me. We made our way back to the office where we found poor Helena sitting alone, tea cup in hand, staring at nothing. She looked up as we came in.

"I don't... don't want to be... to be shot at..."

Poppy was with her in a flash, comforting her. Maisie, after a scared look, moved to sit the other side. I was unsure what to do so did the obvious thing for a Briton in crisis: I filled the kettle and put it on. Between the three of us we calmed her down, telling the full story.

But as normality returned I found that my own nerves were jangling. Something felt different. My hands. I looked at them and found they were shaking. Poppy noticed and sent me to a chair where I felt worse and worse until I had to croak out that I needed to lie down. The floor swam up to meet me and that was it.

When next consciousness returned I was, inevitably, on a bed. Fully dressed, but on a bed. I also felt famished, trembly. Damn. Had events put me back in hospital again? The answer was clear a moment or two after I'd moved. A nurse came in, looking flustered.

"I thought we asked you to attend as an out-patient?" she asked in an annoyed tone. "We really thought you'd have more sense."

It wasn't the reaction I thought a mental patient should receive. A certain amount of normality must have returned already as I found I could ignore her accusation and ask if there was anything to eat, even if it was just a biscuit.

"Hmmm... I know they said you'd been sick, and why." This time there was a half smile which transformed her face. Then the old approach returned. "No one expected you to put yourself in such danger and then behave like a hero. It's not being fair on yourself, having just recovered from a breakdown."

"I hardly went into it and asked for it," I told her, with nearly as much annoyance now as she was showing me.

"That's better," she said, to my surprise. "You seem to have regained a bit of equilibrium. I'll get some biscuits. Actually, would you prefer a Cornish pasty from the machine? Or both."

"Both, please," I said hungrily. "And thank you."

"I'll need some money." Severity had returned.

I dug impatiently in my pocket and pulled out some coins. "Is that enough?"

"They cost £1.40. *Is* it enough?"

I looked. It was. "Keep the change," I said in what I hoped was a mock-sarcastic tone. Again a brief smile.

It took her very little time before she returned with a hospital cup of tea, a pasty and a pack of biscuits.

"Would you like me to feed you?"

This time I really looked at her face. There was nothing there, no antagonism, no sarcasm, no reproach.

"I *think*, after forty five years, I might be able to manage," I said, tearing off the pasty's plastic sleeve. "If you need me to answer anything else, please could you ask the questions before I have a full mouth? I'd hate to open myself to criticisms of bad manners as well as mental breakdown."

This time there was a real smile. "I think you pass the tests, Jack Dyer. We thought when you were brought in that, yes, you were still suffering from the aftermath of the breakdown. It seems that mainly your symptoms were hunger. If you returned your breakfast to the canal there was nothing to…"

"Thanks for the reminder," I said with my mouth open waiting to receive the pasty. Again she laughed.

"You had nothing inside you to make up for the demands of outwitting a couple of criminals and facing real danger. Oddly, working under the influence of adrenalin demands more fuel than you'd expect. You had little. You needed a rest, which you've had, and you needed some food, and I won't stop you any longer. Take a little time afterwards and then try sitting up and see how you feel."

Memory returned and I was shocked that she knew what had happened.

"How do you know all that?" I asked her, worried.

"The Police told us, and insisted that we should say nothing because a lot of people's safety depended on it."

"Oh," I said weakly.

Another brief smile and she went. I took my bite.

I decided when I woke again that it did feel good to have had even that small amount to eat,. Sitting up, which was done carefully, provided no problem. Neither did swinging my legs onto the floor and sitting up from there. A pause, and I stood. Ahhh… maybe too soon. The bed was a better option still.

"What have you tried?" This time it was a male nurse who had entered and awoken me.

"A pasty, four biscuits and a cup of tea."

"I meant in terms of sitting."

"I can sit on the bed, but standing is still very wavery."

"What do you mean by wavery?"

"I mean unsteady."

"Ah. So if I brought you a meal, you would eat it."

Oddly I felt as empty as I had when I first woke. "How long have I been here?" I asked him.

"About seven hours," he said after consulting his watch.

"*Seven hours?* But my sons… they won't know what's happening and I need to be cooking for them! What *is* the time?"

"Eight-thirty. And they've been in, checked you're ok and have gone again. As have your wife and daughter."

"You mean Poppy and Maisie? They're not… oh well, it doesn't matter."

"Is the lady not your wife? It's just that she kissed you when she was leaving."

My head snapped up to meet his eyes and I blinked. I was floored by that, completely floored. But there was a tingle in my arms which I felt could well travel to the rest of my body. Why? And why should she have kissed me?

"I think that meal you mentioned would go down rather well," I said, slightly faintly. "And is my mobile anywhere around, please?"

"You sound different," were Poppy's first words. "Are you all right?"

"Better now I've eaten, thanks, and better to hear that you, Maisie and the boys have been in while I was asleep. I wish you'd woken me."

"We were told not to."

"Oh. Have they eaten, by the way, and do they know what happened?"

"I thought I'd starve them, just for having a father who plays the hero. Yes, Jack, we've all eaten. All four of us, at my house. Thank you for asking though."

"I'm really sorry about this…"

"Don't be an idiot. Do you think I don't understand? And I can cope with a young lady and two young gentlemen on my own, you know. Visitors who help in the kitchen and then do the washing up without being asked are a delight."

"Did they? Good for them."

"They have a good father."

"Poppy…"

"Well, it's true. You are, and I've just reaped the rewards. Can Nat go to the Losardos tonight? With Maisie?"

"Yes, if they're happy to accept both of them. I imagine Phil will be happy to be on his own."

"Do you think so? They're all here at the moment, watching TV. Do you think I should send Phil back when they go?"

"Well no, not unless he's being a pain. I don't know if I'm going to be able to come back to the boat tonight, so could I leave his return to you? And he needs to be there for when Nat and Maisie get back."

"Oh, we've sorted that. If you're not back they're all sleeping here. If that's all right with you?"

For the second time in ten minutes I was speechless.

After a pause I continued, sounding strained even to myself. "That's… that's wonderful. And thank you." Another pause. "I'm… I'm told by one of the nurses here that, and I quote, 'your wife kissed you as she left'. When I get back I'm going to return that kiss."

The phone was silent.

"Hallo? I asked it.

"Damn him. He wasn't meant to see that, let alone tell you. It just seemed… right."

"Thank you, Poppy."

"Good night, Jack."

I felt an odd glow as I lay back, then mentally pinched myself (if one can do such a thing).

I ate, I felt better. I was going to get up and return to the boat. I was told firmly that I wasn't, that my children were being looked after by my wife, and that if I felt strong enough in the morning I could perhaps be taken back there.

"I'm not having you flake out half way through walking back to that marina. Not on my watch," a doctor told me firmly. Protestations that the boat was so close that I could almost see it fell on deaf ears.

I did feel better in the morning and could once again stand up without wobbling, not even a little. In fact I felt absolutely normal. It didn't stop the hospital insisting that I call Poppy to collect me, to my great embarrassment.

Before setting off for the half-mile drive to the marina she looked at me. "You gave us a shock, Jack Dyer."

"Why so?"

"By passing out like that."

"It's not as if I planned it. And I'd had a shock too, if you remember."

She put a hand on my arm. "I'm not criticising, believe me. And I'm not blaming you. But if you knew the concern that everyone showed, from poor Helena to Ian to the other residents opposite us, you would be astonished. Or maybe you wouldn't. I couldn't care less, of course."

It took me a moment. I thought back to our exchange on the phone the previous evening.

"No, Poppy, I quite understand. You made that clear when you were leaving yesterday evening."

She removed her arm. "Damn you."

"Sorry. Actually no. I'm not sorry. It shows that… well, I don't know what it shows, but I know you care."

Had I been in my twenties I suppose I could have jumped to a conclusion in reaction to the look she gave me. But I was forty-five, separated from my wife, had two sons and lived on a boat. A borrowed boat. You're inclined not to jump to conclusions when you're carrying that weight of baggage. I just smiled at her and, for a moment, we maintained eye contact.

"One day, Jack, one day," she said, switching her attention from my face to the car park.

The journey was made in silence. I could think of no suitable come-back to her comment, not one that would have been appropriate. We pulled into the marina,

"Boat and bed for you, Jack," she said. "Hospital's orders, not mine. Maisie will be in at lunch with a meal on a plate for you and to make a cup of tea. No work until tomorrow, and then afternoon only. Again, hospital orders. And no arguments."

I opened my mouth to say something but was immediately interrupted. "Bed! Now!" and she gave me a gentle shove towards the boat.

"Aren't you even going to come and make sure I *do* go to bed?" It wasn't a come-on, just a joke. The look she gave me was yet another of the "old-fashioned" type. Meekly, I turned and crossed to the boat.

Now the confession. A coffee was brewed – by me – and some biscuits found, and they found their way down to my cabin. Two hours later I found the coffee still there, cold. Three hours later there was a knock at the door and Maisie brought me lunch. I ate it and immediately fell asleep again.

25 Equilibrium

The boys woke me on their return from school by being about as quiet as boys usually are – until they remembered being told that I'd be asleep. After that there was an almost comical silence. I woke properly and got up; they were pleased to find me responsive and sounding as normal as I felt.

"You gave us another shock, Dad," Phil told me as Nat gave me a hug.

"Unintentionally," I said.

"And you're to go to the day hospital or whatever it is on Mondays, is that right?"

I nodded. "If there's nothing urgent that I need to do here."

"We think you need to go anyway," Phil persisted. "Poppy, Nat and me, that is. We can walk that way to a bus and go to school from a stop nearer."

"I feel fine," I told them. "I'll go if it's possible."

"Then we need to make sure it's possible," Nat said as firmly as he could. "Poppy will be on our side."

I gave up for the moment. Time would tell.

Later that evening Helen rang, sounding peevish. "I really do want to see my sons," she said. "It's not right that you're stopping me from seeing them."

"I'm not," I told her firmly, "and we've been over this. I'm stopping Jonathan from seeing them given his penchant for assault and attempted kidnap. They don't want to put themselves in danger of that again either. And when we invited you on the boat for a trip so that you could enjoy each other's company, you left them in a huff without saying goodbye. *If* you remember."

"That was different."

"Different from what?"

"From what I want now."

"And what would that be?"

"To see my sons."

Round we go in a circle. Again.

"I'll ask them… no, you can ask them. I'll put the phone on speaker."

I did so, and the first words the boys heard were "…for that. Just tell them to be in a park tomorrow evening and I'll come along."

"You're on loudspeaker and they're here," I told her.

"Oh sh… Why did you do that?"

"I said I was going to, so that you could ask them yourselves."

A pause, then: "Can we meet up tomorrow, when I've finished work?"

Silence from our end, then Nat spoke up. "I can't, Mum. We're at the Losardos' tomorrow."

"And I've got too much homework," Phil said, shortly.

"Who are the Losardos?"

Nat explained, gaining enthusiasm as he gave more and more details of his newly discovered design flair. She interrupted him in full flight. "Nat, you're exaggerating. You never used to do that."

"I'm not exaggerating. And we already have furniture on the boat that I helped design. In fact I sleep on it because I helped design the beds. And..."

She broke in. "I don't care. I want to see you and you need to be in the park, the one near you, tomorrow night. Both of you. Six o'clock."

"Mum, I already said that I had too much homework," Phil told her firmly.

"And I've promised to go to the Losardos' now, and you wouldn't want me to break a promise."

"Then when am I going to see you?"

"Holidays start the week after next. We can fix a time then," Phil said, having a better grasp of dates than his brother.

"So you're... you're rationing the times when I can see you. Even you. It was never like that when we lived together. We were one family."

She must have regretted saying that as the words emerged, because she must have heard my gasp.

"Yes, Mum, we were, weren't we? And then along came our uncle and you threw Dad out. That's why we're not a family any more." This was Phil; a Phil speaking in a tone I'd never heard from him. A Phil who leant over the table and stabbed the phone's red button.

I looked at his angry face. "Cow!" he said.

None of us felt like saying anything for quite a few seconds, until I thought that I had better break the silence. Poor Maisie was looking very uncomfortable.

"It's not up to me to tell you what my thoughts are because I don't want to influence you, either of you. It's for you to make your own minds up and then, maybe, tell me; at least talk over your thoughts. If not with me, then to someone outside the family who has experience of these things."

"We know what you think, Dad. You're as horrified with the whole thing as we are." Phil again.

"You're right. That's the easy bit to think and to say. The difficult bit is how we each view... Helen. I loved her, bought a house with her, had a family with her and aged pretty well with her for years – or so I thought. I don't know what I feel about her now. Numb, I suppose. It's easier to say what I feel about Jonathan... well, actually, no it isn't. We still grew up together. Nothing can change that."

Another pause.

"So if I don't know what to think about Mum, it's all right?" Nat spoke slowly, as if reluctant to say the words, to admit his feelings.

"It's absolutely normal, Nat," I told him. "From what little I know about it, that's just what happens for people who are capable of rational thought. And that describes us. Do you feel that too, Phil? Or can't you really put it into words?"

"She made me bloody angry just now, expecting us to drop everything to see her," Phil said, still with an edge to his voice. "After all she's put us through."

All I could do was nod. What else could I do? Given time we would probably each come to a definite feeling about our relationship with Helen. I hoped so. At the moment it was either painful to think about or our emotions there were – well, numb.

"So long as you know – and I realise I've said this before – that if or when you want to see her, I won't stand in your way. All I need to know is that you're safe and that you are wherever it is of your own free will."

"That we've not been kidnapped by… by *him*, you mean."

"Exactly, Nat. Just so. That's why I think we should all have one of those tracking apps on our phones so that each of us can see where the other two are. And why did none of us think of that before?"

Phil gave a sudden grin, quickly smothered. "Poppy should have it as well."

Was this my turn to give an old-fashioned look? Except that he was right. My employer, friend, confidant, and frequent visitor was a very capable woman. And she seemed to like the boys, amazingly. To get my own back on Phil I told them both so.

"Oh, that's because of our natural charm and good looks," Phil told me smugly.

Maisie's face regained some of its normality. I apologised to her, being really guilty that she'd had to witness that exchange.

"It's all right," she said.

"Not really, Maisie. Not fair on you. But on the other hand I don't see why Helen should have been allowed to interrupt plans that had been made, or the need to do homework."

"She didn't know I was here."

"No," I smiled at her, "she didn't. What has happened to bring you here will be a tale to tell if she's ever able to listen to any of us for long enough."

"Or if she believes us," Phil said with a note of bitterness. "She didn't want to believe Nat's design expertise, did she?"

The subject of that comment said nothing, but his stony expression said volumes. I noticed a movement by Maisie's side. It looked as if her hand had found Nat's again. Once again it wasn't shaken off.

"You're late," I said to my two when they appeared at the marina after school the following day. "I was starting to get worried."

"It's Mum," Nat said. "She was outside the school when I came out, then we had to wait for Phil's year. It was really embarrassing."

"It was," Phil confirmed. "All she wanted to do was talk and find out how we were. If she'd said that last night we could have met her down the road or something."

"Was Jonathan with her?"

"No. Still at work. She had to leave work early to come."

"She should have said what she was going to do yesterday, as you said. Easier all round. Now I feel guilty about not making it easier for her to see you."

"I cut off the phone, Dad, not you. She was being a cow."

"I hope you didn't tell her what you said."

"No," he said, sounding embarrassed. "She told us she was sorry about what she said before I could do that."

"Was… was she all right?" Maisie asked the question cautiously.

"Yes," said Nat, knowing what she meant. "She didn't say anything horrible. We told that you were staying with us for the moment – and that you were there when she phoned last night."

Phil laughed, a little humourlessly. "She was so surprised that we were able to tell her everything that had happened, and that it must go no further. For once she believed us."

Homework was done, I finished work, and Maisie, bless her, cooked a meal – with Phil's help, as she admitted afterwards. During the previous year she hadn't been allowed by her aunt and uncle to do anything around the house. Most of the domestic necessities that youngsters learn as a part of their growing up had passed her by.

The meal itself was interrupted by a call from Inge and Carl to Maisie. She spent a lot of time laughing, to our relief. "They're in a hotel," she said. "They weren't popular with their masters, as Mum put it, because where they're staying is very ordinary. But they told them that the hotel they were at before had spies in it and look what happened afterwards. Anyway, they can come and fetch me tomorrow."

"That's excellent," I told her warmly, "not that we want you to go but it'll be good for you to be with your parents properly. And then you'll have all the excitement of looking for a home. Did they say anything about the two from the cell who were still around?"

"Oh yes, they've been caught. The driver was tracked to a lavatory and was arrested when… well, when they came into the room he tried to get out of the window and his middle got caught on a catch. He had to be taken to hospital. That's why I was laughing."

"Maisie!"

"Well, he was one of the people who wanted to kill my parents. I can't feel sorry for him."

I saw her point.

I told Maisie and Nat that they should leave for the Losardos' workshop and that Phil and I would wash up. He raised his eyebrows and was about to say something about homework, but I forestalled him by saying that I needed help because I was still tired.

The two younger ones returned late, sawdust in their hair and probably everywhere else, and had a shower – separately, despite Phil's coarse suggestion to the contrary which I heard through the thin bulkhead. Maisie's equally coarse rebuttal shocked me until I remembered the obscenities that she'd been subjected to over the previous year. That, I decided, was going to be a problem for her parents to sort out.

Saturday was insanely busy. The first week of the school holidays always was, according to Poppy, who was rushing around like a woman possessed, helping here, cajoling there. I had the usual checks to make and two engine services, so was kept busy with Phil's help where necessary. Nat was on water duty as usual, but on his own as Maisie had by then been collected by her parents.

The air was full of calls, instructions, pleas for assistance and the occasional curse as someone discovered a fault. Part one – refilling, servicing and cleaning – was mostly complete by lunchtime, then we were back to linens, bed making, complimentary packs of tea, coffee and other staples, and the Poppy trademark bunches of flowers to brighten the main dinettes. By the time the car park started filling with new hirers' arrivals we were again all but ready.

One of Phil's jobs, he told me later, had been to paint out this bullet shaped dent in one of the boats. There was a point where I looked over to him and found that he was returning my stare, unblinkingly, his face white.

At the time I wondered if he was ill, but I couldn't leave the engine I was with at the time. I knew that if he was, he would tell me. He kept away until we had finished and Poppy, Ian and others were introducing hirers to their boats. He made his way over to me and without a pause enveloped me in a bear hug, taking me by surprise. A strangled sounding, husky voice spoke by my right ear.

"Don't you ever, *ever*, get into danger like that again." That was all, but he stayed with arms around me, his breathing ragged, until it steadied. He pushed himself away. A pair of very bright eyes looked into mine for a moment and he turned and walked over to our boat.

Poor old Phil. It had taken the presence of the bullet dent to bring home to him the actual reality of the previous Monday's event. His own father had really been shot at, and he suddenly realised what it might have meant. My heart went out to him. I was surprised and genuinely touched by his unexpectedly emotional reaction.

"Can we go somewhere tomorrow?" asked Nat when we had finally seen the last of the hirers depart for their week. Poppy was with us and she also looked up, smiling. It looked as if it was a done deal.

"Can you come, Poppy?" I asked her. She smiled even more broadly.

"Well, I can, but I was wondering whether we could go out for a few days as there's no school..."

It was worth the surprise just to see the two faces light up. Well, maybe three.

"You see," she continued, "it seems that I may have asked Ian if he can man the fort for a few days at some point, and he may have told me that I needed a break and now was as good a time as any. I think he'd appreciate us all being back by next Saturday, though."

Now we were all at a loss for words. Nearly.

"I think you've been planning it all along, haven't you?" I asked her.

"Don't know what you mean. Well, yes," she admitted with a smile. "And then the events of the last week nearly scuppered the whole thing and I thought we'd never get away.

Nat was grinning broadly. "Have we got enough food?" asked Phil, also smiling now, and as innocently as he could.

"Guts," Nat muttered.

"We need to go shopping," I said, thinking that I'd intended to anyway.

"The journey I'm thinking of means that we'd be able to shop in Stratford..."

"Stratford?" Phil interrupted. "So are we really going there then? By boat?"

Poppy looked at him. "Well, you can swim down the canal if you'd rather, but it'd be uncomfortable."

"I didn't know the canal really went all the way to Stratford."

"It does," she confirmed. "That's why it's called the Stratford on Avon Canal."

"Oh well then..."

"I was thinking we could go one way and return another. Look, I brought a map."

"Just a moment," I put in. "Should we go and get something to eat and then go shopping? It's just that I'm sure we're all hungry and these two will probably faint if they don't eat something soon."

"Yeah..." said Phil, with feeling.

So we locked up and visited Poppy's favourite pub again. The map came out when we had eaten and was spread across the cleared table. She traced her route, which seemed to weave its way through more of Birmingham's back streets before emerging into countryside.

"It's not the most direct way," she told us, "but you'll find it really interesting, I think. Not to mention extraordinary. And eventually you'll encounter your first wide locks. But once we get to Stratford it's fun, and the canal to it is lovely. Oh – and if we have time we could go out onto the river."

"River?" asked Nat.

"It's called Stratford-on-Avon for another reason, Nat."

"Ok, ok..."

We digested all this.

"When do we go?" asked Nat.

"When we've got some food," Phil told him, despite having just consumed a large enough meal to keep him going for two days (in my estimation. Obviously not in his).

Our shopping was hedged with indecision. We were no longer hungry, a state which produces a trolley-full if items that hold limited interest, thought it does save money. Poppy laughed at our lack of enthusiasm. "I've seen bag after bag of food being loaded onto boats at the start of the week, and bag after bag being unloaded again at the end. At least you've avoided that. I think."

She knocked at the side of the boat at far too early an hour the next morning, according to Phil; and at a normal time according to me. Nat and I had a d a swift breakfast in Phil's dormouse-like absence.

"'Morning. Ready?" came her greeting as she dumped what looked like quite a small bag onto the deck. In answer to my quizzical look she said just "would you rather I brought a cabin trunk?"

"I have some experience of luggage and a few days away," I said, "and in my experience that would just have held the towels and the things that might come in useful." I was thinking of Helen's attempts to travel light.

"It'd take a bit of time to un-plumb the kitchen sink, but I'll go back and start if you like."

"We have one here, so I'd leave it at home if I were you. Talking of kitchen sinks: Phil?"

"He's in the shower," Nat said smugly.

"When did we last fill with water?"

"Yesterday when I was doing the fleet."

"Good. Everything else is sorted, so we can start."

"What about Phil?"

"The shower was his choice. He'll be out before we hit the city centre, anyway."

With Nat at the helm we turned left at the junction onto the Old Main Line and left again onto the New, towards the city as we had on the disastrous trip with Helen. Phil joined us, looking tousled and wet haired, yawning.

"What we're doing first is to turn left at that roundabout. That'll take us to the first of the locks which end up going under Snow Hill station. It's one of the strangest canalscapes anywhere on the system."

"Why?" I asked, confused.

"We sort of go under Birmingham.

"What?" Phil asked, before Nat or I had the chance.

"What happened is that land is so much at a premium there that blocks of flats and offices were built over the canal's locks. You'll see. We turn left here."

This was to Nat and came a little late, so that we nearly hit the roundabout as we turned. It's not an easy turn, as he said later. There's very little room for the stern to swing into.

His emergency pivoting of the boat had brought us to a very narrow bridge which we squeezed slowly through. The canal beyond seemed to open up. To our left was a lock, and to the right the wide part stopped dead at some moorings; a small marina. With only a little to-ing and fro-ing, Nat brought us to a halt and we jumped off, Phil and I. I turned, hesitantly to Nat and Poppy.

"Do you want to help with the lock?" I asked them both.

"I'll stay on the boat," Poppy called back. "In case Nat asks for advice."

We started down, with Nat doing pretty well. Offices and workshops appeared to our left, a brick wall to the right. Beyond it tall blocks of flats dominated the skyscape. Architecture was an odd mixture of anything from the early nineteenth century to the late twentieth, with a toll booth, bridges, ramps up and down connecting different levels, and steps to and from the canal and its locks.

We walked around the locks as we operated them in a daze of amazement as old buildings and new developments started to hem the canal in its own ravine. The Farmer's Bridge flight is well known to the canal fraternity because of its oddness. We were feeling our way into that fraternity and were still learning the oddness.

Oh, the first few locks are innocent enough, though it does appear as if you're navigating your way to a dead end under high buildings that canyon themselves around you as you drop down. At last the canal gives up believing itself to be a surface route. It allows an office block, Newhall Street and Brindley House to enfold it and to cover it. Operating locks which are surrounded by pillar foundations supporting massive structures over you is highly weird. No matter how much you tell yourself that the whole thing has been there since the nineteen-seventies and is unlikely to choose the moment of your passage to tumble down and crush you, it is definitely unnerving.

"Someone else's turn," said Nat as we were under it. I thought I should let him go and help on the bank; Phil swapped with him.

The grand finale of the lock flight was the tunnel under Snow Hill Station and the road parallel to it. At canal level it's a long, grubby piece of darkness that had me guessing and Poppy and Nat walking carefully using phones to light their way. Once back in daylight we were greeted by some skilful graffiti that announced Birmingham as the Heart of the Waterways. I had been coming to the same conclusion.

The others rejoined us on board at Poppy's suggestion. "It's a fair way to the next locks," she told us.

I made myself useful by putting the kettle on. Poppy followed me down with her bag. "Where would you like me to put it?" she asked.

"Next cabin down," I said. "It's got a clean linen on it."

"But that's yours."

"I'm out here," I told her firmly. "That means I'm in charge of the kettle for a change."

"I didn't want to turn you out of your own room."

"You didn't. I prefer it that way."

I got a look, but she thanked me. We made tea and readied a tin of biscuits.

"I've not had breakfast yet," Phil complained when he saw the biscuits. I took them from under his grasping hand and offered them to Nat. "Oy!"

"*We* had breakfast at eight," I told him. "Those who moulder in their pit until half past look after themselves."

It seemed it was my turn to steer. He went to make toast. "You could start lunch," I called after him. He looked at his watch and exclaimed, then put the bread away.

"What are we having?"

"Salad and cold meats. Maybe bread or something."

He got the loaf out again.

26 Stratford

"Which way, Poppy?" I asked as a wide basin came into view from under a wide road bridge.

"That's Aston Junction," she said. "The locks there take you down the Aston flight to Spaghetti Junction – yes, the Motorway one." She had seen Phil's astonished look. "There are thirteen of them, so that's a route for another day. Turn right and we've only got the six Ashted locks, another six at Camp Hill, and then we'll see."

All these unfamiliar names confused me. She retrieved the map and was about to point out what she meant, but saw that it would be a bad idea as I was steering. "I'll look later," I said, grinning at her. There was somehow more in her answering smile than just a grin. No. I was dreaming. Thinking too much into a simple expression, even after *that* kiss which I never got to experience or return, and our exchange in the car. Maybe one day. It would have be nice to continue that theme, even if it was a theme that she didn't intend to compose.

Besides, I was trying to steer a seventy-foot narrowboat through a series of bridges. Wide bridges.

As we came to the Ashted Locks, Phil announced that the kettle had boiled. Poppy smiled at him – a different smile, I noted – and told him that he had just fallen victim of Sod's Law. "On the canals, whenever the kettle boils or a meal is ready there's a lock or similar waiting to be dealt with," she explained. I was pleased that she hadn't seen fit to soften it for him by calling it Murphy's Law.

He went to turn the kettle off and the three of them went to attend to the lock. What had she called them? The Ashted Locks. After the first there was Ashted Tunnel, actually only a long bridge. Then the rest of the locks. We worked our way down them and made a sharp left turn "…or you end up at a dead end. That's Digbeth Basin where the Typhoo Tea works were."

Now we had time for tea, and to start eating. Inevitably in mid-munch another junction appeared, and beyond it just as inevitably, the first of the Camp Hill Locks. Groaning, we started work again.

"Good," Poppy said as we reached the summit lock. "that's it for the moment. We can finish eating now."

"Workshops?" I asked, nodding to the right as we regathered what speed is possible on a canal.

"The Old British Waterways Sampson Road wharf," she told me. "It's also the last place you turn a wide boat if you're coming north."

I suppose my expression gave away my lack of understanding.

"Narrow locks from here to Birmingham, wide locks between here and London."

The tea, what was left of it, was cold. We started again.

None of the scenery since the bottom of Farmers Bridge Locks had been pretty, hardly surprisingly for a piece of industrial archaeology in a city centre. Much of the canalscape had suffered over the years. The channel had been hemmed in by road developments which criss-crossed the canal like a raised, noisy spider's web. In places it looked onto brownfield sites, ripe for development into… what? And who would have the money? Other parts were still old, still as they'd been built two hundred years previously, but often dank and dirty with added graffiti.

As we approached Solihull, though, there were hints of playing fields and green spaces. To temper their optimism, just as you felt that the countryside was approaching, it seemed that someone had planted another factory – or the massive waste processing site at Small Heath.

Gradually suburbia approached, the channel became tree lined and stayed green for longer. The old Rover plant – the home of Jaguar-Land Rover – raised some eyebrows when Poppy pointed it out. Had it not been almost completely hidden by trees and bushes growing on the bank, we could have missed it. It's vast, stretching away obliquely from the canal into the distance.

Nat: "Would they miss one? If I asked nicely?"

"We can drop you off at their security fence if you want, Nat. If they give you a free F-type you should be able to catch us up."

"It'll probably be a Z-type by the time he's learnt to drive and can afford one," Phil scoffed. Nat put his tongue out.

Soon the country proper, at least as visible from the canal, was with us. We passed some houses, rounded a gentle bend, saw a bridge and moored.

"Catherine de Barnes," Poppy said in response to our wordless questions.

"Is she joining us?" Phil asked, puzzled. Poppy laughed.

"I hope not. She's probably been dead for centuries.[1] There is a pub here, though, and I thought we might save ourselves the washing up if we went there tonight."

We were all pleased with the suggestion, particularly as no one had thought to prepare anything. We tidied ourselves up a bit. Mainly this meant the difficult removal of lock-gear grease from hands (and from Nat's face as some of it had migrated there too) and the changing of the clothes that it had also graced. We walked the hundred yards to the bridge, climbed onto the road and found "The Boat" to be a sprawling but pleasantly refurbished pub-restaurant. At the bar I was about to ask for a table when I was welcomed by a staff member.

"You'll be the rest of the party of seven, I'm thinking? I was asked to say "Emerson" to you."

I gave a start. "Er… well, that means something to us, but we've not made a booking…"

"Ah, but someone else has. The other three are over there, behind that little partition. If you'd like to join them I'll be over to take your order."

With some caution in view of previous events I led the way over, aware of a son at my back. As we rounded the partition and looked, there were Inge, Carl

---

[1] *Note for historians: we discovered later that the name comes from Ketelberne, lord of the manor in the 12thC. There was never a Catherine. In any case the old canal boatmen called it Kate de Barnes, which is nearer that real name.*

and Maisie looking mischievous. A yelp behind me revealed Nat, who went straight to Maisie.

It turned out to be Poppy's doing, she who had arranged the canal trip without telling us. Quietly the Parishes had been asked for their phone numbers as Poppy was thinking to spring such a surprise on us at some point. The reunion looked as if it was pleasing her greatly.

Just as at the Grand, conversation flowed happily. Since the horrors of the attack my mind had constructed a subconscious stigma against the Parishes. I'd not considered it, but it was nevertheless there. Within half an hour of chat, laughter, ordering drinks and food ("No, Phil. No beer.") that stigma had been chipped at, hammered at, reduced to rubble and carted away.

"We can't join you this time, I'm afraid," Inge said at a hopeful mention from Nat. "We're looking at places to live where we can move quickly so as to get out of the hotel. Then we can take our time looking for a real home. Maisie would like to come with you, I know, but we want her to help us to choose somewhere."

It was late when we left and bid the Parishes our farewells. I was watching Maisie and Nat, I hope without being noticed. There was none of the lingering emotion noticeable that I might have expected were it Phil and a female companion, though there was a "regard". It was more than a swift "'bye" from each of them. Unusual for people still not yet thirteen, but then who am I to criticise?

We found our way back to the boat and again I had to counter Poppy's protestations that she should be the one in the dinette. At last she gave in gracefully, and we settled down.

I suppose it must have been about three-thirty when I was woken by the biological need of the middle-aged male. I used the bathroom as quietly as I could, and swore to myself that I'd remember to adjust the catch so it was quieter.

"Are you ok, Jack?" There was a whispered, concerned question from behind a just-open door as I made to return to my bed.

"Yes, thanks. Just needed to commune with nature."

"Oh. Ok. Good night. Again."

"Good night," I smiled.

In the morning, having put the kettle on, I was about to revisit the bathroom when the adjoining door opened and a Poppy-shaped shadow appeared.

"Hallo Poppy," I said quietly, "Sleep all right?" Without her day-time determined look, even though it was almost always tempered by a smile, she appeared ten years younger. I felt my face soften into even more of a smile.

"Like a log, thanks. You?"

"Apart from a call to the loo that you heard, yes. Look, I'd better get some clothes on."

"Don't bother on my account… Oh! I shouldn't have said that."

My grin grew wider. Something subtly changed inside me.

"No, Mrs Watson, you probably shouldn't. But I'm glad you did."

"Why?"

I thought back to when I'd been told about that kiss, and her reaction to the knowledge. "Just because; that's all. Just because."

I returned to the dinette and got dressed, made the tea and converted the bed back into bench seats and table. Poppy joined me, and a few moments later, so did Nat. It was the smell of bacon that brought forth a dressed but bleary-eyed Phil just in time, and only a little later than Poppy had hoped, we set off. It was still fine, although cloudy, and the treetops were moving to show a breeze.

"Can someone take over, please? I'm going to have a shower." Phil had taken the first steering duty. It had lasted less than an hour and I hoped he wasn't going off boating already.

"Can it wait a bit, Phil? We're going to need your muscles." Poppy had a happy knack of saying the right thing.

"Why?" he asked, hesitating.

"Just under this bridge, and you'll see,"

He stayed. Then frowned.

"Just a minute… why's that boat so wide?"

After a raised bank to the right of us there was a boat moored. It looked vast; the same length of ours but about double our width. Ungainly. Unlikely. Out of place.

"Your first wide beam boat," Poppy told him. "Big, aren't they?"

"How do they go through the locks?" asked Phil.

"You'll find out in just a few minutes."

We passed the first few moored boats and saw the start of a lock ahead. A group were sitting on the lock beams and a boat seemed to be moored where we would need to be.

"Ah, good. Slow down now, Phil, and with any luck we can go in with them." Poppy seemed pleased. Phil frowned.

"How?"

"These are your first double locks. They're double the width of the ones you're used to. Two boats can share."

"What – side by side?"

"Yes. And it's good that we can go down with someone else. They're heavy locks and need a lot of turns from closed to open."

"So they and we work them together?"

She nodded.

"And if you've got one of these peculiar wide boats, they fit in on their own."

She nodded again. The gates were opening. People made busy with windlasses. Phil looked uncertain. "Could you take the tiller?"

"You can do it!" Poppy exclaimed. "Just wait until the other boat is completely over their side and then head in as if it was a single lock. You're used to them."

"Yeah… but… I'll take her in this one, and then I need the loo."

He was looking at the other crew, one of whom seemed to be his height. And female. Two others were male and younger. The father appeared to be steering, the mother already at the far paddle gear.

Their boat seemed undecided which side of the lock to pull to.

"When you get there, Phil, just choose the side with the bigger gap. Go really slowly. If the boats touch, don't worry. If you have to push the other one out of the way, do it. But gently."

He was about to do so when both gates started to close. Immediately Poppy's hand was on the horn button. A blare of noise came back to us and the steerer and crew of the other boat all jumped. Five faces turned our way.

Acknowledgements were waved, the gates reopened and Phil chose the wider gap. Fortunately the steerer got the message and pulled their stern over to give us room. Carefully Phil let our motion push the bows over too, and we were in.

"Sorry," said a voice, "we never looked back for anyone else."

Phil and I looked across. I smiled. I couldn't see Phil's face but could almost see the exclamation mark in the thought bubble.

She must have been about sixteen. Long hair surrounded a naturally pleasant face, and it somehow matched the laughter in the voice. As to the remainder of her looks, all I could do was to remember what Phil as a recent arrival at adolescence had said. For him a girl's must-have physical attributes were "big boobs, a stunning face, and legs and a bum to die for." I'd not been able to criticise him at the time because Nat had been there, Helen had been absent, and I had doubtless made just the same remark to friends when his age. Not to my father, though; that would have resulted in either a clip round the ear or a steely silence.

Anyway, I imagined that his attraction level was currently hitting overload.

I nudged him. "Reverse!"

His head jerked back to look at the bow and he engaged reverse with a flourish.

"Concentrate, or you'll have us on the cill as we go down," I hissed. An annoyed look came my way. "Shh! I *am* concentrating."

Yes, Phil. Of course you are. Just concentrate on the item that's equipped with one fender, not two… Sorry, that's an old fashioned thing to say, but it's what floated across my brain in the moment.

The Knowle flight is a pig. It has five double width locks, between each of which each is a short, wide pond. Poppy had 'suggested' to the other crew and to us that we should wait for the gates to the next lock to be open before we started from the previous one. Phil had forgotten that and found himself in mid-pond, being blown inexorably to the side and away from the lock entrance. It had taken him a lot of inexperienced manoeuvring to line the boat up again, by which time his face was red.

I called Nat over to take over on the tiller, with Poppy's help, and turned to Phil.

"You wanted the loo, remember? And your muscles are better helping her on the locks where necessary."

I'm not sure what the look was that he gave me, but he bolted downstairs and bolted up again like a jack-in-the-box with built in delay. At least the blush had vanished.

We struggled down the flight. Nat spoke a little to the two sons when they were nearby closing gates. I chatted to the parents. Phil and the object of his speechless admiration remained speechless, though I think she was aware of his… admiration. I discovered that they were continuing on the Grand Union. Poppy had suggested that we should let them get away first from the bottom lock as we would be turning right at Kingswood. I recognised *that* name, of course, as that had been the scene of my first encounter with Maisie's disastrous "guardians".

It was as the last set of gates were opened that the daughter looked at Phil and smiled. I could almost hear his heart melting, but she turned away down the steps at the lock's tail to rejoin their boat as it emerged. Nat hung back as arranged so that Poppy, Phil and I could close the bottom gates. Phil's eyes were still glued to the other boat as we went to join ours, and he nearly lost his footing on the steps. Thank goodness for handrails.

My turn on the tiller, it seemed. A cup of coffee was thrust into my hand soon after, along with some biscuits, by Phil. We drank and munched in silence for a while.

"Good looking lass, wasn't she?" I ventured, not knowing what to expect. I just got an under-the-eyebrows look and a smile. No words. None were necessary.

"Turn right ahead," came the instruction from Poppy an hour later as we were passing some cottages.

"Where?"

"I think it's just past the houses."

I could see where they ended, and there was a depression in the bank, so I slowed a little. Gradually the right-angled turn became clearer.

"Blimey, it's a bit awkward," I said, engaging reverse to slow down more. The boys emerged from the dinette where they'd probably been scoffing the last of the packet of biscuits. Without a thought in the world (well, maybe one, but she was on a boat ahead of us) Phil stood in front of me.

"Oy! How can I see with you standing there? You're too tall for me to see over your head."

He ducked. I was about to steer in and under the bridge when there was a hoot and the bows of another boat, a hired boat, appeared. More frantic reversing and I stopped in time.

"You'll need to go backwards to give him room if he's turning this way," Poppy said quietly. "Oh damn, he is."

We did get out of the way. Just. The steerer approaching looked shocked when at last he saw us, but nevertheless started to turn our way. I backed further. As he came abreast of us he shouted across.

"You might give me a bit more room!"

My eyes shot up. Poppy kept her cool. "Anyone else following you?"

He shook his head, then faced forward again and ignored us.

"Don't get many of that sort," Poppy said. "It's always live and let live. Maybe we should have answered his hoot, or hooted ourselves first. Probably a newbie on the cut. Usually people are nice."

I made the turn into what proved a heavily shaded, quite short stretch of canal. Ahead was a railway bridge; moored boats lined both banks. The short arm ended at another junction, with brick lined mini-canyons to each side. To our right was a lock. Straight on was what looked like a lock chamber but without gates. Directed by Poppy. We entered it. After the tree shaded, somehow foreboding arm from the wide Grand Union it was lovely to merge into a wide basin and the light.

At the end of the chamber we turned left, and there was the first lock. We were back to the narrow variety which would continue all the way to Stratford. I recognised it immediately as the beginning of our walk down to *Cowslip.* Some of the locks on the flight are close enough for a walk whilst others make you wish you'd not been so enthusiastic.

We lunched on the move, with the locks playing the usual Sods' Law with us by cropping up at the most inopportune moments. It was delightfully rural and delightfully distinctive. Poppy – inevitably – had told us to look out for footbridges with slits between their two cantilevered halves to allow a tow rope to pass through to save untying it from either boat or horse, there being no towpaths under them. The old barrel-roofed lockkeepers' cottages were another feature. We saw and marvelled at both. Phil looked thirstily at the Fleur de Lys at Lowsonford as we passed and wasn't impressed when all we did was to put the kettle on.

Yarningdale fascinated all of us. The towpath dips down to be level with the bottom of a metal tank which forms an aqueduct. Though it's only over a stream it gives an unusual and impressive aspect on passing boats, as both they and the nearby lock are seen from water level.

They had fun with the name of Wooton Wawen, my two, but were suitably impressed at going over a two-hundred-year old aqueduct or two, especially the long one at Edstone. The later part of the day was lock free, and Poppy was looking for mooring possibilities as we approached Wilmcote. We found a place just before the bridge, and stopped. It was half past six and we'd been going for over ten hours.

"That was lucky," Poppy said with relief. "At busy times finding a spot at this time of night can be a challenge. But it's been a good, productive day."

The boys flopped with convincing groans onto the dinette's bench seats. "I don't know why you're groaning. You two are cooking."

"Dad…"

"I'm knackered!"

Poppy laughed. "Welcome to a life outside, with no school desk within miles. It makes you tired, and gives you an appetite. Well, usually. Does that mean you're not hungry?"

"Famished…" Phil sounded ready to faint.

"Well, I suppose we *could* head to a pub again and eat out."

"*Is* there a pub here?" asked Phil, magically revitalised.

"If there wasn't, I imagine Mary Arden wouldn't have been born here and might not have married Mr Shakespeare, and you'd not have been able to study him in Literature."

He groaned.

"He's an acquired taste, Phil," I said hopefully. "Your outlook changes as you age and you start enjoying how words are put together. Unless, of course, you have a closed mind. You haven't."

Crossing the canal bridge led towards the village. At the first junction was the Mary Arden.

"Who was she?" asked Nat.

"Shakespeare's mother," Phil volunteered before either of us could get a word in. "She lived here, apparently."

"Here?"

"Somewhere in the village, I suppose."

"We passed her farm on the way," Poppy said. "That black and white place. Remember?"

"Too hungry," said Phil. "We'll look on the way back."

We ate, then set off on the return walk. The boys were walking ahead of us, passing Mary Arden's farm, and stopped to look. Poppy and I did the same, and took longer. They turned away first, and to my surprise I felt Poppy's hand slip into mine. The surprise was in my eyes, I suppose; that and the smile.

"Shh," was all she said, and we walked on in silence. It was inevitable that as the boys reached the turning down to the footpath they would look back. First one, then a nudge, then the other. And do you know what? I didn't care. I felt her grip loosen, but tightened mine. They waited for us, and I anticipated the barrage of comments that would come particularly from Phil.

We bore down on them and then noticed the smiles.

"Good," said Nat.

"About time," Phil offered, and they turned down towards the gate.

Was that it? Approval? I looked at Poppy and saw the grin start to appear. It matched mine.

"I *like* your two," she said.

"They have their moments. They're not bad, really."

"We heard that!" Phil called back. "What did you want? Wolf whistles?"

I fought down a laugh and let silence return. He looked round again perhaps worried he'd crossed a line.

"No, Phil. What you said was just fine. Just fine. Thank you."

The first few yards of footpath were just wide enough for four people to walk abreast. We did. A couple holding hands, each with an arm round the shoulders of a boy. Neither of them shook them off, either.

We woke late the next morning. It was almost nine-thirty by the time we were on our way. Phil joined us, wet haired, half an hour later.

"Hot water's cold," he announced.

"That'll be because the engine's had no time to heat it." Poppy's simple fact just caused a nod. I decided to say nothing, especially as there was a lock just ahead of us. In fact it was the first of twelve.

The boys did most of the work, though Poppy and I took our turns. It was between two locks when Phil, Nat and I were wandering slowly along between two locks that the boys started were arguing – amicably – about nothing in particular. Feeling himself getting worsted Phil broke off a sprig of the buddleia that abounds on canalsides and held it like a sword pointing towards Nat.

"Oy!" said he, ducking, and harvested his own purple weapon. Returning to the attack the two started duelling as if with swords, even ducking and rolling on the ground to avoid attack. It was so comical that the crew of a boat coming towards us were laughing openly. As was I.

"What are all those blue bits in your hair?" Poppy asked Phil when he returned to the boat.

"Flower injuries."

By the time we had worked our way down those locks Poppy and I were in dire need of a coffee and the boys of a de-buddleia session. Poppy was on the tiller. "It's only fair," she said. "I think there are more locks ahead but can't remember. We don't get down this way very often."

"We?" I asked. I'd felt a twinge of concern.

"Breakdown crews from the marina."

"Oh."

"Who do you think I meant?" she said in a teasing voice. "A husband I'd casually forgotten to mention?"

"Hope not," I muttered, then wondered what I'd said.

The moment was interrupted by drinks and biscuits, then by a lone lock. Roofs were starting to peek through the trees; we were entering Stratford. Just four more locks, some of which were hard work and reluctant to open even with two people. A block of flats by the towpath, houses with attractive gardens opposite, a sweeping right turn, a very low bridge…

Poppy slowed down. "You take her," she said, and all but abandoned the tiller. She called to the boys who were removing still more grease from themselves. "You really need to come up now. But mind your head."

There proved to be just enough clearance under the tunnel-like bridge. Only just. It seemed to be quite bright ahead. A wide boat was moored against the right bank and its stern almost blocked our exit, it seemed. I steered to avoid it, hoping for enough clearance to the left.

We came through, and it was as if the world had opened up to us. An impressively large basin extended in front of us and to our left. People were watching us, pointing, and I wondered for a moment if I'd done something wrong or if we were trespassing.

"Welcome to Bancroft Basin," said Poppy. "Moorings are down to the left, by the Shakespeare statue. It's best to go bow in, especially if people are watching."

"Which mooring?" I asked. It looked crowded, and we were a full length boat.

"Wherever there's a space. I know – how about we put Phil and Nat ashore to find one, then you can hover in the middle until they tell us where one is? It's fairly sheltered today. You'll need to come back and tell us, guys; I don't think we'd be able to see you from the end of one of the pontoons."

They rushed down to the bows and jumped off after I very cautiously nudged up to a short area of quayside. Almost immediately the stern started to swing out into the centre of the basin.

"A jet of forward, and tiller over to the left," instructed Poppy.

It wasn't easy, keeping in one place with even only a gentle breeze blowing the stern out. At last Nat ran back.

"There's one three boats along," he yelled so we could hear over the engine.

"Shall I take her?" Poppy asked. "You go to the bow and direct me to where he means, and stand by with a rope. Get her bow moored and I can sort out the stern."

Poppy, of course was very accustomed to moving boats around her own marina, and getting into mooring slots that were only as wide as the boat. I looked three along, and indeed there was a vacant pontoon. I indicated down to it for Poppy, and experienced the odd sideways movement of the bows as the boat pivoted around its central point. Phil was there, standing on a pontoon, looking a bit nervous.

"It wobbles!" he called, bracing himself on it.

"Catch!" I called back, and threw the rope to him, missing both him and the pontoon. Cursing, I pulled it back in and had another go, but again it tangled up in mid-flight.

"Dad! You're useless," he taunted as the bow drifted nearer. He took the rope from my hands and stepped back with it, pulling. Before I had a chance to warn him he had found the opposite side of the pontoon and fallen backwards. Fortunately the boat moored that side was short so that his head didn't hit it, but he hit the water with an almighty splash. After a short delay he surfaced and swam to the pontoon. I stepped ashore and picked up the rope.

"Phil, you're useless," I said quietly, throwing his taunt back to him as I grabbed his wrist to haul him back.

"Huh! And you can shut up too, Nat," he called down to the quayside where his most concerned younger brother was having hysterics.

"It's ok, Phil, I'll make fast," I said innocently, and walked down the pontoon to one of the double cleats.

"You're not laughing, Dad," Phil accused me, having partially recovered.

"Not externally, no," I told him.

Poppy had already manoeuvred the stern into place and had called out to Phil that he should use the centre line. "We're too long to use the stern rope," she explained. Phil sloshed up the pontoon and did as he was bidden.

"I'm going to have a shower and change, if everyone's had their fill of laughing," he said with a look of daggers at his brother.

"Your *face!* Your face as you stepped back onto nothing. Classic."

I think had I not been there he might have pushed Nat in too, just so as to spread the happiness. But I was, so he climbed back in and was about to go in when I called out. "Could you take your shoes off first, please, and anything else you can? Then there's less to clear up afterwards."

He complied without a backwards glance, then vanished.

We climbed along the gunwale and joined Poppy on the stern. "Is Phil all right?" she asked.

"His pride's a bit bruised, but he's ok. He's having a shower and a change. Shall we start getting some lunch ready?"

"I was going to suggest that, then we can look round the town and merge with the gongoozlers."

Phil reappeared after ten minutes, slightly clothed and still wet. "Who said lunch?"

We admitted our plans.

"I'll swim over there and buy us some ice creams, shall I?"

Where he was pointing was an ice-cream boat. Not a van, a boat. It had windows facing the water as well as the bank, and seemed to be doing a good trade.

"That'd give them a shock. How will you get them back?"

"Swim with them."

"All four?"

He hesitated. "I could give them to Nat and he could walk them round."

"Go on, then."

"Got any money?"

The traditional rolling of parental eyes and I handed him a few coins and a note.

"I don't want to weigh you down. You might drown," I told him.

"Good heavens, he still cares."

"No, I just want my ice cream."

Poppy spluttered into her coffee.

He elected to walk round in the end. "Don't want the note to get wet."

I didn't point out that nowadays they were plastic.

27 The Avon

Stratford has almost the same shops as every other town. Some of them may be housed in much older properties than normal but the chain-store shops are everywhere. Souvenir shops are different, mainly because of the subject on most of the memorabilia. Pubs and restaurants are… well, the usual fare, but sometimes with Shakespearian names,

It's a young place. I suppose kids and teens are dragged there by parents so that the younger element can drink in culture whilst the parents drink in Costa. But the young attract other young people, so for a place which majors on the antiquity of its most famous ex-resident it's a contrast that so many of the visitors are under thirty. Very much under thirty.

Until the episode of the girl at Knowle Locks I'd never thought of Phil as being attractive to the opposite sex. It's not something that a Dad sees coming. I mean, the son is just… a boy you hope to bring up well. Isn't he? Except when he's being a pain.

There had been some evidence of this aspect of Phil when he had hauled himself from the water from the pontoon earlier. And as we walked into Stratford there were young girls everywhere. It was hot, and therefore scant-clothing weather. By that time Poppy and I were in shorts, as were the boys. There were times when Phil didn't know where to look. Well actually, he did; it was more that his eyes – and his neck muscles – were working overtime. Some of the looks, it appeared, were not one-way.

"Shall we split up?" I asked. Something had occurred to me. It was his birthday in two days' time and I had forgotten it completely. I wanted him out of the way.

"See you at the boat in an hour," he said immediately, and was off at the run before Nat could say anything or volunteer to go with him. It was the first time he had done anything like it, and I could tell Nat was miffed. I thought furiously.

"Not polite, but useful, Nat, because I want your advice. It's his birthday on Thursday and I haven't a clue what to get him. Is there anything he's let on that he wants?"

Nat brought himself down to earth.

"Apart from a blow-up girl, you mean?"

There was a muffled cough from Poppy. Nat knew it was a laugh and grinned at her.

"You're as bad as he is," I told him. "There must be something."

"Look at the way he jumped off just then," said the unhelpful one. "It's all he talks about. Girls and food."

"How about music?" I asked resignedly.

"Spotify. No one does CDs any more."

"I do."

"Yeahh... well..."

I missed our music collection from home and was annoyed I never thought to take some of the better ones. At least they were on my phone.

"One thing... he did mention that when he had to replace hoses, it was a nuisance to go and borrow screwdrivers and things."

I registered surprise. "I didn't know he'd been doing that, except with me there."

"Oh yes. If he sees one before you get there he'll swap it over to take some of the weight off you. Especially when you've not been well."

Now I was gobsmacked again. "Did you know this? I asked Poppy.

"Not a clue."

"You two... Just when you think you know everything, one of you pulls me up short again. Yes, we'll find a decent set and present him with them."

"There's Halfords up there," he said, trying to be helpful. I just looked at him.

We found an electrical wholesale place that also dealt with the public. I knew the kind of set I had in mind, and they had them. I also got him a decent head torch, exactly the same as mine.

"Hardly fair to buy him work tools," I said, "but what do you get a lad of his age – or yours, come to that." This was aimed at Nat, of course, not at Poppy.

"He'd like a bottle of wine."

Nat said it in such a rush that I almost had to ask him to repeat it.

"How on earth... Where's he been drinking wine?"

"Didn't say. But he was saying that now he was older he should be able to drink it. And he wants to try opening one."

"He knows..." I went through the usual thing of the brain growing and brain cells being killed off. Nat knew it anyway, as did Phil. I also knew of my own alcohol exploits at 14. "If we did, would you feel very offended if you didn't get any?"

"I'd like to taste it."

I exchanged a glance with Poppy. She just smiled.

We bought a bottle of Prosecco. It seemed to fit the bill and to be suitably celebratory – and had the advantage of a champagne-type cork. We also bought a half-decent red, also with a cork, for him to practice opening and for Poppy and me to drink.

Nat found a 'waiter's friend' that looked a little different from the usual, and bought it. It was unusual for him to buy a present without asking for a loan (a.k.a never-to-be-returned funding).

"I hope we're not raising an alcoholic," I mused as we left the store. "It's hardly the right thing to do, buying alcohol for someone on his fifteenth birthday."

I found myself being looked at piercingly. What? I re-ran my last comment though my mind and found myself blushing at the second pronoun. Oh well. I was starting to realise that something was happening, and it wasn't one-sided.

"You're incorrigible," I told her.

"I never said a word."

"Your eyes did."

"Ah, you notice them, do you?"

Had Nat not been with us and looking at us with amusement we may have continued the conversation. Instead, we made our way wordlessly back to the boat where another thought struck me.

"Damn! No wrapping paper."

"Wrap them in a tea towel, then he'll think it's his turn to dry, and ignore them like he ignores a tea towel the rest of the time." Nat, as usual, with an unusual and early-onset grasp of consequences. Poppy and I grinned and I gave him a thumbs-up. We hid the items in my dirty clothes drawer.

Phil was only fifteen minutes late, and buzzing. He said nothing about his experiences but was notably in a more than usually good mood. His first words were inevitable, though.

"Is there anything to eat?"

We had bought a River Avon licence, so set off to operate the lock down from the Basin to river level. Immediately a crowd of onlookers gathered.

"Gongoozlers," muttered Phil, who had ill-advisedly just put the kettle on. He froze, his eyes on the bridge ahead. I could see why. Had I been fourteen, and had my parents understood more about physical attraction at that age, I'd not just have frozen but whimpered as well.

"Let me off," he muttered. Far too late, Phil. We're lining up for the lock and the stern is in the middle of the basin.

"You'll have to swim," I said in jest.

He looked at me and started taking stuff from his pockets.

"No, Phil! I know she's stunning but you're got nothing else dry. And if you have to walk around naked you'll be arrested."

"Daad..."

As soon as we were in the lock he jumped off and stood trying to look impressive by nonchalantly leaning against the gate to shut it. She was looking the other way, towards the town, and anyway was about twenty. As I looked back to check we were clear of the cill, a large young man came and put his arm around her. They walked away. Poor old Phil!

Nat, at the other end of the lock and in charge of the paddle, had two sisters talking to him and another family of sisters watching. The look on Phil's face was a picture. "How does he do it? First Maisie, now a harem. He's not even good looking."

"Oy! That's my son you're talking about!"

At least it confused him into silence.

"Pick us up on the right, just down there where the hire boats moor," Poppy called as I passed below and onto the river. "Turn right round and come up against the current, though, or she won't be controllable."

I made out towards mid river, thinking about the logic, and saw what she meant. The turn was easy – there was so much space – though at one point I was heading broadside down river and nearly panicked. More power and more tiller corrected that, and we just about coincided, the crew and me, as I came alongside.

Poppy had said something to Phil, and he headed to the bows. Once everyone else was on, he pushed against the wharf and the bow headed to centre stream again. I looked behind him and saw a girl of his age watching him almost hawk-like. He scrambled on board, saw her for himself, smiled and waved. And had a cautious answering wave.

Honour was satisfied. Maybe.

We played dodge-the-swimmer as we reached the first lock. Much of the left side of the river before it is given over to geese, children, swans, inflatables and their parents. The chaos on the river is similar in scale to the chaos of the previous sentence. Trinity Lock is a girder reinforced lock and gave a welcome respite, being comparatively quiet and swimmer-free. We descended it and continued.

Through two more locks we went, round a number of wide sweeping turns, past weirs – suitably distant – but with the occasional panic about which arch of a bridge to head for as often the navigation arrow was hidden. It was all very rural, delightfully so, but with several extremely expensive looking houses, each with a beautiful river view.

We found the *Four Alls* by a honey coloured set of bridges spanning the river. I could hear the questions approaching, but Poppy told Nat at the tiller to carry on and turn when it became wider and bridge-free.

"After this one, you mean." She nodded.

About fifteen minutes later we were heading back under the same bridges and Poppy was looking for the pub mooring. She pointed it out to Nat and guided him in slowly against the current. We moored, ignoring the "No overnight mooring" sign.

"Not really much point in going further," Poppy said. "Not when there's the possibility of a longer trip when the hires are fewer, in September."

"When we're back at school," Nat put in.

"Oh... Blast. Yes, of course. There must be something we can do..."

"Maybe next year when everything's running even more smoothly?" I suggested.

"You mean when we've got so many hirers because the engines never break down and we can afford to hire more help?" asked Poppy with a smile. "It'd be nice."

Once again we decided against thrift and went to the Four Alls. With gasps at the prices of some of the menu we decided on the burgers, and even then the bill seemed astronomical for four people. Perhaps the rates went with the expensive looking houses. They certainly weren't in the league of an engineer or even a hire boat operator.

Dessert was made on the boat on the grounds of thrift. We had a glass of wine too. But not Phil's birthday present.

"It'd be quite good to get through the Lapworth flight, then we can dawdle if we want," Poppy said when she joined me at the kettle the following morning. "Lapworth can get very busy on some days and with inexperienced crews it can take ages."

"Unlike us, you mean?" I joked.

"You have good teachers. Some hirers – and some who own boats and see them once a year – have no common sense at all, and faff around delaying people."

It was an accolade of sorts.

Although a damp-haired Phil scanned the bridge and basin sides of Stratford, none of his idols were to be seen and he had to make do with a party of Guides whose Leaders were singularly unimpressed by his and Nat's posturing on the lock. Yes, Nat had joined in now too. We found our way through the basin and burrowed again under the bridge after its sharp right turn. The canal seemed very constricted after the width of the Avon.

We struggled up thirty locks, and ten hours later made it to the Fleur de Lys at Lowsonford. After the previous night's expense I was determined to eat on board that night. The meal I concocted was the fortunate coincidence of the *Menus for Engineers* and the contents of our larder. In fact it was Phil and me, as I'd given instructions to Poppy to sit and relax.

We did manage to escape for a very quick drink when we'd washed up, just for research reasons, as Nat put it – to Poppy's amusement.

We were passed at high speed early the next morning. The boat rocked violently and a glass fell to the kitchen floor and smashed. As an alarm clock it was very effective. Of course, I got out of bed and walked to the kitchen to look at the damage. Next I was leaving crimson stains on the flooring and cursing, searching as best I could for any more shards that were in the way of my regaining the bed and sitting on it. Blast.

Poppy knocked at the door.

"Hang on," I called, as I swiftly donned a dressing gown.

"Are you all right?"

"Trod on some broken glass. Bleeding."

She opened the door. "Put some shoes on, Poppy. Don't be as daft as me."

I got a look. She returned and knelt to look at my foot. "Well, it's a curved piece, and it should come out all right. Ready?"

I nodded, and she had it in her hand in a second, reached over to dispose of it and picked up a piece of kitchen towel.

"Clean it with that. I'll get the first aid kit and put a dressing on it."

I was prisoner there until she had dealt with me and swept the floor. To try and get dressed would have been unwise. At last I decided that the bathroom was an absolute necessity, but found Nat in it. Cursing again, I stumbled down through the three cabins, apologising to Phil, and used the small toilet in the front. It wasn't until my return journey that I remembered.

"Happy birthday, Phil."

How could he have gone back to sleep in such a short time? Ridiculous. I shrugged and passed through Nat's cabin where he was just re-entering his bed, and then through Poppy's, which was empty. She was still in the dinette, sitting on my bed.

"Thank you," I said, putting the kettle on.

A serious face greeted me when I looked back. "What's the matter?"

"Do you... well, do you think I'm a fool? Am I too old to be... to be befriending a man who's just fallen into my life? Someone who's saved my business, become an employee? Am I acting out of desperation? Or... or what's happening?"

"Should I be answering all those questions?" I said, after a pause whilst my brain reset itself. "I'll answer the first one: You're absolutely not a fool. Neither in business nor in personal matters. If – well, if you treated me or those two any other way than how you have, there might have been room for doubt. But so far as I'm concerned you're as grounded as... as an earth bond."

That got the flash of a smile.

A deep breath. "I think that something must have intrigued me that first time I saw you – when your son was over and you looked so sad. It can't have been only the comparative peace of the marina that I remembered. And ever since, the help you've given the three of us, and I don't just mean offering a broken down mind a chance of a new job, has shown me a lot of your character. We've laughed together, we've gone through a..." I looked for the word. "...an adventure? An event? Anyway, something that most people only read about – together. You've seen me at my worst, when asleep, dressed in nothing but shorts, treated me, let me treat you, and now you've dug a piece of glass out of my foot and bandaged me up.

"From where I stand, that says that here is a thoroughly decent, honest, lovely person I find easy to get on with. To the extent that I was nervous that she might decide against coming away on holiday with me, and quietly thrilled when she did. Did it show?"

She smiled at me, and it was one of those smiles that is guileless, and deeply attractive.

"You kissed me once," I reminded her. "I was unconscious at the time. That gave me no chance to return it. Do you think I should now?"

The smile deepened, if that was possible, and came towards me.

It must have been about forty seconds later that the kettle boiled. A whistle like that is not ignorable for long as it seeps into your very being, even when so pleasantly occupied as we were. Unfortunately it also wakes others up. The door opened and Nat stood looking as if he was about to accuse us of something.

"About time too," he said. "Are you making the tea, or shall I?"

"What do you mean 'about time too'?" I accused.

"You two. Look, can you shut that thing up, please? It's going right through me."

I obliged. "What do you mean, we two?"

"Dad, you can be awfully stupid at times. You two. Together. Hugging. About time. We'd been wondering if it'd happen on this trip."

Both Poppy's and my jaws dropped.

"Are we really that transparent?" asked Poppy.

"It's just the way you look at each other when the other one's not watching. Sickening, really, but I suppose it still happens when you're old."

I looked at Poppy and she at me.

"Would you like to throw him in the canal, or should I?"

He turned and vanished into his cabin. A final kiss, and I made the tea.

Some time later we heard that he'd gone down to tell his brother. Phil had been asleep but Nat woke him by closing his nostrils and blocking his mouth until he struggled, then announced it.

"Good," had come from my elder son, and he turned his back on Nat and went back to sleep.

Oh well, it's still approval.

Despite setting off quite early, we found that others were still before us. A group of inexperienced hirers – not ours – was struggling with the first of the close-together locks. Leaving Nat to steer alone, much to his horror, Poppy and I went off to assist and instruct, and found that we were very welcome. They were heading right at Kingswood, to go onto the Grand Union, and I hoped they'd be ok with the locks. As we lost them, and before we could join the queue for the next batch of locks heading north, two more boats pushed in front of us from the junction canal.

"It happens," Poppy said. "We'll get through eventually."

Rejoining the boat, I sniffed. Bacon? Breakfast? We hadn't eaten. Phil was at the stove, juggling rashers and stirring a saucepan full of beans.

"Happy birthday," I announced for the second time. He looked round and grinned. "Hallo, you two. Nat says you're a proper couple now. Good."

Once again I didn't know whether to be surprised, embarrassed or just thankful that he was in favour too.

"It's not very tactful to Poppy, Phil," I said more in hope than expectation of any apologies.

"Oh, I can be forgiven anything today," he responded. "It's my birthday."

"Or you could join Nat in the canal," Poppy told him.

"Has he fallen in? Is that why we've stopped? Anyway, you're too late. I've played that already." Then as an afterthought: "Has anyone fished him out?"

Poppy explained, then gave him a hug which made him freeze, and wished him a happy birthday too.

We waited there for what seemed like ages as boats came down towards us and others took their places going up. At last Nat's head appeared in the hatch. "Please could someone take over? I need a pee and I'm bored anyway."

Just as breakfast was ready, of course, so was the lock. We left Birthday Boy to eat in peace; Poppy took the tiller and Nat and I went to whistle us up it. It didn't get us very far. The boat in front was still waiting to enter the next one. We moored on the lock landing and continued breakfast with Poppy, two of us outside and two in.

At last we were done, I think just one lock further on. Nat handed the birthday boy a tea towel.

"Oy! The one who cooks doesn't wash up!"

"It's a tea towel, dummy."

"Or dry up... hang on, what's this?"

The waiter's friend, in its box, mystified him. "Thank you," he said in uncertain tones to Nat. "Not sure when I'll get to use it, though."

Nat had stolen our thunder. I rummaged in my drawer and brought the two bottles out with a flourish. "Before you say anything about eighteen years and brain cells, it seems only right that, sensibly, you should be able to celebrate properly later. Fifteen isn't seen as childhood, not really, unless you're a lawyer on duty. What it is, is a halfway point between the start of double figures and reaching the round number of twenty. We felt it'd be good for us all to recognise that with you, if we may."

Only occasionally have I seen Phil speechless, but I seem to have done the trick. The screwdrivers and torch... well, they were good adult-style gifts, the sort of thing I would appreciate in my forties, let alone at fifteen. As gifts go, a bottle of Prosecco is hardly the most generous, but had I deposited a grand into his bank account he could hardly have been happier. The grin that transformed his face gave that away.

"Do I issue a formal invitation?" he asked, eventually. "Or just open it with four glasses nearby?"

"Four glasses and dinner, I should think," Poppy told him. "And if you intend to post invitations and expect RSVPs, good luck."

Phil gave a rare bray of laughter. Nat and I started the washing up whilst Phil, still with a happy grin lighting his way, went outside with Poppy.

28 Home again

The next eighteen locks remained slow going and we were glad to reach the summit.

"Whew!" Poppy exclaimed, "that was worse than I've ever heard it being. You see what I mean about wanting to get that lot done early, certainly in a day. Now it means that we can dawdle a bit, if that's ok with everyone? If so, I have a phone call to make."

Though puzzled, we raised no objections. I did wonder if it had anything to do with Phil, though.

"Don't eat too much," Poppy told us when the boys were clamouring for food and Phil was already delving into a cupboard.

"Why?" asked the delver.

"Because you might just have a birthday meal tonight, and it might just defeat you otherwise. Even you. It's getting on for mid-afternoon, you know."

They made do with three biscuits and a cup of tea. Each.

It wasn't too far to the bridge Poppy was aiming for and we moored earlier than we normally would. We had to take a position opposite a line of private boats, one of which was being washed with a long sponge affair on a pole. The sound of our calls to each other brought the owner of the pole to look above his boat. Phil, still cheerful at the prospect of having his birthday marked by a meal, waved, and received a wave with the pole that made him laugh.

"Going far?" called the pole-wielder in a pleasant southern accent, almost BBC in quality.

"Only here for the night," Phil called back.

"But not for good and all, then. Where's the home mooring?"

"Birmingham. Hockley Port marina."

"We must be neighbours in a way, then. Hockley Heath is down there, where you've come from."

"Are they anything to do with each other?"

"Not so far as I know. I was just remarking on the coincidence."

"Yes," said Phil. "Separated neighbours! I wonder why. Is the Blue Bell a good pub?"

"Very," came the confirmation. "I often eat in there, and they never let you down."

"We might see you later, then. We're going there to celebrate a birthday."

"Yours, by any chance?"

"It is. Fifteen at last. I seem to have spent a year being fourteen and it was getting boring."

The man laughed. "Well, many happy returns, then. And yes, I think I'll need someone else to cook for me after this. It's a lot of work. Then I have to go up to the winding hole, turn round and come back so I can do the other side. Anyway, must get on. I should see you all in there later."

We waved; he waved back and carried on laundering his boat.

We did indeed encounter him later, chatting with a widely disparate group of people. He introduced us as being from a boat, told us his name was John and that he was a retired Geography teacher. We chatted happily until reminded that our table was ready. For once in a genuinely locals' pub we felt that we were being genuinely included in things. John had eaten, so despite our invitation he declined to join us.

It was after we had relaxed, replete, that a small cake with a fizzing candle on it was brought over, and those at the bar started off with "Happy Birthday" in the usual combination of different keys that is typical of most English scratch choirs. Phil was crimson, but grinning widely. There was a round of applause at the end and everyone called for a speech. He stood.

"Thank you! You've very kind. When I'm older and have a job I'll come back and buy a round." He sat down to another round of applause and cheering.

After a while John separated himself and came over, smiling. "Hope you didn't mind, but it seemed a good thing to do. Happy birthday again."

We thanked him effusively but he waved it away. "Good to meet someone of fifteen with intelligence behind him; it reminds me of my career – at least, some of those I taught. But I've got to go now – work calls. Might see you in the morning."

We bade our farewells. It was in a lull in the conversation that Phil mentioned that Helen had phoned him as he had been breakfasting. "She wanted to come and see me," he said.

"Good," I said, to his surprise.

"Why?"

"Because she's your mother, and should see you on your birthday. Or as near it as possible."

"Oh – well yes, that's sort of what I said. I told her we weren't at the marina and I couldn't tell her where we were because I didn't really know. She seemed to think that wasn't good enough."

Why did that not surprise me? "How did you leave it with her?" I asked.

"I said we'd be back at the marina on Friday some time and I'd call her then."

"Okay. I'll leave it to you, then. She knows where we are, but please be careful that Jonathan's not with her."

"Don't worry. If he is, I won't go anywhere near her, and if he is and tries something on I'll hit him. Hard. In the balls if necessary."

"Phil!"

"Well, after what he tried with Nat… I'm not going to allow him anywhere near me."

It was soon after that that we left. The pub was empty of locals by then, and only a few visitors were at tables elsewhere. Phil thanked the landlord for the cake, the remains of which were being taken back to the boat. I offered to pay for it and he declined. "Tell other people about us, though, would you?" he asked.

None of us could face either wine or Prosecco that night, though Phil wanted to try out his waiter's friend. He took in the information that the contents would go flat or stale or both quicker if opened now. "At least wait for a good reason to open it," I told him.

"To celebrate the day-after-my-birthday day? I could do that all year round, he said happily.

"Except that the definite article is singular, yes."

"Ahh."

We didn't see John in the morning. In fact by the time we had breakfasted with comfort and leisure in mind his boat had disappeared too. "He's gone to turn her round so he can clean the other side," Nat said.

"We'll probably see him on the way, then," Poppy observed.

We did, and fairly soon. Phil thanked him for the previous night, which made him smile and made me proud, we waved again and separated.

An increasingly built-up area, one tunnel, a guillotine lock ("sometimes one canal would have higher water, sometimes the other," said Poppy. "These can cater for either.") and a junction, and we were on familiar territory. "If we turned left here," Poppy said, "We'd get to Ghosty Hills tunnel." We remembered the name and Helen's behaviour and turned away from the memories.

After such a long exposure to life in the country, returning to Bourneville, the University and at last to the City centre was at once an anticlimax and a homecoming; both bitter and sweet. Even if, I suddenly thought, the homecoming wasn't really to a home, but to a place to moor our home.

Our home. Would it always be our home now? Would we ever move back into a conventional house? What would happen when the boys grew away? Phil: three more years, maybe, or long absences at University. Or maybe a partner. Or both. Memories returned; the Knowle flight girl, Stratford's manifold female attractions, the girl in the park as he had pushed the bows out. Who know what would happen?

And Nat, getting on for thirteen. Again: who knows? Maybe it would be Maisie? University? A design course?

Ah well. The boat was still our home now. Nat was about to manoeuvre into the space when Poppy called out: "Fuel? Pump-out? You can do the water later." He corrected just in time and we saw to the necessities.

We cooked later, and Phil had his chance to use the waiter's friend. "I won't break the cork next time. Promise," he said looking at the two parts. He enjoyed the Prosecco; drinking it as cautiously as I hoped he would, to my pleasure, and Nat kept him company with a small glass. Poppy and I enjoyed the deep red, and toasted each other for no other reason than we felt we should. But now our eyes met as the glasses chinked together and we smiled, knowing that we were on firm ground, that the journey ahead was more certain, and that two sons seemed to approve of its direction.

The office the next day provided a number of horribly official looking letters, some marked 'Private and Confidential', addressed to me. There were also some stiffer envelopes for Phil, obviously with cards inside. One, certainly, was from

Helen; I hoped my brother hadn't signed it too. But it was Saturday and we all had jobs to do; the post must wait. Much of the fleet was returning and had to be available in a few short hours for the next hirers.

"I hope you don't mind," Ian started when he'd checked how things had gone, "but I got another couple of helpers in knowing how busy it would be. They did an hour or so cleaning while they were here – I said we'd pay them – and they seemed good ones. Friendly types – you know the sort. Just the kind who work well with others."

"Well done, Ian. Thank you. I should have thought of that, but didn't."

"We've had a good few bookings for later on, too. Sounds as if news of the new engine man, and what happened, has done the rounds already." He grinned at me.

"I thought Jack might be useful when he first talked to you and took over that engine," said Poppy, smiling. "I'm obviously better choosing staff than I am fuel suppliers. It's nice to hear of the new bookings, though goodness knows how the news got round."

"Towpath telegraph," Ian said. "Worked two hundred years ago and still does. Like news of two people getting together does too. People seen holding hands, like."

I blinked and tried to look unconcerned. He couldn't be talking about us, surely. There was a faint grin there, though, even if he was looking at Poppy whose face was a picture.

"If that was directed at me, Ian, you shouldn't believe everything you hear." It was said severely, but Ian knew his boss of old.

"Sure it wasn't. They said she was old, or middle-aged, and so was he. So it can't have been you two young people."

The trouble with Ian is that the more he speaks tongue in cheek, the heavier his Birmingham accent gets. At that point he could well have been auditioning for an industrial revolution play.

Poppy glared at him, then turned to talk to the staff who had been gathering, welcoming the two newcomers and detailing people to jobs. Once again I heard an indrawn breath from a certain fifteen year old as he saw the new girl. I hoped he would be able to concentrate on his jobs and not try to seek her out every moment of the day.

We worked non-stop until one o'clock. Sandwiches, cake, tea and coffee, and about thirty minutes to sit; then we were back to the re-dressing of the boats ready for the new batch of hirers. Inevitably some of these were early, keen to experience what their money had bought them for the week, and they had to be nursemaided by our receptionist, Angela, until their boat was ready. They sat outside, watching the work and marvelling. "Won't be long," Poppy said to them with a smile as she scurried past at one point.

"No problem," came the response.

We turned the fleet round and gradually boats left with their instructors. Eventually there was a growing number of the cleaning and refurbishing staff returning to the office for tea. What could Poppy's annual budget be for cake, I asked myself. I was sure she didn't bake them herself.

This time many of the new hirers had been anything but new to the canals. They were experienced, some to expert standard, so needed little instruction. Most of the instructors were back in the office quite soon, leaving only Ian and another of the older casuals still out.

Phil had tried occasionally chatting with the new girl, but so far as I could see without much success. She appeared monosyllabic with him, maybe because she appeared to be a few years older. Goodness knows that's a minor difference, but in your teens it's enough to make the other person unattainable. Yes, I speak from experience. No: no further details will be forthcoming. Eventually he found his way back to Poppy, Nat and me, his eyes returning to her now and again in perplexity.

Poppy's phone rang. "Last two to collect; Ian and Geoff. Before I go, thank you all so much for today. I know I say this every week but I value you all and your ready, cheerful help more than you probably realise. The money will be transferred to your accounts this evening, as always. Our two new colleagues did well, too, settling in with the others, and I'll need your bank details before you go please, otherwise I can't pay you. If you're rushing off, can you give that information to Jack Dyer, please? Stay and socialise if you'd like, though. I must go and pick up the others."

I got the information from the two new ones, Phil's would-be friend and the lad who seemed to be her boyfriend. Ah... that would explain some of it. Phil turned away when he realised. Poor old lad.

At last the others were back, Poppy added the two new ones to her list, did some calculations, pressed a button, and that was that.

"Food," she said. "Then bed. Shall we go to the usual place?"

It was in "the usual place", the Navvy, while we were waiting for the plates to arrive that a quiet Nat floored me.

"Pooooppy..."

You can tell from the tone that something radical is coming.

"Yeeessss Nat?"

"Dad said that when he was on his walkabout, he saw you sitting, looking unhappy, with a man. He said it was your son. Can you... Am I allowed to know what happened?"

He shouldn't have asked it, that much was plain. It was too personal a question. I was torn between telling him so and wanting – no, needing – to know the answer.

But, being her, she answered him honestly, echoing the guilelessness of the question.

"That was indeed my son. I'd written to him to tell him about all the problems we'd been having, and how bookings were suffering badly and how I really wanted to give up." She paused, perhaps to gather her emotions together. "He told me that would be a shame and that I should hire some expert help – an engineer, preferably."

She smiled at me. With what had gone between us over the previous week, my heart melted a little and I smiled back,

"He came over here to look at the books and to understand how the business was doing. I needed him to tell me whether it could really perform if it was more reliable, so to speak. He's a recently qualified accountant, you see. He told me that what we were doing should be a sound business, but that I had some issues to face – which I knew – and a little work to rescue the reputation once I'd done so. He was only here for about a week, so it was complete chance that we were available to be seen by a passing engineering manager."

Again that smile. But the question of Nat's that really floored me was the next one, one that was asked so quickly that I stood no chance of nipping it in the bud.

"What happened to Mr Watson? Am I allowed to ask that?"

"Nat!" I exclaimed, too late.

She looked at him, then at me, then back to him.

"He took over the business when his father retired, way back in 2000. It had started in a small way in the 1970s and when Gordon took over it was doing quite well. He built it even more, but it grew so large that it made running it too much work. It burnt him out and he gradually changed, grew crabby and unhappy. We never took holidays, not even in the winter. He had changed too much; he could only think about work.

"From the start the business was his baby. I only really dabbled at the edges of it, so it was difficult for me to learn what was going on. It became almost a pastime to me, but to him it was life itself.

"It became a divided marriage; he nursed the business, I nursed the baby."

She sighed. "He never stopped nursing the business, micromanaging it. After eight years I could stop nursing the son so much, as he started to thrive on his own with less and less input and more and more independence. It was a good start for him in many ways, but..." she sighed "…but now I think I'd have done things differently. Back then – well, the business consumed first the marriage, then Gordon, and all this suffered because people wouldn't work for him."

There was a silence which eventually I thought I should gently break. But she sighed again. "Lack of staff took its toll. He drank, and drank heavily. Then one day he just left. Just upped and left. I had to take over the business at a stroke. It was so difficult. A learning curve – well, a learning cliff, really. I managed to get a few good staff round me and somehow we kept going.

"As to Gordon, at last I heard that he was living on the streets, had turned almost completely to alcohol, then drugs; both of which involved theft for their funding. But by the time someone had run him to ground for me he was past help. Two weeks after they found him and I tried my damndest to help, he was dead."

Nat, to give him credit, looked appalled, and I could see his hand creeping out to touch hers. I was opposite. She didn't lift her head up to meet my eyes. Phil's eyes were floorward too.

"I was thrust into a world that I only partially knew. The one thing I did know was that I needed a lot of help. Gradually help came, some stayed, some went, and some *had* to go. But the business started to flourish, given the trust that good staff. Until I made the wrong choice about a fuel provider, then the right choice about an engineer."

And now our eyes did meet.

"I'm sorry, Poppy," I said slowly. "Maybe Nat was wrong to ask..."

"No. He's absolutely right. He, Phil and you are now involved in this business, yes, but also in my life. They know that, and I'm pretty sure you do too. And I hope I'm involved in yours. So we should have no secrets, and that's never really been a secret. It's just never been asked by the right person before."

She smiled at Nat, who, to my amazement, jumped up and embraced her. She allowed it, and sat back smiling when he released her.

"You have good muscles," she told him, causing a grin.

"Better than Dad's?" he asked, cheekily.

"Ah well... different strokes." An enigmatic answer, lost on the boys, but I knew what she meant.

The food arrived and we ate, more or less in silence. It was afterwards that I found some courage.

"You don't have to answer this, obviously, and this is not really the time or place to ask. But do you miss him?"

She hesitated. "That's difficult to answer. Running hire boats has taken up every ounce of my thoughts until recently. I miss the man he was. I don't miss the man he became. I'm desperately sad that he ended up the way that he did, even if there was no love left for him by then. It's not a simple answer. But you deserve it, whatever it is."

Poppy decided that she needed to return home that night. "I've run out of clean clothes," she said. I told her she could use 'our' washing machine on the boat, but she laughed and declined, saying that she still needed stuff from home. "I'll be back in the morning. Or you could come to me and have a bit more space for a change."

"Are you sure you want us, after spending all last week with us?" I asked.

All I received was a look. "I'll see you some time after breakfast," she said.

Late it might have been but the first thing we did at the boat was to tackle the post. Phil had a pleasing number of cards, including Helen's which had indeed been signed by Jonathan. I watched as he reached out for a pen to cross the name out so it was a completely black rectangle. Why would my disgraced brother think it was appropriate to sign it after all that had happened? There was at least a fifty pound note in it as well, which I hoped was just from Helen, but the card didn't mention it. Phil took himself down the boat to phone Helen as promised.

The official letters were more worrying. They concerned the sale of the house and I was concerned about their wording. To my untrained eye there seemed little in them that would involve me in setting or agreeing the sale price, and not a lot of guarantee that half the proceeds would be coming my way. Damn. It would have to be solicitors, then.

The last one was a really complimentary letter from Crown, containing a card signed by my ex-colleagues. The ploy I had used in order to wring another month's salary from them had worked, to my relief, so that was another few thousand in the bank. Thanks to having no rent to pay and no rates, and meals that Poppy kept insisting on paying for, we were keeping our heads above water.

In the usual spirit of co-operation I told the boys what it was all about.

"That means our home's being sold, I suppose," Phil said. "I mean, our *old* home." It was said without rancour, and I hoped that Nat thought the same. It also meant that Helen and Jonathan would be living in his flat. Good luck with that, I thought.

"She says it's too late to come now," said Phil, returning to us. "Can she come tomorrow? I told her she could. First she asked me down to the house, but I asked if *he* would be there, and she said that he would. So I'm not going."

"She can come here, of course," I said. "Any idea what time?"

"She didn't say. She'll just turn up, I suppose."

30 The vanishing

It was quite early the next morning that Helen appeared. Both Phil and I checked the car for unwanted passengers and were relieved when none appeared. Both boys went with her – at their own request – and were returned about two hours later. They were uncharacteristically quiet. I knew better than to ask, and it wasn't long before Nat spoke about it.

"She told us she's selling the house. We told her we knew"

I nodded. "I imagine that hurt a bit."

"It's where we grew up."

"A lot of people move house at least once during their childhood. Look at Maisie, for example."

"I know. But it's still… I know it's got to happen."

"How about you, Phil?"

"Same, really. She asked us if we would change our minds and live with them."

My eyebrows raised. "And what did you tell her? Or is that confidential?"

"Dad! It's not funny. We told her that there was no way, not with him there, and…"

He trailed off. "I told her she was mad to ask. That's when she brought us back."

Now I could understand their mood. Even after all that had passed, incredibly she had no real idea what my brother's behaviour really meant to these two. Her own attitude showed that she put little value on their ability to make up their own minds.

Tactfully I put that to them, aware that in a way I was swaying their opinions. But it seemed only right that I should try and explain at least a little of what might be making Helen tick. It might have worked, as they seemed a little happier.

We went to Poppy's house for a change. It seemed odd not to experience that gentle 'give' as I put a foot over the threshold. We had become so acclimatised to a home that was afloat. The house itself was comfortable, although Poppy's idea of a home was more minimalist than our old house had been, with its pictures lining the walls as decoration. But it was pleasant and roomy – a shock to us after the boat.

When she learnt about the contents of my mail and the legal bits surrounding the house sale she was blunt. "If you sign that without talking to our solicitors, you're an idiot. There's far too much unsaid there and they could catch you out at any moment."

"That's what I thought too," I told her. "I could see no stipulation that the sale price had to be agreed by both of us, at all stages from the first advertisement, through offers, to the final sale. And that's just one of the issues."

"We'll phone tomorrow," she said firmly. "None of us wants to see swindling going on."

The boys settled down in front of the television, delighting in its superior size; I helped Poppy prepare lunch. We had done this before, on the boat, and I had enjoyed having to squeeze between the cupboards and her to get something. Her kitchen was wider than narrowboat size, so I had to fake a close pass instead. She looked surprised.

"And what was that for?"

"Just pretending it's the narrowboat galley."

"Incorrigible," she laughed.

"Nice. Well, for me."

She turned and put her arms round me, the first time she had really done so. "And for me."

The hug lasted.

At length the heads came back and each pair of eyes looked into the other.

"Are we stupid?" she asked again.

"It doesn't feel stupid to me."

It was inevitable that the faces should approach each other, should make contact. As they did and we made contact, it felt as if a weight had fallen from my shoulders, a weight whose presence I had failed to acknowledge.

Was it true? Did I now really have in my life a kindred spirit once more? A spirit that attracted me in friendship, bearing, intelligence and physicality?

We were in the kitchen. The boys were in the living room watching a TV of the size Phil hankered after for the boat. It was inevitable that the door should open without our knowledge, a voice should say "Oh!", and the door close again. We disengaged, Poppy opened the door and saw Nat's back about to disappear back to the TV.

"Nat," she called. He looked round.

"Sorry."

"Don't be. Lunch won't be long."

"Ok. Just wanted to see if there was anything I could help with."

"I thought you were watching TV."

"Phil is."

"Not your choice of film?"

He shook his head.

"You could come and chop some vegetables."

"I don't want to interrupt… anything."

"You're not. Come and help."

"But you were… were…"

"Discovering again that we have feelings for each other. Yes. But that doesn't exclude anyone else, particularly not you two."

He smiled, once again showing approval.

Lunch was a leisurely affair, uninterrupted by approaching locks, tunnels or the need for someone else to steer. Instead the interruption came from my phone, and I looked at it casually to see if it might be urgent.

"Carl Parish Emerson", said the display.

I told the others, they quietened and I opened it.

"They've discovered there's another one. Going off grid until found and arrested. She was a link between a European cell and the now defunct UK one. No contact except emergency then with pw."

They listened as I read it.

"What about Maisie?" asked Nat at once. "Will she come here?"

"He didn't ask, so no. Seeing what happened last time, I hope not."

"Dad!"

"Sorry, Nat, but your safety – our safety – comes even higher up. Oh, if they ask, yes of course she can come. But if you remember, last time she was here, she was in danger. And I was shot at. And none of us can take any avoiding action as we don't know who or what we're looking for."

"Except it's a woman this time," Phil said.

I stared at him, then looked at the message. I'd just read the "She links to a…" when the message vanished.

"It's gone. They said it would when they installed the app."

"So what do we do?" Poppy asked. I liked the pronoun.

"Nothing we can do. Just carry on as normal and be wary of any strangers who seem to be hanging about, as before. But women, this time. No, actually, anybody."

"It sounds as if we should be wary of any last minute bookings, then," said Poppy. "Or don't you think they'd try and find them here again?"

"There's just no way of knowing," I told her.

We were nearing the end of the second week of the school holidays and already the boys were at a bit of a loose end. Most of their friends were away with families. I was working at the Marina and at last on some private boats whose care had come our way. Nat had phoned the Losardos and had been told he was welcome to go round there and give a hand in their workshop. Phil suddenly had the idea that he could help me on engine servicing, now he had a decent, professional screwdriver set.

"I know how they work, Dad," he complained when I told him that there was a limit to what he could do.

"That's not the point. There's so little room in the engine 'ole that two people would just get in each other's way."

"I don't mean that we should both do the same engine. I could start things off – you know, wash the gunge off and pump it out of the bilge, then perhaps drain off the oil."

"After you've washed the gunk off the engine, all of it, and got it sparkling, that's when you set it going and watch. And listen. And that's where I come in. Then if it's ok you can drain off the old oil and so on. Fancy doing that?"

His enthusiasm seemed genuine, though I wondered how long it'd last. Working through the holidays was different for me at his age; it had only on Saturdays that my youthful self had been 'helping' at the nearby, long-suffering garage.

There were some more official looking letters waiting for me in the office, but I never had a chance to look at them before people started arriving for work and for conversation. Later would do, I thought.

It turned out that Phil was interested in discovering what his old Dad had learned over all the decades. It also turned out that he was a quick learner, and that he was reliable and efficient at the tasks I set him – when there were no distractions. I wondered if that was how he was viewed at school. His reports from there seemed ok, if unremarkable, just as mine had been all those years ago.

He was hovering over an engine I was listening to, and looked enquiringly at me.

"Just listening for any knocking that shouldn't be there," I called out over the diesel sounds.

"How can you tell, in all that noise?"

"Experience. And if I want to hear more I use a stick."

"*What"?*

"Listen to it. Get used to how it sounds. Now then…"

I reached for my broom handle and held it against the engine's rocker cover, indicating that he should put his ear to the other end.

"Bloody hell, it's loud," he shouted, and held it away from his ear.

"Get used to the volume and listen. Hear that rattling? That's normal. It's really heavy knocks you are trying to hear. I can do the same at the bottom of the engine too, on the sump, to hear how the crankshaft bearings are faring."

I demonstrated, moving to the side of the boat and holding the wood against the sump. "Experience will tell you when it's wrong, and then you can gulp and take the engine out, putting a spare in its place."

"*Is* there a spare?"

"Not yet. At about eight grand it's an expensive luxury for a very occasional need. In our case it's better to find a different boat for the hirer, then buy an engine for it if the boat's not near the end of its life.

It's good working with your son. I just hoped that the other one wasn't being a nuisance with the Losardos. The thought reminded me that it was about lunchtime and I wondered if I should phone Nat and find out if he was returning to eat.

There was no answer. I frowned, and phoned the workshop.

"I think Nat's phone must be on silent," I started after the usual pleasantries. "I was going to ask if he was coming back for lunch – I'm sure you've had enough of him by now."

"But he's not been here," Seppe told me after a pause. "We were expecting him, but he's not arrived. We thought we'd got it wrong and he was coming this afternoon."

"But he left here after breakfast," I told him, suddenly worried. "I've never been to your workshop but I wonder if anyone in the area saw him this morning? Could you check?"

My blood was running cold by this time. Had bloody Jonathan struck again? Or, worse, was it something to do with the Parishes' problems?

I looked at the family-tracking app we had installed. Poppy, Phil and I showed up, but of Nat there was no trace and the software said that the phone had been switched off.

Seppe phoned back half an hour later. "No one has seen him here. They know him by now, so they'd have recognised him."

Blast. In fact I swore roundly, to Phil's surprise. First things first: I phoned Helen.

"Of course he's not here. Do you think…"

I interrupted. "Is Jonathan there?"

"No, of course not. He's at work. What have you done with my son?"

"That's what *I'm* asking *you*. Are you sure he's at work.?"

"Don't be silly. Of course he is"

"Are you at home or at his?"

"At home."

"I'm going to phone him." I broke the connection roughly and called my brother's mobile. There was no answer. Jonathan's mobile was his lifeline. It was his main contact method for customers. For him not to answer it was unheard of. I wondered if he had seen that the call was from me and was ignoring it.

"Phil, can you call your uncle, please? Just pass it to me when he answers, would you?"

He had no luck either.

I lurched out of the boat and ran to the office where Angela must have thought I was mad again, the speed at which I attacked the landline and dialled Jonathan's number. At least it rang.

"Dyer Sales," came the usual voice.

"Where is Nat, Jonathan? What have you done with him?"

"I don't know what you mean," he said after a surprised pause. "He's not with me."

"How can I trust you now after what you've tried to do before? Either put him on the phone or the Police will be visiting you."

"Jack, for God's sake; I haven't got him. I really haven't got him. I've not seen him since… since… well, you know when."

"I don't know when you last saw him. Are you at home?"

"No. I'm at the office."

"Stay on the line." I put the line on mute and used my mobile to dial the landline at his flat. No answer, and I couldn't hear a phone ringing either. So perhaps he was telling the truth.

Why my mind should be so free of panic given the circumstances, I have no idea. But I was thinking straight and I was thinking clearly. I knew that unless he was lying this had to do with the Parishes. And I needed to email them. Now.

"Where are you?" I asked again.

"I said: at the office. Look, what is all this about? Have you lost Nat? Or what?"

"Go to your flat. Now. You're about to get a visit from some officials who won't mess about when they hammer on the door, so let them in quickly. And tell Helen the same thing." I had seen the no-questions-first approach of the Parishes' employers before and didn't really want either my brother or Helen at the wrong end of a bullet, despite all that had happened. My parents – my late parents – would never forgive me.

On my phone with its special app I composed an email to Carl, with the usual 'Emerson' after the address, telling him tersely that Nat was missing and that Jonathan and Helen separately denied having seen him. Both their addresses and phone numbers were given.

A few minutes later Carl messaged: "*Stay with Phil on the boat and I'll keep you updated.*"

I pacified Angela and ran back to the boat where a worried Phil was sitting, staring into space. He looked sharply at me when I appeared.

"Well?"

"He didn't say anything this morning, did he? Nothing to make you worried?"

"No, he was just full of going to the Losardo's workshop. Have either of them got him?"

"They say not. I've spoken to each of them and they say not. So I've told Carl what's happened and he's getting his lot to check – I suppose that's what he meant."

"Are you all right, Dad?"

"No, of course I'm not. Don't ask bloody fool questions."

"I'm not," said my suddenly adult-sounding son levelly. "But I know you've been through a lot and – well, to be honest, you look awful. White as a sheet. I'm going to make a cup of tea."

"Sorry," I mumbled. "I'm worried senseless now. It'd be bad enough if Helen and Jonathan had him against his wishes, but the alternative is that this bloody mob have him. Or something."

With the kettle filled and heating, he started poking at his phone, the instinctive recourse of the mid-teenager.

"Can't you leave that bloody thing alone for a moment?" I snapped. "Your brother's missing, for f… for God's sake."

He looked hurt, but calm. "I was hoping to do it quietly, but I'm looking up the number of the big hospital in case there's been an accident and their Casualty know about him."

Like a pricked balloon I subsided, tears pricking at my eyes.

"Sorry," I said again. I let him find it, and make the call. Maybe a young sounding voice asking about an accident to a twelve year old brother had an effect, but the responses he was receiving were helpful and kind. He had to tell whoever it was that he was fifteen, that he wasn't alone, that he was uninjured, and that the Police had been called and were on the case. His number was taken so that if a twelve year old victim was brought in, he would be told.

Why was Poppy away at a supplier's when I needed her so badly?

An hour later there was a long email from Carl. "*Both addresses visited and searched. No sign. Both persons of interest shocked and worried, and were told to stay indoors. Now tracing all calls they made etc. Other avenues now under investigation, including my brother etc. Please call Police with basic facts and give them this number:"* A mobile number was quoted. *"Don't phone it yourself please. Wait there for more information."* There was just time to save the mobile number before the email vanished. As I dialled 999 I told Phil what the text had said. His face was the most serious I'd ever seen it.

The Police asked all sorts of questions to which there were no answers, but I insisted that they should call the mobile and talk to whatever government-based force it was. They insisted that they would visit both Helen's and Jonathan's homes themselves, a fact that didn't worry me in the slightest, nor did their insistence that they visit us.

Soon after there was a knock on the side of the boat. It was Poppy asking if she could come in.

"Please," I said, with feeling.

"You look dreadful. What's happened?"

I explained, and immediately she was hugging me. When Phil appeared he received the same treatment. Words seemed superfluous.

Two Police officers were next to appear, and we received a grilling, especially about the situation with Helen, Jonathan and now Poppy. They asked to look over her house and she and they all disappeared for a while.

"We've heard of the involvement of the special forces," one of them said cagily, "and there's going to be a limit on what we're able to do whilst their operation is in place..."

"What operation?" I interrupted. "They've told me nothing."

"Nor can I, Mr Dyer. And not only because I have no details."

"Does this mean that Nat is in danger?"

He hesitated. "We know so little about this organisation, just that it consists of some people with extreme political views who have decided to engage in terrorism to force a change in policy making. Of course, like so many extremist attempts it's doomed to failure, but its operatives are blind to that. I doubt whether they would threaten the life of a young child, though."

"They threatened mine," I said indignantly. "They shot at me."

His eyes opened wide. "When was this?"

"I should check with your people. The Police attended."

He looked at me and reached for his radio.

Poppy slept with me that night.

It started off when she said that she wished I had someone who could be with me overnight whom I trusted, just to be a comforting presence. Without thinking straight I said the first thing that came to mind: "The only person I'd want is you."

A long, level gaze into my eyes. "All right," she said in a voice so quiet I could hardly hear it. "But I meant actually *with* you, there to hug you while you dropped off to sleep, and stay there in case you woke up."

My last few words echoed round my head, and they sounded good.

"So did I."

Preparations for sharing were awkward. It was not like young love where there is a frantic physical rush to be intimate at the cost of any other considerations. We gained the bed separately, with circumspection, and lay there side by side.

"I don't know If I'll be able to sleep, you know," I whispered. "I'm still worried sick."

"I know. So is Phil. So am I. But we'll be doing him no favours if we are useless tomorrow for lack of sleep, shall we? And it's not being disloyal to him to sleep, either. It would be disloyal if we were unable to think clearly tomorrow, or to be useless when Nat returns."

She was right, of course. And we did both get some sleep, helped by innocent physical contact. Which honestly did help a lot.

We were woken by the sound of the water pump next morning, as usual. Before we could wake and get out the door opened and Phil appeared, only to stop short as he saw us obviously having slept together.

"Oh."

It was all he said, but it was the hard tone he used that got to me. He vanished again down to his cabin. I looked at Poppy helplessly.

"Leave him to me," she said, put on a dressing gown and followed him down. I heard a knock at his door and a depressed voice answering.

They were back soon after. Phil was better – at least, he was still depressed at Nat's absence, but was normal with Poppy and me. A week or so later I asked her what she had said to him.

"I told him that you wanted – no, needed – a comforting presence. I was going to tell him that in the old days it would be Helen but had only got a little way into that when I decided it wouldn't be appropriate. I said that I was there, and that you said that – well, that I could help. He accepted that I was just hugging you having told you that sleep was essential to keep a clear head." She laughed. "I told Phil that I wished that I could have magicked someone to do the same for him, or do it myself, but that it wouldn't be acceptable. That seemed to calm him down."

And Phil? He just told me that it had seemed gross for us to get together when Nat was missing. But he said that now Poppy had explained it, it was ok.

All that Friday Poppy was hovering near the office phone and I was scared witless that I wouldn't hear my mobile. Phil was mooching about, although I wished he would involve himself with something, just to keep from worrying. The Losardos appeared at around midday, very quiet for them, and asked if we knew anything. They had endured visits from both the Police and some men 'who looked like the Mafia' but who gave the right answers to questions the brothers had asked so as to check their motives. Both groups had searched their workshops and homes, and asked questions.

"Sorry," I said without thinking.

"It had to be done. Don't worry. We told them that the area around our workshop is quiet, so it may have been there that he… disappeared. Or it could have been anywhere. They're searching for any CCTV footage. Well, actually they searched for any cameras, but there aren't any.

There was no contact from anyone else apart from a Police officer who introduced herself as the family liaison officer. She was sympathetic, but had no more information.

At least my efforts in keeping busy had paid off and the fleet was ready for the following day's change over. I ran a depressed Phil to earth and made him eat, aware that he'd had the appetite of a sparrow since Nat had been reported as missing. To have to persuade my hollow-legged elder son to eat was a new experience.

31 Nat

I groaned when we woke and I realised that I had to be nice to people, to be normal and cheerful, and to work hard and quickly on engine checks.

Over a hurried breakfast I tactfully asked Phil if he felt he could face doing what he usually did on a Saturday.

"Yes. It's all got to happen, hasn't it? Do you want me to do the water tank filling too?"

It was a gut-twisting question. That had been Nat's job, of course.

"Yes please, Phil. If you can," I said as calmly as I could manage. Poppy nodded.

Gradually the seasonal and permanent staff arrived. It was difficult to keep cheerful alongside the barrage of casual conversation and teasing and I was pleased when Poppy started off with her usual Saturday pep talk. Apparently someone was ill, so we were one short, so she had reorganised the jobs to cope with it all, as far as possible. Initially I thought she was talking of Nat, but this was someone else.

But then she mentioned Nat's absence, and gave a potted version of what we thought might have happened. She explained that the kidnappers were trying to pressurise us into admitting the whereabouts of some people who they thought might have been involved in busting a cell of terrorists. "What they don't know is that we have no idea where they are, even if we had met them, but that they had since vanished. We're in no danger, but if you see any strange men or women who aren't hirers, please let Jack or me know straight away. Or, of course, if anyone asks the whereabouts of anyone you don't know, please also tell us."

It caused a buzz of excited conversation. We all started on tea and cake. I found Poppy.

"Who's missing?" I asked.

"One of the new ones. I think he's her boyfriend." She nodded at the good looking, youngish girl who had caught Phil's attention the previous week.

"Just what we need."

"Quite."

We coped with the morning's returns, and I was relieved to see Phil darting around like a boy possessed, filling the fuel tanks, filling the water tanks and recording each on the sheets we used. Both as a result of our worries and because of his workload he had no time to scope out the object of his previous attraction. I wondered if he would, with her boyfriend absent, sick.

Snatching a cup of tea somewhere between the final checks and the new arrivals, I noticed the two of them talking. She seemed to be quite attentive and concerned about how Phil was feeling. Understandably, despite our situation he was flattered by the attention of an attractive girl, and seemed to be opening up to her.

Finally our part in the day was over. A few of the experienced staff were away with inexperienced hirers and the rest of us gravitated to the office for the inevitable tea. Gratefully I sat, a tea in my hand, thankfully half hidden from most of them by a filing cabinet. I was in no mood to be sociable. Phil was out of sight, but I could hear him chatting to the girl. It appeared he had at last learned her name: Trishia.

Although I was trying to relax it was impossible to keep my mind still. It was weighing up all the possibilities in its efforts to try and think where and when Nat could have been taken. The circle of worry and thought was starting to take hold of me, I knew, and yet another corner of my mind was starting to think that I might be about to suffer a recurrence of my mental problems. Though I wasn't listening to Phil, a snippet of conversation came to me.

"What do they know about your brother? Are they any nearer finding him?"

"No," Phil answered flatly. "No one is saying anything. It's horrible, not knowing."

"And do you really not know where these people are? What was their name? Parish, Poppy said, wasn't it? If they are friends of yours, surely they gave you a hint."

"No," Phil said after a pause. "No hint at all. We haven't a clue."

I noticed after those words that there was an edge to his voice. His comments after that were even more flat, and I wondered at it. Soon afterwards he excused himself and passed me with a glance on the way, I thought, to the lavatory. On his way back he stopped and asked me if I was all right, but before I could respond he checked to see if he was in Trishia's view. I suppose he wasn't, because he mouthed at me: "Wait a bit, then follow me." He told Trishia that he was just going to start cooking for our meal later and would be back in a moment.

"Doesn't your Dad do that?" she asked.

"He's too worried about Nat to think about it," he replied over his shoulder as he went out.

I gave it a few minutes, wondering what was going on, and then casually picked up my bag of tools and followed him.

"Is she following you?" he hissed as I entered the boat. I hadn't checked, but took a look from the window as I passed it.

"Can't see her… what's the matter, Phil?"

"She knows their name. Parish."

"I overheard part of your conversation. Sorry. Of course she does; Poppy told everyone."

"*No, she didn't.* She said that someone had kidnapped him but didn't mention the name of the people the kidnappers were looking for. She knew it."

"Trishia did?"

"Yes. Look, I've emailed Carl and told him. He emailed back as I was coming out and she's going to be followed when she leaves here. But he asked for her home address in case they lose her. Can you get it?"

If I was to go and look at the computer it might be suspicious, I thought. Angela had access… and if she didn't I could give her the password. I called the office landline.

"Angela, it's Jack. Don't acknowledge me because someone's listening who I don't want to realise what we're doing. Can you get Trishia's home address without saying anything or mentioning her name? It's on the computer. Can you access it?"

Apparently she could. "What shall I do? Write it down and bring it to you?"

"No, go to the stores, or the bathroom, and make sure nobody follows. Call my mobile and quietly tell me, then go back to the office as if nothing has happened."

She just said "ok" and rang off. Five minutes later there was a suitably echoing call presumably from the toilet, and I had an address.

"Did you see which way she left last week?" I asked Phil, suddenly remembering there were two possibilities.

"I think they went up the little path to the gate," he said. "I'll go and check on her and email Carl when she goes."

"I'll come back with you, after a gap," I said.

"Why?"

"So it doesn't look as if we've been planning things. I'll come back with clean hands so she thinks I'd come back to the boat for a wash."

"Ok." He was off.

When I emerged he was watching her, waving, as she headed towards the same path that he thought she'd used the previous week. When she had vanished from sight he dodged back into the office and I found him hurriedly punching at his phone. "Damn autocorrect…"

He finished and looked up. There was a fierce look on his face, maybe a look of hope. At least we felt that we were now involved; we had actually done something to help. Frustration receded a little.

There had been no messages still by the time the boat instruction crews returned late in the afternoon. Each of them asked us for news, but we thought it best not to mention our suspicions. When Poppy returned, last of all of them we took her into a now-silent office and went through it all.

"God, I hope it'll be the news we want when they do contact us," she said. "I miss him so much."

I think both Phil and I looked at her with surprise.

"What?" she asked. "No, I'm not his Mum, but he's a friend, someone I like for himself and for the raw life he has in him, and for the potential he has in him too. As do you." This was to Phil, who smiled faintly, not embarrassed at praise for a change, and mouthed 'thank you' to her.

We were about to close the office when it occurred to me that its phone was one of the contact points that could be used. Phil volunteered to go and prepare sandwiches for all of us, and return with them. When he reappeared his eyes were suspiciously red. I took the plate from him and went outside, shepherding him.

"Come on you," I said gently, "what's up that I don't already know about?"

"I've not stopped before," he said slowly, "but when I was making sandwiches I wondered if… if we weren't going to see him again. And what we'd do if that happened."

Hugs between the two of us seemed to be far more common these days than in the previous five years. It wasn't surprising given all that we'd had to put up with. Once again we found comfort in each other.

It was not until an hour later that my mobile rang. Carl. A real voice and in a tone that sounded positive, making my heart give a jump. "He's safe," he said. I gave a gulp and started breathing hard. "We've had a stand-off with those two in a house a short distance from the marina. But it's over now, we've got them, and Nat's on his way to the hospital. Then if they find nothing that they need to keep him in for, he'll be back to you with the Police and two of our people. They need to talk to him when he's ready, but I insisted that he saw you and Phil first if at all possible."

I was aware that the other two were watching me with wide eyes. "He's safe," I said, and felt my knees were giving way. There was a chair behind me and, thankfully, I collapsed onto it.

"Thank you, Carl," I said weakly. "Thank you so much. When do you think that'll be?"

"Give it a few hours," he said, "then look out for a car." We made sure that the gate remained open.

It was late, nearly dark, when a blue car appeared along the quayside. It revealed a police officer who opened the back door. A slight figure unfolded itself and walked stiffly over to us. A bruised, thick-lipped face gave a painful smile.

Once again I gave a gulp and knew my eyes were misting over; this time it was with relief. He allowed himself to be hugged, though there was an exclamation as I squeezed him to tightly.

"Ow. I hurt a bit."

Now it was Phil's turn, to his surprise, and by this time none of us was dry eyed. Poppy joined in the hug session, and he seemed to spend a longer time in her softness than with either of us. Ah well, I couldn't blame him.

"I suppose any checks by us about whether you are his family are a bit irrelevant," said a voice when at last he was free and we were all looking at him, to his mounting embarrassment. I ignored the officer and spoke for the first time. Even I noticed there was an edge to my voice.

"What did they do to you?"

He shrugged his shoulders and winced a little. "I tried fighting them off, and Trishia – that's her name – lost her temper and started hitting me. Hard. If it had been Will I'd have hit back, but – well, I couldn't hit her, not really."

"So she took advantage of that," said Phil in a voice that I hardly recognised. It sounded both hoarse and near-treble again. "And to think that to start with today I was thinking she was nicer than last week. And then she cocked up." He trailed off, swearing at her under his breath. For once I agreed with every word.

"What do you mean, she cocked up?" asked Nat.

"She mentioned the Parishes. Poppy hadn't told anyone the name, just that someone had kidnapped you and that if anyone asked for a name we didn't know they should tell Dad or Poppy. So I emailed Carl."

"So you started off the rescue?"

"S'pose so."

"Thanks, bruv."

For a few moments Phil's face was as mobile as a cinema screen, but in a moment Nat was in yet another embrace, a gentler one this time. "I'm a fool," he said, "but I've missed you so much, you annoying little... *brother*." He released him and turned away. A suspicious sleeve came up to eye level. Nat watched him gravely.

A throat was cleared – an unspoken request to be heard. One of the police officers looked at me.

"I'm really sorry to interrupt, but we need to ask some questions so that we can start to investigate properly. And at some point, soon, we'll need you and your son to take part in a formal identification and a recorded interview. It's the only way we can make a case and present it to a Court."

"Ok," I started. "Nat, do you feel up to some questions?"

"If I can go home and have a cup of tea."

I smiled the first real smile for two days. "I think we can manage that. Bring as many people as you need over to the boat and I'll put the kettle on."

Poppy locked the office after us and we set off down the quayside. I almost knew what was coming, and I wasn't disappointed. It happened as I turned to climb onto the stern.

"Is this it? I mean, your home?"

"Yes, we live on a boat." The stock answer I'd given so many times.

Two officers and one of the 'special forces' men performed the interview. Poppy and Phil made tea, then disappeared down to the bows. I was the 'appropriate adult', in police terminology. We were just about to start when something occurred to me. I shouted down the length of the boat to the others. "Phil – can you phone your mother and tell her the news? I'll call her later and she can talk to Nat. If all that's ok with you, Nat?"

Nat nodded.

Carefully, the police asked the questions. Nat had been in the quiet area of street between the main road and the Losardos' workshop when he noticed a parked car. It was quite unusual to find one in that area as there were almost no businesses or homes there. It almost by a semi-derelict building – the sort of brown-field site that still exist in the city. He admitted to having been puzzled, though not enough to be alarmed. As he was about to pass it the door opened and Trishia greeted him. He was pleased to see it was someone he knew. They were talking about the boatyard when there were footsteps behind him; he turned and saw Will.

"I knew there was something wrong," Nat said. "He looked... cruel."

With no ceremony the man grabbed Nat whilst Trishia opened the back door. They bundled Nat inside despite his struggles. He tried the opposite door but it was locked. "Child locks," he said bitterly. He told us that it was at that point that Trishia punched him on the face and, despite his struggles, managed to cable-tie his hands together. He could see there was little point trying to get away then as Will was outside the door and would have joined in if he carried on fighting.

Will had driven them some way away and at some point in the journey a blindfold was put over Nat's eyes. He was told to lie quietly with his head on Trishia's lap. At last the car stopped, there was a wait, and then he was pulled out of the car. It was then that he started fighting again and when Trishia set about his face and body with her fists.

"She didn't knock me out," Nat told us, "but I was dazed and winded by the time she had finished."

He was marched up what felt like four flights of stairs, a door was unlocked, and another one inside opened. They had thrown him on the floor, taken his phone, cable tied his ankles and told him they'd be back later to ask questions. He was left there for hours, aching, and bored out of his skull, but had listened to any sounds he could hear.

Later the questions were asked after threats were made, but all he could do was to tell them that the Parishes hadn't told any of us where they were staying. He gave them their email, though; obviously without the 'Emerson' part. They left him in the room.

"It was near a junction," he continued. "I could hear traffic stopping, some hooting at times, and quite a lot of trucks. When I could I crawled around and found the wall by the window and leant against that. Then I stood up and sort of felt my way round the room. There didn't seem to be much in it, but what there was I tripped over and started hurting again. That made so much noise that they came in and started swearing at me so I told them I'd stop if they took the blindfold and cable ties off. All they did was laugh."

The only time he had left the room was when he thumped against the door to ask to visit the toilet. They let him do that, at least, even undoing his hands for the few minutes necessary. At last they gave him some water, but no food. He slept that night fitfully, lying on his back; no pillow, no coverings, nothing, and again just some water the next morning from a mug held to his mouth.

He thought that they would both be at the Marina as it was Saturday and set about trying to break the window. But the noise he made trying to use his elbow on it brought Will up again and this time he was cable tied to a chair. "I should have thought earlier and used that to break the window," he said regretfully. "I could have thrown the chair out too. That should have brought the Police."

He endured another boring day, with the constant cutting of the plastic ties around his wrist causing pain. He called out frequently for Will to come and ease them off, at least, but he refused.

At last, when he felt he couldn't endure it all much more, he heard voices outside. It took some time, but eventually the Police broke down the door to the room and cut him free. "I nearly hugged them," he admitted. He had been taken to a hospital where he was examined and had his injuries exposed and, embarrassingly in some cases, photographed. His wrists were bandaged; he refused to let anyone deal with his bruises and declined everything else except food and drink, saying he just wanted to get back home. Amazingly neither the Police nor the hospital insisted that he stay, nor did they call me and tell me to come and look after him in hospital. Perhaps they thought he was older than he was, or had passed whatever test of medical self-competence they have.

All this took some considerable time, two cups of tea and a packet of biscuits for all of us, but at its end they thanked him, switched off their recorders and put away the notebooks.

"Where are the two bastards who did this to him?" I had been seething with anger since the details started coming out and only now could my frustrations be let out. Before, I would have been caught by the recording – and had been warned that this must not happen.

"They're in custody. And they'll stay there until the hearing, and I hope they'll stay there after that too. With any luck they'll plead guilty, probably with mitigating circumstances..."

"What fucking mitigating circumstances are there to torturing a 12 year old boy, my son?" I shouted. "They are animals – no, they're worse than animals. Animals don't treat their own species as items to be used in a game of chess. These are ruthless maniacs who need to be put away until they're too feeble to do anything like this to anyone, let alone kids who don't yet have the physical strength to fight back."

One of the police officers held up her hand. "Would you believe me if I take your part completely? If Nat was my son I would be as angry as you, and feel the same need for revenge as you do. And even with my Police experience I am with you all the way. But – and there always has to be a "but" – we need to ensure that Nat and you give enough technically correct evidence, of the right quality, to put these people away for as long as possible. There's a science to doing that, and to follow that science is an absolute imperative. If we fail, and let their pleas for mitigation be given weight, then we would lose a lot of the impact of the case."

Along with most of us I've watched enough courtroom dramas to realise the truth of that, and knew also that my instinctive, angry protests would have little effect on hardened lawyers.

"Sorry," I muttered. "You tell me, and him, what evidence you need and we'll provide it."

"We've got the gist of it just now. Now we need to get that in writing, Nat comes in, checks it, adds what he wants and corrects it. Then he signs it. Then it's your turn to give your part of the facts – in fact your other son should do the same."

"What about the other group, the people who thought I was Carl Parish and shot at me?"

"We know about that, of course. You'll have given statements on that..."

"No. Never been asked," I said indignantly.

The officer looked at one of the others, the special forces man of Carl's department.

"Never struck us that the Police wouldn't," he said.

"And we were told it was all top secret that you didn't want us involved at that point, except for custody reasons."

"Then we'd better talk to everyone who had anything to do with it, including you," said the police officer, feathers ruffled.

This could go on for some time, I thought, and I'd had enough for one weekend. I knew that Nat would be hungry; in fact by now I was too. Ravenous, in fact, having had no appetite and little to eat while Nat was missing.

"Enough," I told them all firmly. "We've had enough for one day and we're all hungry. You tell me when you want me to give a statement and I'll go wherever you tell me. But right now I want you out of my house – my boat – and we need to get back to normality."

They made apologetic noises and I was about to shove them out – figuratively speaking – when I realised I'd forgotten to thank anyone.

"Just a moment," I called to their retreating backs. They turned. "I'm grateful beyond my capability of expressing it for what you've done to rescue him." My breath was getting ragged with emotion. "He's very precious to me. To us all. Thank you."

They appreciated it, I could tell. So did Nat, whose astonished look and sudden slightly painful smile brought me back down to earth.

They went. I fetched the others from the bows and asked how we were going to get something to eat at this time of night. It was nine o'clock.

Poppy put an arm around Nat's shoulders. I think it's time to raid my freezer," she announced.

"What about Mum?" Nat asked suddenly. "She knows, I suppose?"

"She knew you were missing. They had visits from the Police and from Carl and Inge's people. Apparently it wasn't very pleasant for them, especially as it came out that Jonathan had tried to kidnap you. But Phil phoned her earlier to tell her you were safe."

"Phil..." He gave a smile.

"Shall I call her?"

"Of course. She needs to hear your voice. Borrow mine."

Her terse response to the call floored Nat, though the tone changed for the better when she realised it was him, and got the confirmation that he was safe home. It was an emotional conversation from both sides. She ended by telling Nat that she was coming to see him.

"We're just going to eat," he told her. "Poppy, can she come to your house to see me?"

"Of course."

He told her how to find it, and that we were just setting off. She arrived ten minutes after we did.

To give her credit, her reaction to seeing him was genuine and loving, and she went up in my estimation a notch or two. Nat's story was told again and apparently apart from a few exclamations she was silent, appalled and attentive. And angry, as I discovered when they emerged from the room where they had talked alone.

"What is being done to these people? And are the boys safe now? I'm horrified that anyone can be so evil as this, I really am. How can you keep them safe? I really think they should come home."

"They're in prison, on remand," I told her. "And I share your anger and horror. We're told that those two are the last of them, although we've heard that before. We have to go to visit the Police next week for Nat to sign his statement and for Phil and me to make mine. We'll talk to them and to Inge and Carl later to make sure there are no more and to find out what started all this."

"Until we know they're safe, I don't want you to take your eyes off the boys. I still want them to come and live with me for safety…"

"But they're almost thirteen, and fifteen, and active in mind and body," I told her. "They can't be wrapped in cotton wool. That'd be almost the same as imprisoning them."

For once, somehow, she saw sense.

"But I will be taking them in the car wherever they want to go in future, even if it's just to the Losardos' workshop. Yes, and bringing them back. Thank goodness for mobiles and cars, eh? I'll have to get a new one for Nat. God knows where the old one's gone."

32 Normality: our version

I think we collapsed into bed at about one. Even the boys. Nat's mind was still buzzing up to the last possible moment, the moment when he appeared suddenly to run out of battery. Phil wouldn't go anywhere unless his brother was there, partly because he hadn't wanted to miss any part of the story and partly, I'm sure, because he felt that he'd so nearly lost his only sibling. His instinct was to make sure they were together. It's an odd thing, the psyche. And it's not age related – or is it? As an adult, would I have felt the same about Jonathan if he were in danger? Oh God, Jonathan…

My dreams were troubled. Poppy was with me. That was fact, and I was glad of it. It seemed right that she should be there now. What woke me? Was it a continuation of the thought process about my brother, the trusted one, who had proved so successfully that he was anything but?

It was a noise from the corridor. Alarmed, I jumped out of bed (Yes, pyjama bottoms) and opened the door. Muttering I heard, one treble and one light tenor voice. I passed the bathroom and knocked at the door. It opened. Phil.

"I heard voices," I said. "Everything all right?"

"Dreams. Nightmare I suppose." Nat's speech was quick, unnaturally so.

"I heard him and – well – just needed to try and… and…" He gave a huge yawn. I nodded, being better able, perhaps, to wake and make immediate sense of the world.

"Nat, your brain's been through a lot, more than most people ever get to experience in a long lifetime. And I mean older people, and I mean a full lifetime; let alone when you're young…" I stopped, wondering how to put it. "Just as alcohol affects the brain more when it's less than eighteen years old, so do unpleasant memories. It's all right to work through it all when you're asleep. That's what sleep's for."

"I didn't want to wake anyone," Nat said unhappily.

"You're right that sleep is something that we should try not to interrupt. But when your son or brother has a nightmare –" I looked gratefully at Phil who was looking shell-shocked "– everyone who loves the sufferer is happy to wake and help. It's what families are for."

His smile was tired, still in something like shock, as he laid his head back on the pillow. Phil and I exchanged a glance.

"Do you want me to stay here until you've gone back to sleep?" Phil asked.

The pillowed head shook slightly. "I'm all right."

"Yeah… Like hell. If you didn't snore, I'd offer to sleep here."

He was just enough awake still to give his brother a V sign. The smile returned.

"Good night, Nat. Good night, Phil," I said quietly, and went back. Unsurprisingly Poppy was awake.

"Are they all right?" she asked drowsily.

"Nat had a bit of a nightmare. He's ok now, I think."

"Not surprised, poor kid. He's been through a lot."

"I know. I wonder if he needs to talk to someone."

"He does. You. Phil. Maybe me too. If he doesn't settle down in a day or two perhaps we could think about it. But he's tougher than most, I'd say."

"Unlike his Dad who goes walkabout with a nervous breakdown, you mean."

She hoisted herself up and propped her head up on her hand. We had been quite circumspect about going to bed, pyjamas, and so on, so to see her tousled, marginally exposed and vulnerable was an epiphany; the lie to her vulnerability lay in her wide-awake and surprised expression.

"Jack, that's not what I was hinting at, and you know it."

"I know. I know. Just stay like that for a moment, would you?"

She looked down at herself laughed quietly. "Incorrigible."

"I admit it."

"Go to sleep."

"I need comforting."

"That was Nat. Remember?"

"It's a strain for me too."

"Go to sleep."

Defeated, I laid down properly and closed my eyes. There was a soft touch to my mouth.

We kissed.

It was some time since I had enjoyed a comfortable, intimate waking up knowing that I was in love with the person next to me. It was hardly surprising, then, that I lay awake for some time enjoying the moment. That deep contentment is seasoned with excitement; a version of the amazed depth of feeling of a teenager's first love that is still available to those of full adult age.

Poppy was still asleep. To watch her with her face at peace was to me new; and lovely. The sight added another level to my complete contentment.

At some point we had to wake and to start the day. I breathed a deep sigh, and immediately she was awake, startled, before smiling and relaxing again. I kissed her. She smiled more and returned it.

"You're wonderful," she whispered. "I'd almost forgotten how good it is to be with someone."

"Shhh..." I stopped her saying any more in the simplest way possible.

We were interrupted by the sound of the shower pump, an evil morning necessity. One of them was in there, meaning I'd have to squeeze past his brother on the way to the small bathroom. There had been no answer to my knock at the first door so I entered cautiously. His absence proved that it was Nat in the shower, first as usual. I discovered after knocking at the further door and waiting for a non-existent answer that, as usual, Phil was still asleep.

We started making breakfast, wondering when we would become a family of four again. Had it not been the smell of bacon cooking it would probably have been late morning, but the yawns and groans announced a teenager and a near-teenager who gulped mugs of tea and became near-human and awake. Awake enough to eat, at least.

"Did you sleep all right?" I asked Nat.

Phil was about to answer but, to his credit, saw that there was a reason I was asking only his brother.

"Yes, after… well, you know."

"No more nightmares?"

His shoulders lifted. "Don't remember any. I'm stiff this morning, though, and things still ache."

"Good. I mean, good that you slept, but not good that you're aching. It'll wear off, though."

"Hope so."

"I slept ok," Phil added, "just not long enough."

"Have a nap this afternoon like an old man," I told him.

"Like you? Ok," he responded. I blew him a raspberry.

"Are we doing anything today?" Nat asked as we were washing up.

"I've been thinking about that," said Poppy. "I think we talked about it when we were near there in the boat, but what about visiting the Black Country Museum? Are you up to that, Nat? I was looking at it last week before things started getting unpleasant. It's huge. If we left now we'd have only half a day there, and we'd never see it all in that time. Not properly. I was wondering if we should get a family membership – it's only a little more expensive than a day ticket for all of us – so we could go back whenever we wanted to."

"What's there?" Phil asked.

Poppy drew breath. "There's a colliery, the canal arm and tunnel entrance and boat trips, trams and trolleybuses…"

"What are trolleybuses?" Nat interrupted.

"Like ordinary buses but electric. They…."

"They're modern, then."

"No. They pick up electricity from wires over them, hung from poles like trams do."

"But not trams."

"No. They steer and have rubber tyres, but there are two poles on top instead of a tram's one."

I could see he was intrigued.

"And there are old shops, sweet shops, tailors, cigarettes, fish and chips, pie shops, electric shop – you name it. They're all in a little village near the canal. It really is interesting."

"Let's go!" She had intrigued Phil, anyway, who was heading for the door having surreptitiously hidden his tea towel.

"When this lot's finished," I told him – as he knew that I would.

"Are we going by boat?" he asked, undaunted.

"It'd take about three hours," Poppy said. "Maybe visit again midweek when we can, and tie up nearby overnight. Or, if we're not too big, get towed through the tunnel."

That started off another chain of questions. Poppy forestalled them by suggesting that they ask when we were there about mooring at the Museum, and about getting measured for a tow through the tunnel.

It was a great success, that day. I don't know who was more interested, Poppy and me with the social history, or the boys with the technical side of it and, naturally, the fish and chips, sweet shop, and all the other things guaranteed to separate money from kids (i.e. parents). They both wanted to return, and to bring the boat for measurement to see if it would fit through the tunnel. I had my doubts. More importantly, so did Poppy. It was a successful half day, but like the previous night's sleep, not long enough. Nat was absolutely shattered by its end and vanished off to bed as soon as he could.

To my pleasure, Poppy returned with us to the boat for the night. "I can't trust you people on your own," she told me with her smile half hidden.

Monday brought normality and work, and yes, after a phone call Nat went to the Losardos' workshop. He was accompanied by me, to his disgust. With no engines due for service I was at a loose end so allowed myself to help with jobs as mundane as cleaning an oven, washing windows and other somewhat mind-numbing things. There were only three boats which weren't out on hire.

Poppy was busy trying to find staff to replace Will and Trishia and was making calls. I asked Phil if he knew anyone.

"I only know people in my year," he said, "I suppose they've got to be older."

"Over sixteen, Poppy says, or it's a lot of work to get through the child employment legislation."

"They might have older sisters," he said, brightening up. "I'll make some calls."

Many long calls later, during which the story of his holidays so far were recounted to each friend, he announced to Poppy that he'd only been able to discover someone's sixteen year old elder brother who was bored and needed something, anything, to do. Poppy phoned him, invited him to visit, and was pleased when he said he could be there in an hour. He was as good as his word, turned out to be an engaging type who loved his first experience of a narrowboat.

"I was christened Attila," he admitted reluctantly, "But I refuse to answer to it. Everyone calls me Till – at least, if they want anything done." It was said with such a disarming smile that even Phil liked him. Not bad for someone who had been intent on finding a girl to brighten up the marina one day a week. Poppy also found a local, middle-aged woman who was looking for a job now that the last of her offspring had left home. "Though they never really leave," she told us. "She'll be back with armfuls of washing, and phoning for cooking advice."

There was a call from the Police later in the week asking us to visit a Station, to sign our statements and make others. Nat, Phil and I were asked to complete witness impact statements too, our opportunity to tell the Court how our experiences had affected us. It was a job I was looking forward to getting my teeth into.

"I don't want to do one," Nat said suddenly. "I don't want to remember."

I thought a long time, looking at him, before it struck me. "You know when I was in hospital? They got me to go over and over what had happened, every last detail of it. And the need to think about it and remember and put it into words was one of the main things that helped me back to normal."

"Do you think I'm not normal?"

"That's not what I meant at all. But the brain plays tricks on its owner sometimes, like mine did on me. Anyone who's had an experience like you went through will benefit from a proper debrief – look at it as a soldier getting treatment for PTSD. Most of them welcome it. *I* think that if you made yourself do the same, even if you tell me and I write it down for you it'll help you get it out of your system, and maybe avoid more disturbed dreams."

I could almost hear the cogs turning.

"I do get dreams," he said slowly.

"Then let's have a go together, just us. Then we can both make sure the Court has the information it needs to put those bastards away for even longer."

He grinned, suddenly more cheerful. We set to that evening, leaving Poppy and Phil in the front cabin with the TV. It was not a pleasant experience for him to go over yet again what he had suffered, nor for me to hear it, but I summarised what he said in writing, slowly, as best I could. It seemed only fair that I should tell him what had happened from our angle at the boatyard, and spared nothing of the anguish I had felt, and how much it had taken me to avoid descending back into my own previous mental issues.

He looked gravely at me. "Are you all right, Dad?"

"Now you're back and they've got those… those people behind bars, yes. It's made me think just how lucky I am to be here, and cured, and have you two looking after me."

"I thought you were looking after us."

"And I'll counter that by saying it's mutual. And that's the healthiest way of being in a family. I think that's all the work we need to do, don't you? I'll tell the Police in the morning that we're done, and they'll have all they need."

The visit to the Police was… well, boring, like most police station visits unless you're being investigated and have something to hide (no, I have no experience). It was made as low key as possible, so much so that I had to remind the interviewer that Nat was nearly thirteen and mentally tough. Nevertheless I bought us both an ice-cream on the way home.

The two new staff, Till and Maureen, were soon put to work the following week. It wasn't until we discovered from another of the staff that Maureen's nickname was Mo that someone put the two together and said how agricultural it sounded. "We'll be getting Plough and Scatter next," Nat quipped.

Over the usual evening meal Poppy asked when we might feel like visiting the Museum again, this time in the boat and making a long weekend of it.

"I thought we were too busy for that," I ventured.

"Ian can cope, and we have enough people on call now who can come in if there's an emergency. You forget that we can get to a bus route or book a taxi to bring us back here very quickly if we really need to respond to a problem ourselves. It's not as if we were going to another town."

She was right. She had to be: it was her company. "I'm very happy to go.

How do you feel about it?" I asked the boys. They were enthusiastic too.

"Another thing I wondered," Poppy continued. "How about asking the Parishes? It would give them the opportunity to tell us exactly what they know, what they knew, and what dangers there may be in the future to them and to us – if any. It'd give Maisie a cruise as promised, and give her parents a taste of life aboard."

"I'm not sure," I answered. At that moment the Parishes were once again an unknown quantity, people who brought danger with them. They had done so twice, so their track record was dubious in my estimation.

"I'd like to see Maisie," Nat ventured.

"I know, Nat. But it seems that every time we've involved ourselves with them, one or other of us has been put in danger."

"But it's not *their* fault. They're trying to stop it and live ordinary lives. And it's only for two days."

Any minute now, I thought, Phil was going to make a comment about his little brother wanting his girlfriend with him. But he seemed just to be following the conversation.

"In any case, do you really think that they could all just pack and be at the boat tomorrow morning?"

"Don't you like them, Dad?" Phil had spoken at last.

"It's not that I don't like them. In fact they're pleasant people and good company. But…" I let the sentence hang.

"How about calling them now, asking them, and particularly asking if they think it would be safe or if there are likely to be still more of this – what? Gang? – out there looking for them. Don't forget they're the ones in real danger, not us. We're just the people who the gang thought could lead to them." This last point of Poppy's was well made. Surely if there was any danger they wouldn't risk Maisie's safety.

"You're serious, aren't you?" I asked her.

"Yes. They've proved themselves friendly types, and I don't think it'd be fair just to cut them out of our lives because of what others have done. It means, somehow, that whoever it is has won."

I thought for a long time. In fact it didn't need much thought, because I knew she was right. Let's just say that I let it sit in my mind for a time, by which time Phil was saying that Till had been really useful in the marina that day, and that Mo had been liked by everybody too.

"All right, then," I said, apparently out of the blue. "I'll call them,"

It took a moment for the others to back-track, but they all smiled encouragingly. I dialled them and Carl answered almost immediately. There was a silence after I'd put the proposal to him, then an exhalation.

"I thought for a moment you were in trouble from yet someone else," he started. "And I thought that after what's just happened… how is Nat?"

I looked at the subject of the enquiry. "Carl wants to know how you are, if you've recovered."

"I'm fine," Nat lied. "Still a bit bruised and stiff, but I'm ok."

Hardly surprising. He'd mentioned it before, but not complained. And really I should have checked him over, even if a hospital already had.

There was a laugh at the end of the phone. "I heard him. Most of the details have come my way, and from what I understand 'being ok' isn't quite true. That young man may be at the age when he repairs quickly, but he really means that he's soldiering on regardless, so as to look tough. Forgive me if that's too personal, but I'd hate the idea that he's really gone through the wringer and is now trying to demonstrate his toughness."

He made me feel guilty, and I vowed to get Nat to show me his remaining bruises in private when he made ready for bed. "He's said so little about it after we'd done the victim statements that I'd just hoped that he'd carry on levelling with me." I was speaking to the phone but looking at Nat, who averted his eyes.

"No more interference from me," said Carl. "Maisie may have something to say, but that's up to her. Now, to go back to my initial alarm when I thought there was another problem, my – er – ex-employers have asked a lot of questions of the remainder of the mob who shot at you, and will in due course be following the same tactics with this Will and Trishia. Pressure has been brought to bear on the first lot and we are now convinced that after these two there are no more. If any more are trained up, it'll be done in the EU or USA and none of them will know the name Parish, let alone Dyer. So we're absolutely sure that now we are out of danger."

I hesitated. "The problem is, Carl, that you thought that last time. Then these two bastards crawled out of the woodwork and basically tried torturing my son."

"Jack, I know, and for that I am truly sorry. I was acting on the best information we had been able to extract from the gang by then. Without going into details, we have better psychological methods of interview than even the good specialists in the Police. More time and applying these skills got us to the bottom of the British cell. Honestly, we are all safe."

He was obviously sincere, and his tone was – again – one that I felt I could trust. Even then my cynical brain was whispering to me that he was trained in persuasion, but where do you stop disbelieving people? He was not deliberately using my family as a buffer against his. Nor was he using us as a titbit to bait a trap. I believe that I would have been able to tell.

"Ok, Carl. If you're able to level with us some more and open up about where these people come from and what their aims are, we'd like you to come on a short voyage with us on the boat. Actually, we'd like you all to come anyway. All we're going to do is take the boat to the Black Country Museum and have a second visit. And we want to see if she'll fit through the Dudley Tunnel or not. What d'you think?"

"Wow… I know someone who's going to be jumping up and down in a minute… what, Maisie? Yes, I know you're old enough not to… Let me talk to them. When were you thinking of going?"

"Well tomorrow, ideally. But it could be Monday."

"Tomorrow… Wow… Look, can I call you back?"

"Of course."

It took them ten minutes before Inge phoned in an amused tone. "Maisie's gone to pack already. She did jump up and down, just once before the solemnity of age kicked in. A question, though: will you be all right for accommodation?"

"Yes we shall, now. Things have, let's say moved on, since you were here last. So It'll be Nat in the front on an inflatable if you can supply one, then Phil in his own cabin, Maisie in Nat's, you two in the next one and us in the dinette."

"If you're sure… I don't like to displace you."

"It's better like that, because we can be in charge of the kettle."

Inge laughed. "In that case… thank you. We've actually got a car now. Can we park it in the marina, please?"

"All the hirers do, so yes, certainly."

"Last questions: anything particular we need to bring? And what time should we get there?"

"It's summer and Birmingham, so bring waterproofs. Breakfast will be served at about ten, so any time around then."

I'd made a sudden crazy decision to get our lot out of bed earlier than the usual Sunday lie-in. Poppy was signalling to me. I raised my eyebrows. "Get them to bring bedding and towels. Makes it easier."

Message relayed, we looked at each other, I tried not to see Nat's Cheshire cat grin or Phil's look of resignation to it.

"We'd better go shopping," I said.

Carl's first word in the morning when he smelt the bacon cooking was another "Wow!" Even the normally hibernating Phil-shaped hedgehog was not only awake but clothed and drinking tea as they arrived. We all know – as does he – that the hedgehog spines recede as the mug drains. When it's empty he will have achieved something approaching human normality.

"This proves one thing," said the ex-hedgehog once the bedding and light luggage had been dumped onto beds, "We need another of Nat's magic inventions in the front cabin. When are we going to get a decent TV?"

He was right, I supposed. With everything we'd had to put up with, finishing off the boat had been the last thing on our minds. A few camp chairs and a bench were the only things we had. Only hardened TV watchers spent much time in there.

"Some people have wood-burners," Phil added.

"Do you know, that's not such a silly idea," Poppy said. "There's your central heating, but in case of problems a stove would be a good idea. It should be reasonably easy."

"You're very practical," Carl told her.

"I had to learn, and learn fast, Jack'll tell you my story. The hire boat world can be full of problems, so you soon learn to come up with solutions. If you just wring your hands and whinge, nothing happens. Besides, Nat has a way with design. All he needs to do is to read through the safety regulations and he'll be all over it, I'm sure."

The purring noise was someone else's engine, not due to the Cheshire-cat grin wearer.

Breakfast was a leisurely affair, complete with decent coffee – a gift from Inge and Carl. We were nearly groaning when we had had our fill. Except the ex-hedgehog, of course, who was actively casting round for more.

We set off. This time we took the more boring New Main Line that avoided the locks on the Old, but also avoided the covered motorway part that had fascinated and deafened us on our first trip. The Parishes were intrigued, even at the idea of the railway running beside the canal just behind a fence, and the industry that seemed never ending.

I was wanting to bring up the subject of the shared problem, the gangs of people who had caused us such agonies. There seemed to be no opportunity when the stern was crowded. There were seven of us, after all, and not everyone could fit on. So everything remained unsaid and questions remained unasked. Maybe it was for the best, as voices travel and it was not something I felt that we should broadcast.

Just as the modern factories and warehouses gave way to something approaching countryside, Poppy told me – I had wrested the tiller from a reluctant Nat who had been showing off – to turn left under one of the old lattice sided bridges. This was new territory, the Gower Branch canal – as Poppy reminded us. We had seen its other end as we had started our first trip. The junction we'd just turned into we had only seen when approaching it from the opposite direction.

At far end are three locks in quick succession, heading up to the Old Main Line. This was our guests' baptism of fire on operating locks, even if they had seen them from a distance.

"It's so simple," said Inge, "until you think that it was all built with picks and shovels; no machines then. All the saws for the gate woodwork were hand saws, all the metalwork was cast or wrought individually. It really is quite an achievement if you look at it like that."

I suppose none of us had, really. The whole system must have been a wonder of the world when it was first built. And the surveyors, with such basic measuring devices, had engineered water as if by magic. Ground breaking stuff. Literally.

We turned right at the junction. I relinquished the tiller to Maisie who steered under Nat's direction, to Phil's pretend horror. Seeing her efforts, and how quickly her eyes glazed over, made me understand that we, at least, had some useful experience under our belts. Soon we were crossing over the Netherton Tunnel branch, to the excitement of all the Parishes who had never seen a canal tunnel.

Poppy and I had quietly made arrangements for a mooring at the Museum, on the Dudley Canal near the end of its forbidden tunnel. We were, after all, taking the boat there to be measured to see if we could fit through, and therefore towed through, the tunnel. Even if not, we had plans, and we could access the Museum from there anyway.

"This is different," Phil observed as Poppy turned left into the Dudley Canal.

"We went right last time."

"Indeed we did, Phil. But we're going to get the boat measured by the Tunnel Trust to see if we can get through under tow – remember?"

He nodded, and I thought I could detect excitement.

33 Phil and the tunnel

We didn't know how far in toward the Museum we should go, so stopped before a long bridge – we discovered later it carried Birmingham New Road's four lanes. Poppy and I walked under it towards the main Tunnel Museum and found someone in their reception to ask.

"Oh yes," she said. "Can you bring the boat down and moor here? We can measure up, then either you can turn and moor, or just moor and we'll take you through tomorrow. And if it won't fit, you wanted to join one of our long tours, didn't you?"

"Yes," said Poppy, "but don't tell the others that yet, please. They don't know about the trip boat yet."

She smiled. "I see. Ok, bring her down and our team will be out to you."

"We've got annual membership. Our friends haven't. Can we get into the Museum this way?"

"Black Country? Yes, you can. Just cross the swing bridge and follow the signs."

Our home made its cautious way to the quayside she had shown us. We had just tied the last hitches when three people appeared, introducing themselves as wanting to take "the lady's vital statistics, please."

Well, they measured (the boat, not Poppy or Inge), scratched their heads and re-measured, then looked at us. "She won't fit, I'm afraid," said the one who had introduced himself as Mikey. "The sides are too upright. If they were more slanted inwards she'd just do it, but – well – she'd scrape and probably peel back quite a lot of metal before coming to a shuddering halt. Worse than that, she'd damage the tunnel, which is even more important. To us."

Poppy smiled at him, understanding Dudley humour. "Well, without a major rebuild, we're a bit stuffed, then. Ok; thank you for trying. We'll get busy on winding her. But how do we book for your long trip, all the way through and back via the Netherton?"

We were on our own by then, the others having trooped back to the dinette with some disappointment.

"If you're asking me," he started.

"I am," Poppy said with a grin.

"Then I'll get the bigger boat and take you myself. You'll have to pay at the office, but tell them Mikey says 'mates' rates'. I know you, you see: you're Poppy Watson, and one of us."

Even Poppy was floored by that. "I had no idea I was famous!"

"You've made a go of that business, and I hear you've got a real good engineer now who's sorted out your fuel problems. Must be costing you, but I admire you for doing it."

I was trying to avoid laughing. It wouldn't have been right.

"It's cost me a boat," said Poppy, "But it won't fit through the tunnel."

"That boat?"

"That boat."

"How's it cost you that?"

"Because I need the engineer on site, and that's become his home."

He looked from one of us to the other, and my smile broke through.

"I've been had, haven't I?" he asked at last. "You're him."

"I am," I admitted. "And at last I love the job that I'm doing." I was conscious of Poppy's sudden look at me.

"You could come and have a listen to some of our old boats," he said. "Not the electric ones, though."

"Couldn't help with them," I laughed. "But any of the old ones, I'd love to. When I get time."

"Hard task master, is she?"

I was tempted, but no… "No, she's not. Not now we've got the engines under control. But you tell me when there's a good day, and I'll come down. Maybe with my elder son who's starting to take the same interest that got me into engineering."

"You're on."

We explained to the Parishes what winding a boat meant and gave the honours of demonstrating the move to Phil. Although he'd turned our boat only a few times, he had been allowed to practise in the marina when we weren't busy, with some shouted supervision from one of the experts on another boat. By the time of our visit he knew what he was doing – more or less. We had been lucky since starting our live-aboard career that the weather, and particularly the wind strength, had been fairly kind. It seems that with a wind of any note, turning a boat is a nightmare.

Poppy was watching him like a hawk; Maisie watched him like a star-struck child. I thought that wouldn't go down well with Nat, but he was too busy watching, waiting to suck in air between his teeth at the slightest collision, that he never noticed. Phil succeeded, and started looking smug, before hitting the side with a bigger bump than I think he intended.

The smug look vanished, changing to a momentary wince. The others jumped ashore and moored. I put the kettle on and Phil joined me.

"Ouch?" I said, casually.

"I hoped no one noticed."

"Only just. Not enough to worry about."

"Yeah, but I should…"

"You just gained a bit more experience, that's all."

A steady look, then a grin. "Ok."

"We've got annual membership for the Museum," I said when the others had returned. "It's only a little more than a day's worth and we've got three hours today before they shut. We could leave it until tomorrow, but then we may want to go on the trip boat into the tunnel…" I was deliberately saying nothing about having booked a trip for us all the way through it, round to Bumblehole, and back through the parallel tunnel.

"It seems ridiculous to live near Birmingham and not support something like this," Inge said. "We'll go for an annual membership too and - well, how long are you able to stay here?"

"If I'm needed back at the ranch I can nip on a bus. Or get a taxi," Poppy confirmed. "We could spend a couple more days here if we want. Or come back by car another day."

"Well, we're here now, and tomorrow I think we should take one of the tunnel trip boats," I said firmly, seeing a possibility that our undisclosed trip might be in danger. It seemed to interest them, so we went to the Museum's booking office.

Everyone was amazed to be able to ride on a trolleybus, later on an old-fashioned tram, and to look at the shops and old workshops as they passed us by, so to speak. We spent a happy three-and-a-half hours there, then returned to the boat before the swing bridge denied us access to the Museum's pub. Damn.

We consulted Google, bless it (sometimes). "Curry!" Carl exclaimed. "There are two really highly rated places quite near. Everyone happy with that?"

It turned out that we all were, with Nat and Maisie only slightly dubious. They were told that they could choose something that was only slightly spicy, or an English dish, so they perked up.

Discussions about the mob and the couple who had given us so much trouble were put on hold yet again as being unsuitable subjects for a crowded restaurant. It was encouraging that its clientele seemed to consist mainly of people of Indian origin, those who should recognise good Indian cuisine if anyone did. And in a city whose food outlets major on anything from tiny curry take-aways to high quality Indian cooking establishments, this one was excellent. Even the slightly dubious younger members were complimentary.

Our return to the privacy of the boat with two bottles of wine from the Parishes was enough to set tongues in motion. This time there were no potential eavesdroppers to make explanations unwise. Carl put up his hand to ask for an opportunity to speak. We quietened.

"Everyone remembers the National Front, itself the successor of the British Fascists. Not so many know about the various spin-off organisations and cells that were created after they were banned. Most of these new ones are now themselves illegal, despite which there are still some really awful racists and fascists out there. Their aim is to get their message across and to cause protest, disruption and worse. Their aim is to purify – their words – the British race. They ignore the naturally mongrel nature of Britain and the fact that all decent people are against them.

"They are the people – thugs, really – who protest and chant appalling threats to any group who by their twisted logic is not "British". That is, anyone with a skin that isn't white, or anyone who looks different from what they chose to describe as British. They've made threats of murder against a number of prominent and ordinary citizens, and some atrocities have probably been carried out in their name. Ironically for those with beliefs like that, they have sympathisers in other countries in the EU and USA."

He paused for breath and a drink. The rest of us were silent.

"Wherever you get those who become – rightly or wrongly – fanatical about a cause, you will find others who will take revenge on any politicians, government departments, police or members of the public who try to act against them. Revenge is seen as strength, and to them it often equates to murder attempts."

He stopped and looked round at us all. "Inge and I had been recruited into a branch of the government which – well, let's just say that it collects information, makes deductions and acts on the results. If you assume that's the secret service, then those words must never be mentioned in the same breath as our name. If it is, we shall be in danger. Maisie, Inge and me.

"To continue with the story, the whereabouts of cells of these people was known. Our employers swung into action. They did so because they could see that other, weak minded people were being influenced. The police aren't equipped to investigate such a semi-hidden set of organisations effectively so we used our alternative methods and managed to bring a lot of them to justice.

"It made us very unpopular, as you can imagine. It made us unpopular with the more naïve right-wingers – fascists by another name. As if dealing with that reaction wasn't enough, we had also needed to infiltrate one particular cell to eradicate the organisers and persuade their supporters that their beliefs were not acceptable anywhere, that they would be treated as terrorists and dealt with accordingly. We were quietly successful and have left many languishing in prison. Others are no longer with us as they chose to die rather than to be captured. That does not please us, but when it is a question of a terrorist's life or yours, or the life of a colleague or friend, there remains no contest."

My mind flew back to the incident in our marina and the reaction of the secret service man there. He had not been uncaring, but had hardened himself to the idea of "us or them", innocent or terrorist. The innocent had to be protected. Were it otherwise terrorism would be seen to win out. If it had, I should be dead.

"Weeding out any mob like this takes time," Carl continued. "Despite our successes, others still remained; we knew that. But we had done our bit and we felt that had we stayed it would expose us too much. Inge and I had all but decided to leave not just those investigations, but to leave the service of our employers. That was for a reason that you know about: Maisie.

"We were about to contact our employers when the phone rang to tell us that the arrangements we had made for Maisie had gone very sour. It focussed our minds. We returned from… where we'd been… in a hurry and met these wonderful people who had saved our daughter and befriended her, even to the extent of looking after her in the safety of their floating home. We hoped that we'd covered our tracks enough so that even those left in the cell couldn't find us. It's extraordinary that those remaining, who were really only on its periphery, would still try and silence us or get information from us.

"Could we have anticipated that the low-power idiots left would do that? I don't think so, not knowing the state in which we had left the cell, and what had been achieved by other officers elsewhere. Apart from the well-known mouthpieces who sound off in the press and on TV, and who wouldn't dare take direct action, nobody was left who would be a danger. Or so we thought. Now, we know better.

"Have our lot, our ex-employers, learnt? All I can say is that they were put on their guard by what subsequently happened, and once they have a case they will cling on to it like sh… like a bulldog onto a pair of trousers."

There was a long pause whilst this story sunk in to our minds. The events of the previous months now hung together better. Gone was the feeling that there might still be an unknown danger that could leap up at us, shark like, from a calming sea.

"Like shit to a blanket," Nat murmured so that only I could hear. Then to Carl: "Is the danger really over now?" He had a vested interest in the subject that was greater even than that of the rest of us.

"Our employers are keeping tabs on each and every one who's known about, here and abroad, and are doing the same with every friend or acquaintance of the two who mistreated you so badly – and I mean *every* acquaintance. They will keep contact with us, even though we've resigned, and will tell us if any more people become of interest, along with where they are.

"I'm levelling with you, Nat, and with everyone else, because you deserve to know. I trust you because you're intelligent and are not gossipers. You will not be tempted to tell anyone outside this circle, to discuss it with anyone else. That's going to be difficult for you all when it comes to Helen Dyer and Jonathan Dyer, who also have an interest. Please just tell them that the danger is over, that they are not under suspicion, and that you and they are safe if they keep their mouths shut about their experiences."

"I've let Carl do the talking," Inge put in. "We were equal partners in the Service and now we'll be equal partners in normal life. But someone had to take the lead in explaining things to you and he's the better talker. I'm now a mum, full time, and in fact always have been even when we were away for such a long time." She looked at Maisie with a grimace of regret. "Any mum, any parent, hates the idea of harm coming to their children or to the children of others, especially friends. So we *will* continue to be honest with you so long as you all keep every bit of this to yourselves. That's the way to public safety and to your and our safety."

Once again there was silence.

"What's going to happen to Trishia and Will?" It was Nat again.

"They will be tried in Court for kidnap, causing actual bodily harm to a minor, child cruelty and anything else we can think of," Inge said.

"Try a charge of counterfeiting references so as to gain employment," Poppy said. "If you don't, I might well go to the Police myself, just so that I can feel better."

"I think we would, Poppy, if it wouldn't make a connection to you, your company and its engineer. They will receive a prison sentence, and given the antipathy of the public to anything to do with danger being caused to children, I think that part will attract a long tariff. I should be surprised if they were freed before ten years is up, by which time Nat will be in his twenties. Given the bruises he caused Will when he struggled – and Will complained about them in the interviews – by that time he should be able to flatten him with one blow."

"Unless a gun is involved," I said drily. The comment silenced everyone.

"We – I mean The Service – will be ensuring that those two are well watched when they are released," Carl said. "And we – the Parishes – will ensure we know what's happening. Trust me on that."

At some ungodly hour of the night there was a soft knock at the door between "my" cabin, where the Parishes were sleeping, and the dinette where Poppy and I were.

"Hallo?" I answered quietly. Poppy was instantly awake too.

"Carl," said Carl. "Sorry, but Nat's having a nightmare, we think, and I didn't know whether to ignore it or tell you. We decided you'd want to know."

"Thanks," I said. "Can I go through?"

"Of course. I'll be decent by the time you are."

Once again Phil was there before me and was talking quietly to his brother. Both of them looked up as I knocked and came in.

"Sorry, Dad," said Nat in a small voice.

"Nothing to be sorry about. Families still help each other out when in need. Nothing's changed since before."

He smiled gratefully and sank back onto the pillow.

"All right now?" I asked.

"Yeah… Thanks."

"Good night. And well done, Phil."

"Yeah… thanks, bruv," added the dreamer.

Another knock at the door, this time the stern door to the outside world. It was light. I woke, shocked. "Who is it?"

"Nat. Can I put the kettle on?"

I looked at my watch. Nine o'clock. *Nine* o'clock? When did I last sleep that late? Poppy was watching me.

"You've been twitching for ages," she murmured. "What have you been dreaming about?"

"No idea. I didn't even know I was dreaming. Come in!"

"I can't, Dad, it's locked."

Of course it was. I hurriedly pulled on some trousers and went to open it.

"Aren't you two up yet?" exclaimed Nat as he climbed down into the galley.

"You woke me up, apparently," I said. "I was well out of it."

"Sorry."

"It's as well that you did. We have a boat trip to start at ten, and we need to have breakfast before we go."

Another knock, this time on the internal door. "Can we come in?" It was Inge. I thought.

"Give us both five minutes or so and we'll be alive. Sorry. And Nat, can you do the same? It's not fair on Poppy to get up when the world's watching."

"It's only me, Dad..."

"Yes, but I meant anyone watching, really."

I half expected some sort of come-back, but he grinned and left again. We got up. Breakfast was a cereals-only meal, and at nine-fifty we were heading towards the Canal Trust's office, already quite busy with tourists. Mikey was waiting, chatting to the man on the desk. He looked at us as we arrived.

"You survived, then? Our resident ghosts didn't get you?"

In response to the inevitable questions he told the story of two youngsters who tried paddling their way through the tunnel on a raft and were drowned. "They're sometimes seen as if they're standing on the water, waiting to be picked up by one of the trip boats," he finished.

"Is it true?" Phil, the sceptic, asked.

"When did it happen?" Maisie asked, wide eyed.

"Well, the story's been going around a long time, longer than I've been here," Mikey said. "I heard it from one of the old boys whose father used to be a Number One – a skipper of his own boat. He said that it was just known about. So it goes back to the early 1900s, I'd say. Canal tunnels often have ghost stories – Harecastle and Crick for two have stories of a Boggart. It's not just something out of Harry Potter.

"Now look, about today: I wanted to tailor the price down for you so I've got none of the food on board which we would normally offer. If it's all right with you we'll head off down through the tunnel, then go on the No 1 Canal to the pubs at Waterfront, have lunch, turn and then head for the Netherton and back. That all right?"

It was the first that our lot had heard of the plans, and I could see they were interested. We agreed and walked out to the trip boat with Mikey. A younger man was at the tiller. Mikey introduced him as Pete, his son. We were about to cast off when there was a shout from the office. Mikey looked round.

"Mikey, we've got a party who were booked to go tomorrow, but they've turned up a day early by mistake. And they went to the wrong entrance as well. That's why they're late. Any chance you could fit them on?"

"It's a sort of private trip, really," Mikey called back. "The lady's Poppy, from Poppy Narrowboats. Besides that, I've got no food on board – we're stopping at Waterfront for a break."

"Oh..."

"We don't mind, Mikey," Poppy said hurriedly.

"You sure? Don't really like messing people about, but they are customers – even if they're tomorrow's."

"You go ahead," Poppy said. "Ok, Jack?"

The more the merrier, I thought. I'd been expecting more on the tour anyway. "Of course," I confirmed.

Mikey called back. "I've only got teas and coffees, so warn them first what's going to happen. Make sure they're happy to get their own lunch, then we can do it."

The message was relayed, and soon a group of six people climbed on board and looked round apologetically.

"I hope we've not caused you too much trouble," said one, a man of about my age. "We made a complete cock-up of the whole thing, thanks to my well-meaning Dad who booked it for us.

I was about to mutter something about it not being a problem when a quiet voice from amongst the group piped up.

"Aren't you Phil Dyer?"

I was conscious of ears being pricked up near me. Odd how a parent is alive to these things. "Yes," admitted the owner of the name. "Oh. Hallo. You're Year Eleven, aren't you?"

"When I'm at school, yes. But normally I'm just Erin Bradley."

"Hallo Year Erin," he said, recovering swiftly. "You've come to experience our world, have you?"

"My world too. I'm as Birmingham as you probably are."

"I mean my world of canals."

"They're my world too, just as they are yours... just a minute, what do you mean, your *world*? You make it sound as if you live on them."

"Well actually..." Talk about the gift of a conversation starter being dropped in your lap. "... Actually we do. Our boat is just up there a bit."

"Well? We hire boats too. Every year."

"We live on ours," he said casually, as if dropping a name.

Turning slightly, I could see the look of surprise on her face.

"*Well,*" she said eventually, "that sounds really exciting. But don't you find it cramped.?" It wasn't said condescendingly, though I did wonder to start with. Phil took it at face value.

"No, not really. It's good. We all have our own spaces, rooms and that. My brother designed a bed that makes a sofa, a desk that comes out of the floor, and a bench seat opposite that drops from the bulkhead. We've both got one."

"Clever chap," she said. "Studying design at Uni?"

"No. He's Year Seven at our place. He just has a way with design. That's him, over there."

She looked over with surprise at the subject of the compliment. "He's Year Seven? Tall. But is he always bruised, or have you hit him?"

He paused and looked at her seriously. "He's just been returned from being kidnapped by people who were trying… who are evil. No. I don't hit him. At least, not often. And not hard."

"You don't mean they were trying to… kidnap him for…"

"No. Look, it's difficult and we can't talk about it."

Her expression was one of astonishment. To give her credit, she apologised genuinely for putting her foot in it. Phil smiled.

"May I come and look at his work some time?" she asked.

"On the boat, you mean? Yes, why not. Come and have a look when we get back."

They moved away from our little group. I wondered, as parents do, if this could be the start of a meaningful friendship although I hoped it wouldn't result in long absences from us. He had proved his worth to me during the period of my mental fragility and his brother's absence; and was now very useful with manoeuvring our boat as well as helping everyone by being at the marina. Even as my mind was working on this I knew it was a selfish attitude to have.

Mikey had rejoined us and was preparing to tell us about the tunnels we were visiting. We quietened down, sitting ourselves at the tables to gaze out at the tunnel sides. Floodlights had been fitted along the boat's roof, so we could see the tunnel's stonework clearly. Those of us who didn't know the tunnel were surprised when it proved so short, opening out onto the sides of a mine before continuing. We had settled down again when once again we came to the open air.

There were two exits. We explored one which we were told was the Seven Sisters mine, then backed out and swung so as to enter the left exit. Inside, three other turnings to the left were seen and commented on, but we kept going, straight as a die.

Mikey went to start brewing teas and coffees to order. The boat-illuminated darkness continued, and continued, and continued...

We sipped our drinks. Phil was still evident by his absence. Indeed, he only reappeared from the family's table nearer the bows when we emerged into the light and the boat slowed.

"We've got some locks ahead," Mikey announced. "Any experts here? We have windlasses."

There was a scramble, Nat and Maisie, Erin and Phil, and two others. "I think we're redundant," Poppy told me with a smile.

The six were told that there were three locks before the junction and one after it. They spread themselves out and amicably worked us through them, past some quite wide stretches of canal, and on towards Brierley Hill. The Waterfront proved to be a wide area of canal containing a small marina and several pubs. One of them was expecting us and we hungrily trooped in. Carl and Inge, Nat and Maisie, Poppy and I all gravitated towards a large table. Phil and Erin looked at it, looked at her parents and friends on a table of five, and hesitated.

It was a moment of indecision writ large. Choose one? Separate to the family? Which?

To give Phil his due he noticed a table for two and looked enquiringly at Erin. She smiled broadly and shook her head, saying something quietly.

They separated. I drew up another chair to ours and Phil sat on it, looking defiant.

I said nothing. Nor did anyone else, except of course Nat.

"'Bout time."

Phil looked sharply at him, then at Maisie. I wondered what was coming next. But he just smiled sweetly at his brother and reached for a menu.

The boat was turned in the basin and we retraced our steps to the last of the locks we'd passed earlier, with its adjacent pumping station. Immediately to the right, at Blowers Green junction, was the start of Dudley No. 2 Canal. We turned down it and increased speed.

Phil was seen to talk to Mikey, and Mikey to Pete, who nodded with a grin. The next thing I knew was that Phil and Erin were standing at the tiller and Pete was holding a coffee, watching our course warily.

He was about to rush to intervene when the two were watching the huge Netherton Reservoir go past, but Erin corrected Phil's hand on the tiller and we avoided the bank. Pete relaxed again.

We passed another junction. This time Pete was on hand to show Erin the way. She had somehow wrested the tiller from Phil. I saw amazement and a grin on Phil's face, and a moment later knew that it had to do with the mention of the Bumble Hole Arm and junction. Pete took over and the other two came down again.

"Tunnel next," Erin said happily to us. "I'm sorry if we're ignoring you – but he's interesting to talk to."

Was he? I could think of many descriptors of my elder son, some complimentary, but 'interesting to talk to' had not hitherto been one of them. Before I could say anything, Nat had to comment, naturally.

"Thanks for keeping him away. It's been nice and quiet." It was said gravely, but I couldn't see his face from the angle I was sitting at.

She grinned: behind her back Phil gave him the finger.

Mikey gave a few details of its history as we entered Netherton Tunnel. Its width came as a surprise to us as novices; it even had a towpath each side to add to it. On a tunnel that's almost a mile and three-quarters long it must have added so much to the construction cost and effort. Quite some engineering achievement, as Poppy observed. This time Erin had joined us too, and was pleasantly conversational about family, school, expectations and other matters. Phil engaged in it all, fully, so we managed to avoid taking her over, so to speak.

There's a limit to what can be said about millions of bricks passing around you as part of a long, uniform tunnel, and as Mikey said, once you've gone through the Netherton's vital statistics you have to stop talking and leave conversations to occur naturally. It was a relief to get out of the darkness and into Birmingham rain. Thank goodness for covered boats. We just felt sorry for Pete on the tiller, and I noticed that this time none of our party rushed up to take over from him.

We ended up joining the New Main Line near Dudley Port station, then headed back to Dudley down the three Factory Locks. This time our lot did go and help, fortunately, otherwise Poppy and I would have had to.

Altogether we were away for almost seven hours. It had been fun, though tunnels, we decided, can be boring. We bid our farewells to Mikey and Pete with thanks.

Phil took Erin by the hand to lead her to our boat, but she shook it off. "Don't you want to see our home?" he asked, injured.

"Oh... sorry. I thought you were trying it on." I was on the edge of hearing this, and smiled to myself.

"Bring everyone, if you'd like to," I called to him, no doubt causing embarrassment.

Between them they managed to attract all six of their party and we engaged them in a one-way trip through the boat. They spent some time playing with the adjustable furniture in the cabins, to Nat's delight, and he was congratulated six times on his ingenuity. When they climbed off the bows it was obvious that Phil didn't know what to do, whether to stay and help prepare food with us or escort Erin to the car. In the end the two parted, and he watched like a sad fawn as her back retreated.

He was a bit non-communicative that night.

34 Museum and return

Wednesday – most of it – was spent at the Museum. There's so much there and if you have an interest in your own city and its past you could spend even longer than we did. But around mid-afternoon we found our way back to the boat and wondered whether to make a move or to stay another night. We decided on the former.

The Old Main Line was an experience for the Parishes, and we'd not navigated it in an easterly direction. It was effectively new to all of us except Poppy. The return to the Marina was at about eight-thirty and we decided to eat out. Seven people trying to fit round our table was too much of a squeeze, we'd decided, and there was nothing much down at the front – that Nat had christened the Stateroom – to enable eating. Our usual little pub was pleased to see us, if a bit fazed at having to provide a table for so many.

The next morning farewells were said, and it was Nat's turn to wave the car out of sight, and to be less communicative than usual for the rest of the morning. Poppy and I went to the office. I remembered the letters that had arrived early that Saturday morning and started looking at them, only to jump in the air with an obscenity when I read one of them.

Poppy looked at me with surprise and I apologised. "Bloody Helen," I started. "She's only gone and told me that she'll make the decisions about the house without asking me or telling what price she's after."

"She can't do that, surely. Your name's on the mortgage and the deeds, isn't it?"

"Well, yes. But she seems to have missed that, even if the solicitors have told her."

"How about keeping a look out on Rightmove or Zoopla or similar, and when it comes on find out who the estate agents are? Then you can write to them and explain that a sale without your involvement would be illegal."

A pause.

"Why do you always talk sense? Thank you, that's exactly what I should do. I'll write to Helen to tell her to look at the solicitor's letter again and read it, so that she knows it'd be illegal."

"But don't tell her about my idea, or she'll try and sell it privately. Have you told your building society your new address? And how about the Land Registry?"

"Neither. Actually, I also need to calculate the value of the house and tell Helen what I expect from her."

"Good idea."

I set to. It's difficult writing letters when you're furious with the recipient, and it took many drafts before I presented what I hoped was the final wording to Poppy, as if she was my class teacher. She approved it, but pointed out two typos.

It took two days before Helen phoned me.

"How dare you tell me how to sell my house?" was the gist of it, yet another of the "how dare you…" conversations we'd had. By that time I'd calmed down and told her that just as the boys were mine as well as hers, so was the house. "Don't forget it was your taking on a live-in lover and changing the locks that excluded me from it," I told her. "I've not abandoned the place. If you want to move out, the boys and I will move back if we can afford it, always assuming that you've kept up the mortgage payments, that is. Have you?"

Silence.

"You haven't, have you?" I asked in incredulity. "Do you want to be homeless? Or don't you care about your and the boys' future?" There was a click as she ended the connection.

"I have none of the paperwork," I told Poppy, who was in the boat with us. "I can't… oh yes, perhaps I can. I'll call the broker we used and get the information from them – if they're still going after all these years."

"How long?"

"I think we took out the mortgage about ten years ago."

She opened her laptop. "What was their name?"

Amazingly, given more recent financial turbulence, they were still in operation, online, and had a working phone number. Not only that, but they were helpful, once the reason for the call was understood, and found a contact for me within the building society.

It seems that Helen had missed only one payment up to that point, though how many others she would be unable to pay, going forward, I had no way of knowing. The contact left a note on the file about the reason for the difficulties, and I told her that a sale was very likely.

Next stop was at Poppy's and my solicitor who was helpful but said that there was a limit to what they could do without being professionally engaged – another way of saying that if I wanted them to do more, I needed to start paying them. She did say, though, that whoever was looking after the children for the greater part of the time would normally expect a Court to allow them to occupy the property. "But, of course, the mortgage would still have to be paid," she said to finish.

"I suppose it's not surprising," Poppy said when I told her. "They have to earn a living too, and solicitors aren't cheap."

"Tell me about it," I said, thinking about the fees when we had bought the house.

I looked up the likely value of the house and my eyebrows shot up. Wow. It had increased a *lot* over the years. If we could get anything like that… Another letter to Helen was concocted, and I made it more conciliatory than I really wanted to given the tone of her phone call. She now knew that I was concerned about the missing of a mortgage payment, that I knew the worth of the house and what I expected my share of its sale to be. Again I sent a copy of it to my solicitor (and told her I'd done so, of course.).

"Where did you get that value from?" were her first words on the phone the next morning when she'd read the details.

"The various property selling websites that give sold prices for other places near it. They all agree, more or less, but feel free to do your own research. Are you going to put it on the market, or shall I? Or do you think the flat would raise enough to make that figure?"

"Look, this is getting ridiculous. I want to keep the house."

"Then you need to see what Jonathan's flat is worth. If it's more than fifty percent of that value, sell it and the boys and I will take that figure. If it isn't, you'll have to make up the difference."

"I can't do that."

I decided to drop my bombshell. "My solicitor tells me a Court would expect that whoever was looking after the children of the marriage should occupy the house."

The silence was deafening.

"I'll get back to you," she said, and there were thumps and a click as the connection broke.

"Perhaps she knows that you're serious now," Poppy said when I told her what had been said. We were in the boat. The boys were doing homework, for a change quietly. "But if she gives up the house, will you be able to afford the mortgage?"

"No, certainly not. But then she will be obliged to pay her part of it." The Solicitor had divulged that too.

"So that means that you could return and live with the boys there," she said, and I could tell that there was worry in her voice.

"I suppose so." It was said reluctantly. We had all acclimatised to narrow living. We had all acclimatised to Poppy's more-than-frequent presence. I had more-than-acclimatised to Poppy.

"I need to think," she said abruptly, and turned to go.

"No, you don't, Poppy," I said hastily. "We're happy here. I'm very happy with your presence here. I don't want to go back there now. This is home, this boat. There are too many unpleasant memories back there; arguments that I want to forget and a mounting – no, actually a complete coldness affecting what was once a real relationship." A deep breath. "All the time we've been here, the boys have been happy, I've been happy, and I hope to goodness you have been too. And still are."

She turned back, thank goodness, and just looked at me. "I… I'm an old fool. I…"

She was speechless for a change. I crossed to her and gently hugged her, to find the tenseness still there.

"I'm not going back there. Not unless you… No, not even then. Too many negative vibes. I'm happy here, as I said. If you want, we can…"

Her head came up.

"We could make a go of it, if you think we could. If we know each other well enough in this short time."

"Are you saying what I think you're saying?"

I thought, furiously. Was this something that I should talk to the boys about first? Or was this something I could do for me?

"It is," I told her, throwing caution to the winds. "And I believe you feel the same."

We embraced. Again. It seemed the right thing to do, and it seemed that we each wanted it to happen.

"This is going at a speed," she said quietly. "I like those two. A lot. They're each independently minded and intelligent, but more than that, they're good people. I wouldn't want to cause them to give a shocked gulp before accepting me as a… a replacement Mum."

"That's a difficult one, I admit. But so far they've been very pro you. And pro us, which is even more to the point. Do you really think they'd object if we – well, if we really got together as a couple?"

"I don't know. I don't think so. But what would they think about my effectively being their Mum, if not their actual Mother?"

"I think that's best left to them to decide. My guess is that they'll still just call you Poppy."

"Jack, you can be silly at times. I don't care what pronoun they use, but I do care how they view my having a measure of control over them."

"But you do already. At work, on a Saturday, and when we're cruising on the boat you give them instructions."

"That's different."

"No. It's the same. "Take her into the lock, Nat, please," is the same as "Homework time, Nat, please. Oh, you'd probably phrase it differently, like "Shower, Nat, don't you think?"

"I'll have one later," came a voice from the door, causing us to wheel round sharply. A grin appeared, attached to a Nat.

"How long have you been listening?" I asked coldly.

"Since Poppy mentioned pronouns. We don't mind being bossed around by Poppy, because she doesn't."

"What?"

"She doesn't boss us around. She just makes sensible suggestions, like you said. Is there anything to eat?"

At Crown I was paid to take in information quickly, process it quickly and produce a reaction quickly. Nat's *non sequitur* had me temporarily bamboozled.

"I suppose I'd better start cooking," I said, weakly.

"Can't we all cook?" Poppy asked, looking at Nat with a smile.

"Might as well," said that one. "If we all muck in it'll be ready quicker. So are you two going to get together properly?"

Blast the butterfly brained boy.

"What would you think if we did? What would you *both* think? Really?"

"We thought you already were. What are we having?"

"Macaroni cheese ."

"Bacon? I mean, you're sharing a bed."

"I know, but…. But yes."

It was his turn to look confused. "Was that 'yes' about sharing a bed, or bacon?"

"Yes," I said again.

He smiled. "Good. I'll go and tell Phil."

"What? About the bacon, or about Poppy and me?"

"Yes," he said, and headed for the door.

"Just a minute, Nat. Let him finish whatever it is he's doing without interruptions, then you can both go and talk about it. You can both tell one of us what you think about it. It's not something you'd want to have to announce to both of us, especially if the answer's 'no'.

"Are you talking about bacon still?" he asked innocently.

Poppy gave a snort of laughter.

"Nat, you are…"

"Incorrigible. I know. It's fun. Anyway, I'm glad."

"Bacon?"

His face was suddenly serious. "You two."

In fact, three people trying to cook in a small kitchen doesn't work. We did what we could, but Poppy was supplanted by Nat who took it on himself to prevent the boiling macaroni from sticking to itself and the saucepan. It seemed to be a messy, sloppy business and I was pleased when Poppy laughed. "Is it you who are going to clean the hob after all that sloshing around?"

He glanced at her; an unwise move as still more boiling water removed itself from the pan and onto the hob, causing him to jump.

"It's only water," he accused her.

"With starch and salt in it, which sticks to the metal and attracts bacteria."

"Oh well..."

I think the point was made.

Once the dish was browning happily under the grill and the vegetables cooking, he vanished down the boat, not to reappear until we called them both to eat.

They sat at the table. We served up.

"Yes," said Phil.

"Yes what?" Poppy asked as she plonked a plate in front of him.

"Thank you. Yes we like the idea of you two getting together properly. We approve of Poppy…"

"Phil!" I said, shocked. It seemed the right thing for me to do.

"Well you wanted the truth, didn't you? We approve. She makes you happy. And she seems to like you, for some reason. As Nat says, she doesn't boss us around. She's the complete opposite to Jonathan. Yeahh… we like her."

I looked at the object of his comments and took in the grave, pleased smile. "Am I allowed a hug?" she asked.

"Who from?" responded Phil with the hint of a grin.

"Both of you," she answered, and closed the gap between them despite the hot food in front of them.

"If you're going to be… to get married, will we have to call you Mum?" asked Phil.

The subject of that overheard pronoun looked horrified. "Phil, Nat: the idea that you should even think that either of us should tell you what to call us – well, it really horrifies me. We're not in the Victorian era any more, you know, nor are we American. You call me what you want to call me. If it's 'Poppy', fine. If it's something rude, then you'll probably get an old-fashioned look. If it's rude and in front of Jack then he might have something to say. But I have no intention of sneaking to him. I fight my own battles." She tried to look severe, but it didn't work.

Phil grinned. "Thanks."

Just one word, but given the conversation it was enough.

"So..." I started cautiously, "do you think I should ask your mother for a divorce?"

Two slightly shocked pairs of eyes met the question with silence. It was Phil who broke it.

"If you don't," he started slowly, "you two aren't going to be able to get married, are you? So really, I suppose, 'yes' is the answer. Is that what you think, Nat?"

"I... I think so, I suppose it has to be. In fact, really, I *know* it has to be. It's just..."

"A big step?" I offered.

"Yes. That. You startled me, that's all."

"Me too," Phil added. "I suppose we both knew it had to happen, but..." His turn to trail off.

"It won't actually alter anything, not practically," I told them. "Nothing about our life will change. Poppy will, I hope, still be here and we shall live as we have been living, between here and her house."

Another silence.

"A bit hard," Phil said at last.

I sighed. "I know, Phil. It's a decision that has to be made, though. It comes with a jolt to the system, that's inevitable. But..."

"I don't mean that. I mean sleeping between here and Poppy's. The ground's hard."

A tableau: two open adult mouths, a youthful grinning one, and a slightly older one that was trying to keep straight.

"Idiot," I said as Poppy and I joined in the laugh, in our cases a relieved laugh.

We started eating. Never had I seen my two with full plates in front of them choosing to talk for five minutes without eating anything. It's certainly never happened since.

"I think we'd better let the house sale get sorted first, and make sure the funds from it are split and in accounts before we start mentioning divorce. Maybe that's over-cautious, but if there are legalities to consider – which there are in any house sale – it'd be helpful if they weren't muddied by still more legalities."

"Is Mum going to be all right?" Nat asked suddenly. "I mean, will she have somewhere to live? Or will she be poor?"

"She didn't worry whether I'd have anywhere to live when my brother changed the locks and refused to give you a key," I flashed. "But she'll have half the sale price of the house, less half the mortgage owed, and will be able to live with Jonathan. They're both working, and Jonathan has afforded the mortgage on the flat up to now, so they'll be fine."

"What about us?" Phil asked.

"We'll have the other half of the house sale as a deposit, my income from the company that employs me and any from any consultancy work that comes my way."

"So..." Phil was about to ask more, but Poppy held up a hand to stop him. She continued, in a voice so quiet, uncharacteristically quiet.

"If we do get married, it means that Jack becomes co-owner of the hire business and you two stand to inherit it if – when – we die."

This time the silence extended for what felt like an age. I could hardly marshal my own thoughts. Surely the boys would be similarly dumbstruck?

"I never thought in a million years that I'd end up helping to run a boat hire company," Nat said.

Poppy looked at him sharply. "We're not dead yet!"

He coloured, and looked down. It was the first time I'd really seen him embarrassed. "Sorry," he muttered.

"I don't know what to say." I too was talking quietly. "It never struck me that... that..."

"Well, Jack, as far as I know all successful marriages share everything if the partners in it trust each other. And I'm certainly not going to put mine at risk by keeping the main family income to myself. Why would I want to? Gordon took himself away and is now dead. Tim's over in Canada and will soon be earning good money if he isn't already. He has no wish to return to England to practise, in any case. I suppose I'd better talk to him, but he's been very independent since he left.

"You three are here – we four are here – and are already engaged with the company. It doesn't mean that either of you two is tied to Poppy Narrowboats, not by any means. Each of you is as free to follow your own interests or life direction when the time comes. Just as you'd have been free to make your own career choices as if Jack had never seen a narrowboat in his life."

I could now smile. "Or an engine," I added.

"Or an engine," she echoed.

"Well," Phil started, "I think for once you've silenced us both."

She nodded. "Your food's cold by now. I should eat it and let it settle in. You too, Jack."

"Yes Poppy."

"Let what settle in?" Phil asked with what I knew as a cheeky grin. "Food or the news? And shouldn't we be celebrating with some wine or something? I mean, I suppose you've asked Poppy and she's accepted? Or is this all just... just rhetorical?"

We laughed. "It's real. I did, sort of; just not very conventionally. And yes, she accepted. And yes: how else would you celebrate other than with macaroni cheese and red wine?"

Phil went to the cupboard, looked at the bottle, said "yay!", then rushed down to his cabin to fetch his birthday present. To give him credit, he drew the cork perfectly.

35 The Lift

The next few weeks followed the same pattern. Saturdays were manic, weekdays less so. We managed the occasional trip out, just from Saturday evening into Sunday or Monday so as to be fair to Ian who had to hold the fort whilst we were away. Occasionally Helen came to visit and to take the boys somewhere. It seemed that she had finally realised that each of them would be very capable of escaping and returning to the marina by bus, or of phoning me to collect them, should Jonathan appear. He didn't, fortunately.

Erin didn't make contact with Phil, which caused a bit of a depression in that area. It didn't affect him too badly, but I was aware of some distance-staring and a straight face from time to time which I imagined to be the result. Keeping him busy helped, though. Once, fortunately midweek, there was a knock on our cabin side and we found the Attwoods, the couple who had been so hospitable when the Smiths had made themselves a nuisance. They wanted to see if the marina could look after their boat for a while, and whether they could moor with us.

Discussions with Poppy agreed that temporarily they could moor alongside us and that she would press the Trust for a proper mooring for them. "It's about time we got this sorted out," she said. The presence of their boat gave me a caretaking job with a retainer attached and near carte-blanch to spend money without reference if necessary. It gave Poppy a mooring fee which we described as a "facility fee" as we weren't then permitted to profit from mooring boats privately.

At odd intervals the Parishes reappeared, to Nat's joy. Actually it was to everyone's joy since the more they relaxed into civilian life and the more we got to know them, and the more we were all at ease with each other. Helen and I had befriended a goodly number of people over our years together, from areas local to our home and from work. Some were on really good terms with us, but none of them were as easy to like as the Parishes.

I mentioned it once when we had enjoyed one of those uproarious teasing matches that can only happen between family members or those so close as to be regarded as family.

"I hope we're not pushing the boundaries," Inge said, suddenly serious.

I laughed, as did the boys. "If that's boundary-pushing, you push away!" I said. "Being able to relax completely is an absolute tonic, and that's what we all do when we're together. Your presence just adds a different dimension to it and we thoroughly enjoy it."

We were on one of our mini-trips on the boat at the time, and were surprised to see a middle-aged couple on the towpath turn and smile at us. We'd forgotten how much we had to raise our voices to hear each other over the engine as we were in progress. We smiled back.

Later Carl asked me quietly how my recovery was going after the earlier problems.

"I'm inclined almost to ask you 'what problems?'" I started. "To be honest, the change of pace and – " I chuckled – "the reduction in trip length from Birmingham, Alabama to Birmingham, West Midlands have done the trick. It's only on the really exceptional – and rare – occasions when I get stressed I know that there is something remaining there." I paused.

"It's like knowing there's a deep well at the bottom of your garden, hidden from view; a thing all but forgotten about. Sometimes life drives you to search through the undergrowth towards it, and maybe you even glimpse it. It's not something you hope ever to be drawn to, to approach voluntarily. I suppose my mind has developed strategies to keep me away from leaning over and looking into it, or, worse, hanging over the edge. I know it's there, but knowledge is the first defence, if you like." A humourless laugh. "I suppose you'd say 'know your enemy'."

He looked me straight in the eyes. "That's deep, Jack. And I don't mean the well. I mean the notion. And the 'know your enemy' was rule one in the trade we've now left behind us. But like all trades, it leaves traces. No matter where we go, what room we find ourselves in, training kicks in and you're always looking for a second, third or fourth exit, for things to use as shields against an incident. You really don't want to know all that, to get involved. But it's training ingrained from day one and you can never get rid of it. We, too, have our version of the knowledge of the well, but so far have never located it, let alone looked over the edge. And certainly not since resigning."

I wondered if he knew that to hear him share that side of him helped me put further distance from my own usually hidden dark well.

The house went on the market at a price that Helen and I finally managed to agree after discussions with three estate agents and a lot of online research. Jonathan seemed to have come to his senses too and had made good the missing mortgage payments. I imagine that the sudden outlay stung him into quick action to seek a sale.

I had thought long and hard about the boys' inheritance of the house and concluded that at whatever age they would be when the inevitable happened, they wouldn't want to go through the long procedure of selling it as executors, to try and afford a joint mortgage or to share a house together. It was best sold now. Helen and boyfriend could go and live in his nice, much smaller, flat. And good luck to them.

I made no mention of a divorce: nor did Helen. That would be for later.

As school holidays neared their end Poppy and I thought that for the last week we should take some time out – in the boat, obviously – and Ian good-humouredly agreed to look after the marina and the decreased number of hires that were booked. Guided by Poppy we looked at the options – the four of us – though we hoped that the Parishes would come too. Poppy had a glint in her eye which already I knew meant that there was a surprise in her plans. Inge, Maisie and Carl jumped at the chance and with their help we were able to set off after one Saturday's efforts were over, and reached a pleasant enough mooring near the Dudley branch for that night. Trains from the nearby railway kept us awake for a while, but you can't have everything.

We knew there were locks to work the following day, and were looking forward to them. As we wove our way to Wolverhampton it started to rain and we were thankful that only one of us had to be outside on the tiller.

The first lock appeared after Broad Street Bridge and after that the remaining twenty were as unrelenting as the rain. Murphy's Law ruled again; we were all but done with the locks when a brighter disc appeared above us and the rain reluctantly eased. We joined the Staffs and Worcester canal on its way up from the Severn. Here the canal is in an overbearing cutting, and we were glad to turn left onto the Shropshire Union and, via a single lock, to gain higher ground.

We wrung out our wet clothing. Actually, that's an exaggeration, although the drying cupboard was in full use and people reappeared looking different. Birmingham had been mourning our departure, no doubt.

There were no locks in sight, nor was there a pub. That was discovered when we sent Maisie and Nat up to the road at Pendeford and were told categorically that we could buy furniture nearby but there was no pub. Phil just looked at her.

"Do they sell narrowboat furniture? TVs, anything like that?"

"They were shut," Maisie told him. "If we moor here, when the noise wakes you when they start, you could go and find out."

"He won't wake!" Nat said, "He's a dormouse until about ten thirty and then needs to be woken with tea." He was Looked At.

We carried on for a mile or so before mooring, resigning ourselves to be self-sufficient that night. It was actually a pleasant change to be totally in the countryside, in peace and quiet. We relaxed.

The next day there were still no locks. Time was spent finishing off clothes drying, playing cards, watching scenery, learning that the M45 is noisy, that Brewood is pronounced "Brood", that there is such a place as High Onn and that the G in Gnosall is silent. More importantly, the Anchor Inn at High Offley is still as wonderful as in 1990 when I visited it, and appeared not to have changed at all. I bought a pub T-shirt back then which had obviously shrunk in the wash since, so I joyously replaced it with a larger version. The visit was bittersweet: back then it was when a friend discovered he couldn't throw darts reliably any more. Later he was diagnosed with a disease that killed him at thirty.

Ow.

I silently raised a glass to him.

When Poppy had planned the route, one of our overnights would have been at Tyrley which had once been a major wharf. Since we were about three hours in front of ourselves we tackled the five locks that start to drop the canal to the lowness of the Cheshire Plain. Further on is Market Drayton, so we stopped at what we hoped would be a quiet mooring, and so it proved to be. We even walked into the town to satisfy Phil's quest for a pub – actually the adults were glad that he'd mentioned it so that we could blame him. We ended up eating there too.

The weather was overcast next morning, though dry, as we headed into the wilds of Shropshire, down the Adderley locks and the first eleven of the Audlem flight. An attractive little town is Audlem, and friendly with it. We shopped at the general store.

Down the remaining three of Audlem's locks we regained flatness again until the two Hack Green locks. Nat's forehead wrinkled. "What's a Secret Bunker?" he asked.

"I can't tell you," Poppy replied straight faced. "It's a s…"

"Yeah, ok," Nat interrupted with a grin. We discovered that it was a Cold War shelter and command post; a reminder of precautions taken in case of what might have been all those years ago. Chilling stuff.

Nantwich proper – ignoring the new developments to its south – appears over an attractive aqueduct which crosses a road. Immediately there's a bend and the start of a long line of moored craft on a long embankment that gives treetop views of – well, trees. Houses peep shyly from between them occasionally.

On and on, bridges, no locks, attractive countryside but not a lot of interest until a bridge blocks the view of what appears to be a sheet of water. There's a huge bank ahead and to the left. Also to the left is a lock which Poppy told us leads into the Llangollen Canal.

"As in Wales?" asked Maisie.

"The very same."

We continued. The immense bank is there to hold back the water of Hurleston Reservoir, and we were very glad it was still successfully doing so in view of the reservoir's size.

"At the next junction, turn right," said Poppy in her best Google Maps voice to Inge, who was steering at the time. "That's the Middlewich Branch and we can get a little bit along that before we need to moor."

"Any pubs?" asked Phil innocently.

"None," she said with mock severity. "Think of your liver."

"Liver?"

"Liver. Too much alcohol over too many years gives you sclerosis of the liver and you don't want that."

I don't think that the comment had much effect.

There's one lock on it, and a queue of boats was waiting for it. "At least it spaces them out so that the lock at the end shouldn't get too busy," Poppy told us. Mooring a little later gave us a good view of a river which we identified on the map as a young River Weaver. "You might be meeting that later, when it's bigger," Poppy told us, "but I won't say any more about that yet."

Another grey day brought us to the lock at the end she had mentioned. It turned out to be at the start of the world's shortest canal, the Wardle Canal, all 154 feet of it. as we discovered later.

"Why?" asked Phil.

Poppy shrugged. "All it could do was wardle a short distance? Who knows. The only other reason is that the map says so."

Cautiously, having posted Maisie and Phil at the bow as lookouts, we nosed out onto the Trent and Mersey canal, turning left. The first lock afterwards gave onto a sharp left hand bend, and inevitably there was another boat moored in the bend just where we needed to swing our seventy-footer round to straighten up. It took a bit of hurried manoeuvring by Carl, helped by Poppy, before we realised we had no option but to ask them to move. After some blustering, they realised that they would have to do so if we weren't to remain wedged against them. People!

"They're not all like that," said Poppy in a not-so-quiet voice as we finally squeezed past them. I looked back. Not only had the steerer heard, and was looking daggers, but the boat following us had closed the bottom gates on the previous lock and was already filling it, so delaying them further. What goes round, comes around. Happy arguing.

Two more narrow locks and then the last of what Middlewich had to offer, Big Lock. For some reason it's a wide lock and seems very out of place in a canal classified as narrow.

The Cheshire Plain is nearly as flat as the name suggests, though patches of trees disguise the fact. The canal wanders, and there are some expanses of water that we christened inland seas as they were so unexpectedly large after the canal.

"Flashes," said Poppy, the fount of all knowledge.

"Who is?" Phil asked as innocently as he could.

"Twit. Salt has been mined here for centuries. The land sinks in places and water fills the depressions. There are some even bigger ones around too." As if to prove her right we passed the Lion Saltworks Museum, though Poppy was in the cabin at the time.

"I think we need to moor just along here," she said. We had rounded some bends and were passing what appeared to be a belt of trees with a busy car park alongside it. "You need to walk along the towpath and go into the Reception – it's obvious – and tell them you're booked for an hour's time."

Those of us who could fit on the steering area looked surprised. I smiled, knowing by now that Poppy liked to arrange surprises. I had no idea what this one was. We did as bidden. Whatever was ahead kept itself to itself until we were nearly on top of it.

An unremarkable, modern commercial building announced itself as being the Anderton Boat Lift and once again our brows furrowed. I think in the distant past I'd heard of such a thing, but its whereabouts were unguessed – unless this was it. No sign of the Lift was visible. As we entered the building, heading obediently for Reception, a large display appeared in front of us. We breathed a collective "Wow!" as we saw a model of what looked like a Meccano structure assembled by an overactive thirteen year-old (sorry, Nat). If the thing itself was nearby… just a minute; Poppy had said that we were booked for an hour's time. I left the others exclaiming over it and found Reception. Quite nonchalantly she ticked us off on a screen and asked us to come along to the mooring outside in forty minutes. Suddenly childishly excited I nodded my thanks and rejoined the others who were looking through one of the windows.

In the flesh, it was even more impressive than in the model. Together we worked out what happened, more or less, and I became even more excited. The engineer in me was screaming to be let out to look at the workings.

Time passed, I looked at my watch and nudged the others. We needed to move the boat. When we found Poppy I gave her a hug, knowing that she'd planned this for us. We moved up to the "holding" mooring as directed, with another, shorter, boat between us and the entry to the basin. At last two boats emerged from it, we were briefed by one of the staff, then followed our neighbours in.

We seemed to be on the edge of the world. Behind us were the ordinary canal, ordinary homes, an ordinary road, and a high footbridge across the basin entrance. In front of us were two black guillotine gates against a background of other black structures, and as a background to *them* a distant, grey concrete factory building. To the right, trees. To the left, not a lot apart from a view over a river far below us.

"What do we do now?" Maisie asked.

"Follow that boat," Poppy said in an American accent. It was lost on Maisie and the boys but the rest of us grinned.

We found ourselves on a sort of aqueduct. A gate closed behind us, a man walked past and opened the seal to the caisson in which we'd be descending to the river level. We entered and secured the boat as instructed. The guillotine gate closed behind us, sealing us in a bath shared with the other boat.

Machinery hummed. The boat moved downwards in small bounces, to our amusement, bounces that became less as we descended. Half way down we passed the other caisson on its way up. The panorama to left and right through the lift's supporting superstructure – the Meccano bits – grew less impressive as we neared the river and were cut off by a concrete storage yard one side and high banks the other. At last machinery quietened, staff unhurriedly made ready, the guillotine gate in front of us lifted and we followed our neighbours out. To the left were the visitor moorings.

There was a limited time we could stay on the river Weaver as the younger element had to face school the following Monday. The journey back to base would take a few days of that. We moored, and returned to the museum, discovering as we climbed the steps just how high above us the canal was. There was a common shortage of breath as we gained flat ground, and a decision was made that lunch in the museum would be a good idea.

"I didn't think to book a return trip," Poppy admitted as our enquiries for one at the office drew a blank for that day. "We're going to have to go some when we get back up to the top tomorrow. Long days, I'm afraid. Sorry. "

I slipped an arm round her shoulders and she looked at me, startled, before her expression softened. "I'm still not used to that, not after all these years."

"Shouldn't I do it? I was just showing support."

"Don't ever stop."

The more I thought about that comment, the more I liked it.

Poppy negotiated a passage for the following day and returned to where we were waiting, looking at some more of the history of the Lift. "I've booked for eight o'clock tomorrow morning. Sorry, Phil."

He looked at her and worked out what it would mean, then smote his forehead with his palm theatrically. "How *can* you, Poppy? It doesn't exist."

"I'll start cooking bacon at half past six."

"Half past *six*? That's worse… with fried egg? And tea?"

"Maybe."

He groaned, similarly theatrically.

We returned to the boat and decided to head downstream to a rural mooring point we'd been told about, one that was within easy cruising distance from the Lift.

"What's "easy?" Phil asked.

"About twenty minutes," said our informant.

"That means…that means getting up even earlier! This is child cruelty."

"Just as well you're not really counted as one then, doesn't it?" I told him, and enjoyed seeing his mouth open and shut as he took that in.

We set off, negotiated a narrow road swing bridge that was fortunately high enough not to have to be swung for us, and found our moorings.

"Now the fun bit," Poppy announced. "It's not strictly necessary because the river's not busy enough or fast enough moving. But what we should do is to turn round to point upstream. To tell people what we're going to do we use the horn. Four blasts means that we're turning completely round, and another two blasts tells that we're turning to port. Got it?"

"Where's the horn?" Maisie asked before anyone else had a chance.

"The button marked 'Horn' on the panel." Phil was nearly dismissive.

"Now?"

Poppy looked round behind us as well as in front. "Yes."

Seventy feet is a long way away to hear a horn that's facing frontwards anyway. We found it underwhelming, but a fisherman on the bank nearby gave a start and looked at us. Phil was on the tiller at the time and swung us round, then back towards the obvious straight bit of bank.

We moored.

Once we had cooked and eaten, Poppy suggested a brainstorming session to see if we could come up with a plan for the front cabin, our stateroom, which Phil told us was a TV lounge really. "And we want a good big TV," he said. Yet again.

"We need to make sure it won't drain the batteries," Poppy told him. "It's all right when you're plugged into the mains, but if you use the inverter you might use more than they can put out."

"But can't it run on 12v?" he asked.

"Not a big set, no. It has to be mains voltage."

"Oh. But can't the inverter cope?"

"Yes, but the batteries hold a certain number of amp-hours, and once you've used them, no TV, no lights, no cooker ignition."

He thought for a moment. "We just need a good, long stretchy lead from the marina, then."

Poppy put out her tongue at him.

"You probably won't use the TV during the day," Carl said suddenly, "so why not have it across the front doors? It could swing out of the way when you needed it to."

I could see his logic, but that would mean installing seats behind seats, such as in a bus, so that when we had seven people on board – like then – they could all see.

"Well, assuming a large set is *de rigeur* the only place where it can be seen by everyone is at one side," Carl responded. "That means a long seat opposite it. If you want a double bed there too, that wouldn't be long enough."

"Er..."

Nat was looking intently at the side where the seat would be required.

"We could do a futon type thing, but with non-moving bits at both sides of it."

Carl's eyebrows raised. "You mean like those that you have in the cabins."

"Yes. Should be possible. And storage underneath of course."

"You could have single futons at each end instead," Phil said happily, "then we could convert it all and have an orgy."

Later, when the others were talking about something else, I explained to him that you do not make jokes like that when your brother's potential girlfriend has her parents in the room. It took him a moment before the penny dropped, he coloured up, said "good night" and took himself off.

Tact, my son, tact. Develop some.

36 And back again

It was a distressingly early start given Phil's tendency for late rising. To be fair, it wasn't much better for the rest of us. Mist clung to the water like Phil to his bed, and we chugged off cautiously upstream towards the Lift. There was a short delay before it was ready for us. Upwards we dawdled, from the misty Weaver to the sunlit canal. The growing warmth made us feel increasingly awake as the southward journey started.

At Middlewich we continued south, passing the end of the Wardle canal that we'd emerged from the previous day. The lock straight ahead was in use by a stream of boats emerging from the Middlewich Branch. There were two boats waiting for the narrow lock ahead so the opportunity was taken to fill our water tank.

At a lull in the traffic we passed quickly through the lock and continued upwards, ever upwards. Locks came sporadically at first, giving a sense of false security; at Malkins Bank the locks have you believe that they're within walking distance from each other, but often are not. We reached Rode Heath, moored, and collapsed thankfully into the Broughton Arms with twenty-three locks and twenty miles under our belts.

"Who's cooking tonight?" Inge asked, yawning. We looked at her until she raised both hands in surrender. We ate in the pub.

Phil was noticeable by his absence in the morning. We set off, Poppy and I cooked breakfast, we ate breakfast in shifts of two at a time with one on the tiller and four locking. After six locks the dormouse joined us, demanding tea, and Poppy pointed him towards the kettle.

"Have I missed breakfast?"

"And a load of locks," she said severely. "Make your own, and wash up."

"What, everybody's?"

"Everybody else has been working the locks, steering or cooking."

"Oh *Poppy*..."

"Your choice, not mine."

"But..."

When Poppy looks at you, you *know* you've been Looked At. He withered, put the kettle on, had a bowl of cereal and groaned as he saw the mountain of plates, mugs and frying pans in the sink.

We were in a lock-free stretch at the time, I was in the bathroom. When I returned, Poppy was helping him. You've got to love someone who does something like that, who understands. They were on the best of terms, too. Well done, Poppy.

Eleven Locks. Easy to say, but time consuming when they're spread out. At one point we emerged from the cocoon of fields, trees and undergrowth into urban sprawl and busy-ness: Kidsgrove. A junction, ("That's the start of the Macclesfield Canal," said Poppy) and several bridges later, the water grew more red.

“We’ve seen this before,” Inge said. “It’s the effect of iron ore tainted springs. That means we’re nearing Stoke, I think.”

“We are,” Poppy agreed. “And we have a long tunnel to go through. I’ve not booked, so I hope we don’t have to wait too long.”

“Wait?” I asked. “Why?”

“It’s a narrow tunnel. There’s a one-way system in place, otherwise two boats would pile into each other.”

We joined the back of a thankfully short line of boats and waited. After about twenty minutes our chat was interrupted by a cheerful “Mornin’!” and we asked for passage. Details were taken, a safety briefing given and we continued waiting. And waiting.

Half an hour later a headlight appeared at the tunnel entrance and the first of six boats emerged. With those cleared the first in our queue was given the signal to start. We plunged into the darkness after our neighbour.

Thirty minutes later we were aware of a low roar. It increased in volume over the next ten minutes and then – hey presto – slowed to a stop and a door ahead of us opened. We blinked in the stream of light and emerged into a cutting. Phew. As if we were caged birds at dawn, we all started talking again.

Potteries, Westport, Etruria (“There’s a carvery!” Phil exclaimed), the Caldon Canal junction, an incredibly deep lock leading to the remainder of the Stoke on Trent flight and we were in countryside again. All this was peppered with cups of tea or coffee, the occasional snack, and the careful construction of braised chops by Maisie, Nat and me. As we approached Stone the smell from it was starting to tantalise those on the stern and I swear Phil started dribbling at one point.

Finding a mooring spot in Stone was difficult and we ended up some way from the pubs, to Phil’s disgust, and were late with the meal. A trip back to the lock and the Star was a necessity, though. We were late to bed that night.

“We’re doing all right,” Poppy said next morning.

“You and me, or were you talking about getting back on time?”

“Yes.”

“Which?”

“Both.”

Downhill all the way… as far as Great Haywood. Then we turned right onto the Staffs & Worcester canal, through the impressive and disturbingly wide Tixall Wide, through Penkridge and as far as Gailey whose distinctive ‘round house’ lock-keeper’s cottage even I had seen from trundling up and down the A5.

Poppy had spent a bit of time on the phone, it being Saturday and change-over day, and was concerned about one of the parties of hirers whose token female member had been taken ill. “I’m sure that’s what she was,” she said, looking worried. “It leaves an all-male group, and we don’t accept them. They’re so often trouble. But Ian didn’t hear about it until they were on board and ready to go, and it was too late. He said that they were sensible and reasonable people, so perhaps it’s all right.”

"No pub." Carl had been examining the map. We ate on board again and finished off our stock of wine and even the low-alcohol beer that had been on offer.

Sunday… the last day. "Keep going at the first junction and turn left at the second," instructed Poppy. "We're on home turf now. Only the Wolverhampton nineteen to come down and then run for the marina."

"It's not turf, Poppy," said Nat sagely, looking down at the water. "Please don't try walking on it."

"Yes, Nat," she responded as if under instruction. He grinned.

On we sped, at a hair-raising three miles an hour.

"We'll use the new main line, it's quicker," said Poppy as we emerged from Coseley Tunnel. Three more locks, upwards now, and we were on the finishing straight, the shallow-cutting-surrounded, boring, straight waterway that evades Dudley and West Bromwich on its way to Smethwick and the city centre. At about 7.00 pm we were home and moored.

"Pub!" said Phil, hopefully. Tired out, we agreed.

"We mustn't be too late," Inge said. "We have to get a good night's sleep and make sure everything's ready for the morning."

The morning… it suddenly hit me – as it must have hit the boys. School. A new school year. Nat would be thirteen two days afterwards – although he'd been behaving as a fourteen year old for the last six months, in my view. At least he would be in year eight.

The three of them were quiet for about fifteen minutes. We walked to the pub, the usual one that Poppy had introduced us to all those months ago. It was something of a hurried meal and return; the Parishes loaded their car and goodbyes were said. Phil made no comment as Maisie and Nat hugged.

I made them get their school clothes out and was horrified to discover that in six weeks Nat's trousers had become too short and that Phil's were an even more skinny fit than intended. "I was going to tell you…" Nat started.

"We either get up at silly o'clock tomorrow or you'll have to have a day like that," I told them.

"They're not too indecent, are they, Dad?" Phil, conscious of being shape-hugged.

"Not if you like that sort of thing. They're too short as well, though. Tomorrow night. Or else."

"Or else what?"

"Or else you carry on wearing them until one of the teachers complains. Or a seam splits."

"Ventilation," Phil said dreamily. "And embarrassing. Tomorrow. Do I have a long enough jacket?"

Seeing them off the following morning, after breakfast on a much quieter, more roomy boat, made me feel really lonely. Yes, it was peaceful, but a buzz of people around you is easy to acclimatise to and I missed it. As nine o'clock approached and Poppy appeared it felt better. We met up with Ian and went to face the day. Via coffee.

"Have you fuelled yours?" Poppy asked half way through the morning.

I had an engine to service, and knew I had to fuel the boat it was in too. "No, I could do that at the same time as I did the hire boat. Same with the pump out. Even with two toilets I'm glad we used the facilities at Anderton."

"It can get a bit *interesting*," Poppy agreed.

Servicing done, we were about to break for lunch when there was a phone call.

I could tell from Poppy's cautious tones that this was potential trouble. Then "*What?* Oh, for goodness sake! Are they still there?"

When she'd disconnected I looked enquiringly at her. "I think bloody *Cowslip's* becoming a gremlin. CRT say that she's been speeding down through Bourneville, onto the Stratford and has crashed into a boat at Kingswood junction, causing a child to fall off the roof of the other craft."

"Where are they now?"

"They refused to stop and have headed on down to Lowsonford. With any luck they'll have stopped at the Fleur de Lys."

"Hang on – that's only a bit faster than the Smiths did it. And they've been speeding?"

"Yes. They must have spent a long time moored, probably by pubs."

"How's the child?"

"Shocked, and wet. But ok."

"Thank God for that."

"The mum is hopping mad."

"Not surprisingly. Have they got the Police involved? I would have phoned them had it been one of the boys in the water."

"I think it's a good idea. They're moored at Kingswood, I suppose recovering. Look, could you meet up with them and get details, and I'll go straight to the Fleur and heave them off the boat?"

"You're going to *evict* them?"

"Most certainly," she said forcefully. "They were trained properly, told, persuaded, cajoled; just like everyone else. And for the first time in God knows how many years I'm going to chuck someone off."

The phone had been ringing again. She answered it.

"Who? Oh yes, I remember. Would you like to talk to Jack? Here you are." She covered the mouthpiece. "It's John, that teacher from the Blue Bell – you know, he organised a cake for Phil."

I nodded and took the phone.

"Hallo John. Jack here. Good to hear from you."

"I hope you'll still think that when I've finished," said the distant voice. "I'm afraid one of your hire boats moored up here last night and I've just discovered that they behaved very badly indeed in the Blue Bell. They got drunk, ended up swearing at everyone behind the bar, and left without paying for their meal. I wonder if it would be possible for you to intervene somehow?"

"I suppose the boat wasn't called *Cowslip*, was it?"

"Yes. Someone followed them down to the canal and watched them get on board. Do you know of them? And why did you hire to them? It's not really fair on the rest of us."

"I agree completely, John, and I'm very sorry. They've caused other issues too. We think they're at a pub further down and are just about to go and evict them from the boat."

"Well… good. It sounds serious."

"It is. I'll tell you more later when we know more. A visit to the Blue Bell tonight is on the cards, I think. Actually, it's my younger son's birthday on Wednesday so I'll call in, book an early table for five, to include you if you're available, and apologise on their behalf – the hirers' behalf, not my sons' – and pay their bill."

"Well… well that would be very gratefully accepted by them – and the invitation is gratefully accepted by me. But you must let me pay my way…"

"Not at all, John. You bought a birthday cake – remember? I'm grateful to you for that and for your welcome there. You'll be our guest."

"Then thank you, and I shall look forward to it."

I looked at Poppy when he had gone and explained. "Oh God. They sound dreadful. Let's get going. Ian and me to the Fleur, you to Kingswood and then to the Fleur with Police alerted if appropriate. Then to the Blue Bell. Ian and I will stay with the boat to make sure they don't trash it, then see them off in a taxi. Can you get back to the marina and muster any troops you can find, tell them the situation and protect everything?"

"Ok," I promised. "I take it we're talking about the all-male group, are we?"

"Well no," said Poppy. "Oddly it's two youngish couples. Not the types you'd worry about normally. How you weed them out, I don't know. Perhaps we should circulate a black list of hirers around all our competitors."

I drove to Kingswood. Some bystanders at the junction gave directions to a nearby boat and knocking on the side of it brought a woman up from the cabin, She looked at me suspiciously.

"I'm really sorry to bother you," I started, "But I'm with the company owning the boat whose hirers crashed into you earlier. Canal and River Trust have told us what happened and I've come to apologise. We're about to visit the hirers now."

"They're animals," she said. "Absolute animals. We'd just come out into the basin from the junction and you can't see what's coming."

"I know," I told her, "we've done it."

"We were going dead slow. They just roared out of the lock straight at us and never even tried to take avoiding action. And as my daughter – who was on the roof at the time – tripped and fell in because of the collision, they actually laughed."

I could tell that she was so stressed about it, still, that she was nearly in tears.

"Is your daughter all right?" I asked.

"She's bruised where she tripped over the rail. Fortunately I've got a ladder I can let down, so she climbed up that and got on board. There's a nasty bruise on her shin, though."

"Have you called the Police?"

"Police? No. Should I?"

"I think it might help you – and us. You see, my colleagues have had complaints elsewhere too and are about to find the party and evict them from the boat. If you can make a call to the Police, tell them what happened and what we're about to do, and that they didn't pay for a meal in the Blue Bell last night, I think they might be prepared to attend."

"It never occurred to me."

"Well, as I said, it might help. It might help you two as well as us, if only to get a crime number for an insurance claim if necessary. You have a bump on your paint where they hit you, you see."

"Have I? Oh no – I've been so concerned with my daughter that I never looked. I'll phone them at once."

"Could you say that the hirers concerned may be at the Fleur de Lys at Lowsonford? And tell them the action we're taking? There might be some resistance and Police help would be useful." I had a brainwave. "I'm also going to get CRT told so they can come and help if needed. That large a posse might frighten them."

She agreed. I told her I'd return with news, then made my way down to Lowsonford, parking in the large pub car park. I could see Poppy's van but of her and Ian there was no sign. Boats were moored opposite the pub and I could see from the map that there was a lock and a bridge further down. A short walk down the road brought me to both, and *Cowslip* was moored – on the lock moorings. Poppy and Ian were examining her.

"Much wrong?" I asked.

"Mainly paint," Ian told me. "We don't know what the cabins are like yet."

"Have you seen the hirers?"

"No. They'll be in the bar, no doubt," said Poppy. "I suppose we'd better go and see them. I want to bring them outside to argue – because they will – and not make a scene in a pub. How did you get on? How's the child?"

I gave the news. "It occurred to me that we might call CRT back and tell them what we're doing, maybe give them the other details that they don't know and ask if they could – well, let's say "make sure that no more boats or Trust property is damaged by the hirers."

Poppy liked the idea and started jabbing at her phone like a teenager. Fortunately she just had to mention 'potential damage to a lock' and 'disruptive hirers' to be given the number for a local team. An irritated, out of breath voice answered, but calmed down when he understood who was speaking and what the problems were.

"We're only at Knowle," he said. "We're not meant to put ourselves at risk from the public, though."

"But this isn't doing that. There's three of us, the Police may be attending because of the girl at Kingswood, and if you were able to come down and make sure the lock can't be operated, so keeping them here, you wouldn't be at risk."

There was a pause. "Well, if you put it like that…"

We returned to the van and waited. About twenty minutes later and almost simultaneously a Trust van and a Police car appeared. We compared notes.

"You'd best leave us to remove them from the pub," said one of the Policewomen. "They might think better than to refuse us. If you can be the presence out here, with Mrs Watson as the official representative from the hire company, we'll join you and make sure they behave themselves."

"Thank you," said Poppy. "I need them to get all their possessions out of the boat. Jack, can you get the boat away from here, through the lock to somewhere remote, then walk back here, please? Then we can take the van back to the marina and make sure nothing unpleasant happens there."

"How do we get the boat back to base?" I asked.

"Well, first things first, but I think that could be a job for your two if they'd want it."

My jaw dropped. "On their own?"

"Well, yes. They're very capable."

"But that'd mean waiting for the weekend."

"We can swap boats round. It's not a problem if she stays there for a few days – I can talk to CRT about over-staying on the mooring. Take them down on Friday after a meal, give them food and money and they can sort themselves out."

One of the two Officers cleared her throat. "Should we get on with it, do you think? We need to get back to the city when we've dealt with these people."

They disappeared into the pub. We waited near the entrance for them to reappear, as we had decided amongst ourselves.

I should have said that Poppy Narrowboats staff wear polo shirts with logos. We are quite recognisable. When the four miscreants emerged from the pub, shepherded by two police officers, it was quite comical to see their reaction to the three of us plus three Canal and River Trust badged people.

Before anything could be said by them the Police officers told us that the four were under arrest for theft from both the Blue Bell and now from the Fleur de Lys. Apparently they had refused to pay for the meal that had been served to them as they were being arrested.

Poppy interrupted. "They have been reported to us for steering a boat erratically, for causing an accident by deliberately steering at another boat thereby causing injury to a child, and for excessive speed on the canal in contravention of the restrictions imposed by the Canal and River Trust. As such, we are recovering our property – the boat – and they will need to remove their possessions from it immediately, and remove their car from our marina as soon as it is practically possible."

At this, pandemonium broke out. I was glad that every one of us said nothing until they had run out of words.

"We have radioed for transport for them," said one of the Police, ignoring the stream of invective. "They need to attend a Police station to make statements and be formally arrested. We can't release them back to the boat until that's done."

"And I'm not letting them near the boat again except to remove their possessions," said Poppy when a further outburst had died down. "I think it's probably best that they find their way to the Marina, collect their cars and go home. Once the boat has been returned by our staff we will email them to retrieve their possessions."

The language was quite choice. We let it wash over us.

"I suggest that you cease making a fuss, as any more outbursts like that will result in a further charge causing fear and distress under the Public Order Act. And yes, we can do that. You have no option now."

"What about our deposit?" asked one of the party.

Poppy answered that. "We need to carry out repairs on our boat, to offer compensation to the injured girl and her mother, and to pay the fine that the Trust will levy on us for your behaviour. If this pub and the Blue Bell don't want to prosecute we will pay your bills there too as I'm sure you would want us to. I can't say how much will be left, or whether we need to invoice you and pursue it in the Small Claims Court if need arises."

"Can't we just go to the boat and get our stuff?" asked one of the men.

"No," said one of the officers, "once arrested, you are taken for processing as soon as it can be arranged. And we have transport arriving in about half an hour."

"What about our meal?"

"The one you haven't paid for?"

He shut up. We waited. As there were four of them there was a tacit agreement that we would stay to support the two Police officers. Eventually a van appeared, they were bundled into the back and driven away. We were given a case number and asked to give witness statements over the course of the following week, to which we agreed.

"Well, that alters our plan a little," Poppy said. "If we take the boat into the wilds a bit, and moor her, would it be all right if she stayed there until Saturday when we have some staff who can bring her back?"

The Trust men agreed that they would turn a blind eye and tell others to do the same. "There's a good bit of bank between the two locks, and some decent people on one of the continuous cruising boats there. Tell them the story and they'll be pleased to keep an eye on her until the weekend." He mentioned the boat's name.

We thanked him and made our way back to the boat. A thought struck me. "How do we get in?" I asked.

Poppy and Ian grinned. "We do have duplicate keys, you know!"

37 May

"You had to do *what*?" asked Nat when I told them later, having asked how they'd got on in their new school Year. I explained, with interruptions.

"Wish we'd been there," Phil complained. "I might have learnt some new words."

"So that you, too, could be arrested for causing fear and distress? Good idea, that. Of course, if you carry on wearing those trousers you'll probably be arrested for indecency anyway. Tonight, we need to get you some new school clobber, and I thought we might eat at one of the supermarkets' cafes. Good idea?"

"With Poppy?" Nat asked.

I hadn't been going to burden her with a clothes shopping expedition, but if he wanted her there… "Go and ask her. She's still catching up in the office. But before you do, there are two more things." I took a deep breath. "Firstly, Nat, what do you want for your birthday? Apart from a meal on Wednesday in the Blue Bell – I asked John as well, by the way. Hope that's ok."

"Well… ok. And Poppy?"

"And Poppy."

"Good. I don't know what I'd like. I'll have to think. Something to do with carpentry. Or design. I need to talk to the Losardos."

"So do I," I remembered. "We need to get that front cabin sorted. And the other thing is that Poppy and I have a job for you both."

There were two questioning looks. "We've got jobs," Phil said.

"This Saturday there aren't many boats out. We can manage. Your job is to be taken to *Cowslip,* go down the canal a bit and turn, then bring her back here. If we go down on Friday after a meal, with sleeping bags and enough food, you can have two nights on her and work up Lapworth flight, turn right at Kings Norton and come through Gas Street to here. How does that grab you?"

"On our own?"

"On your own."

Looks passed between the two.

"Yes, ok." "Yes please." No points for knowing which came from which.

"Can you manage the locks on your own? There are a lot of them."

"Of course," Phil growled. "My superior strength will make short work of them. He can steer."

"Good," Nat rejoined. "Suits me."

"Are you sure you don't mind being on your own?"

"Dad, we're not kids any more. We can cope." It wasn't strictly true, of course, but they both had good sense. That was clear from how they managed when steering the boat and using locks, and how they had reacted whilst I'd been in hospital.

"Ok, then. And thank you. It was Poppy's idea, by the way."

"What was?" came a voice from the open hatch. "I'm not interrupting anything, am I?"

"No. Come in. You don't need to ask." That was Nat, saying what I would have said. He received a radiant smile.

"What's my idea?

"Bringing *Cowslip* back from – from where, Dad?"

"From the Fleur de Lys at Lowsonford – just below it, actually."

"Ah, yes," said Poppy. "That's really what I came over to ask. Are you happy to do that?"

"Very," said Phil enthusiastically. "Best thing that's happened all year."

"What?" Poppy and I exclaimed together.

I continued. "You've just had a long cruise up to Anderton Lift and you say that?"

"I meant the academic year," said Phil, unfazed. "It's only just started."

"I've never heard anyone dig themselves out of a hole so quickly," Poppy laughed. "You win."

He grinned.

"Can Maisie come?" Nat asked.

"We can ask, but I shouldn't bank on it. Even the Parishes might baulk at their only daughter being alone at night with two rancid teenagers."

"*Dad*!" A unison accusation of unfairness.

"You know what I mean. She might have a lot of studying to do too. She spent a long time being barely home-schooled, don't forget."

That was a part of it they most certainly could accept.

"Poppy," Nat started, "we're going to have something to eat in a supermarket and buy some new school stuff for us two. Are you coming?"

"That's the best invitation I've had all the academic year," she said.

Nat's birthday evening meal was a success. We enjoyed an early, leisurely dinner, and John proved to be a mine of anecdotes – frequently with himself as the butt of the joke. He is one of those people, like Poppy and I hope like me, who treats those younger than himself with the same courtesy as he treats his contemporaries, yet is not above teasing when appropriate. He had us all in stitches at times with his tales of boarding school life.

This time I had arranged the cake. It was actually a trifle, with some very worried looking candles in large holders somehow holding their own on the sliced-strawberry covered cream. I knew this would intrigue Nat, who loves trifles. It made the rest of them laugh. Nat was thrilled. "That's another story for you, John!" he said.

Time passed, and despite having arrived at the Blue Bell at six thirty it was nine o'clock when I next looked at the clock. I interrupted the conversation. "Does anyone have homework tonight?"

Two voices admitted that they had. We ended in a hurry and I hoped that Nat, particularly, would stay alert long enough to complete his work adequately. John told me again that he felt that he should pay for himself and there was a chorus of "no!" from the rest of us.

"Then if you two are bringing this boat up on Saturday and manage to stop anywhere near here, knock me up and I'll return the compliment."

We thanked him for his generosity and made our way home, arriving late. They got their heads down in their 'studies' and... well, studied.

Waking them up next morning was something of a task, however; even Nat. They didn't so much walk off to the bus stop but stumbled to it.

"Ready?" I called down the boat the following Friday evening.

"Just about. Have you packed enough food?"

"Enough for an army. An army of two, anyway." Maisie couldn't come it seemed; she had started school later than the other two and, as I'd suggested, had a lot of catching-up homework to do.

We took them to the Fleur de Lys and helped them carry their belongings and supplies down to the boat. Poppy had the spare keys.

"It's a mess," she said as she walked back through the cabins. "We all need to pitch in and get their stuff down the other end so that it's out of the way. If you want a TV you'd better bring it up here to the other aerial socket. The bow cabin's going to be full."

With our Marigolds on – we all agreed we didn't want to touch the ex-clients' personal stuff, especially the more intimate clothing they'd been wearing – we shifted it all to the front cabin. Phil elected to wash up, there being about two meals' worth of it still in the sink and around the galley. We dried up for him when we'd finished.

"There's a lot of food in the cupboards," he said. We groaned, having forgotten that they would have brought some with them, and set to taking that to the bow as well. "More in the fridge," he announced as seven-thirty approached.

"It can stay there," Poppy decided. "Best if you don't use it, but it'll probably be past its use-by date by the time they come and get it. If you do use any of it, make sure it's all right first."

"Ok. Anything else you want to tell us?"

"Just that there are seven locks to go through before you reach a winding hole."

"*What*?"

"I only realised that last night," Poppy admitted. "It's all a bit longer than I thought. Are you still up for it?"

"Oh yes," Nat said. "We are. Aren't we?"

"Of course. Anything to be rid of these two for a weekend."

"Thanks, Phil. Nice to see the back of you two as well," I told him mock-severely. "Tell us where you are when you get a chance, and if you hit any problems, give one of us a call. I suppose one of us could come down and help you up the Lapworth Flight tomorrow."

"We can cope, Dad," Nat objected.

"You'll be on the tiller! It's all right for you." Phil was more pragmatic about it.

"I want us to do it on our own," Nat countered. "But I suppose..."

"Tell me when you're two locks away and I'll try and get free," I interrupted.

"Would that be all right, Poppy?"

"It's not too busy tomorrow. So long as there aren't any engine faults, it'll be fine."

"We'll talk later, then," I said, now reluctant to leave them on their own and realising that they were both quite young to be doing this.

"Ok. See you. We'll stow our kit properly and then get going. We should get to the winding hole before it gets dark, shouldn't we?"

"Yes," Poppy told him. "But please don't take any chances. Remember there are only the two of you and I really want to see you both again. Alive."

"Thank you, Poppy," Phil called as he turned to enter the cabin. "We love you too."

That, it appeared, was the end of the conversation. We turned and made our way back to the car. "I hope we're doing the right thing," Poppy suddenly said. "They're very capable, but they're only just fifteen and thirteen, and it's young to be doing this on their own. Nowadays."

"I suppose back in the day Phil would be steering the boat all day."

"He'd be on the locks and Nat would be steering. Maybe they would swap now and again, but they'd certainly work the boat together if the parents were away, or dealing with another boat."

We were back on the boat, in the middle of the second glass of wine when the phone rang.

"We've just moored," said Nat. "We'll do the actual turn tomorrow 'cos it's getting dark now and we didn't want to cock it up."

"You're at the winding hole, then?"

"Yes. Just having a sandwich before we switch the TV on. Do you think they'd miss one of their beers?"

"They most certainly would," I said hurriedly. "That would be theft, no matter how attractive they look."

"Oh, ok. Phil was asking, that's all." There was a muffled comment in the background.

"We'll talk tomorrow. See you at the junction."

"Ok. G'night."

And that was that. For some reason I felt lonely. They'd not been away from me except at school since I'd left home. School… well, they were away then and I never worried, so why now?

Poppy and I finished our wine and had another.

"Where are you?" I asked the phone at about midday. The call had come about forty-five minutes previously.

"At the second lock," came Nat's voice. "It's all right, we've got help."

"Lock keeper?"

"No. Phil's pulled, big time."

"*Pulled*? What do you mean pulled?"

"You know that girl who fell in the water? This boat hit theirs? Well, it's her."

My brain did a backflip. "I thought she was a child."

"She's sixteen. They saw each other from boat to boat and Phil went all soppy. It was like something from an old film."

"Well, I'm glad you've got help. I'm here now, though, so I'll come and see you."

"We can manage, Dad!"

"I know. But I don't want this to have been a wasted journey. See you in a minute."

It was actually more like ten of them by the time I caught up with *Cowslip*, there being towpaths and bridges to negotiate. Nat was waiting behind two other boats in the lock queue that Poppy had told me would be inevitable. "Everything all right?" I asked.

"The turn was tight," Nat said. "The bows stuck on the mud, but we got her round and reversed off all right. And the locks were set for us."

"No incidents, then."

"Not until the junction. There was this boat moored there, and as we were joining the queue this girl shouted "Oy!" at us and then just looked. And Phil looked too. And that was that."

"And suddenly she's helping work the locks for him," I said.

"Something like that. She came over and the first thing she said was 'you're not the people who steered straight for us last week.' Phil explained what we were doing, and she got more quiet the more he said, and at the end she was looking at him like he was a film star. He was going soppy over her, too. They both went up to the locks and left me to sort out the boat."

I nodded. "Looks like the bottom gates are opening. Do you want a hand moving up?"

"I'm ok," said Nat as if he'd been a boat handler all his life. "You'd better go and throw a bucket of cold water over those two." An oddly adult – and old-adult – thing to say, but I remember it had come in a book somewhere. Apparently two dogs were getting a tad too friendly.

I met them, busy working the locks… No. In fact they were sitting on a bench talking, whilst other people worked the lock. There seemed to be an invisible barrier between them and reality.

"I thought you were meant to be helping people to get *Cowslip* through the flight quicker," I called, without preamble or tact.

The barrier must have crumbled at the sound of my voice. Not that I could see it, of course.

"Hallo, Dad. I am. We are."

"So I see. Hallo. You're the girl that our hirers deposited in the water the other day, I guess. How's your leg now?"

"It's better, thanks. Just a bruise. You must be Mr Dyer."

"At your service. Glad to meet you, even if my son hasn't introduced us."

"I'm May Wynne," she said. "Don't laugh. It was my father's idea."

"And you've said that a few times over the years, I bet. Good to meet you,

May. I gather you've met my son."

She couldn't help the blush. "We – er – saw each other… I mean, I saw *Cowslip* and was going to have a go at them. Then I saw that it wasn't them and came over to find out what had happened."

"And then he persuaded you to help him work the locks."

"Actually, May offered," Phil interrupted. "Is that woman on her own? The boat coming down? Do you think you should help, Dad?"

"I think *we* should help, Phil. The three of us. I imagine there'll be plenty of time to chat when there's not a boat to return to base and clean."

I must have sounded severe, because I had an eyebrow lift from Phil and a slightly guilty look from May. But they knew I was right. We crossed to the single-hander and found that she was totally alone, so I volunteered to work the locks for her as far as the junction basin.

"I'll come back here and help Nat through," I told them, more to make sure they knew that I wasn't abandoning them to the bench and reconstruction of the invisible barrier. By the time I returned they were indeed locking for Nat, and Phil was almost back to his normal self.

The lock flight passage was a slow process with so many boats in each direction. It was late in the afternoon that I finally saw them near the top. "It's five o'clock," I called to the elder two. "I'm heading back now, or Poppy will wonder where I am."

I was half expecting some sort of comment about being under the thumb already and was almost disappointed when none came. What did come, though, was a gasp from May.

"I never told Mum where I was!" she gasped. "My phone's in the boat so she'll be worried sick."

"Do you want to come back with me?" I asked. "I can explain, perhaps."

"Yes. Yes please. Bye, Phil. I'll… I phone you."

"I'll give you my number… better, I'll walk back with you."

"That won't work, will it, Phil? You can't leave Nat to do the last two locks on his own. Unfair."

He looked straight faced. "Ohh…" on a rising tone. But he realised it wouldn't be right and came over to her. I almost expected a kiss, but they held hands for a moment before she pulled away to follow me. I'd already said my farewells to Nat, and to him.

Mrs Wynne was concerned, but not as frantic as May and I thought was likely. "My neighbours said that she'd gone off with a couple of lads on a boat called *Cowslip*," she explained. "I knew it couldn't be the same four who were on her last week because they were older and she'd have steered clear of them anyway. I did try phoning her, but you left your phone in the boat. Again!" This last was obviously to the daughter.

"Sorry, Mum. I…"

"I know you, don't I?" Mrs Wynne was obviously not one to let her daughter speak.

"We spoke at the time about the accident, Mrs Wynne. The hirers were pitched off by us at Lowsonford and my sons are taking the boat back to base. Once we've sorted out the financial side of things I'll be back to talk about insurance and compensation from Poppy Narrowboats. Well, from the hirers actually, but they don't know that yet."

"It was your sons on the boat, was it? Do you know them, May?"

I leapt in. "May saw the boat and was about to give the crew a piece of her mind. When she got to them and found my lads, she and Phil found they had a lot in common, and May very kindly helped them up the flight."

"She's never done anything like that before, have you May?"

"He's… he's a really nice boy, Mum. You'll like him."

"I should give you his mobile, shouldn't I? Shall I send it to yours?"

"Yes, please."

I knew that I'd be lucky that night to be able to speak to Phil. He'd be spending all possible hours of inactivity on the phone to her. When I reached the car I called Phil.

"She's got your number. If you stop at the Blue Bell tonight, please remember not to talk or message her while you, Nat and John are together. That would be really rude."

"Yes Dad."

"And don't forget Nat could do with some company. Don't just leave him to moulder while you two talk."

"Yes Dad. Or should that be no, Dad?"

"Phil… I know what I was like when Helen and I…"

That was enough.

"Ok, Dad. Is her mother all right?"

"If you're asking whether she's fit, I don't know. She's not my type and anyway I have Poppy. If you're asking whether she was panicking that some young stud had run off with her daughter, no. She'd heard it was only you."

I could hear the cogs turning as he weighed up whether that was an insult or not.

Poppy welcomed me with open arms. Literally. Inevitably we went to the usual pub for a meal.

"Lost the boys?" asked the landlord, "That's careless."

We had to tell him the saga as well, but I left the love-interest until I was alone with Poppy. "Just as well she didn't ask if she could complete the journey with them," she said. "I bet Phil will be quiet tonight if his emotions have been 'all shook up' like that."

I remembered back to those early days and the intensity of the attractions. There had been times when… Suddenly I felt sorry for my son. Not so much for Nat and Maisie. His hormones hadn't had a chance to do much more than stretch themselves and ask what there was for breakfast. But Phil – well, maybe his were chomping at the bit and already looking for dinner and bed.

Their arrival around mid-afternoon on the Sunday was a great relief, despite all my suppressed concerns. May wasn't with them – I'd half expected her to be

– and they were still talking to each other; an added bonus.

The conversation of greetings approximated to "Hallo, where shall we put her? Is there anything to eat? Can May come over?"

We jointly ignored the last two and told them where to moor. Poppy vanished into the office to phone the ex-hirers to tell them to collect their belongings. "Bloody cheek!" she said when she emerged. "I told them the boat was back and asked if they would please collect their possessions and they told me it would be after work tomorrow. I had to tell them that we needed to clean the boat and would empty it and put everything of theirs in a workshop, for which they would be charged." She paused. "Their language hasn't improved. I think we get everything off the boat, including the perishables, and they can take their chances."

"Have you circulated their name as being undesirable hirers, and why?" I asked.

"There's no such thing as the 'Don't Hire List'. If there was, it could be held as defamation of character. No, I haven't not circulated the details yet, but I'll make sure I don't do it tomorrow."

It took me a moment.

"Was the information about the Smiths… er… not sent in the same way?"

"I never did not send that. The timescale defeated me, and in any case they should be in prison. I'll not send that at the same time I don't send these people's information."

Nat was in fits and Phil was grinning widely.

"Anyway, didn't you stop for lunch on the way?" I asked the boys.

"We took it in turns to make a sandwich or two."

Nat nodded. "I didn't not cut my finger with the bread knife."

I looked at his hand, and the little dressing. "Did you clean it?"

"No, I rubbed it on the earth. Of course I cleaned it. It stang."

"Stang? Past participle of 'to sting'?"

"Yes."

"No."

"What is?"

"Stung".

"Doesn't sound right."

I shrugged. "Sorry. Blame the past."

"Have you two finished the English lesson?" asked Phil. "If so, can May come over and can we feed her?"

"She can, and you can. And the rest of us. That's dinner for five, unless her parents are coming."

"Dad's left them. Do you want her Mum?"

"It'd be considerate to ask her, especially if she's bringing her over."

"I thought you could go and get her."

"Did you now? It's a three-quarter hour journey, each way!"

"Oh… Shall I ask?"

"I suppose so. What time will you have the meal ready for?"

"Daaaad..."

"Oh, go on then, but you can help."

It turned out to be one of those team efforts. By the time May and Lizzie (Mum) arrived we were just about ready.

Lizzie is a talker.

Lizzie interrupts everybody.

Lizzie doesn't believe that sixteen year olds have emotional feelings.

Phil looked embarrassed.

Nat looked amazed, then fed up.

The food was good.

Next time Phil wants May to visit, I'm going to fetch her. Lizzie can return her if she wants.

They left at about eight o'clock, blaming school the next day. We breathed a collective sigh of relief. Phil didn't know what to say. I think his evening had been spoiled.

"She's hard work," I said to him in support.

"She's a bloody embarrassment," he burst out. "God, I hope May doesn't turn out to be like her."

"She might say something when you phone later."

He paused. "I... I'm not sure I want to."

About eleven o'clock, when he was theoretically asleep, I heard the phone ring. He still had the ringtone on full volume so as to be heard over the engine. Of the ensuing conversation, no sound.

Over breakfast he announced that she'd phoned him and apologised for her mother. "She gets so excited when she meets new people, apparently. May wouldn't have brought her if she had a chance, but she'd been invited, so she didn't think she could refuse."

"We'll know in future. I take it there will be a future?"

He paused. "I think so."

38 Progress

We had a conference one evening when homework should have been the priority. Seppe and Ifor had been asked to drop in and give their view on the suggestions for the front saloon. With Nat's input, of course.

"Why two static seats either side of the convertible one?" Ifor asked.

"Style," said Nat. "And when you're asleep it's something to stop you rolling out."

There is a logic to this that can't be denied.

"It'd cost more," Seppe told him.

"But look better."

"And cost more."

"Oh. Well, perhaps not, then. I see what you mean about cheaper. Two double covers are cheaper than two singles and a double. And I suppose the woodwork's easier."

"But will we be able to have a good big TV the other side?" Phil asked me.

"Maybe…"

"That's all you say!"

"It depends on money. If you want the latest tech, costing a grand or more, then no. If you're happy with a perfectly good normal set, then probably."

"Have we got a grand or more?" Nat asked.

"Not for a TV, no."

"Oh. It'd better be as good as we can afford, then."

"So when do we expect you to come and help with the design for the bases, Nat?" Seppe asked, regaining more familiar ground.

"Whenever you want," Nat responded, with a look at me. "If that's all right."

"Tomorrow night?"

"And welcome."

"Fine by me," I confirmed. "I suppose it's safe for you to go alone now. There should be no more danger."

Nat paused a moment. "No, no more danger."

"Have you put that app on your new phone? The one that tells where you are? If not, can you download it before you go, please?"

"Ok," Nat said. Good. I'd been half expecting resistance.

"I'll make sure mine works too," Phil volunteered unexpectedly. "Then I can find out where you are as well."

"And I can find you," said Nat.

"Oh… well, I suppose the sacrifice is worth it."

The look between the two was quite telling, really. We got busy downloading.

Nat vanished after an early meal the next evening and returned at a time by which my concern was starting to grow, despite my being able to see he was static, at the Losardos. At last the trace started moving and before long he was back.

"I wish you'd get some of that sawdust out of your hair before you leave there," I said as usual, more to cover my relief than in censure.

"Sorry. I saw it was late so just hurried away. I thought you'd be worried."

I relented. "I was, despite the phone app. Good to have you back, but could you brush your hair over the water, please, rather than wash it off in the shower?"

A fat envelope awaited me a few mornings later, containing the papers for the sale of the family house. All seemed to be in order, but I phoned Helen to ensure that she had the same information. She had. "It's quite a good price," she told me.

"So it is. It's in a nice part of the city and a good house."

"You're telling me."

"I'm agreeing with you."

"I don't want to have to sell."

"Just as I didn't want to fall out of love. But we each have, and need to be realistic. We both know that the house has to be sold, as do the boys."

"Why do you keep talking to them about our affairs?"

"I think 'affairs' is an inappropriate word to use, don't you? I include the boys because what we do now will become their business when you and I are dead."

"They're too young to understand."

"With Phil becoming adult in three years and Nat in five? I think not. They have grown up a lot… over the last months." I had been about to say 'since being with me' but had stopped myself in time.

"So you're going to sign the papers, then?"

"The sale papers? Yes, after chatting to my solicitor."

"There's no need for that, surely?"

"Why not? Is there something you don't want me to see?" It was a dig and I was immediately ashamed, but her comment had made me cautious.

"Don't be ridiculous. I don't want to waste money, that's all."

"Nor do I. But I want the contracts to be correct."

"Well, you're going to do what you want anyway, aren't you?"

"If it means safeguarding the boys' futures, yes."

She ended the conversation, if not in a friendly way, then at least with the usual courtesies. I brewed a coffee and went to talk to Poppy, who agreed that a solicitor's eye on the contract would be essential.

"I'll phone them later and fix up an appointment," I said. She lifted the phone, gave me a look, dialled the number and wordlessly handed the receiver to me.

Two o'clock that afternoon was the appointment on offer, to my amazement. I looked quizzically at her by way of seeking permission from my boss and she put her tongue out. I accepted the appointment.

They found no issues and acted as witnesses to my signature. Poppy must have sway with them because they told me that the fees would be minimal and that they trusted me to make a payment only once the money was in my account. "Though I'd recommend two or more accounts, with different banks," I was told. "Nothing's likely to happen to any of them, but you should be aware that the

Government only guarantees a balance up to eighty-five grand."

Put like that, out of the blue as opposed to just seeing figures in writing, made me realise that our liquid financial situation would be the best it had ever been, and by 'our' I meant the boys' and mine. And Poppy's.

And Poppy's?

"Are you all right, Mr Dyer?"

"Sorry – yes, just thinking. You're right, of course; it would be sensible."

"You might want to invest in another property and let it out to gain an income. Lower value residential property can be awkward, but garages in the right place can be a good bet. We'd be happy to act for you in any sale, of course."

Garages! Well, that was new one. I thanked them and made my escape.

Poppy and I discussed it later. "You need to decide how you're going on from here," she said after some thought. "Maybe wait for the sale to complete, then decide once… once the situation between you and Helen is… er…" She tailed off.

"You mean, what happens after the divorce goes through," I said bluntly.

"If that's the way you decide on."

"It's inevitable, Poppy. And it's what I want, now."

"Now?"

"Now I've met you."

"Why should that make a difference?"

"You're not making this any easier, are you?"

"No."

"I want to be free to ask you to marry me properly." There. I had said it, and I knew I meant it.

There was silence for such a long time that I started wondering whether I'd been wrong all along, whether she was looking for the right words to let me down gently.

"Is that a formal proposal?" she asked quietly.

By that point I felt thoroughly rattled.

"It's not the way I would want to make a proposal," I told her slowly, as if forcing the words out. "That would be in a decent hotel, with music, flowers and a ring. But it's a declaration of my wanting to clear the way for me to do so."

"So if I were to say that I wanted a clear way to accept, would that answer your question?"

This time the silence was mutual.

It was by then mid-afternoon on a Wednesday, near the time when Ian might come in for a tea (and cake) and for Helena to return from her break to take over the reception again. Had they chosen that moment they would have seen a middle-aged couple in a long embrace, an embrace that some might call a clinch and my sons would call making out. It ended, finally, and there were two gentle smiles facing one another.

A knock at the door. Hurriedly, we turned. Ian. Damn.

"Is it safe now?" he asked.

"We thought you'd done that a long time ago," said Nat when I'd explained the course of the conversation to them. "When do you get married?"

"Don't be daft," his brother told him. "They've – there's got to be a divorce first, otherwise they'd be bigamists or something."

"We don't want that and get chucked in prison," I agreed. "We have a business to run."

"Are we going to live here when you're married?" asked Nat, "or are you moving into Poppy's house?"

"One thing at a time," I said. "Firstly we get the money for the old house, secondly there's a divorce and thirdly we make decisions. All of us."

"Do you really mean that, Dad?"

"When have I not consulted you since we all moved out?"

"So will you be a partner in the business?" Phil this time.

It hadn't occurred to me. I thought a moment. "I might want to stay an employee. It's less hassle. And that's up to Poppy."

"Yeah, but…"

"Something to be left to her, Phil. And before you ask, as yet I don't know what'll happen to the money from selling the house, though I'm pretty sure it'll be held in trust for you two if we don't need to buy a home."

"Somewhere it gets lots of interest," said Phil. "I like the idea of getting money for doing nothing."

"I was thinking of buying garages and letting them out," I said. "An income with no need to deal with blocked drains."

"*Is* there such a thing?"

"There are 'wanted' ads in all the papers. I've been looking."

"Is that good, then?"

"Contrast the interest rate the banks give against £60 a month's rent for a garage. We'd have enough to buy about twenty garages, I should think."

"But that's… that's… a lot of money!"

"Exactly."

On the strength of it we went to buy a TV. A large TV. So large that we had to think about how to protect it from hurriedly passing legs on their way to moor the bows. Nat was seen standing looking at it with his head on one side, so we knew that the problem would be solved.

Over the next fortnight the new carpentry for the stateroom's convertible seating and the associated paddings were installed and tested, and found to work well. It was a stateroom when Nat had anything to do with it, but was relegated to 'TV room', 'front cabin' or even 'the front' by everyone else. We soon found that the futons, when extended, presented a threat to the TV screen. "I should have seen that coming," Nat said, furiously.

Seppe took one look at it, laughed as only Italians can, and told us to buy a mount which would raise it to arm-height when necessary. "That way you can watch the telly in bed," he told Nat.

"You and Maisie," Phil called from his cabin. Nat raised two fingers – which his brother couldn't see, of course. "You and May!" he countered. The lack of reply was deafening.

By the end of the week the front stateroom was finished. "We just need a log-burner," Phil told the rest of us smugly. Poppy raised her eyebrows at him. He cowered theatrically and raised his hands to protect himself.

"Something occurred to me the other day," Poppy said, ignoring him. "Since you came, we've just referred to this boat as 'The Boat'. The previous owner never named her, though I think there was a name before we took her over. I'll have to see what she was called when we bought her."

"So long as she's not called 'Dunromin'," Phil said, now recovered.

"Dad's Desire," Nat suggested.

"How about Jack's Breakdown?" I put in.

"A bit pointed. Especially as she's not going to. And nor are you."

"You hope," I said to Poppy.

"Poppy's Engineer", she countered. "Let's have a look at the old name and see what you think."

We discovered next day it had been *Myrtle*. "Oh God," said Phil. We set about choosing another; a brainstorming session that produced much hilarity but no decision.

The house exchanged, eventually. Thanks to my solicitors' stipulations – which were thanks to Poppy's insistence – the distribution of the proceeds went without a problem. As soon as our funds hit the bank I set about starting more accounts so as to distribute it safely.

"Now for Helen," I said to Poppy one night.

"Are you sure?"

"Of course!" I was slightly shocked that she might doubt my intentions after all this time. "Or do you want that romantic evening in a good hotel with me on one knee, a rose in my mouth and a ring in my hand, proposing?"

The grin on her face widened. "How about a macaroni cheese on the boat with the boys? You could pop the question with your mouth full and then just ask me what date we should choose."

"How romantic."

"Well… it's not as if we were young lovers with any doubts between us, is it? We proved pretty soon that we talked the same language, both have what my parents would have called 'horse sense', and are happy in each other's company. No frills needed."

My eyebrows raised, and I said no more. The next day I wrote to Helen at Jonathan's address.

Half term had arrived and we had begged another cruise. Phil asked about May, who had been an irregular visitor, and Nat about Maisie and her parents. But May had to be at home studying and the Parishes were on holiday abroad. We went alone.

This time we yawned our way through the Netherton Tunnel, then down the Delph and Stourbridge lock flights and through Kidderminster to Stourport. The still unnamed boat was moored there and we walked down to the river.

“We’re not venturing out on that!” Poppy said decisively.

After a very wet October the river was “interesting”. The water was high, fast, and carrying so many heavy tree trunks and associated foliage that we were stunned into silence. We were glad it was closed to navigation and left us no doubt about taking our boat on it.

We chilled out, had a curry, overnighted and returned the same way.

The Monday after our return, Helen replied to my letter. Just a text with no sign of a letter which I’d have thought would be the decent thing. “Got a problem. Can we leave it for the moment. Will contact later.”

Puzzling. I left it, hoping it wouldn’t be too long. But it was. The delay turned into a fortnight. Annoyed, I phoned her.

“I… I can’t tell you,” she said.

“Something’s very wrong, isn’t it?” Estranged beyond breaking point we may have been but you can’t spend years with someone without learning them.

“I’m worried,” she admitted.

“About… him?”

“Yes… look, I really can’t talk about it.”

“Is he mistreating you?”

“No. At least… No. I really don’t want to talk about it.”

A lack of knowledge is a bad thing. It leaves the mind racing, trying to imagine scenarios. Physical abuse? Rape? Lack of sex? Someone else? I hoped he hadn’t managed to get his hands on the proceeds from the house.

It was a full two weeks later when she phoned again. I suppose you don’t know where Jonathan is?” she asked, without preamble.

“He’s hardly likely to make contact with me, after all he did. Is he missing, then?”

A long gap. “I haven’t seen him for a fortnight. There’s no answer from his work, or his mobile. In fact his work number wasn’t even ringing today. It was unobtainable.”

“Have you contacted the Police?” That, to me, should have been the obvious first step.”

Another pause. In almost in an embarrassed tone she admitted that there had been problems and she was so disturbed that she hadn’t.

“What sort of problems?” I asked.

It took so long for her to answer that I was wondering about the phone connection. “He… well, he moved into the other bedroom,” she almost whispered.

Now you know how I felt when you all but threw me out of our shared bedroom, I thought. It seemed cruel to mention the coincidence.

“I see,” I said, though I only partly understood. I wondered where the origins of the split actually were.

“We’ve not seen him here. If either of the boys had seen him I’m sure they’d have said something. Absolutely sure.”

“Should I tell the Police, then?”

“Well, yes. Tell them the full story, though, including what he tried on with the boys. Even if it makes it look bad for me."

"Why should it?"

"I have a grievance against him. They'll want to investigate that side of it."

"Oh. Well, if you're sure..."

"Of course. I might not want to know him any more, but unfortunately he's still my flesh and blood. I... well, I owe our parents that. He's still family."

"Thank you, Jack."

I hadn't been expecting that. "It doesn't mean I want to see him, just that I wouldn't wish him harm. And I'd be sad if anything had happened to him."

"Thanks. I'll tell you what happens."

She had called during that time before the marina closed for the night and before the boys returned from school. When they were all with me again I explained what Helen had said and what my views were. Later, when we had settled into bed, Poppy said something that worried me.

"You're not having second thoughts, are you?"

I turned to look her in the eyes. "What about? Jonathan?"

She smiled. "No. Helen."

"Poppy, she's cooked her goose with me. That happened months ago. You know that."

"But now she's... well, unhappy, needing help. I just wondered..."

"Don't wonder. There's nothing to wonder about. She and I are no more. There's only one woman for me, and she's lying next to me."

A smile that melted my heart.

"I just needed to know."

"And you do know. Too much has happened between us for us to be a flash in the pan. I found you... I felt an attraction to you when we first met, though I was in no position to want a relationship. That happened over the months. I love you, you see."

It seems that was the right thing to say. We may be in our forties, but we were very late getting to sleep that night.

Inevitably, the following day the Police visited. Poppy came to the boat with them and the first few minutes were spent explaining the relationships. They understood, but insisted on speaking to each of us alone.

It was slightly uncomfortable, but I told the full story, omitting nothing about what Jonathan had done to the boys or what I had done to Jonathan. The officer's eyes raised when he heard about what I described both at the time and at the interview as Jonathan's kidnap attempt on Nat.

"You should have reported it," he told me.

"I was ready to, I was so angry," I replied. "I know my brother well – we'd been close up to that point. And I hoped that I knew him better than to think he was trying to do anything except take Nat back to Helen."

"So there's no history of anything untoward with your sons, or with other children?"

I bristled. "Good God no. Never entered my head. And we grew up together. We were all but inseparable until I went to Uni., and even then were together in the holidays."

He went on to ask about Jonathan's other girlfriends but all I could tell him about was Jeanie, the ex-wife. "And no, I don't have any details for her. Maybe they're in his flat somewhere."

Thank goodness that the account given by Poppy corroborated mine. There was no second questioning. It wasn't until they had left that I remembered that I had an old notebook – a work notebook – from a much earlier era. Might there be a chance that Jeanie's phone number was in there? It was. I reached for my own phone, sat down, alone, and made the call.

"Good heavens!" was her greeting after I'd identified myself. "Well, I never thought I'd hear your voice again."

It was not said in a friendly nor a welcoming tone.

"It almost sounds as if there was a problem when you and Jonathan broke up, one that involved me," I said with as much lightness in my voice as I could muster.

"Well you should know."

"Well, I don't. I imagine there was quite an unpleasant time when… when you split up and it seemed best that I should leave it to you to make contact when you were ready. Maybe when things had settled down a bit."

"I was afraid that you were going to contact me and accuse me of all sorts of things," she said, astonishing me completely.

"Well, hardly. I had nothing to accuse you of. Relationships break down – God knows, mine has – and the only ones who know where the fault really lies are the two concerned. Even then they often won't or can't admit it to themselves."

Silence.

"I'm sorry to hear… does that mean that you're no longer with Helen?"

I told her the saga.

"Oh. Oh, I never knew that."

"No reason why you should. It's all pretty recent."

"Yes… yes, but you were always the strong one. You two were invincible. How are the boys? Or don't you get to see them very often?"

I hadn't mentioned that part of it. I explained a bit more.

"And you live on a *boat*? And are the boys happy to be with you? Or are there problems?"

"It was their choice to be with me," I answered, again starting to bristle. "And they're happy. I treat them as trainee adults, as partners. They have a say in everything that goes on. It's Helen who thinks they're too young for that."

"You've confused me completely," she admitted after another pause. "When he and I separated he said that you had the same … well, let's say 'attractions'… as him. I nearly went to the Police about both of you."

This was starting to sound ominous. "What sort of attractions?"

"Are you sure you don't know what I'm talking about?"

"I'm absolutely certain. But whatever it is sounds unpleasant."

A long silence this time.

"Nobody likes to hear that their recently acquired husband also has an attraction to young men. And to teenagers"

"*What*?"

"And he said you were the same."

"He… "

It was my turn for silence.

"He told you a whole tissue of lies," I said vehemently when I had got to grips with my anger. "If you knew how untrue that was you would be appalled that he said it. So that's what you meant when you were talking about the boys. Well, trust me that they are entirely safe – from me. Maybe not from him. And Phil's fifteen… Oh, bloody hell." I paused. "If our parents heard what you've just said they'd – well, they'd be mortified."

The door opened and Poppy came in.

I continued. "As it is he tried to kidnap Nat, but we all believed him when he said that it was to get him home to Helen.

"How are your parents? I suppose they *don't* know about Jonathan?"

"They're dead," I said briefly. "And I'm sure they never did know."

"I'm so sorry to hear that…"

"The pandemic. One after the other."

"Oh God."

"Look," I carried on, desperately, suddenly fighting an emotion I'd not felt, really felt, for years, "for the boys' safety I'm going to let the Police know. Can you give me your address, please?"

"Yes, but what's brought all this up now? Has there been a problem?"

I explained that he was missing.

"Oh God," she said again. "Of course. I'll tell them what they need to know, though it's little enough after all this time." She rattled off an address. Poppy wrote it down at the second repeating. "Who's that?" asked Jeanie.

"Poppy Watson. She's my employer and, once Helen and I can divorce, I hope she'll be my fiancée."

"You haven't wasted any time!" she accused. "Employer? Oh, of course. You left Crown. You said."

"I did, so as to regain my sanity. And things happen. She attracted me when we first met and things have developed."

"Well…" It was no longer accusing, just an exclamation. We promised to keep in touch and I confirmed that I'd be contacting the Police.

Poppy was horrified when she understood. "So it could be that the boys are in danger from him."

I nodded. "I suppose he can't help the attraction. But if he starts to act on it – he may already have – it's completely different."

I called the Police, and finally spoke to someone on the case. "You told us that you didn't have her details," he said flatly. It was an accusation.

"I didn't think I had. But there was an old work notebook I thought she might be in, and she was," I explained.

"Does your wife know this?"

My eyes widened. "I shouldn't think so. If she had, she'd have been as horrified as me and would have warned me to keep our two safe."

"And are they?"

My eyes widened again. "They should be on their way back from school. Just a minute."

I was about to look at the app on my phone which told me where they were, but he interrupted me. "Don't you fetch them?"

"No. Haven't for years. The bus service has always been so good, it's safe."

"Maybe not any more."

"If they get on it, he'd have to kidnap them off it or snatch them between the bus stop and the marina. And that's not far. He doesn't have a key for the gate, anyway."

I found the app whilst he was on. Nat was moving, it told me, and was on the bus route nearing home. I told him.

"Where's your other son?"

Suddenly alarmed, I widened the search area. It showed Phil in the opposite direction from the school, stationery, in a built-up area. In a voice now tight with worry I told the officer the area.

"Phone him, would you? And have you got someone who'll collect the younger one from the bus?"

I was about to end the call to do so when I remembered Poppy was there. "Phone Phil, would you, and ask him where he is and if he's all right?"

Her expression told me everything. She jabbed at her phone.

"Is someone calling him?" asked the officer impatiently.

"Yes. Hang on."

Poppy was speaking. She jabbed at the phone again and Phil's voice came through on the speaker. "…fine, thanks. What's the problem?"

"Where are you, Phil?" Poppy asked.

"I'm with a friend, sorting out some research. What's up?"

"You're not with Jonathan?"

A pause. "*Poppy!* I said a friend. No, I'm not. What's happened?"

"He's vanished."

"Vanished? Where to?"

"If we knew that… Phil, this is serious. You're sure you've not seen him? He's not contacted you?"

"No! If he had I'd have hit him, then told Dad."

If any comment was going to reassure me that my bloody brother wasn't there threatening him, that was it.

"Ok, Phil," I called to Poppy's phone. "Call me when you're ready and I'll come and fetch you. I'll tell you what's happened on the way."

"Ok, but can't you tell me now?"

"No. I've got the Police on the other line."

"Police? Why? Oh… ok. I'll wait till you get me. We won't be long."

I returned to my phone. "Did you catch that?" I asked.

Poppy mouthed about going to fetch Nat off the bus. I mouthed a 'thank you' to her.

"Yes," answered the officer. "He said that he would hit your brother if he saw him. Why was that?"

"Because Jonathan hit Phil when he thought he was being rude once, soon after he and my wife had got together. It was one of the things that persuaded them to ask to live with me, not with them."

"So far as you know, has he ever touched either of your sons?"

"If that had happened he would still be in hospital now. No, officer, neither of them has hinted at it. Nor has their behaviour changed as we're told youngsters' behaviour can if they're being abused."

"Has your brother even baby-sat for them?"

"Years ago. I'm talking about three or more years or so when Phil – that's the older one – was under age for being on his own. But even then they were all right. In fact in those days they enjoyed going to his flat because it was a change and they said it was fun."

"Thank you. So we believe there has been no abuse."

"We're sure there has been no abuse. Have you tried Jonathan's number?"

"Frequently. Just as Mrs… as your wife has."

"I'll try too, shall I?"

"If you do get an answer can you call us on another line, please? While he's on the phone?"

I agreed.

Poppy brought Nat in. We were in mid-explanation when Phil phoned to say that they'd finished. "If you do want to come and fetch me," he added. I assured him that I needed to. He gave me the address. On the return trip explanations were given.

"So do they think he's… he's got someone? Some boy or other?"

"No one knows, Phil. I just don't want it to be you. Or Nat."

"Do you think he might?"

"I have no clue. But I'm sure as hell not going to take any chances."

"I can look after myself."

"But can you look after Nat as well as yourself? If… oh, I don't know… if he hit you and dragged Nat off, would you be able to help?"

"What would happen if he knocked you out you and dragged us both off?"

"If he tried that, you'd hit him, just as you said you would on the phone. Who were you with, by the way? They must have heard the conversation."

From the gap I thought there might be some embarrassment. For a moment I thought he was going to admit it was Jonathan.

"Erin," he said. "She's been through what we're doing at the moment so I thought she might be able to give me some pointers."

"Sorry but who's Erin?"

"That girl we met on the tunnel boat. Remember? Your memory…"

"Is as good as yours, just not as attuned to young girls."

"She's not a young girl, she's older than me."

"You know what I mean."

"I can't get over Jonathan being... well, whatever he is."

"Nor can I. It's not something I want to think about, either. It's not as if there were any signs when we were kids, or even later. And I'm sure I'd have realised."

He shrugged his shoulders.

39 Finality

Explaining to Helen all that Jeanie had told me, and the questions from the Police, was uncomfortable. "I don't believe it," she said. "He would never… he and I were…"

"I don't want to know," I told her abruptly. "Have some tact will you? Do you really think I need to know about how often you shagged, in my house? Whilst I was away? No. Tell the Police. But if you see your precious boyfriend, tell him again from me that he's got to keep well away from my sons and from me, or he won't know what hit him."

It was unfortunate that I had called her whilst in the galley, and that Poppy and the boys heard everything. They were very straight-faced, and shortly after a very quiet meal they vanished to start their homework (Nat) or studies (Phil), a subtle difference which I'd learnt from Phil's scornful comments since the school year had started.

I apologised to them when they returned, individually. Nat just nodded, eyes downcast. Phil was more direct. "Well, you and Poppy are, so it's the same thing."

"No. We didn't take advantage of someone else's absence to get together. We knew we weren't breaking up a marriage and a family. We knew that you two were aware there was a growing attraction and you were in favour – you've both said so. It's totally different."

The point was made. I just hoped that when he'd had a chance to think about it, to weigh up the pros and cons for himself, that it would eventually sit easier with his emotions.

We had a very quiet meal that night. I made sure the boat's doors were locked, secure marina or not.

The next week and a half passed without incident. There was no contact from Helen about my request for a divorce. There was no contact from the Police about Jonathan. I'd been quietly scanning the local papers and social media for missing teenage boys or young men. Nothing.

At half past one on a Tuesday morning my phone rang. Helen. An angry Helen.

"Your bloody brother just phoned from India. He's gone to live there."

We two had just reached the deepest sleep of the night, or so it felt, and many seconds passed before the news sank fully into the cotton-wool of my psyche. So long, in fact, that she almost shouted "Hallo? Hallo? Are you still there?"

"Just a minute." I really couldn't make sense of what she was saying. "Did you say he'd phoned from India? How do you know?"

"Because he bloody said so," she spat. "Do you think I'm an idiot?"

"Just because he said so doesn't mean it's true," I told her. "If he can mislead me about all the things he has misled me about, he might be lying. Did he give a number? An address?"

"Don't be stupid. He doesn't want to be found. I told him that we knew about his... his *peccadillos* and he went quiet. Then he said that he was with someone who made him happy. Happier."

Well...

"Did he give a gender or an age for this person?" I asked cautiously.

"I told you he wasn't a nonce," she said defiantly.

I was now almost fully awake.

"That didn't answer the question. Who's he with?"

"He didn't say."

"Then why India? Is it because it's a place you can lose yourself easily? Why there and not – oh, I don't know – Spain?"

"He said he wanted to make a clean break. To get rid of the flat, his business – which he said bored him – and 'everything'. By which he means me, of course."

Another pause while I thought. "Where's he been for the last few weeks then? Since he left the flat?"

"He didn't say."

"Look, if he's really gone to India, made a complete break, what's he doing with the flat?"

"He *said* that I could keep it. But..."

"But that's ridiculous! You can't just give a property to someone. It's - well, how does he propose to transfer it into your name if no one knows where he is?"

"Jack, how the hell do I know? The man's genuinely unbalanced."

"Is he?" I asked, shocked at her sincerity. "What makes you say that? Was he showing signs of it when you were together?"

There was a silence.

"He did, didn't he? And you never told me. What did he do?"

"I don't want to say. And I couldn't tell you then, either. He's your brother, even if you didn't care what happened to him."

"After he'd hit my elder son, just as you hit the younger one, and then tried to kidnap them, I shouldn't think you can blame me."

"He... I'm going to carry this on in the morning."

"It is morning. And I'm going to call the Police. If there's a chance that he's taken some kid to India who doesn't want to stay there, they need to know. You'd better expect a visit. Good night."

Poppy was also completely awake, of course. "I can't believe what he's done," she said quietly.

"I've got to call the Police," I told her. "Sorry."

I did so. Having given brief details I discovered that, not unnaturally, the investigating team were off duty. They'd make contact with me the following morning. With that I had to try to be content.

I didn't sleep well.

They called at eight thirty – fortunately the boys had groaned their way schoolwards by then – and I passed on what Helen had told me. "We'll try and correlate the date of his disappearance with any missing persons enquiries. When was he reported missing?"

I couldn't remember. "More important is when he actually failed to return, surely? And only Helen can tell you that. Aren't there records of people leaving Britain? Isn't it possible to search using his name?"

"It doesn't work like that. We can't. What phone number did he call from?"

"Helen can tell you that. I assumed it was his normal one. She's the one who has the most up to date information about him. And there's his business. He said he was bored with it. Whether he's just left it or if he's sold it I don't have a clue."

They wanted the details of that. A quick investigation answered the question; it had been sold, and with no reference to Helen. It was and is a quite lucrative sales consultancy business, an occupation which had always puzzled me as a severely practical man. Jonathan, obviously more different from me in more ways than I realised, had built it up from scratch. The proceeds from the sale had funded the flight and the presumed change of lifestyle.

It took three weeks before the mobile number used to call Helen was traced to a small town in India. Its user explained that an Englishman had given him the phone, told him to ignore any calls coming from England, and that when the SIM had run out of credit he would need to get his own. Apparently its owner had been with a much younger man, 'not much older than a boy.' He had not seen either of them again.

We were back in limbo, though more secure in the knowledge that Phil and Nat were safe from an uncle who increasingly came to be regarded as a loose cannon.

"What am I going to do, then?" asked Helen when I broached the subject of a divorce again.

"Whatever you want, I imagine, and better than I would have done when you and Jonathan locked me out of my own house," I responded hotly. The boys were with me at the time and I was aware of both sets of eyes looking alert. "That's not something I can forget. So I shall be quoting adultery and unreasonable behaviour as grounds."

The silence was deafening. I checked that she was still there.

"We've sorted out the house. We've sorted out the money. I'm making no claim against you for child care costs, despite what I said at the start. You have a job and somewhere to live. The boys have made their choice, you have access to them when they agree and I won't try to stand in their way. We don't need solicitors and I'm glad, because the costs would count against their financial wellbeing. As it is, there's a fee to pay for the divorce proceedings."

More silence. Then in a low, almost muttered tone: "All right."

"So you don't intend to contest it."

"I can't, can I?"

"No. Because you know what I've outlined is true and because you would be depriving the boys financially if solicitors were needed, as I said. All right, then, I'll complete the thing online and you'll hear from the court in due course." We ended the conversation.

I looked at the two grave pairs of eyes watching me. "Look, Poppy's not here. You can say what you like without risking offending her. Am I doing the right thing? The right thing in your eyes? They right thing for me?"

"I suppose it had to happen, didn't it?" asked Phil. "We both knew it. It's just that it seems so… so final."

Nat just nodded.

"It's only final legally," I said slowly. "Practically it changes nothing, as I've said before. We'll still keep in touch as much as we do – which isn't much, she and I – and you can obviously still see her when you and she want. She's still your mother."

"You and Poppy can get married," Nat said suddenly.

"Yes, we can. And we want to. Are you still happy with that?"

Two heads nodded. "You've asked us that before, Dad," Phil told me.

"I know. But it's more than important to me that you're happy with it too, and that you haven't changed your minds."

"But if we had, you'd still get married." Nat's just too mature for his years.

"We could live together. You know, a sort of common-law marriage."

"And the divorce wouldn't be needed."

I thought. "Well yes, it would. For my sake. Because I've been treated so badly."

"I think I'd rather you got married," Nat said unexpectedly. "It seems more – more secure."

An interesting choice of word, and Phil was nodding too. "More as if you really mean it," he added.

"I do mean it."

I completed the online form and reluctantly paid the heavy fee. Online forms… it seemed such an insignificant way to end such a meaningful thing as a marriage. The significant parts would be done behind the scenes, of course, and would ultimately lead to the very significant, freeing, Decree. But still I felt an air of regret. Not regret that the marriage was to be ended; but regret that all that it had meant once, for the greater part of the time, had somehow been wasted.

Had it?

No, it hadn't: the boys. Their existence gave the lie to any thoughts of it having been a waste. I smiled at them, though with their heads in books and arms writing in folders they were unaware of it.

"Anyone want to go to a pub tonight, rather than cook here?" I asked suddenly, wanting to mark the occasion with something less routine.

Hands stopped writing, heads looked up, surprised, and nodded. Later Poppy arrived.

"Hallo," I said. "I've just completed the divorce application online. Shall we go out tonight for a change of scenery?"

I'd not been expecting a hug, but received one anyway.

Christmas was approaching. Poppy and I were engaged and would arrange a wedding once the twenty weeks of waiting that the law forces on you were at an end. The Parishes were frequent visitors, we had occasionally weathered the storm of Mrs Wynne when May came to visit, and had also met up with the Bradleys when Erin was brought to us "for a studying session, Dad."

I made no judgements, nor did Poppy. Erin and May knew that each visited; neither seemed to object, though they never met.

We spent our time between Poppy's house and the boat. In fact they are only a few minutes' walk apart, an ideal situation when the boys want to watch something on TV that doesn't interest us. Christmas itself was spent at the house and we went to town on the decorations. Boxing Day saw the entire staff join us, with their families, and it was interesting to see them relax and be themselves. I think the boys and I did Poppy proud, and she was beaming happily along with the rest of us. Toward the evening when some of them started to drift away, the Parishes appeared, unannounced, bearing food, wine and gifts. All very welcome and somewhat guilt-making as we'd done nothing for them. We seemed to start proceedings again.

It was the small hours before the remaining staff friends left. We offered boat cabins to the Parishes as they felt that driving would be inadvisable, and crawled happily and thankfully into our respective beds.

On the Poppy Narrowboat front Poppy had decided in early Autumn to commission two new boats. "This is on the back of your arrival, Jack, not to mention the lack of serious breakdowns since."

No pressure there, then. Build time was six months from the start of the build 'slot', so early summer it should be. We gleefully added them to the new brochure which, I'm happy to say, bore a photo of each of the marina's staff and mentioned me as the engine guru who ensured reliability.

Again: no pressure.

We sent out the brochures to three years' worth of customers with a letter describing the reasons why up to last year the engines had been less than reliable. Under a week later the phone started ringing. "I really hope the two new boats arrive in time," Poppy said nervously on more than one occasion. In fact we were keeping a weekly check on progress and all seemed to be good, despite a few materials shortages which threatened delays.

I even managed to talk to my old boss at Crown to reintroduce the company to him. He was intrigued, and said he'd think about a booking.

With enquiries, bookings, detailed questions, requests to visit the boats before deciding, and the more run-of-the-mill calls, Poppy and I were kept tied to phones for a lot of the time. And yes, for every booking we took, we referred to the Red List of bad hirers. Which, of course, doesn't exist. "It's such a relief that it's not here," said Poppy as she put it on one side again having told one of its subjects that we were full.

One particular morning we were just looking forward to coffee when the phone interrupted yet again. My turn to answer it.

"Jack? Is that you?"

I looked in astonishment at Poppy, who raised her eyebrows.

"*Jonathan*?"

"Yes. I'm back in Britain. Living in Brighton. Look, I'm sorry. That's all I can say."

My mind was in turmoil.

"We all thought that you… that you and *he*…" I accented the pronoun "…had vanished. Just upped sticks and gone."

"So you know."

"We know most of it. Jeanie and…"

"*Jeanie*?"

"Well yes. The Police were called, I found her number and she told us what she knew. Helen still hasn't said anything about it. I should think she's just too embarrassed for herself. How the *hell* didn't I see this coming when we were in our teens? Or later?"

"I'm sorry. That's all I can say."

There was so much that I felt should be said by me; for me, for Helen, for Jeanie, even for the boys. The one thing I needed to know was whether the boys would be safe.

"I don't know how much I can trust you now, if at all, but there's something I need to know. For my sake and theirs, please just tell me the truth. Are you still attracted to my two?"

"*What…*? Attracted to… good God no. I've never been attracted to them, at least not in the way I think you mean. I like them – liked them when I was allowed to see them – but attracted to them? Absolutely not."

"Then for f… then why the hell did you try to snatch them? You nearly succeeded with Nat."

"I was trying to get them back to Helen. I was trying to do what I could for her. I never meant to scare them."

"You didn't scare them, you bloody fool; you made them – us – angry. Angry to the extent of being about to call the Police to arrest you for attempted abduction with paedophile intent. Did you not know? I thought Helen told you. I certainly told her to."

A gasp, then a silence.

"I knew the first part, but not the second. Is that what you all thought?"

"What the hell do you think? Anyone who… who's done what you did, then grabs a boy off the street like you did is an immediate suspect, don't you think? Brother or not. Estranged brother."

"I never thought of it like that."

"You mean, you never thought. You're attracted to men, young men, yet you make up to Helen, your brother's wife…"

"She complained to me that she was out of love with you. It was – it was silly of me to accept her…"

He petered off.

"So our marriage would have ended anyway? Maybe, but you didn't make it any easier. And to exclude me from my own home! I needed a place to crawl back to and recover, and you had deliberately locked me out. No, Jonathan, you never thought. You never cared. You listened to my tale of woe about Helen and all the time you were shagging her – well, I suppose you were, but now I'm not so sure. And you're such a good actor with me, the one who knows you best of all. Who thought he did. It's hardly surprising that I don't trust you, isn't it?"

"I shouldn't have done that, I know," he said in a pathetic tone. A tone that so far as I knew could still be the product of an acting attempt.

"Too right. And your contrition now sounds hollow. Once an actor, always an actor. I have no way of knowing if you're telling the truth or not. And by the way, have you done the paperwork which gives Helen your flat?"

"No."

"Then you have unfinished business with her. Expect to hear from her. Or you can do it today and send me copies of what you do. That's the only way I'll believe you. Got it?"

"Yes. I'll try."

"I want to see progress within a week. And I'll tell Helen too. Anyway, how old is this boy?"

"What boy? Oh, you mean my partner. Twenty-one."

"And you're nearly double his age. Well, I hope you'll be very happy. But you'll realise I want as little as possible to do with you, and you are to have nothing to do with Phil or Nat. When they're 18 it's up to them to contact you or not. But if anything ever happens to them at your hands… Well, trust me: the Police will be the least of your worries."

"Nothing will happen. Good bye, Jack."

With a shaking hand I replaced the receiver. Poppy had finished one call, had looked at me with raised eyebrows, then been interrupted by another. I went outside, ignoring a further call, and breathed deeply to get my mind back onto an even keel. A walk down to the marina gate and back improved my mental state and thank goodness the office was quiet when I returned.

The coffee machine can be a useful distraction, especially when your boss puts her arms round your waist without warning and causes a near miss with hot coffee. I explained what Jonathan had said and she was as short of words as I had been.

"What a situation," she said at last.

"What an arse," I corrected. "It's worse because he didn't level with me or anyone to start with."

"He's bisexual, then. Must be, I suppose."

It was the only explanation, that or something like it. It's not something you can really put even to an estranged brother. Not even when he's excluded you from your own house and shacked up with your wife, and lied so convincingly.

"I get that," she said when I had explained. "That's the worst part. To go through all that when it's a sham, if it was, and lie so well; it's just – well, I don't like to say 'unforgivable'."

"Nor do I. But it is. He's gone against every last vestige of trust I had in him. And we grew up together."

"And you're hurt."

"I'm angry and hurt. And let down. So badly let down that I'm even more angry."

"Do you want me to be a punch bag?"

I just looked at her. Slowly the anger, the hurt evaporated and I started almost smiling.

"I could do with a hug bag… no, that sounds horrible."

The hug came anyway.

Later, carefully, I told Phil and Nat.

"If he's gay, why did he… go with Mum?" asked Nat.

"I wish I knew. We wondered if he was bisexual, not gay."

"Oh."

It was less of a surprise to them than it had been to me. Sexuality has to be taught in schools now so that people don't get bullied like they used to. I hoped.

"So he's not going to try and kidnap us and rape us?" Phil, blunt as usual.

"He says that neither of you were ever in any danger of that from him."

"But you don't believe him."

"He really sounded genuine when he told me. But we know he's a good actor."

"A liar."

I sighed. "Yes."

"Oh well, if he's in Brighton we'll probably not see him. What are we eating?"

And that was that, so far as they were concerned. Chapter over.

A month later a fat envelope arrived. "Decree Absolute," it said. I showed it to Poppy and a slow smile lit up the office.

April: very few hires, fortunately. We were performing deep cleans and very full checks of every aspect of every boat. That frequently included me and one particular afternoon it was doing so. I was using a vacuum cleaner in a cupboard when I was aware of a presence behind me, so looked round.

Helen. *Helen*?

"I'm not staying," she told me. "But I thought you should know that Jonathan has made over the flat to me."

I knew. He had been as good as his word – for a change – and had kept me abreast of events by sending images of the documents.

"Well, at least he's done something decent," I retorted.

"I know that you know," she said, surprising me. "He told me that you insisted that I made good and kept him informed. I hate what he did to me, how he led me on, and what he did to you. But if he's at peace with this Justin person, then he might be able to get his honesty back."

"It will take a lot of proof before I can accept that's happened," I told her. "And I'm afraid your collusion in 'what he did to me', as you put it, doesn't leave you in a very good light with me either. But I'm glad you have a home."

She nodded slowly. "Thank you for that, at least," she said.

A silence.

"Can I hang around and see the boys?" she asked suddenly. It was late afternoon, the end of the working day was approaching, and they were actually probably back already.

"Be my guest," I said. "They'll be in the boat if they're back. It's locked but they have keys."

She nodded again and turned, then turned back.

"We had some good years," she said quietly. "I'm grateful for that. And I'm sorry it didn't work out."

It sounded to me like a softening up attempt, something I wasn't going to accept. It was my turn to nod slowly.

"We did. Pity it ended as disastrously as it did."

I turned and switched the vacuum cleaner on again.

Three weeks later we dragged the boys out of school ("Very ill-advised, Mr Dyer. It's the most important time of the school year.") so that we could all go to a hastily arranged civil wedding service. It had to be so because the main hiring season was just round the corner. We couldn't afford to wait until a summer Saturday and didn't want to wait until the end of the main hiring season. What had been possible the previous year wasn't so now. Poppy Narrowboats was just too busy.

Poppy, the boys and I, and one or two from the marina – including the long-suffering Ian and his wife – met up with ex-colleagues from Crown Engineering, with the Parishes and some friends of each of us, and completed the simple, dignified ceremony. We had arranged a minibus to take us to the Grand Hotel for a good lunch. I'm pleased to say that their management had felt so guilty about the lack of a decent screening process for drivers which had led to the discovery of the Parishes, that they gave us an apologetically low price. Indeed the reduction extended to a dinner for us and the boys and the evening entertainment.

Disgustingly late, the boys departed by taxi back to the marina, the first time they'd done anything like that. To provide another room for them was a cost we felt wasn't justifiable. They had school the following day any case.

One of the Grand's huge (after a narrowboat cabin) rooms helped us sleep in quilted comfort and to wake late the next morning. We had been considering actually getting out of bed when I thought of something.

"How about a Church blessing once the summer has calmed down?" I asked.

"Complete with bells?" Poppy said drowsily.

"With bells on," I assured her, and received a dig in the ribs.

We named the boat *Hockley*. Pronouncing the *H* is optional and depends where in the world you were brought up.

That September, one Saturday, *Hockley* was moored at the Blue Bell. Our simple blessing took place in St Mary, Lapworth. With bells. The Blue Bell provided something akin to a banquet for us, and our guests that evening included John.

During her move to the flat of my disgraced brother, Helen had gifted me quite a few pieces and pictures that wouldn't fit there, along with personal items that included my music collection and the boys' Lego. The former have pride of place at Poppy's – as the house is still called – and the latter is hidden in a cupboard there, out of sight.

The February after our wedding Poppy and I named our third and maybe our last child Amy. She is so loved. She, two parents and two mid-teen boys alternate between a seventy-foot narrowboat and a nearby, comfortable house as the mood takes them. Yes, we still live on a boat; just not as permanently as we used to.

A sketch plan of the boat.

Drawn by Nat, then 13, to show his friends how we had arranged things and to prove that living on a 70 ft by 7ft * boat is not only possible, but comfortable too.

* (21.336 x 2.133m. Happy now, Nat?)

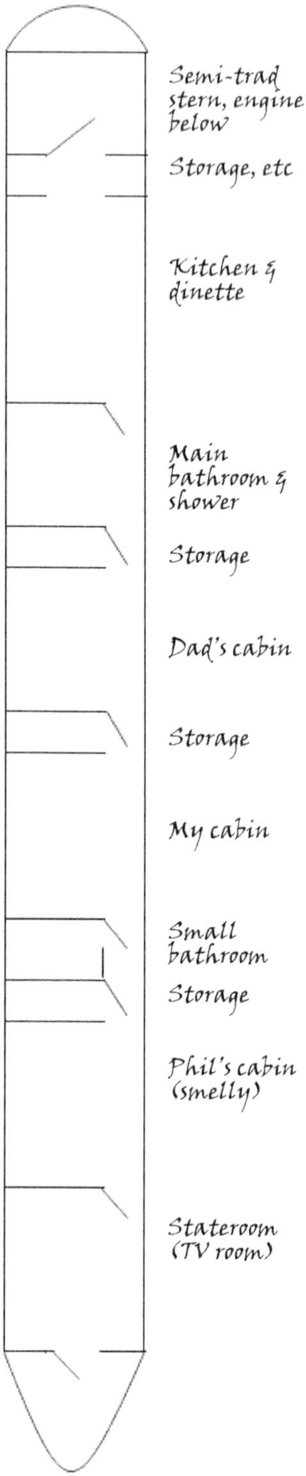

Printed in Great Britain
by Amazon

36035651R00188